"Go as far as you can see; when you get there, you'll be able to see farther."

-J.P. Morgan

"The best debut novel that I've read in recent memory."
-Lawrence Cohen

"Full of substance, and grossly entertaining—a book for the ages. Will leave you questioning your own morals."
-Darlene Perón, E-Reader Café

"Harrison Charles will bring you to tears during this harrowing journey into the minds of some very persistent individuals."
-Tim Garrity, H.W. Garrity Investments

"It will be a great disservice to the world if this book isn't turned into a major motion picture."
-Chance Morehead, Queen's Dominion Battered Women's Shelter

"I haven't been this satisfied since that unforgettable Anglo Saxon chap back in '91."
-Bridgette Bordeaux, The de Gaulle Boutique.

COMING

OF

THE

HOUR

Harrison Charles

Second Edition

Buttress Publishing Company
2448 Broad Creek Dr.
Lilburn, Ga. 30087

All Buttress titles, imprints and distributed lines are available at special quality discounts for bulk purposes, for sales promotion, premiums, fundraising, educational or institutional use.

Buttress Publishing and the Buttress Publishing logo Reg. U.S. Pat. & TM Office.

ISBN 978-0-9903079-3-8

Second Buttress Trade Paperback Printing: January 2016

Printed in the United States of America

0 9 8 7 6 5 4 3 2 1

Acknowledgements

First and foremost I would like to thank my Grandmother who never gave up on me. I would not be where I am today if it weren't for her love and effort. My lovely wife (Feedie) for giving me the daily inspiration to follow my dream of becoming a published author. I'd like to thank my uncle for his lessons in life. To those who were down and out; as I once was: Never let the past determine your future.
And lastly, I'd like to thank my parents, who had more impact on my development, and who I am today, than anyone.

COMING

OF

THE

HOUR

Harrison Charles

Second Edition

Prologue

"You think they knew he was doing this all along?"
"They always know, he was insulated by the cloth. The ranks of evil have swollen exponentially until the world is now rife with their kind—eradication is the only means of establishing an equilibrium."
A misty sheen agglutinates the air with dense condensation, meandering trials of dew trickle down the window's pane.
A cautious survey of the area reveals two playful youths engaged in a two-wheeled duel across the paved lot; obviously enjoying the muggy weather. Thus far, it's been the wettest month in Atlanta on record.
When will the time come when she'll be able to conceive? Maybe a

new baby will rekindle their happiness, reckons the co-conspirator. "The fucker uses all these degrees and scriptures to hide behind," staring at the many plaques and awards atop the fireplace's mantle.

In his free hand is a micro-cassette recorder. And despite being paused at the moment, the preceding lengthy session has just about drained the batteries.

"Telling from this photo, it looks like he used to be a coach or something as well. I'm ready to resume our work, I hate pigs like these. The only problem I have with Robin Hood is that he didn't have the guts to kill the sheriff. As the old adage goes: Never do minor damage to a major enemy."

And picking up the video camera says: "Always be conscious of our mission, focus on what you're doing. Take no mercy when enacting retribution."

"I won't. I'm quite ready to finish him off."

"Just follow my lead. Don't be so eager to attempt something, even if you have experience with it. Mistakes happen when confidence runs amuck. Now hold this while I look for something."

Passing his cohort the camcorder, he searches under the sink.

Exhausted whimpers are coming from somewhere in the sprawling loft.

After a final look out of the window, and another glance at his wristwatch, the two vigilantes are ready to continue.

"Let the defrocking resume."

SLAM!

Goes the cabinet.

Five short steps and the door opens with a creak. In the center of the floor sits a naked man bound to a chair; a ceramic sculpture of the Apostle Paul lay shattered on the floor. The bookcase of religious texts is turned on its side, and from his neck hangs a stained glass rosary—the congealing words: *'False Prophet'* etched into his chest. Although the room is in shambles and reeks of sweat, the windows are covered and tightly shut; the adjoining patio's blinds drawn and dusty.

He steps forward and glares at the wannabe evangelist; disgusted by what he did to that innocent boy's. Today he'll be recompensed for his repulsive transgressions.

"State your name for the audience," holding the vintage voice recorder to the man's lipless, herpetic mouth.

His companion powers on the camera's light, training it on his mug.

And he presses the play button: a robust concerto piece.

"J-Joseph," he managed to say. *"Joseph Tangier,"* lips trembling from the uncertainty of what's next to come.

"What do you do for a living Mr. Tangier?"

Sobbing.

"Say it!..All of it!"

"....I'm a placement advocate with family and children services," he admitted sadly.

"And?"

"….I pastor a church."

The captor extracts a picture and shows it to him.

"Now you know what this is for. How much have you profited from exploiting children you were supposed to help?"

Shame won't allow him to respond. All he can do is hang his head and cry.

"Remember them!"

He reaches for the electric iron and places it against his bare chest; the microphone vividly capturing his pain and agony—part of his velvet pulpit robe stuffed in his mouth.

Scattered around his feet like cigarette butts; charred wicks of twisted Bible were ignited and used to sear him.

The swath of cloth does little to dampen his screams, as his eyes roll backwards, and his teeth clenches the expensive fabric.

The captor removes the iron, and details his work into the device; wanting the authorities to have a clear picture into his suffering. In his quest not to omit the smallest detail, he places the machine to his mouth, and notifies the listeners: "No one is exempt from accountability."

In the final act, a revolver ends the pedophile's life.
The recording session is over.

All that remains is Mozart's genius, the playing children's laughter, and the calm breathing of the murderous composer—what an exhilarating performance.
He ejects the cassette, and drops it on the floor.

Chapter 1

Stockton pounds on the slab of lumber!
"What took you so damn long?" is the greeting he gives her as she holds the door.
"Don't start Stow! I'm not in the mood for it today! Is there one day when you're not mad at the freaking world?" she replied.
"Working at that prison is making you crazy."
"It's not the job that's making me crazy," he hinted.
Kathy decides against saying anything else, having experienced too many times what that leads to.
"One of those inmates stole my fucking keys, probably waiting till they make parole so they can come steal all our shit."
"I doubt it."
"You always think stuff can't happen to you."

The de-facto twosome live in a newly gentrified neighborhood in the historic Summer Hill section of Atlanta. The house is a small, three bedroom structure in a neighborhood occupied by other small three bedroom ones. The home's generous furnishings remains in top condition thanks to them both, but mainly Kathy. The kitchen is fitted with an array of high end appliances, as is the rest of the home.

Stockton goes straight to the living room, flops down on the recliner, and grabs the remote.

"You don't think you're overreacting Stow? There just some keys. You'll probably find them tomorrow, I bet someone's already found them."

He ignores her and flips to the evening news.

She gives up on conversation and returns to searching the pantry.

Stockton Billings, Kathy met him ten years ago, back when he was the missing ingredient. He was affectionate, hardworking, barrel chested and devilishly handsome. He was the perfect catch. But just not for her. He made every attempt at sweeping her off her feet just as she was healing from a nervous breakdown. He footed the $150 an hour bill for her countless therapy sessions, despite never knowing what happened. Whatever it was almost pushed her over the brink. During this time, he fell madly in love with her, but could always sense she never let go of the past. She repeatedly explained that she cared deeply about their friendship, but just wasn't ready for another shot at love. He insisted that he could *make* her better, and after enduring years of repeated proposals, she reluctantly accepted—well sort of. By doing so, she thought it would help her forget about the past. But the past traumatized her entire soul. So for almost the last decade, she's been playing house with a man she knows she'll never love. She doesn't love Stockton, and he knows it. Despite treating him kindly, deep down sits the stark reality that she's in love with something, or someone else. However, he's unwilling to move on, and continues living with the notion that, he and time can make her better.

"Anything you want from the store?" she asked.

"Nothing in particular."

"Okay, I'm gone."

"Bye."

She opens the door.

Bright sun ray stream in, warming the foyer with light.

Turning she says: "Cheer up. They're only keys."

Making for her modest Camry, Mr. Vickers waves from across the street, wishing he was eons younger so he could request her hand in marriage. It isn't hard to see why Stockton has such a hard time ungluing himself from Kathy. At thirty-two years of age, and 5'9" with brunette hair, the old war vet thinks she's the goddess of his dreams.

But what he's not aware of, is that she's gone to tremendous lengths to keep her past hidden from him, and anyone else wants to get to *know* her.

A selfish thing indeed she thought, situating her designer shades in the rear-view, and backing out the driveway.

Fair or not, no one can ever learn the truth about the enigmatic Kathy Billings.

News Flash

In an effort to stem the skyrocketing murder rate—including new legislation on violent crime, while in the face of wide spread criticism from human rights groups: The state of Georgia has ceased the use of death by lethal injection, in favor of death by electrocution.

The raucous effect of dozens of doors simultaneously opening, and the guard's voice echoing throughout the cell house, he's rescued him from his daze.

"Count tiiiiiiime!!" repeated the shouting behemoth, as if the inmates don't already know the annoyingly repetitive procedure; they've been performing the exercise four times a day for years. Many welcome the thought of it all coming to an end. This is Georgia's infamous death row unit, where the condemned rot before being strapped in "Old Sparky's" lap. The fog of hopelessness and despair hangs so thick, that one would think it's being pumped through the ventilation system.

"Parson!" said officer Harry Fawell, standing outside of his cell holding a clipboard.

Dressed in the traditional sky blue button down, and gray polyester slacks that all Department of Corrections officers wear, his face is tanned and weathered with deep stress lines, permanent bags are under his eyes, and an unkempt gray nest perches atop his head—effects of working death row for twenty eight long years.

"Still here, same as yesterday," replied Parson.

Harry's a good guy among the seventy one men awaiting their turn to repay society for their crimes. But he's violated the cardinal rule: Never become friends with the inmates.

Having lost his only son to malevolent prosecutors in Texas, he doesn't think they're all scum.

Douglas Parson, EF#-8071613, returns to his thoughts as the rusty bars slide shut. He's played the tape in his head thousands of times, even has transcripts of it. First hearing it eleven years ago when the district attorney played it, he'll never forget how it brought the jury to tears, and made him the most hated man in the state—convicting him of the murder of highly esteemed bishop, Joseph Tangier.

"Fuck it," and rises from his mattress.

Only to be greeted with a look of contempt from the person staring back in the mirror.

He scans the cell.

His heart rate quickens!

"Talking to yourself again," came a husky voice from next door.

"I look like hell."

Visitation is in two minutes.

"And you smell like it too," joked his neighbor.

"Parson! Visitation!"

A reverberating call over the PA system.

Avoiding eye contact with the mirror, he hurriedly combs his hair, grabs his prison I.D. card, and waits at the bars.

The old pulley system slowly turns the sprockets, and the dusty chains pull the door back.

Clank.

Clank.

Clank.

Until it's halfway open.

He squeezes through the remaining space, and exits the cell. Walking down the tier, he looks into eyes similar to the ones he encountered moments ago. Not wanting to look so many hopeless faces, he lowers his gaze and focuses on the often-buffed floor.

SPLASH!

The warm mixture collides with his skin!

Considering the empty cup rolling around on the floor, and the wetness seeping down his face; the unmistakable stench of urine and feces is evident.

Gus "Sheephead" Beasley, the man who raped and killed eight women in one day, doused him as he passed his cell.

"Awwww shit! You motherfucker!!"

"BwaaaaaaHahahahaaaa!Hahahah! Wooooooooooweeee!" he bellowed. "Yo ole' lady gone luvta see yo' perdy lil' shit covered face!" displaying his badly decayed, and missing teeth.

Parson spits in his face, and tries to punch him through the bars. Harry yanks him around the corner.

Sheephead shouts obscenities, as he ushers him away.

"Bring dat bitch back! I wanna fuckeem!"

"Let it go. There's nothing you can do," Harry advised. "Just wash it off, and go see your people."

Breathing angrily, he goes into the supply room and refreshes.

Stockton hasn't moved muscle, not as much as batted an eye since Kathy has made the thirty minute trek to her favorite store.

"I hope they have the nerve to use those keys," speaking through clenched teeth.

"Be my guest," and strokes the .44 Magnum®.

He retrieves the remote from the hidden compartment and starts flipping. Coming upon a documentary about a dead musician, he presses a button in the vicinity of the cup holder.

The chair hums to life, adjusting to a reclined position.

Now with his feet elevated, he unbuckles his leather belt.

Thunk!

His pride and joy meets the carpet.

The program's narrator speaks mightily from the surround sound system. Mixed with this, and the comfort of his $1,100 chair, he succumbs to a much needed nap.

Stockton Billings, a Georgia native, born thirty five years ago to Lewis and Ibsen Billings—the only child they managed to produce throughout their on again-off again marriage. His mother was a sweet and caring woman by nature. But repeated blows from Lewis' right hand had hardened her heart; placing a strain on their relationship. In her pursuit of a better life, Ibsen would frequently leave, taking little Stockton with her. But as luck would have it, she never found it. Each time she left, she'd shortly return. And each time Lewis would greet her with open arms and false promises; each time becoming increasingly violent.

Dependent, depressed, trapped and abused was part of her plight —discernment wasn't. She knew exactly what she wanted. Problem was, she didn't know how to get it: love. Unadulterated, unequivocal, and everlasting, a never ending cascade of bliss and companionship; not emotional carnage. Her soul had been massacred, her heart trampled upon like dirt at a horse racing track. Nevertheless, she continued to patiently wait for fate to release the valve on her stream of tranquility. Sadly for Ibsen that never happened. She never discovered the happiness she yearned for, only sank deeper into despair. That was up until a debilitating disease took her life at forty three, five months after being diagnosed with ovarian cancer.

Stockton was left with only fond memories from the twelve years he'd known his her, and the uncertain future he now faced with his father. It didn't take long for him to see just how worthless and sorry he really was—the kind of person that made you wonder what purpose they served. He would've been more useful as manure dropping from a donkey's ass; at least that way he would've helped grass grow. The only effort his good for nothing father put forth was cash the monthly check he received from his wife's annuity.

On the other hand, Stockton worked all sorts of menial jobs—when there were no laws to limit the time, or scope of labor a minor could perform.

Until the winds of change blew the ominous cloud hovering over his life away, he busted his tail. Every pair of pants he wore, every shirt he'd washed, and every pair of sneakers he muddied, he bought. Four and a half years after his mother's death, he was adopted by the proprietor of the farm he worked on; his boss was now his father—a better situation for everyone. Sharing chores with his new brother Alex was nothing strenuous, basic stuff, normal things kids do. Despite having things better than he ever had, he felt out of place. Waking up to breakfast was foreign to him; he shied away from things like that. Taking hot baths, being hugged, and playing baseball was odd. He had a hard time adjusting to coming home from school and not having to toil till nightfall.

But in time, he transformed back into a regular boy, and started enjoying life. Unfortunately, his heart never changed towards his father, but became as hard as a billiard ball.

One evening, after his seventeenth birthday, and exactly one day before the anniversary of his mother's death, Lewis Billings was found stabbed to death in the parking lot of a bar. According to legend, he smarted off to a patron earlier that day, and the guy supposedly came back and ambushed him. However, none of this was ever proven, and the culprit was never caught. The case was marginally investigated and quickly forgotten—fine by Stockton and everyone else who regrettably knew Lewis Billings. Someone had done the town of Rex a great service. Whoever it was will always be remembered as the unsung hero of that town.

Moving away and joining the Atlanta Police Department proved to be a step in the right direction. At twenty one, he was the youngest person to be accepted to the academy. After eighteen weeks of training he graduated at the top of his class, and quickly climbed the ladder. Without the usual antics employed by others in their quest for advancement, he accomplished his by being good at what he did; a natural, he had a knack for leadership. This caught the attention of his superiors, and he was quickly promoted, much to the dismay of everyone else. Long gone were the days of being just another uniform. He now had a title: Sergeant Billings—a force to be reckoned with.

The department erupted; many resigned, refusing to work under someone so inexperienced. His twenty five years of age too much for them to handle. They'd been brown nosing their entire careers, and yet to be rewarded.

They eventually they got their wish. Internal Affairs tarnished him with allegations of police brutality, and prostitute rapes. His demise drew rave reviews from his peers, and left him with no choice but to resign. Whispers of a frame job ensued, but there was no evidence to support it.

Unable to land a job with a different department, he was forced into the penal system. Reluctantly, he accepted a position at the Atlanta Federal Penitentiary, badly wanting revenge on the A.P.D., especially that conniving bitch who spearheaded the investigation. He'd done none of the things they'd accused him of. He was indeed the victim of a strategic set-up.

Along came Kathy Easterbrook, and she changed everything.

Stockton awakens to the mating rituals of the African Elephant, the camera man thorough in capturing every intimate detail.

He rubs his eyes to be sure he's seeing clearly.

There seems to be a fifth leg hanging from the mammal's under-belly. Then he sees it's the animal's gigantic member.

A glance at his wrist tells him it's 5:45 in the afternoon, prompting him to lift off the chair, yawning as he walks to the kitchen.

After grabbing a beer from the fridge, he stands at the sink gulping while watching kids play basketball in the street.

How many times did he get that opportunity.

However, he finds it easy to recall how many times his father was sober.

He takes another gulp, but pours it out when he pictures his sperm donor doing the same thing.

"Dipshit."

Now it's about her, about how distraught she was during their early years. If it wasn't for him, she'd be a basket case by now. She swears the reason she can never tell him what transpired is because the ordeal caused her to lose parts of her memory, and what she can remember is much too painful to speak on. Her psychiatrist recommended that he not try to jar her memory, fearing it may cause further damage. Whatever happened, her brain removed recollection of it.

But Stockton has secrets too, a past he's also gone to great lengths to conceal.

His heart flutters at the sight of his reflection on the glass.

The death row visitation area is a ghost town. Not many people care to once labeled a diabolical monster; the occasional letter is a miracle. Once found guilty of having committed some heinous act, erasure from memory is the usual result. Somehow Parson has beaten the odds, even staff members are perplexed.
In the third seat on the opposite side of a three inch slab of Plexiglas®, sits a striking blonde. Her eyes glisten like blue sapphires in a kaleidoscope, she possesses perfectly symmetrical features, and impeccable skin. Wearing a hound's-tooth pantsuit and crimson heels, she makes his heart sink; truly a sight for sore eyes. Much too gorgeous to be wasting her time visiting a condemned man.
"Hi baby."
"It's a pleasure to see you again," he speaks into the black phone.
"The pleasure's all mine. Stand up and let me see you."
He stands up.
The 4 ½ ft. wall below the glass makes it impossible to see anything below the chest while sitting down.
Two years ago, a man received a visit from a pastor who brought along his elderly wife. While they engaged in prayer, the prisoner decided to partake in a quick masturbation session. The misses opens her eyes to see veins popping out of his head, and him geyser all over himself.
She fainted.
Determined to thwart future occurrences, the warden had the

wall installed the following day.

"You just saw me last week," his teeth as white as hers.

"I know."

Getting right to business, she grabs the briefcase and removes a thick folder, which produces dozens of photos of different people. None of them knew they were being photographed. She takes one labeled *#1*, and places it against the glass—fingers along and elegant, nails freshly manicured.

"This is her."

Using an index card, she shorthands the name, address, and occupation of the woman.

Knowing their every word is being recorded, they say as little as possible into the phones, and instead employ code words, and advanced sign language. At even this very moment they're being eavesdropped on. The four correctional officers stationed at opposite ends of the long room are supposed to be there to ensure no prohibited acts are performed. But the real reason are as spies for Warden Stuckey; he's highly suspicious of their activities. The fact that she's been coming to see a condemned man every week for the past decade isn't normal. Each time she comes, she always has some kind of information, and always carries that briefcase—never coming empty handed. Stuckey has yet to discover what all the hushed meetings are about, but vows to find out what. Douglas Parson is very peculiar, doesn't talk much, always reading something, and always studying. He's not interested in what's going on inside the prison, but is good friends with inmate Matthew Grainger. Maybe it's because they're part of death row's elite. Both have been convicted of brutal crimes, and both deemed psychopaths by the same noted psychologist. From day one the investigators adamantly believed Parson had an accomplice when he tortured and killed Joseph Tangier. They also said it's quite possible that it could've been a female. Blonde hair follicles not matching his, or the victims were recovered from the scene, including other tell-tell signs of feminine involvement.

"How'd you come up with her?"
She smiles.
"I think she can be a great asset to our cause. I spoke with her and she's willing, in direct accordance with all of our ideas," her manicured hand shooting off fluent sign at blazing speed.
With a crooked brow he studies the photo.
"I don't know. Are you sure?" his sign equally fast.
"Positive."
"Who's the others?" he asked, nodding at the stack face down on the cold steel table.
On one photo is a man wearing an expensive suit standing between a man and a woman with his arms draped over their shoulders. The man on the left looks to be in his mid-forties, and wears blue overalls and a straw hat. The woman about the same age wears a yellow paisley sun dress and brown moccasins. All three are smiling.
"This is the couple I told you about. The man in the middle is…"
She picks up an index card and shorthands the name.
"How much does he want? I'm sure he's not doing it out the kindness of his heart."
"Nothing, as long as I come up with something new, stuff he can use."
"What do we have that's new?"
"Not much at the moment, but I'm working on it. Have I ever let you down?"
He shakes his head no.
Parson knows she loves him immensely; would even go through hell and back for him—even climb Kilimanjaro barefoot if she had to.
But….
The question is for how long? How long will it be before she wakes up and realizes what she's doing? The situation would've already crushed him had it not been for her steadfast devotion.
The puzzle slowly seems to be coming together.

But will it be too late?

It can happen as long as he keeps her on his team.

"Just believe in me like I believe in you. I know this is going to happen for us. No one, or no *thing* will compromise our mission," sounding very sure of herself.

She stares into Parson's piercing eyes, thinking of how much she loves him, how much she's infatuated with him, and how much she lusts for him. How long has been since she's made love? How long will she wait?

Forever.

What had they done wrong? What could they had done different? If only they could get a second chance. Someone's going to pay dearly for what they've done to them, even if it means paying with their life. She taken a vow to avenge the demise of Douglas Parson and Christine Chase.

A lone tear falls from her eye.

"I hate this happened to us," her glossed lips beginning to quiver.

"You gotta stay strong….How are you doing out there?"

"I'm doing all right I guess, just concentrating on doing my part, trying to make sure everything goes to plan," while shuffling through the folder to remove a document.

He reads it while she holds it against the glass, nodding his approval; they don't care who sees this.

"Make sure she doesn't change her mind."

"She won't, I'm very persuasive," replying with a mischievous grin.

"You become more beautiful with time."

"And still all yours….Last photo," she said. "I know this isn't exactly what you wanted me to get," holding it up. "But I feel a bit more comfortable with this one."

Parson examines what he sees, confident she'll be able to handle it.

"The rest of these are just these are just shots of the same things. I took different angles so you can get the full view."

She lets him see them all, closes the manila folder, and places it back inside her briefcase, locking it with a click.

With her elbows resting on the counter, and her face cradled in her hands, she smiles with those sensuous lips.

"So, how did I do?"

"Splendid. We'll shock the world."

They spend the reminder of the time in idle conversation, all of which they speak through the phones, until one of the guards signals the two minute warning. They say their goodbyes, and she stands to leave.

"You think I should've gone with the semi-auto?"

"No. What you're comfortable with is always the right choice."

Waving goodbye she blows him a kiss, and vanishes as quickly as she appeared.

"She'll do fine."

The spies shackle him for the long walk back to death row.

Chapter 2

On one wall hangs a ridiculous, 6' x 3' oil painting of Gordon Stuckey, surrounded by awards, plaques and other accolades from associations involved with the prison industry. There's also shots of him posing with local businessmen, politicians, judges, and other upwardly mobile individuals. On the adjacent wall are a bank of video monitors, and other state of the art surveillance equipment; providing him a details view of the entire facility. Open blinds cover an enormous floor to ceiling window, allowing sunlight to stream in. Mounted on the wall behind his desk is a twelve point, moose head.

"Shit! That's it! You mean ta tell me they spunt forty…," pausing to look at the timer on the video monitor.

"Forty-one minutes and sixteen seconds talkin' about nuthin'!" shouting as if they're puppies being chastised for soiling the floor. "What do you want me to say sir?"

He berates them with his heavy southern accent for several minutes, sighing and shaking his fat head in disbelief.

"We tried to the best of our ability," said Officer Roy Starns, 6'2" and built like a bull. And with just enough hair to tell it's brown.

"But they communicated in their usual sign language. And even if we did know it, we wouldn't have been able to understand it because they did it so fast. The woman wrote some stuff on index cards that she shielded us from seeing."

"Yeah, I noticed," Stuckey grumbled.

With a full head of gray styled to perfection, and those untrusting eyes, Gordon can pass for any number of politicians.

"We did get a little something of Parson."

Gordon's face brightened at the mention. Finally he'll get a piece of what they're up too.

Starns reaches in his shirt pocket and retrieves a small notepad. Flipping it open he says: "He mentioned something about making sure a woman doesn't change her mind, and something else abo-"

"Stop-stop-stop! Did he by chance say any of this into the phone?" holding a feigned smile.

"Yes but…"

"*BUT SHIT!*" he yells, jumping to his feet. "If they said it in the phone, then dat means I already got it over dere, you freakin' idiot!" pointing to the area where the bank of monitors sit.

Starns fumbled with a spec of lint on his leg realizing his stupidity.

"Whatchu got?" referring to the spy who's taken the silent approach.

Shane "Salvo" Salvatore, a young hot head from New York City. His ear length jet hair shimmers with styling gel. With broad shoulders, and a permanent smirk, he resembles a Bronx wise guy. Rumored to have mafia connections, he was an instant hit with Gordon. He loves the underworld.

"Sorry Mr. Stuckey. I don't have any more than you've already got."

He talks like one too.

"Guys, we gotta find out wuss goin' on. It's obvious their upta somethin', and their vera seruss about keepin' it a secret," massaging his forehead. "I don't need anything happnin' between now and the end of my term. It'll ruin my chances at makin' governor."

Scandal is Gordon's middle name. He's already survived two criminal investigations: One stemming from misuse of office back in his city councilman days. Allegedly, he misappropriated eighty two-thousand dollars; claiming the money was used for repairs. The other was for extorting a foreign proprietor of a successful grocery store chain.

"Lord knows I don't need no more investigations," thinking of his past brushes with the law.

"Find anything useful in his cell?"

While Parson visited with the mysterious blond, the two minions ransacked his cell. They've dug a few dozen times in the past but never once hit pay dirt.

Starns opens his notepad, and flips back several pages.

"Nothing of use. He has a few books on hypnotism, and another on psychology stuff, and an autobiography by a man who escaped the gas chamber by fooling a shrink into thinking he was retarded. Personally, I don't think he's stupid enough to leave anything incriminating around. One of the inmates said on numerous occasions they saw him flushing shredded paper down the toilet," flips it close, and places it back in his pocket.

Gordon shakes his head, and walks over to the window overlooking the main entrance. The evening sun is reflecting blindingly off the cars windshields. A woman bucking a child into a car seat catches his attention.

Jackson State Prison houses 71 death row inmates, and 1,021

others, with sentences ranging from a year, to quadruple life. If Stuckey had his way, the woman will have no reason to bring herself, or the child, because he'll abolish visitation. He watches as she backs her emerald green Honda® out of the space and makes for the exit. He's observed her perform the same weekly exercise for the past three years. Out of curiosity, he found out who she coming to see. It turns out to be her husband who's serving a five year bid for drug trafficking. The visits for death row inmates are held on the back side of the prison, along with its own separate parking lot. The only way he catches a glimpse of the flawless Christine Chase, is on the video monitors. Of course there's always the other option.

Years prior, he decided to introduce himself as she walked back to her car. Surprisingly, she was very polite. He asked if she had a moment to talk over coffee and she obliged. He indirectly attempts to pick her brain about the purpose of their visits, but she quickly recognized the ploy, and gave him the run around. She babbled on and on about how she wants only the best for Douglas, and will do anything for him, and that she has faith that they'll one day be reunited. From that day forward, he's convinced she's the unidentified accomplice the detectives spoke of. To him, she's just as bizarre and psychotic as Parson. A drop dead gorgeous blond in love with sick fuck like that spells trouble. Unfortunately for him, all he can do is sit on his hands and wait for the shit to hit the fan.

"And probably right around election time."

"Excuse me sir?" asked Salvatore.

"Nothing.....*Nothing goddamn it!*"

Storming back to his desk, he sits in his buttoned leather chair. Spinning around, he unlocks the resistant file cabinet in the corner, slides open the third drawer, and thumbs through the tightly packed folders until he finds the one he wants. Pushing the drawer close with his foot, he turns back to his desk and slams to thick folder down in front of him.

"Go get his ass!"

Parson waits at the end of the corridor for the guard to come out of the control room and frisk him before being allowed back in the cell-house. Each time an inmate leaves death row, upon returning, they're subjected to a full body search. There are six guards that escorted them, and the only time an inmate is left unguarded is for the twenty two ft. span from one set of sliding bars leading into the corridor from the main hallway, to the other set leading out of the corridor, and into the cell house. Of course there's a camera perched in the corner of the ceiling while they're left "unattended".

Parson places his cuffed hands on the cinder block wall and spreads his legs. The iron door buzzes open, and out comes two correctional officers slipping on leather gloves. He'd prefer deal with Officer Fawell, but he's gone for the day. After removing the shackles and conducting their search, he signals for his co-worker in the control tower to let him in. The towering iron gate squeaks as it grinds open.

There before him, half the length of a football field, and wide enough to park eight VW® Beetles bumper to bumper across the floor, is the cell-house. On one side are two levels of cells stacked one above the other running from end to end—two tiers. Each inmate has his own cell which helps cut down on the sexual activity. On the opposite side are Plexiglas® windows reinforced with iron bars that start midway up the wall, and to the top of the thirty foot ceiling. Directly up the center are ten rectangular stainless steel tables bolted to the floor with four seats wielded to both sides, and one at each end. Two 25 inch color televisions are bolted to the wall at either ends of the building, each with its own cushion-less, stainless steel sofa bolted to the floor. Six shower stalls are located midway down the wall beneath the windows. The often-buffed gray concrete floor shines like a sea of glass.

A prisoner wearing a hair net hands him a tray—slop with the usual beverage: Punch spiked with an anti-erectile agent.
He takes it and heads towards the stairwell, amid the echoes of televisions and noisy inmates.
Grainger yells from the shower.
"You had uninvited guests again, just the two normal butt heads. I told them you weren't home, but they went in anyway. Must've been the spare key you gave 'em."
"Yeah? Fuck them."
And continues to his cell at the end of the tier. Adrenaline courses through his veins as he remembers he may've forgot to put the screws back inside the light fixture! That's where he stashes all of his contraband.
Peering through the bars, he's indeed left them out.
"Twenty-Three!" hands cupped around his mouth.
The door opens and he immediately moves to the bed. Looking over his shoulder, he carefully removes the access plate while making sure not to touch the live wires.
There it is, his prized possession: A folding, four inch buck knife. He lifted it off a rookie guard; the very reason staff members are strictly prohibited from bringing any kind of sharp objects to work. If found in violation of the rule, they're immediately re-lived of their duty.
After the CO realized he'd been pickpocketed, he notified the C.E.R.T. Team (Corrections Emergency Response Team) that his "cellphone" had been stolen. They literally tore the place apart, cut open mattresses and ripped apart pillows. After they

were done the place looked like a tornado had got trapped in-side. They found shanks fashioned in everything from rusty nails to sharpened toothbrushes, a number of water filled latex gloves used as masturbation devises, known as "Fe-Fes", were also dis-covered. The final determination was the phone must've been flushed down the toilet. Afraid that his phone would be used against him, he transferred to another prison the following week.

Checking again to make sure the coast is clear, Parson quickly replaces the plate, reaches down and removes a chunk of con-crete from the floor, revealing the crude bit he created by burn-ing a toothbrush, and packing the melted plastic inside the head of one of the screws he'd lubricated with margarine. After the plate is safely secured, and the bit back in its proper place, he sits on the bed and eyes his tray.
"*There baaaaaaaa-ack!*" a harmonic warning from Grainger mimicking the little girl from Poltergeist®.
Parson sticks his head out the doorway. Six guards are standing in the corridor waiting for the gate to open. His heart skips a beat when he notices that one of them are holding a milk crate of chains and shackles.
E-house!!!!
The building prisoners are quarantined once the date for their execution has been set; usually two weeks before the big day. He's having a warp speed picture show of memories, visions of Christine and their plans flash through his mind.
Another flash!
Images of his childhood.
Flash!
Tears running down his mother's face.
Flash! Flash! Flash! Flash!
Carnage! Bloodshed! Mayhem!
Aftermath.
"Parson! Warden wants to see you!" shouts Starns, standing at the bottom of the stairs.

The words hit him like a splash of cold water, snatching him from his daydream. The hideous images dissipate into thin air. A huge sigh of relief escapes from his chest, as his heart returns to its normal pace.

"You all right man?" Grainger standing beside him with water dripping from his hair.

"You're dazed like you saw the devil or something."

"I did," and walks away.

They shackle his ankles and double cuff his hands, ending with a mask over his face.

"Let's go," ordered Salvatore, after checking everything.

Due to the short chain around his ankles, Parson can only muster baby steps.

"I can hardly move. At this rate it'll take an hour to get there." Starns looks at him and laughs.

"You've got nothing but time, dead man walking."

"Hey, can you get the bags out the car?"

Sitting the three she carried in on the kitchen counter, her keys dangling from the deadbolt. It's almost dark when she returns from the store. Stockton gets up and pulls the keys from the door, and gets the rest of the bags while she puts the things away. After everything's out, he returns to his favorite chair, and flips the liquid crystal display television.

....and tonight we bring you a tragic story about a man who

spent seventeen years of his life in prison for a crime he didn't commit............"

"Turn that up a little please?" asking from the kitchen.

"I hear lies like this every day. I don't care to hear them when I come home."

"But I'm interested in it," taking eggs out of a Styrofoam® carton, and placing them inside the refrigerator.

"And secondly, how can the courts keep making mistakes like this anyway? This isn't the first time I've heard of something like this happening."

"It's life," showing his displeasure with her interest in the story. But turns it up anyway.

"Michael Isakson lived on the east side of Chicago with his wife and three sons, where he worked as a truck driver to support his family. On October............"

As soon as a commercial comes on, she says: "Now don't you think that's sad? The guy had a family depending on him."

"What a shame."

"Have a heart Stow!"

"I do. It's just immune to shit like these sad prison stories. All you do is sit at that desk all day, yapping on about feeling sorry for the world."

"Whatever, it doesn't matter how you feel. Ironically, I met this lady at the store today. We were in the check-out line, and she starts telling me about how she has a loved one in prison, and how she's stood by him the whole time he's been there, and that she's found a way to get him out. She swears he's not guilty of the things they say. I told her I work in a law office and gave her one of my cards; she was really nice. Funny thing though, all I keep thinking about is how pretty she was. I don't think I've ever met a woman blessed with that kind of beauty."

"I'm transferring to another prison," without acknowledging anything she said.

"Say what?" raising her voice over the running water she's using to loosen the lid on the jar.

She turns it off so she can hear him. Holding it in her left hand she asks him to repeat himself?

"I'm transferring to another prison, I need a change of scenery. The warden says there's room at a camp about forty miles of here."

"And you aren't going to think this over?"

"Nothing to think about, I'll be starting sometime this week."

"And what might the name of this new place be?"

".......Jackson State Pri-"

CRASH!

She drops the jar, spattering spaghetti sauce everywhere. Shards of broken glass, chunks of tomatoes, and green peppers blanket the tile floor.

Stockton leaps up and runs to the kitchen!

"Are you okay, what happened!"

Kathy frozen like a statue.

"Kathy!"

Nothing.

Her heart is racing!

"Kathy!"

No response.

"KATHY!" shaking her.

She doesn't bat an eye.

He runs for the phone, and just as he's about to dial 911, she comes out of it.

"Sss.......Stow......Stockton, I'm fine," stuttering the words.

She just realized she dropped the jar.

"Aaaaaah!"

Her manicured hand clutches her breast.

Fear envelops him like a hungry anaconda. He sprints from the glass end table, and back to the kitchen. Crossing the floor, he tramples through the sauce, crumbling glass under his boot. His chest rapidly rises and falls, drawing in as much oxygen as he can! With her hand in his palm, and his eyes glued on hers, he dials 911. A tear fall from her face as she winces again. Her eyes roll backwards, and her body turns into the Leaning Tower of Pisa.

It's like a bad dream!

As if it's happening in slow motion, her head falls sideways into the side of the refrigerator, and slumps to the floor.

"Nine, one-one, what's your emergency?" came a drab female voice over the phone.

He tries but can't speak. A grapefruit sized lump of fear is lodged in his throat.

"Nine, one-one, what's your emergency?" the female dispatcher repeated.

His vision becomes blurry, his head grows heavy and unstable! His chest exhales the last of its oxygen reserves, and suddenly everything becomes dark!

Chapter 3

The sound of shattering glass brings him back to his senses. His head feels like it's been bashed by a falling bowling ball. Feeling the cold wetness against his face and smelling it, he knows he's lying in spaghetti sauce. His vision gradually returns as the image of Kathy comes into view, causing his heart to flutter as it all comes back to him.

"Police!" shouts a man from somewhere inside the living room. Stockton rolls on his side with his hair matted with Prego®.

"Help!"

The first officer spins into the kitchen in a crouched position stiff arming a 9mm pistol!

His partner leaps from behind the wall and onto the, floor pointing his gun at Stockton!

"Freeze!" skittish, like this is his first day on the job.

"I think my wife just had a heart attack!" blood tricking from his forehead.

His partner is already checking her pulse.

"She's alive," said the larger one, who radios EMS before asking more.

Deciding there's no clear and present danger, he returns his weapon to its holster, but doesn't take his eyes off Stockton as he sits up.

"She was standing there talking to me while I is sitting over there," pointing to the recliner. "And I hear her drop something. I jumped up and ran in, and she's standing there not saying a word, she just fainted. I called nine-one-one and that's when I remember getting real lightheaded."

He pauses for a moment, and says embarrassingly: "I must've fainted too," realizing that's the only plausible explanation for him waking up on the floor.

"Are you *sure* that's all that happened?" the officer not quite buying his story.

"Damn right that's all that happened!" offended by the little scary man's insinuation.

The other cop gestures his partner to stand down.

"Well give me a detailed run down?"

Stockton does, and by the time he's finished, he hears sirens coming down the street. Moments later paramedics are coming through the door casually pushing a stretcher as if it's just another day at the office. The EMT passes him and goes directly to Kathy and checks her vitals. Smelling salt is waved under her nose, causing her to slowly regain consciousness.

"What's your name ma'am?"

She winces and rubs her forehead.

"Kathy….uhm…..Kathy Easterbrook," she whispered, about to

say something else.

"Can you feel your hands?"

"Yes," blinking her eyes in an attempt to clear her vision.

The EMT rolls the stretcher over to her, tracking red footprints and wheel tracks onto the unscathed portion of the floor.

"Ma'am, we're going to take you to the hospital to make sure everything's okay. It can just be a bad case of heartburn, but we won't know for sure until the doctors take a look at you."

She shakes her head in agreement.

"How about you sir, are you okay?" finally paying attention to Stockton who's holding a bloody towel to his head.

The EMT patches him up while Kathy's rolled to the ambulance. Mr. Vickers is standing outside in his pajamas trying to figure out how he can lend his sixty six year old, arthritic hand. The police broke the window beside the front door so they could get in without having to kick it off the hinges.

Once outside, Stockton asks Vickers to keep a watch on the place while they're gone. He quickly accepts, pleased that someone has honored them with the task of protecting their property. One has to admit, weighing in at a beefy 138lbs., and armed with Centrum Silver®, he's quite a force to be reckoned with.

With Kathy safely tucked inside the ambulance; sirens waking the dead, Stockton in his Silverado, and the cops taking up the rear in the squad car, the convoy pulls away from the brick house en-route to Grady Memorial Hospital. General Vickers crawls into his foxhole and awaits the arrival of the Viet-Cong.

Upon further examination, it was determined that Kathy hadn't suffered a heart attack, but rather a mild stroke or "brain attack" as it's sometimes called. Despite finding no signs of blood on her brain, or blocked vessels, the physician gave her a date for a follow-up appointment before discharging her after performing a battery of tests. A prescription for Plavix® was given as a precaution.

They ride in silence while traveling along I-20 East. Kathy stares at the spectacular Atlanta skyline pegged with sleek skyscrapers, extravagant hotels, and elaborate office buildings; still suspended in a state of disbelief, his words echoing in her mind. She looks at him, his eyes are glued to the road not noticing her stare. He seems to be in a world of his own too, one that keeps replaying the events of today. Her hand begins to trembling and she has the sudden urge to vomit.

"Stockton," she said, as he pulls onto the exit ramp. Welcoming the thought they're almost home so she can puke in private.

"Yeah?" waiting for the light to change.

"I....I don't feel it's good for you to work at that place."

"It's no different than the Feds."

The light turns green.

"And besides, I can't undo it. I already gave the warden the go ahead. My replacement's scheduled to fill my position tomorrow, I'll be all right. It's not like I'll be working death row or something."

Harry travels north on I-85, the speedometer on his '86 Caprice holding steady at 55. He's in no rush to get to his destination, cruising in the slow lane enjoying a much needed day off. After his wife lost her battle with cancer, and his boy railroaded by the savage beasts of the Texas justice system; he decided to be part of something. He decided to make a stand, refusing to sit there and watch what happened to his son be done to someone else. Months after his son was murdered, as he calls it, by lethal injection, a lawyer hand delivered a sealed package to the Travis County Sheriff Department, the prosecutor who tried the case, and one to the local newspaper. Inside was a video recording of a man who'd contracted HIV and had less than a week to live. He confessed to the murder, rape, and robbery of the old woman Harry's son was convicted of. He gave the location of the missing murder weapon, the specific date, time, and method used to kill her. Also in the package were three plastic pouches. One contained a sample of his semen, the other contained follicles of his pubic hair, and in the last was a patch of the slain woman's hair. The body was exhumed to see if the hair matched. It did.

The semen sample initially thought to be his son's was DNA tested.

It wasn't.

However, it *was* a perfect match to the one provided by the confessed perpetrator. It was determined that Harry Fawell Jr. had been wrongly accused, convicted, and executed for a crime he didn't commit. The story made front page news, and exposed vast errors on the prosecution's behalf. As one might expect, he promptly sued—blaming the sheriff, the judge, the prosecution, the police department, the Dept. of Corrections, as well as a long list of other agencies who he believed were responsible for the murder of his only son. A settlement offer in the amount of $750,000 was received by his legal team; of which he declined, stating: It's not about the money, but the principle—he wants the world to know his son was innocent. And also wanted

to convey the message that this is what happens when people put career advancement before finding the truth. The Supreme Court awarded him eight million dollars in damages, fined the state anther five million, and ordered them to suspend all executions until each case was reopened and thoroughly reviewed.
Nine additional men were found to have been wrongly convicted, and that was just on death row. Harry invested nearly three-quarters of the award money into various watchdog organizations, wanting to make certain no other people fall victim to overzealous prosecutors, and less than honorable judges.

He gets off on the swank Lenox Rd. exit, Atlanta's version of Rodeo Dr. Instead of being known as Beverly Hills, this slice of the peach state is named 'Buckhead', a place where noses are held in such a way that the sight of nasal debris is a normal part of the grandiose ambiance. Entertainers, entrepreneurs, professional athletes, orthodontists, executives, and other well-to-do's who make this their stomping ground.
The old steering pump whines as he turns into the parking deck. After taking a ticket from the machine, he pulls into a space beside the elevator.

He doesn't have one designated with his name on it.

The NOFTWA Agency or, National Organization For The Wrongly Accused is located on the 13th floor of the black granite edifice. NOFTWA is one of the agencies he founded. After exiting the elevator, he pushes through the clear glass doors, and is greeted by an enthusiastic receptionist.
"*Heeey* there *Harry!*"
Deborah Williams, a buxom African American college student with a genuine smile.
Before he can return the greeting, she comes from behind her desk with open arms, hair intricately braided into a beautiful crown.

"Long time no see stranger!"

Hugging him to the point that he can't breathe.

"I've been working a lot, haven't had much time to do anything else. Some of the other agencies needed a hand."

"You're always trying to help someone. I wish there were more people like you."

"So what's been going on? Any new developments?"

Her smile disappears.

"We just got a date for one of the cases were looking at."

"When is it set for?"

"June, twenty-fourth."

"*Damn,* that's in thirteen days!" consulting his G-SHOCK® wristwatch.

"I know. The board has gotten in the habit of releasing dates at the last minute, giving us less time to fight for a stay. Bad news is that we may've had a chance to get his sentence reduced if we can somehow convince the governor that he wasn't in a sane state when he committed the crime."

"Matthew Grainger," he said automatically.

"How'd you know?" going back behind her desk to answer the phone.

He knows all of the men on death row, and exactly what they've been convicted of.

Matthew Edward Grainger, born April 19th 1959 in Marietta, Ga. Apparently, his wife of fourteen years was having an affair with a man that turned out to be the father of the son he believed to be his. The child was ten at the time, born four years into the marriage. Out of the blue, he received an anonymous letter informing him of the truth about the child. After approaching his wife with the letter she admitted he's wasn't the father. Grainger was devastated, but forgave her and continued the union without incident. Sensing infidelity was still an issue, he secretly tailed her to a motel where she entered a room with the child's biological father. He kicked in the door, caught his wife on her knees performing oral sex, and shot them both.

"More bad news," after hanging up. "That was Kenneth Myers, the court appointed counsel for Mr. Grainger. He said that he just left the capital and Yates isn't budging on this one. He told him he's already heard the temp insanity excuse, and it's nearing election time, and is keeping his promise to remain tough on crime."

"Politicians are sonofabitches! Let that would've been his boy, he wouldn't have gave a rat's ass about no damn constituent! I'm going in here to speak to Sivan about organizing a rally. Thanks Deb."

"Sure thing, it's good to see you again."

"You to darlin'!"

Heading through the brown double doors, his comfortably worn Cole Haans® sink into the thick carpet—the walls lined with awards recognizing NOFTWA as one of the leading human rights organizations in the country.

"Hi Harry!" speaks a squat blonde stopping to give him a hug before continuing down the hall.

Each open door he passes brings similar results.

Sivan Goldstein, (pronounced see-VAHN) is a modern day Joan of Arc. After receiving her masters from Harvard, and widely being considered one of the best legal minds in the country, she resigned from her six figure job as partner of a highly regarded firm in Manhattan, to come and work for him. Since joining NOFTWA nine years ago, she's won acquittals for two hundred and fifty two men, and eighteen women. That was before the case that brought her national acclaim: She proved an Iranian immigrant had been wrongly convicted for killing a Philadelphia police captain, who coincidentally happened to be Jewish. Harry knocks before entering. Her name in brass cursive adorns the stained oak door. She's just ending a heated conversation when he walks in.

Before her window overlooking Buckhead sits her desk, the adjacent wall showcases her many degrees and accomplishments. The second she spots him, she rises from her high backed leather chair.

"You have the uncanny ability of showing up right when I need you! Must've got my telepathic message?" pushing her chair out of the way, and coming around the mahogany slab of lumber.

Sivan wastes no time in continuing the ritual of trying to squeeze the life out of him, her silky hair resting against his chest the way a daughter would her father.

"You've got to stop being such a stranger," speaking with perfect English.

"You know I work a lot," taking a seat before her desk.

He informs her about Grainger, and his idea for a rally.

"That bastard Yates! I hope he never runs for president. He'll be just like his war crazed uncle!" resentment bitter in his voice.

"It'll probably be the end of the world, nuclear missiles flying everywhere."

"Tell me about it. I think a rally will be the exact thing he doesn't want," flipping through her vintage Rolodex®.

"Here it is," and dials the number into her cellular.

Sivan is a "classic chick", and quite stuck in her ways.

"Time to redeem a favor," she stated, waiting for an answer.

She talks for several minutes, writing on a Post-It®.

"That was my contact at the Atlanta Journal®. He said he's going to dig up all the dirt he can find on governor elephant ears. How about I treat you to lunch. By the time we get back we can salivate over Dumbo's naughty deeds."

"I'm starving."

Parson lay face up on his bunk, counting the ceilings mildew stains once again. The visit with Stuckey was nothing more than an interrogation laced with threats of *"I'll make your time a living hell if you don't tell me!"* and *"Confess or I'll have her arrested!" I'm already living in hell!"*
What can be more like it than being confined to a concrete bunker no bigger than a high school gymnasium? What can be more like it than waking up every day in an 8 x 8 cell; physically abused until tamed, treated like an animal—let out of your cage in the day time so you can be studied and watched, then herded back inside after the spectators are gone?

What can be more like hell than being an innocent man and this be done to you?

In the blink of an eye, life snatched away, given a serial number; warehoused until you become fatted calf, and sent to the slaughterhouse. Parson has watched two men he believed to be innocent die. Nevertheless, he can't pretend to be of those unlucky souls. The evidence against him is to damning, too much. It's no subterfuge he can employ to snake his way out of this one. It's widely believed that the state has got it right on this one. The system finally did its job.
"Douglas Parson is undoubtedly the heinous murderer of Joseph Tangier," were the prosecutor's exact words.
And there's no way the judge, the governor, or even the president will believe different.
He dreams about the murder, reenacts it, remembers the way the bishop's body was slumped over in the chair with a gaping hole in the side of his head, brain matter and pieces of skull fragments still attached with hair spattered on the wall behind him.

Killers live to kill again.

He's going to see to it that his life doesn't end because of deceased pervert Joseph Tangier. He and the devout Christine Chase will show them something they've never seen!

The animal gets off of his bed and walks onto the tier. The cell house is a buzzing with activity. A large group of orangutans engage in a raucous game of spades below. At the other end of their unnatural habitat, a crowd of silverbacks jump up and down after the Falcons scored a touchdown against their cousins the Eagles. Sheephead Beasley is locked in his cage, much too dangerous to mingle. The zoo keepers sitting in their fortified control tower keep a close eye on the primates.

Meanwhile, Grainger is sitting on his bed buried deep in some romance novel. He looks up when Parson walks in.

"Man, you know this stuff is better than porn. I mean this lady is screwin' like there's no tomorrow. And this lady here," flipping to the back jacket to show him a picture of the author. "Ain't leaving out nothing. Makes me wanna go take Fe-Fe in the shower," looking like he just might do it.

"You know they say too much jacking will make you blind," informs Parson.

"Yeah, I'm just kidding. So anyway, how was the visit?" using a comb to mark his page.

"We talked about how we're going to rake these cocksuckers over the coals."

"Let me know when so I can rake they butts too."

A cryptic grin comes over Parson's face, his voice grows low.

"The whole state will know when it happens. You or anyone else won't be able to miss it. I'm going to rip Georgia a new asshole."

"Rip it then! I hate this state!"

And cuts his hand through the air.

"You must be planning to get one of these CO's or something?" Parson doesn't say a word.

"Well whatever you do, they deserve it!....Just like the slimeball I went to court with who molested five autistic kids, and they only gave him three years. I shoot my no good wife and her lov-

er—who very much deserved it, and I get sentenced to death.....
Let me ask you a question, it may sound strange considering
we're waiting to die; but do you thinks the death penalty's fair?"
"Fair how?"
"Like do you think it's right to kill someone."
Parson doesn't have to think about it.
"Yes. Some people deserve to die."
After a long pause, Grainger says in a voice full of sorrow: "This
mess been really weighing on me lately man, I'm having night-
mares every night now."
Pause.
"The sight of her sucking that jerk off made me lose it…I mean,
she has a kid by the guy after we'd been married for four years,
and tells me it's mine. What the hell!"
Another pause.
"I did everything for them, I was a real dad. Baseball games,
fishing trips, walks in the park, I mean the whole nine. I treated her so good that she didn't even have to work. I was the
man so I took care of everything; you know, like a man should.
Sometimes I worked sixteen hour shifts to make sure she had
everything she needed. I bought her new clothes when I didn't
even have nothin' for myself.…...Then she goes and does some
mess like that to me. *Maaaaan,* people are messed up! You reach
down to help a person up, and as soon as they get to their feet,
they turn around and stab you while you ain't lookin'."
Looking away, he wipes his face.
"After I found out that boy wasn't mine, I was crushed.….…But
I had so much love for her that I forgave her and continued to
treat her like my queen. How stupid could I have been!"
A tear rolls down his face and falls to his lap.
"No way she should've done me like that. It hurt me so bad
when I caught her in that hotel room, I mean it was like my
heart had been ripped out and steamrolled. When I knocked on
the door, and she opened it and saw it was me, she slapped me
in the face and started cursing me out, saying I was spying on

her…Man can you believe she slammed the door in my face and went back to what she was doing like I wasn't even *there?* I could hear them from outside. I just stood there like a dumb ass and cried while she got her brains fucked out!"
Punches the bed.
".......You think I deserve to die?"
"No."
"You think I was wrong?"
"Yes," realizing this is the first time he's every talked about that night.
"Me too."
The dam no longer able to hold back the mounting pressure breaks, allowing years of pain to flow unrestricted down his face. He shakes his head like he has water in his ear, misting Parson with tears.
"Man, I went to the car, the one that I bought for her, and reached in the glove box, and grabbed the gun that I gave her and went back in there, and I just killed them both. I just shot 'em man, and waited there holding the gun until the police came."
He wipes his nose with the back of his hand.
"I might be a killer or whatever, but I got a heart. I would never do nothing like that to somebody," tears squeezing from his tightly shut eyes, running over his cheeks.
"Hey," Parson said, laying a hand on his shoulder. "I don't care what anybody says about you. You're all right with me you hear. This system isn't designed to be fair Matt. This is the same system that considers it legit business to hostilely take over a company, fire all the workers, then turn around and sell it for a profit. This is the same system that says it's okay to take from the poor, and give to the rich. This is the same system that says it's okay for pharmaceutical companies to charge patients thousands of dollars for the medicines they need to survive. If you'd would've been some rich cosmetic surgery prick out of Dunwoody, they would've charged you with involuntary man. Your fast talking

attorney would've pushed for temp insanity—and since you're part of society's elite, you'd have done about two years in some exclusive mental hospital, and all your sins would've been forgiven."

After pausing to take a deep breath, Parson continues.

"Life just isn't fair man. Life's never been fair, and it sure as hell ain't never gonna be fair. Life is dirtier than that woman could've ever been."

Grainger swipes his sleeve across his face.

Abruptly, all of the noise and in the cell-house ceases!

An eerie silence is cast over the place!!

Parson peeks over the top of the guard rail, and notices all of the motionless inmates are looking toward the corridor.

His heart drops out of his chest and slams into the pit of his stomach!!!

He knows exactly what's about to happen.

Slowly, he takes a step out onto the tier and closes his eyes. He can hear the gate sliding open—the sounds of chains dragging across the floor ricochets off the walls. Saying you'd rather be dead, and actually getting ready to die is two different things. Parson opens his eyes.

"Matthew!.....Edward!.....Grainger!"

The words hang in the air.

The seven guards are already coming up the stairs, chains banging as they come. Something must've grabbed the hands of time, because each step seems to last an eternity.

Parson's muscles no longer move by his command, the floor feels like squishy rubber beneath his feet.

"Excuse us!" demanded a guard he's never seen before.

He's never known them to come get a man without prior notice. Watching in disbelief, they begin the process of chaining Grainger around his ankles, shackling his wrists, and running a big chain around his waist; an iron ring dangles before his belt buckle. They chain another around the links between the hand-cuffs, through the ring around his waist, and down, hooking it to the chain connected to his ankle shackles.

It's now impossible for him to lift his arms from his waist. Steps more than ten inches can't be made.

Just like that it's done. No goodbyes, no words of encouragement—only the collection of the beast. They walk him out of his cell and down the tier. The new guy gathers Grainger's belongings, and hastily stuffs them in a clear garbage bag.

"Be careful with his stuff," speaking to the CO as he walks past. Billings is stamped on his nameplate.

He's almost to the stairs when Sheephead gives him a nice warm welcome to the row.

SPLASH!

Excrement and piss all over his brand new uniform.

Deafening laughter erupts throughout!!

"You fuckin' dickhead! Ahma bash your fuckin' brains out, you fuckin' asshole!"

Evidently, being doused with body waste triggers the same reaction in everyone. Billings spits in Sheep's face.

A small brown turd sits on the toe of his boot.

Three COs run back and grab him. Since they have more pressing tasks, stomping a mud hole in Beasley will have to wait. And besides, new guys don't mean that much to the vets anyway.

"This ain't over faggot!" and spit in his face again.

"I know it ain't," Sheep replied, and uses his finger to wipe the saliva off his face, and the tip of his tongue to lick it off.

"Cuz ahma get yo' perty lil' ass era time I lay eyes on ya. Bitch!" Then forces his hand down his pants, exposes his penis, and begins fondling himself.

Billings kicks the turd back inside his cell and walks away.

"And ahma stick dis here bananer in yo' tailpipe fo' I get fried Dougie boy!" and licks the rusty bars.

"But I'll have already have gutted you like a pig," Parson standing inches from his face, voice cold as ice, mouth a tight hard line.

Although Beasley is a stone-cold killer in his own right, he chooses not to engage Parson, knowing he means every word. "Fuck you punk!" before walking away.

Parson returns his attention to Grainger who's being double checked, chains snake around his body like vines of kudzu. Grainger looks up at him with a blank expression.

Parson raises his hand and places it over his heart. The action causes a domino effect as each man follows suit. There they stand, like soldiers pledging allegiance to the flag. But there is no flag, and they aren't soldiers. They're condemned men awaiting their turn to receive a similar farewell. The chances of Grainger being seen alive after he passes through those doors are slimmer than burning a Quran at the Kaaba and living to tell about it. The iron gate rattles open.

He turns his back and steps into the corridor.

BANG!

Slammed shut against the frame.

The hands all fall back to their sides!

The second gate opens.

He steps out the corridor and into the hallway, and looks at Parson for the last time.

BANG!

The second gate returned to its normal position.

The faint sound of chains dragging across the floor is all to be heard, as Matthew Edward Grainger became nothing more than a memory.

Chapter 4

Stockton pushes his '06 Chevy north on Interstate 75 doing well over the 65 MPH limit. Today has been a disaster to the second power. Aside from the fact that one of his peers found his keys in the break room back at the federal pen, it's been horrible. The fuzz-buster detects enemy radar up ahead!
He eases his foot off the accelerator in time to see Georgia State Patrol parked between two short hills that were seemingly made for cops to hide behind, and spring out on unsuspecting motorists as they fly by.
The second he's out of sight, he eases back on the gas thinking that blowing off steam on the big V-8 will make him feel better. Suspecting the A/C is robbing him of needed horsepower, he

flips it off. The metallic silver pickup instantly shows its gratitude, by dropping the orange needle on top of the 100 MPH mark.

The sun is high, and the skies are clear.

He lowers the power windows and feels the clean country air. Smelling cattle, he notices them grazing on a dairy farm; conjuring memories of his childhood. Alex, T-ball, camping, his adopted parents, his good for nothing father, his chronically depressed mother—more steam billows from his smokestack. He pushes the Silverado harder.

At the last minute he sees the exit coming up fast on the right, and slams on the anti-lock brakes, swerving across two lanes, narrowly missing a tractor-trailer hauling freshly cut pines.

A red Caravan packed with kids is exiting the highway as he cut in front of the semi!

Left with only a split second before he careens into the back of the minivan, he slings the truck to the right, the deep tread tires screech as they slide across the pavement! The truck goes airborne off the side of an embankment, sending a gravel infused dust cloud into the air, doing a 360 before coming to a bumpy halt feet from a light pole!

The lady in the Caravan calmly turns left off the ramp, and continues on her merry way, unaware that she'd just missed being involved in a collision that would've sent unbuckled youths flying everywhere.

The dust is just starting to settle when he spots the state patrol car coming over the hill.

"Mind your own business cop," watching the blue Crown Victoria like a hawk.

But police never mind their own business.

The officer hits the lights, pulls behind his pickup, and gets out.

"How you doing officer?" stupid grin on his face.

But he's not smiling. The black campaign hat, dark tinted shades, and bushy mustache gives him the 'I don't have time for bullshit' look.

"You been drinking?"

"No...Not really," his voice giving him away. "Well I drunk a beer after work."

That's all he needs to hear. He grabs the door handle and opens the door.

"Please step out of the vehicle sir," but it's not a question.

Stockton thought that with his uniform on and all that he might get a break. He doesn't. But he does as instructed.

"You have anything in the truck I should know about?" his words full of suspicion.

"I have a pistol in my glove box. *And* it's registered," speaking with a tad too much cockiness.

The officer stares for a moment, and retrieves the firearm.

The gun comes back registered. Stockton gives him an edited version of how he got turned backwards on the side of the road. He's given the option to blow into a Breathalyzer® or go to jail. He chooses to blow, which shows that he's just below the legal limit. The officer returns his weapon and continues on his way, no apologies.

Back moving again, he makes certain not to exceed the posted limit, as he enters the small town of Rex. He pulls into the parking lot of *Fat Man's Bar and Barbecue*, formerly *The Crazy Horse*. The same lot his father was found lying in a pool of blood after being stabbed seventeen times.

The vehicle now sports a fresh coat of red dust and grass blades. Before entering, he walks to the side of the building were the dirt lot once was, and still remembers how his father looked laid face down covered in blood.

He hawks up a loogie, and spits on the ground.

Alexander Zarbin now owns the land and the joint known as Fat Man's. Business is slow this time of day. Only a few locals man the torn, faux leather barstools. Garth Brooks sings about the pain of a broken heart from somewhere on the other side of the room. A stocky guy wearing a cowboy hat and knee-high snake-skins taps across the hardwood floor en route to select another tune from the same Jukebox that's been there since the Crazy Horse days. Several squeaky ceiling fans circulate stale air stale throughout the building permeated with the odor of cigarettes. Photos of NASCAR® greats, iconic race tracks, classic muscle cars, and neon beer logos adorn the pine wood walls. A giant fieldstone fireplace sits midway between the bar and the rest-rooms.

Alex is just coming out of the kitchen when Stockton takes a seat, but he doesn't notice him sitting there, as he grabs a dish towel and dries mugs.

"Let me get a Bud in the bottle when you get a chance."

"Sure thing," not turning around.

He looks the same as when they were kids. He's been 5'10" from the time he was in junior high. And for some reason hasn't given up the lame haircut, but still slim and trim under the dingy apron.

"Man hurry up with my goddamn beer!"

Alex spins around about to say some choice words!

Smiles.

Throwing the dish rag on the counter, he shakes his head, glad to see his buddy.

"We don't serve city slickers here."

"Why didn't you return my call the other day jerk?"

"Sorry man, I been so busy I haven't had the chance," handing him a frosty brew.

"That's on the house."

"I wasn't paying anyway after what I just went through."

"What?"

"I was testing out the ole hag, and damn near hit a van full of kids. Then some hard ass cop tries to get me for DUI," pausing to take a sip. "On top of that, some asshole threw shit on me at work."

"You ain't kidding. You *have* had a wild day," leaning over the counter.

"Guess what I got?" holding a mischievous grin.

"Some stank ass breath."

He reaches into his pocket and produces a finger sized joint.

"That's because I've been smoking this. How about we grab a couple beers, and go in the office and get fucked up like old times?"

"I'm all for it."

Alex grabs 4 beers from the cooler, tells one of his employees to hold things down for a while, and they make for the kitchen in route to his office.

After thirty minutes of some good, slow burning, California green, they crack the beers—the cotton mouth is intense.

"Maaaaan…That-was-some-good-weed." Stockton barely able to see Alex behind the desk, whose red eyed and silly looking.

"Maaaaan…My mouth is dry as hell. This beer ain't doing shit," speaking as if he's thinking about what he's going to say as he says it.

Stockton stares at him for a moment, and bursts into laughter, pointing at Alex.

"Hey!….," laughing. *"Hey!…Stop doing th-,"*

He doubles over holding his stomach, knocking the empty bottle over on the desk.

"Alex!" he said out of breath. "Stop! You're making my stomach hurt," hanging his head.

Alex abandons using his natural resources and stumbled out of his office. When he returns, a glob of Vaseline® is on the tip of his index finger, and commences to smearing it on his puckered lips, but he puts too much. When he's done, it's unevenly spread and unflatteringly glossy.

Stockton falls to his knees and knocks the bottle to the floor. The room is spinning, and he's laughing so hysterically that his eyes are watering. After catching his breath, he uses the desk to pull himself back up.

"*Aah shit*. I'm faded, I gotta go home…..Help me up."
Alex helps him to his feet.
Walking to his truck, they converse and say their goodbyes. Alex gives him a bottled water, and offers to chauffeur him home, but he declines.

Stockton pulls in beside Kathy's Camry, having already cured the redness with a few drops of Visine®, and the cannabis odor with a splash of cologne. The house is permeated with the scent potpourri.
He hates potpourri.
"So how was your first day?" asked Kathy in a drab voice, slicing Vidalia onions and organic bell peppers.
"I got doused with shit," he said flatly.
She gives him a quick up and down.
"You look pretty clean to me. Why'd they do that for?"
"I need to take a shower and change clothes….Cause they're sub-human filth, that's why. Why don't you come back here and help me out of these clothes so I can relax and forget about it."
Still holding the knife she says: "You can handle it."
"So that's how it is? A man asks his woman for a hand and she flakes him off. I've done things for you that I didn't want to do. How about some compromise, or maybe a little gratitude."
She sighs, already knowing he's waiting for her to protest so he can lay the guilt trip on her, and throw a tantrum if she refuses.
"Give me a sec."
He signs again.

She puts the knife down, and walks out the kitchen.

He grabs her by the hand and walks to the bathroom. Sitting down on the side of the garden tub, she stands there.

"Here we go with this again."

Reluctantly, she reaches over and twists on the water.

The tantalizing scent of her perfume teases his nose. He studies her soft skin as she unlaces his boots, pausing to push a few wayward strands behind her ear.

The fact that he knows she doesn't want to do it encourages him more, moving him to stand. Taking her hand, he guides her to unbutton his shirt.

The sight of his muscular chest does not heighten her senses. All it does is move her to recall how long it's been since she's experienced true intimacy. Making love is not what she does with him. That experience is saved for someone else.

She tosses the blue correctional on the floor, his arms bulge under the XXL T-shirt. Using her petite, silk-like hands, she quickly slips them under—unable to establish a connection, unable to become interested. Touching her, he caresses her chest upward, feeling his accelerating pulse. Holding his arms in the air, she removes the V-neck. Steam from the shower casts a thick fog over the bathroom, covering the vanity mirror with condensation. His desire moves him to cup her face, he attempts to taste her lips. But she turns away, and instead offers her neck instead. Behind those iridescent blue eyes, she fantasizes about a similar scene, but with a different suitor. Slowly, he slides a finger down her chest, and unbuttons her lace blouse revealing her perfect breasts. Her nipples don't stiffen when he traces them with the tip of his tongue, but his member does. Breathing heavily upon her, he fights to rescue her from her slacks—she pushes his hand away when he tries to feel her.

"Get inside. I need a second," anything to stall the moment.

He obliges, hurries himself from his garment, and jumps inside. She hates this.

Feeling the hot steam against her skin, sweat trickles down her back. Telling her mind to enjoy it, she tries to convince herself this time will be different; more obligation than anticipation. She imagines a different plot, a different show; one of hopes and dreams falling like drops on the window's pane. What stroke of fate destined this scene, this act of a bad play. Feeling like a miner forced to pick worthless gems, she puts on her hard hat, and goes under.

As if she's made of the finest china, he takes her into his arms, his heart pounding wildly. Running his hands through her wavy, brunette hair, he gently lifts her legs.
If only she could be with that special someone.
She doesn't speak.
Only he touches, jerks, trembles, and tastes the salt on her skin; only his sounds of ecstasy fill the room.

His seed goes down the drain.

Standing alone before the mirror, Kathy curses herself. Just as always, she feels a tremendous sense of guilt after having sex with Stockton; knowing her heart isn't with him, but in a faraway galaxy—another dimension. The one in which she continues to live until she's positive that it's something that'll never again be.

It's 2 a.m., and Stockton's lying in the bed staring at the dresser reliving the day's events. He looks over his shoulder at Kathy, fast asleep under the covers. After the time in the bathroom, they got into a heated argument about her chronic reluctance to have sex, and again accused her of having a guy on the side. Things got ugly, he pushed her again too. She responded by pushing him back and refusing to cook.

His stomach growls at its emptiness, moving him to slide out of bed, and pull on an old high school sweatshirt, and blue jogging pants. The fridge holds nothing but leftover pizza, an uncooked pot roast, and an array of other unappetizing half eaten dishes. He grabs his duffel bag, places the items inside, and heads for the door.

Christine Chase lay in her empty bed thinking about Douglas. She longs to be with him, badly craves his touch. How much she'd love to kiss his lips. This is the night she'll complete another phase of their plan, the continuing start of a new era in their lives. She has no doubts about whether he'll do what he said. Wondering if he'll execute the first phase sometime this week, she rolls out of bed, and goes to the closet. Lifting up the carpet, she opens the secret compartment, and extracts her backpack.

Unzipping it reveals a .38 caliber handgun. After making certain she has all the necessary tools, she closes it, replaces the carpet, dresses in all black, and slips out.
After backing out, she disappears into the distance.

Holding a flashlight, she circles the locations in red ink, thankful she followed his advice and got the windows tinted. Getting off on I-20 West, Christine goes several miles before to Windsor St. Downtown Atlanta is deserted at this hour, only a few cars here and there—a lone homeless man tries to get her attention as she traverses down the boulevard. Picking up the map, she marks the first one with an X. And after taking several pictures of the brick structure, speeds off. A uniformed man standing in front of the adjacent building smoking a cigarette looks suspiciously as she coasts by taking more flash-less pictures. Speaking into his walkie-talkie causes her to pull away. Placing the fresh Polaroids® on the seat, she heads for the expressway.
After driving a short distance, she's off again. A patrol car sits in the parking lot of a deserted gas station on the left.
The blue lights comes on!
The car pulls forward!
She grabs the pistol!
But it shoots out, and heads the opposite direction.
Relief.
The two-lane highway grows darker as she drives farther from the expressway—a deer darts across the road, and disappears back into the dense forest.
Using the flashlight, she consults the map to make sure she's going the right direction—a scene from the past materializes in her mind; Douglas is all she thinking about.
Would you do all this for me?
A street sign causes her to check the map.
This is her turn!
The first sign of life she's encountered in miles. Lined with old country homes with big yards, and pickups in dirt drives, her

heart rate quickens; light poles with dark stretches between.
She checks her weapon: Seven hollow points at her disposal.
Breathing deeply, she creeps towards the address; dead go the
headlights. Releasing the accelerator, the car to rolls on its own
power, rocks rumble beneath the tires.
2728.
A small house wrapped in peeling white siding and gutters over-
run with leafs. Stopping about a block up, and void of hesitation, she turns it car off, grabs the backpack, and looks at couple
on the photograph.
An elderly couple.

◆◆◆◆◆◆◆◆◆◆◆

"What a workout that was."
Stockton's still perspiring when he walks into the bedroom after
secretly storing his duffel bag in the unused hallway closet. He
showers and slips into bed hoping not to wake her. He's come up
with the perfect explanation for his late night travels. Being that
he's an insomniac, he routinely works out at a 24-hour fitness
center. Certain she's fast asleep, he quickly dozes off, exhausted
from his "work out."

Kathy lying with her back to him, listens to him snore. Glancing
over her shoulder at the unsuspecting man, she gently slips out
of bed and hides her weapon. Returned to bed, she doesn't doze
off to dreamland.

You never know, she may have to kill him.

Harry grabs the pot off the coffee maker and fills his Thermos® with hot Maxwell House®. Sitting at his dining room table, he's ready to receive his sustenance of Honey Bunches of Oats®, a banana, and a butter soaked Thomas English Muffin®. The morning newscast begins as he starts to eat.

"This morning we begin with……..," the anchor began.

Kathy sits on the edge of her bed trying to slide on the stockings without adding another run.

"Shoot!" her fingernail catching the delicate material.

"I'm already late. These will just have to do," standing before the mirrored closet door.

She assesses the damage, grabs the remote off the nightstand, and increases the volume.

Stockton has punched his timecard, and stands in the break room trying to figure out what to get from the vending machine. "Come on slowpoke," joked the masculine female behind him. He looks back.

That's a big bitch!

The break room teams with people beginning their day, and others glad theirs is ending. An old television sits on a table beside the drink machine. The familiar tune of the morning news fills the room. The anchor is just starting to speak when he grabs his Lorra Doone® shortbreads out the machine, and turns to leave. "I'll *take* those cookies," and laughs.

"…..*with the gruesome discovery of a couple brutally murdered at their home. We now join Kale Savage live at the scene…….Yes Lisa, as you stated, the bodies of a man and woman were found around six-thirty this morning, when their neighbor noticed the front door was open and went to see if anything was wrong. He yelled inside but got no answer, and decided to call police, where ultimately the bodies were discovered. I asked one of the investigators if they*

have any information as to how, or why they'd been killed? He said they'd both been shot multiple times, but offered no clues as to motive. Although, he did say the couple seemed to be heavily involved in something. An unspecified amount of cash wasn't taken, and the names of the victims aren't being released."

Chapter 5

Parson stares blankly at the television mounted on the wall. A few dozen inmates scramble to get the best seat as that all-too-familiar piano melody fills the cell-house, signaling the start of *The Young and the Restless*. He watches the noise of movement and idle conversation cease, as the couple engage in a heated argument on the brink of their umpteenth divorce. Seeing all these convicted killers with their eyes glued to a daytime soap makes him wonder how these same people had the heart to take someone's life, some several. Parson usually reads during this period, because it's absolutely the most peaceful time of all the twenty four hours. Anyone brave enough to attempt more than a whisper will be quickly reprimanded, or face repercussions. Eight months ago, a guy convicted of decapitating a rival drug dealer decided he's not watching "this bullshit", and snatched the remote from another guy, and turned it. Before he could even sit down, a heavy-duty mop ringer connected with the side of his face, shattering his jaw, breaking his nose, and causing him to permanently lose the ability to hear out of one ear. Since, he's become an ardent supporter of the program.

Parson opens his book: *Abnormal Psychology and Modern Life*. He reads book after book on the behaviors of serial killers, dictators, and cannibals. The minds of these people intrigue him. He wants to understand their train of thought, see what led them to commit such atrocities against their brethren. According to study, most had been raised in dysfunctional homes, or either abused physically, mentally, sexually, emotionally, or all the above. A substantial number had grown up in foster care, group homes, or with relatives. Since every person on death row has been convicted of killing at least one person, he decided to take a survey of the willing participants. And provided them a list of multiple-choice questions pertinent to these theories. Astonishingly, ninety eight percent of the fifty nine participants had experienced some form of abuse, or alternative living arrangement as a child or teenager. Eleven had spent at least three months in a mental institution, thirty eight had lived below the poverty line for a minimum of five years, and only three out of the fifty nine stated that their fathers were in their lives. Fifty had no more than an eighth grade education. Only Matthew Grainger had been raised by both parents, lived a healthy middle class lifestyle, had never been abused, and holds a high school diploma. Unfortunately, his only brush with the law came the night he killed his wife and her lover.

"I almost gotcha girly!" shouts Sheephead, faced mashed between the bars.

"Juss keep own lookin' at me like dat!" trying to get a good look at a women who's just gotten out of the shower, penis is in his right hand. No one flinches when he cries out in ecstasy from his second tier cell.

Parson shakes his head and wonders had Sheep been born a psychopath. Flipping through the fat book, he pauses to look at the images of slain people, triggering thoughts of Joseph Tangier. He mumbles something as he gets up, walks to the intercom, and stabs the button with his pen.

"What'cha need Parson," a scratchy Harry from the speaker.

"Heard anything on Grainger?"

"I don't think Yates is budging on this one. Says it's too close to reelection; gotta to keep the public happy."

"So the chances of him coming out of E-house are pretty slim huh?"

"That's how it looks right now. But were still working on it." After pausing to answer the phone, he continues.

"If it was some way to stall it until after the election, he'd probably have a good chance of getting a stay. But that probably won't happen, especially since Gordon's promoting himself as a no-nonsense candidate who promises to be even harder on crime."

"Man Harry, he got a bum deal, they railroaded him. How can they claim pre-med when he didn't even bring a gun. Hell, he didn't even know she was going to the hotel to meet the guy. And on top of that, the guy that he shot......You listening Harry?"

"Yeah, go ahead. I'm listening."

"Anyway, the guy she was messing with, his damn sister was on the jury."

Harry's voice instantly changes.

"How'd you find that out!"

"He said he remembered her from a time she dropped the boy off."

"Why the hell didn't he say anything at the trial!"

"That's what I asked him. He said he didn't know it was illegal."

"Illegal! That's grounds for a mistrial! She had to have lied to get on that jury! They tell all potential jurors to notify the judge if they're related to the victim or the perpetrator so they can

be excused. That's contempt of court, and she should've been charged."

"If he would've had a half decent lawyer it would've been discovered.

Harry is speechless. All Parson can hear is him breathing.

"I gotta make a few calls!" he said finally, and shut off the intercom.

Parson can see him through the glass snatch up the phone and start punching numbers.

He gathers his things and heads up to his cell for a snack. While chewing, he thinks about how unfairly the lower echelons of society's totem pole get treated. Only the high and mighty are granted the rare privilege of obtaining real justice.

"It should be spelled: just us."

Looking at the men gathered around the trick box, (prison slang for television) he wonders how many of them received a square deal.

But not everyone is wronged.

"You're telling me the guy's sister was on the jury, even though it's a violation of law?" Sivan not believing her ears.

"Nobody knew. Luckily he told one of the inmates."

"He shouldn't have had to. His attorney should've done his job and investigated if not the entire jury pool, at least the final twelve. That also makes me wonder did he make any strikes, or just let the prosecutor have a field day and pick them all," upset

by the lack of effort put forth by the state appointed counsel.
"What did he do, just sit through the trial and pick up his check? Thanks for the information Harry. I'm going to make a few calls, especially to Mr. Myers. Call me later okay and I'll give you the news. Love you, Bye."
No sooner than she hangs up, she's snatching the receiver back up ringing Kenneth Myers. After five rings a woman answers.
"Fulton County Public Defender's office."
"Shouldn't it be more like public swindlers?"
"Excuse me?"
"Ken Myers please? Sivan Goldstein."
"One moment."
After a very long moment he answers.
"Kenneth Myers, how can I help you?" a nervous tone to his voice. The receptionist must've warned him that the caller on the line isn't happy.
"This is Sivan Goldstein, NOFTWA. I have a few questions concerning the Grainger case."
Judging from her tone the secretary was spot-on.
"Pertaining to?"
"Did you know the victim's sister snuck her way onto the jury?"
"*What!* Where did you get that from?"
"Straight from the horse's mouth!"
"I don't believe that. Even if that is the case, why didn—"
"He shouldn't have had to tell you! You should've investigated the pool for yourself, especially in a death penalty case!"
"I had I a hundred and seventeen cases at the time! What wa—"
"Don't give me that garbage Ken! You better drop whatever you're doing and find that jury list! Find out her name, then go directly to the courthouse and convince the judge to pull some strings! And maybe I'll think about not calling the bar on your incompetent a—"
But slams the phone down before it came out.
And starts rummaging through the towering case files strewn across her desk until finding the one she wants. Her contact at

the Atlanta Journal and Constitution® has dug long and hard into Yates' past. Surprisingly, there isn't much she can use to blackmail him with. He's been pretty clever at hiding his dirty work. There's only rumors of cocaine use and bribery, but nothing concrete. The only thing that she can use, but not against him, is the fact he's only communed one sentence since being in office. She searches the file for something juicy.

"What's this?....*A DUI!*...He hit another car!"

She's onto something.

"Charges dropped the following day."

The woman testified under oath that it was her who ran into him shortly after leaving a bar, though the field sobriety tests showed no traces of alcohol in her system. She even offered to pay for the damages. Yates declined and didn't file charges.

Sivan sails the file into the wastebasket.

After thumbing through her Rolodex®, she dials a number and after two rings, a man answers.

"Governor's office," in a stern voice.

"Yes. This is Val Dupree, Vice President of Cain Solutions. I'm one of Hal's top contributors, and it's very important that I speak with him. I've got some information I think one of his opponents may've gotten their hands on."

"Well he's unavailable at the moment. I'll take down your information and forward it to him. If he sees fit, I'm sure he'll contact you."

"No, that's not going to work! It's imperative that I speak with him *immediately!* Due to the sensitivity of this information, it can't wait. Either you find a way to get him on the phone, or there'll be a motorcade of his core donors parked at the mansion's gates demanding answers. I'm sure that'll be great for the news. We here at Cain will have no choice but take our million dollar offerings elsewhere; you get my drift? Maybe we'll cross the aisle and back the Dems candidate. I'm sure you've heard, due to the changing demographic, several analysts are projecting Georgia to turn blue in the coming years. You know the new regimes never keep previous staffers."

".....................One moment."

She can hear it in his tone: panic, confusion! Someone has gotten their hands on something detrimental to the campaign's health. *My job? I'll be unemployed!*

Sivan imagines the expression on Yates' cowardly face, sweat bullets running down the back of his neck. He'll be ecstatic when he finds out who it is.

Seventy-nine seconds is all it takes.

"Governor Yates speaking."

Just like she figured, he's shaking like a crap game.

"Well hello Mr. Governor. I hope I didn't disturb anything. If I did, I am truly sorry," disguising her voice.

He's silent, attempting to put a name with the voice.

"Who is this may I ask," polite but suspicious.

"You know who this is Hal! Stop playing games!"

"Goddammit Sivan! Couldn't you have left a message? I'm very busy."

"I didn't *want!*...To leave a message; thank you very much. And besides, it's important."

"Don't tell me it's something about the Grainger case."

"You must have ESP?"

Yates is quite perturbed. She's tricked him into talking to her, knowing he didn't want to. But he won't dare hang up on her. He completely understands Sivan Goldstein's power and influence. If she begins openly speaking out against him, he'll certainly lose votes, not to mention millions in donations. A horrible stench will be cast over his reelection campaign, possibly costing him his seat.

He sighs.

She hears it.

"Life's tough isn't it?"

"What do have that's so important?"

"As I recall, it's unconstitutional for a victim's immediate, *or* non-immediate family to be allowed to sit on a jury in a case

against the accused perpetrator of the crime against the victim?"
"Sivan, what are you talking about? Can you please get to the point becau-"
"Don't you raise your voice at me Hal!..I'm a lady, mind your manners!"
Then pauses for effect.
"The victim's sister was on the jury," she said flatly.
No one's exempt from her ferocity.
"Where did you get that from? And anyway, how can that happen? The courts are aware of relatives on juries."
"Grainger told me, that's where I got it. And the courts do screen them, but she lied on the questionnaire. And as I recall, that's contempt of court, and it's illegal. I'm going to have a talk with the media before I call the bar on the judge and entire prosecution. I also think the paper will love to get hold of this kind of malfeasance. All the fingers are going to be pointing at someone higher up the food chain. And guess who that'll be? And right smack dab in the middle of your little re-election campaign."
The heat seeking missile finds its target, and the impact is devastating.
On the other end Yates can feel his hopes at a second term slipping away. He can see Gordon Stuckey, the self-proclaimed warrior against crime, taking this and smearing it everywhere. He'll look like a fool in the eyes of the public. But if he communes Grainger's sentence, he'll look like a wimp. If he doesn't, he'll look like an idiot.
"Excuse me sir?" Sivan pulling him from his thoughts. "Are you still there?"
"Yeah, I'm here. Look, I'm not going to make any promises. I'll check on what happened. Give me a call tomorrow and I'll tell you what I have."
"*Oh*, You can have a lot done when you want Mr. Yates. But I'm not going to keep pestering you. I think I've given you enough to think about for one day. I'll just wait and speak with you tomorrow; and with all due respect sir, don't let me have to come

down there and show my behind. You have a nice day now you hear. Ciao!"

And places the receiver back on the console.

Leaning back in her chair with her fingers laced behind her head, she relishes the fact she's just thrown a monkey wrench into the governor's day.

"Some men are so weak."

Grainger doesn't want to speak to the chaplain. He feels he's already gotten right with the man upstairs. No one has been to see him since he's arrived at the "death house", no one cares. Maybe if his mother and father hadn't already passed, they would've paid him a visit. However, none of that matters now, he'll be dead in two weeks.

"I wonder if I'll get to see you guys in heaven?"

Quietly sitting at the brown desk bolted to the wall inside his cell, he stares at the picture of himself. He was only eight, riding his father's back while his mother laughs in the background.

The television sits outside the cell, but he has no interest in watching it.

"Mom, do you forgive me for what I did?.......What about you dad, do you?"

Tears well up.

"Dammit Matthew, we ain't gone keep crying like a little girl. Straighten yourself up, be a man," his lips quivering the words.

A tear traverses his cheek and lands on his mother's face. The resonances of pouring rain are all to hear inside the building sized liked a small house. This is the final punishment before be-ing executed—placed in a cold concrete cave with nothing but a television, and the thing that's sometimes his dearest friend, and others his worst enemy: his conscience. It knows his innermost thoughts, knows the name and size of each and every skeleton he keeps under lock and key, it possesses the ability to relentlessly gnaw at the most delicate parts of his soul, it doesn't care about making him cry, it ridicules him about things he doesn't want to think about, bothers him at night when he wants to be left alone. There's no defense from it. He can't cover his ears when he doesn't want to hear the truths it speaks. It's always there, lurking in the back of his mind; ready to lift him with pride, or suplex him with shame.

Matt puts the photograph in his shirt pocket, and goes to the sink. After a few splashes of cold water, he stares at himself.

How did I end up like this?

Trying to fight off the demons, he grabs the remote, and turns on the television.

ESPN® is airing highlights from the Miami Dolphins® miracle season of '72. He remembers that year like yesterday. His dad was the biggest Bob Griese fan. Each Sunday they'd sit and watch the game together. He'd always root for the other team just to irk him.

Larry Czonka's the best damn back I've ever seen.

He still remembers how he jumped out of his chair and spilled lemonade all over his coveralls the day Czonka broke the fran-chise record for rushing yards in a game.

Matthew looks at the tiny camera situated in the ceiling.

Men have been found hanging from the bars in this cell, unable to deal with the prospect of being cooked alive. Others have been known to deprive themselves of food and water. But that tactic is never successful though, considering ten days is the max an inmate can be confined to E-house before the sentence is carried out. They'd be close to death, but holding on just long enough to feel the straps bind them to the chair. Stuckey now requires the guards make sure an inmate drinks at least one cup of water a day. If the prisoner refuses, they're restrained to the bed and fed intravenously. He doesn't want the easy way of suicide being the cause of death, wanting them to feel the electricity course through their body. He adores the fact that he has his very own torture chamber. It's even rumored that after the body's removed, he lifts up the hood covering their face to see if their eyes have popped out. It's also rumored that he's drastically reduced the amount of voltage output. Instead of the process being done in the neat and timely fashion at full power, the result is a slower, more painful procedure. This way it takes longer to stop the heart from functioning. One observing an execution would equate it to a live fish being dropped into a vat of hot oil. It splashes and twists until can it no longer fight, and succumbs to being fried to a crisp—three minutes, depending on weight and size. Amazing how the same principle applies to humans. The larger ones take a little longer to cook.

Grainger doesn't sleep at all that night.

Chapter 6

Honk! Honk!
"Come on lady! The light turned green ten minutes ago!" Kathy giving the person in front of her a piece of her mind.
"You SUV drivers think y'all on the road."
And wheels around the beefy Escalade.
This is the second consecutive day she's going to be late for work; thanks to Atlanta's wretched traffic that seems to worsen by the day. Even with the subway, the city buses, the car pools, *and* express lanes; weekday mornings between seven and ten, expect all major interstates to be congested, and road rage rampant. She decides to sit back and accept the fact that she'll again have to hear her boss's mouth. She turns on the radio hoping to soothe her pain.

"This is Tony Thomas with your morning news report. New details have surfaced concerning the early morning shooting of the couple found dead in their home. According to a source close to the investigation, the man determined to be in his mid-fifties had been shot three times about the head and face, making it impossible for him to be identified at the scene. The woman of similar age had also been shot multiple times. Neighbors say they had only been living in the house for about a week, making it difficult for police to get much information about them. No one knows them, or where they'd move there from. Anything that could be used to identify them had been taken. Police are in the process of trying to locate dental records, and believe this was not a random act of violence. These people were targeted for a specific reason. No suspects have been named in this case."

As the station begins airing a statement from the police chief, the friendly blonde from the store appears, and is trying to say something.

Kathy lowers her window just as the city bus pulls away from the curb, engulfing her car in a noxious exhaust cloud.

"Hey girl!" she yells, waving her hand. "What are you doing out here in this mess?"

"I'm supposed to be meeting this guy from a modeling agency to talk about doing some commercials."

Even a looker like Kathy admires how beautiful she is. With those cheekbones, and that figure, modeling's an excellent choice.

"He asked if I have any friends that would be interested. You could easily land a top spot," declared the blonde.

"I'm too old for that kind of stuff. Plus, I don't think my size will allow me to make the cut."

"You and I both know that's not true," her car rolling forward.

"I'm thinking about going back to get my law degree. I think I'll

make a better lawyer than model."
"I'm sure you will. Which reminds me, what's a good time to reach you? I've got a few questions to ask?"
"Anytime!" she yells, coming to the intersection of Peachtree and North Avenue.
"Call me anytime! This is my turn!"
"Okay bye, drive safe. It's good seeing you again. Maybe we'll talk over lunch; my treat."
"Great!" and speeds down the hill.

The woman watches Kathy until the black sedan becomes a speck; smiling at the thought of getting to know her. She can possibly be the missing piece to the puzzle. But can she be trusted? She'll have to test the water before deciding to swim; considering she's not one to easily disclose personal information. Nor is she dumb.
She grabs the pack and lights up, clearly in rush to make it to the so called modeling appointment.

It's 9:18 and Kathy's almost twenty minutes late when she steps off of the elevator, and onto the 27th floor of the Equitable building. Her heels tap across the marble floor as she hurries through the double doors being held by a coworker.
"Good morning, thanks."
"You're late," said the receptionist. "Again."
"Hush."
And scurries through the lobby, and down the hallway.

Her dark office is cold and uninviting; which moves her to flip the lights on. Under her desk are two pink, fluffy slippers that welcomes her feet after retiring the Nine West® pumps. She reaches down and turns on her portable space heater; the relentless air-conditioning blowing from the window seal is an effective sleep deterrent. After logging on to her computer, she turns on the radio, plugs up her phone, and begins sorting case files. Listening to her messages, she wonders how long it will be before she calls. Kathy doesn't make new acquaintances often, but for some reason she feels drawn to this woman. Seeing her this morning vivified the somber mood she's been in after again hearing what some crazy did to those people.

"Knock, knock. Anybody home?" came a cheerful guest from the hallway.

"Come on in Megan."

"It's about time you got here," said the middle-age woman wearing a red, hip hugging pant suit; borderline inappropriate for work. Open-toe hills display her matching nail polish, a low cut shirt offers cleavage.

"I know, I got caught in that," pointing over her shoulder at the gridlock.

"Yeah right. You're probably late due to some early morning frolicking."

"Girl I wish. You're the forty-eight year old who thinks about sex like you're twenty-one."

"That's because I don't get any dick."

"Megan!" Kathy gasped.

"Ever since my husband went over the hill, he's lost his spunk. Viagra® won't even bring his little soldier to attention. His boring ass don't even want to do any….," flicking her tongue between two fingers in a peace sign.

Kathy gasps again, her mouth an 'O' of disbelief.

"I guess that's what I get for being married for nineteen years. I think it's time for me to trade my old horse for a new young stallion."

"I can't believe you said…uuuhm…I'm not going to even say it. But girl you need help."

Megan flips on the lights and makes herself comfortable.

"You're right. I need a pipe layer with a strong back. So what do you have planned for today since you don't wanna talk about the fun stuff," grinning.

"Probably just organize these files, and call few of Vincent's clients. Unless something else comes up, that's about it."

"Your day sounds as uneventful as minds. All work and no foreplay."

"Me-gaan."

"Okay, I won't say anything about candle wax, or leather whips and cuffs."

She laughs at her co-worker. It's never a dull moment with Megan around.

"You hear about those people getting murdered yesterday?"

"Yeah, It's all over the news. They say they believe the person might make a habit of it."

"Just what Atlanta needs, another serial killer," said Kathy. "Wayne Williams number two."

"Makes you wonder who did it huh? Especially when they say they don't have a clue as to who it might be. To tell you the truth, it makes me look at everyone suspiciously," giving Kathy a sideways stare.

"What me? Megan please, I'm a woman. The person doing this isn't. We don't do things like that. Only men are that sick."

"Oh okay. Just ruling out my best friend…You know what I think? They know the guy that's doing this, but don't wanna say too much thinking it might scare him off. You know they don't tell the public everything."

"That kinda scares me. I hope it's not somebody I know," Kathy replied.

"You remember Bundy, the suave intelligent law student who up and decides to go on a cross-country killing spree. And we *do* just so happen to work in a law office."

"You're right," pausing to digest the fact that she can be talking to a killer every day.

He could even be considering making her a target. Not willing to accept nonsense, she shakes the thought from her mind and changes the subject.

"I have a new friend, I met her at the store the other day. I'm supposed to be helping her with some legal stuff."

"That's nice," Megan uninterested in talking about some lady she met at the store.

"Hey Kath, you still know that detective guy?"

"Yeah I still know him, why?"

"Because I was thinking that since he's got the hots for you and all, you think he might give you something about the case? You know, something they didn't tell the press."

"I've never asked him about anything that doesn't pertain to a client."

"Well try, use your God-given skills," she said in a seductive voice.

"Oh stop it Megan!"

"You're about as fun as my neutered husband."

Kathy adjusts the temperature on the heater while she thinks about Megan's suggestion.

"Guess it wouldn't hurt."

"That's the spirit Kath! Behind every good legal assistant is a nosy secretary."

"I'll give him a call and see what he tells me."

"He'll tell you all you want to know if you play him right. Girl don't feel bad, men have been deceiving us forever. Look at it like you're evening the score."

"You're evil."

"I'm a woman, I've been this way since I coerced Adam into taking a bite of my *wet, luscious,* fruit. That's what he gets for thinking with the wrong head."

The composition disturbs the silence, moving the languid stillness with undulating waves of exhilaration. Precise, methodical, melodies serenade the entranced inhabitant with fervor. C.P.E. Bach lives on as his fingers stop, then gracefully adagio to the opposite end of the ivory coast. Passionately, he caresses each note, sashaying along the worn trails of the grand piano. Suppressed emotions reign free on this exceptional fantasia, exemplifying the sensitive style of Empfindsamer Stil. Nimble hands execute an effortless waltz of fluid motions, producing an effervescent blend of sophisticated sounds, and shape-shifting notes.
As devious shadows flicker against the wall like a mischievous puppet show, three red candles illuminate the room with unnatural glow—clandestinely, the soul of the listener is captured.

Photos of a slain man and woman lay face up on a table. The being stands and admires the naked body presented before the mirror.
"The bodies have been discovered. I am at the pinnacle of the human genome," whispered the voice.
"It's been so long since I've involved myself in the hunt. They deserved to die for their sins!.......The lies! The deceit! The exaggerated claims they made against him!........This is the day of which I has no doubt.......The day of reckoning! The day of which is now upon you all! These hands have sought and received retribution from thine enemies. My endogenous rage has laid dormant long enough.......*Now!*...The votary of death has returned to feast."
A barely visible photo of a woman checking her mailbox is placed before the candle. A wet tongue roguishly fondles her body.

"I'm whispering at you. I'm touching your hair. Can you hear me as I speak ever so softly?......My heart pounds for you."
Lips gently kiss the picture before the tongue mops across her face.
"I've honored you with a taste of my love........Your scent heightens my desire....Can you feel the passion in my touch?....Can you feel the raw lust on my breath?......Do you understand the reason for my whisper? I do so because I have uncovered your secret. It has drawn me to you, I know that which you know not.......I have looked into your remarkable eyes...There's a part of you that yearns for a certain.........Aaaaaaaaah!.............I am an actor of death, and you are my leading lady. Everything will be made plain to in due time. For what lies in the shadows of darkness, shall soon come out into the exposure of light."

The naked figure ejects the small cassette from the device and presents it to the photograph.
"This is my gift to you. It will be personally delivered by none other than yours truly........Until we meet again my love."

"Sivan, You have Kenneth Myers holding on line one."
"Thanks Deb," and presses the button beside the blinking light.
"I hope you have good news Mr. Myers," talking into the speaker.
"Well good morning to you too Ms. Goldstein," his voice holding a hint of brash.
"I'm afraid it's about to make a turn for the worse if you don't

start talking."

"Unfortunately, I don't have any good news. I did a little search-ing into the jury report, and found there *was* a lady named Iona Triplett, who became juror number seven. Her mother was involved with a man by the name of Dwight Springfield, whom she shared a mobile home with for about fourteen years; Iona lived there with them. About three years after the three of them had been living together, his son from a previous mar-riage named Jeremy Springfield decided to stop living with his mother, and move in with his father. Jeremy of course was the guy Grainger shot."

"What's the point of you telling me all this?"

"Let me finish and you'll see."

"Careful Ken."

"Jeremy and Iona lived there until graduating high school. They considered themselves brother and sister. Before Edith met the Dwight she'd been legally married to a Wilford Densing, the biological father of Iona. She left and took her daughter and ul-timately met Dwight. Problem is, she never divorced Mr. Dens-ing, even after a fourteen year relationship with Dwight. Mr. Springfield also never divorced his previous wife, which makes and Iona and Jeremy nothing more than friends."

Sivan's silent, the gears in her brain working to add credibility to this trailer park fiasco.

Ken interrupts her train of thought.

"I know what you're thinking. I've already tried to see how it can be justified. Common law's no good because they were both still actively married couples, thus making their union nothing more than a full-time extramarital affair."

"But she can still be charged with contempt because she knew, better yet *lived* with the victim for several years. That alone is grounds for a new trial. Have you located this Iona lady?"

"Yes, she's been in the cemetery for the last six years; died in a car accident, making it impossible for us to prove she intentionally lied to get on that jury. Then there's the statute of limitations thing," before excusing himself to take another call.

After several moments he returns.

"That was the clerk. She said the questionnaire's nowhere to be found."

Sivan is fuming.

"Mr. Myers, I am furious with the representation you gave Mr. Grainger. If you had done your job correctly the first time, he could've possibly avoided the chair," her voice filled with fire.

"Ms. Goldstein, it was a mistake, I'm human! I was swamped with over a hundred cases at the time, I couldn't do everything at once. The state's indigent defense system is a big pile of unorganized, poorly funded mess. I did the best I could with the tools I was given, especially coming fresh out of law school, and quite inexperienced. I told my supervisor I wasn't qualified to adequately defend a double murder case. But he could've cared less. All he was concerned about was closing cases. Sivan *please,* give me a break. I did the best I could. And for your information, I do have a heart, and do not want to see Matthew Grainger put to death."

Sivan hears the compassion his voice, and understands exactly what he means. She too experienced similar situations in New York; straight out of law school working as an indigent defense attorney. It's a cruel way to get familiar with the ins and outs of legal system. On their backs strategies are devised, the less fortunate used as lab mice, tested and experimented with; skills honed upon. If you lose a few cases, so what, no one cares. They're just criminals who can't afford to hire private representation. Attorneys get on-the-job training, and the defendant gets a free lawyer to lie for them.

But it's often accuses who pays the ultimate price.

"I know what you mean Ken. I apologize for my attitude. I went through the same stuff early in my career. I just hate to see things like this happen when they could've been avoided, that's all. This is the exact reason why I joined the agency. I got so tired of seeing people railroaded by heartless prosecutors only interested in conviction rates. Again, I do apologize for my rudeness Mr. Myers."

"Thanks Ms. Goldstein. That means a lot to have one of the best lawyers in the world apologize to a peon like me."

"No problem. But hey look, I'm thinking, could the DA have known Triplett was friends with the victim, and still allowed her to sit on that jury? That would've given her an advantage over the defense, because I'm positive she investigated every one of those people she picked. And also, do you by any chance re-member if you struck Iona or not?"

"I do remember. I'd already used all of my strikes. I was at the prosecutor's mercy. She handpicked all six of hers and it was nothing I could do. That was a trick I wasn't aware of back then."

"I'm willing to bet you the she purposely got rid of those ques-tionnaires to cover her butt in the event you found out about Triplett."

"I forgot to tell you something. She was also the foreman."

"*What!*" shouting to the point it made his ear itch.

"*Iona Triplett was the foreman?*"

"Unfortunately so."

"One second Ken."

Sivan put him on hold, and get up to pace the floor. After re-gaining her composure, she returns to her desk and presses the hold button.

"I had to take a few seconds to breathe. This trial was a flim-flam from the start. How could they even seek the death penalty in a case like this. I see no evidence of the commission of any felo-nies that would warranted such a harsh punishment. Makes me wonder how many of jurors were against it before she persuaded them."

"More bad news."

"What?"

"About three months after the trial, one of the jurors called and stated that she and two others had received threatening phone calls saying that if Grainger wasn't convicted and sent to death, they'd be severely punished. Upon mentioning it to Mrs. Triplett, they were allegedly advised not to worry, and that they should not tell anyone until well after the trial, because she didn't want anything to happen to them."

The phone buzzes, Deborah notifies her that Yates is on the other line.

"Hey Ken, that's the governor. I'm going to have to call you back."

"Okay, keep me posted."

Sivan pokes the 'Line 3' button.

"Good afternoon Hal," she said politely, knowing he too has found out about Iona, and is calling to rub it in her face.

"And the same to you Sivan."

She can see him on the other end grinning, enjoying the defeat of the great Sivan Goldstein.

"I've already heard about Triplett. You don't have to repeat it," bursting his bubble.

"Well there's no need for us to talk. I'm sure you already know where I stand on things."

She loathes brown-nosing, especially clowns AWOL from the circus.

"You're right, I do. And that's exactly why you should stand up for what's right, and get off your belly, and quit slithering around like a snake in the grass, willing to do whatever to devour some extra votes!" her tone sharp as a sickle.

"I'm disappointed to hear that you think of me in such a disparaging light. However, this is for the citizens of Georgia. It's for those who live in fear, terrified of the heartless criminals that roam our streets. It's time for me to step up and take charge, guide this state in the direction of peace and safety," sounding as if he stood in the mirror half the night reciting it.

"For God's sake Hal, he didn't even get a fair trial! You tell me how could he when the guy's sister, or friend, or whatever you want to call her sat on the jury. We both know they knew each other. I can't prove it, but you know the DA intentionally put her on that jury to guarantee a guilty verdict. That's wrong, and it's unconstitutional. You should have enough integrity to pull Grainger's sentence!

"None of your claims have been substantiated, and therefore my hands are tied."

"Oh don't give me that garbage! You know good and well that he should've never been tried on pre-med in the first place. If he would've had a qualified counsel, he would've easily been found to have been temporarily insane. How about you catch your wife in a room with some jerk's cock in her mouth and see how quick you lose it."

"Sivan I understand, I really do. But that doesn't change the fact that he murdered two people in cold blood. Millions of people deal with adultery, they don't go around killing their spouses."

"True! I'm not disputing that. What I'm saying is that he did not, I repeat *did not* get a fair trial under the guidelines of the United States Constitution!"

"I need hard facts Sivan. You have nothing but hearsay," going back to his defense lawyer days. "Okay. Let's say they did know each other. That doesn't mean she lied to get on the jury, or even knew it was illegal. I can't subpoena her now because she's dead, and the questionnaire's gone. And lastly, there's no guarantee the verdict would've been any different."

He's right, she thought. Without any physical evidence there's nothing she can do.

"Do you know Grainger at the age of twelve spent nine months in Georgia Mental Health Institute, better known as GMHI?"

"Yes. And he was diagnosed with a chronic depression disorder and ADHD, *not* deemed a psychopath, sociopath, or schizophrenic."

"Mr. Yates," she begin softly. "Aren't you trying to win an election?"

"I most certainly am."

"How about we make a deal? You reduce his sentence to life and I'll promise you that everybody who's anybody in the legal community will endorse you. You scratch my back and I'll scratch yours. How about that?"

He weighs the pros and cons of her offer. With her on his team, he'll win by a landslide. But what if the plan backfires and he's seen as a sellout? All of his Republican allies will turn against him. No more campaign dollars, and no endorsements from the senator. He'll have to look to the Democrats for help, and that won't be good. He can't do it, it's too risky. He's going to have to pass.

"Sivan, I'm sorry, I can't. There's just too much at stake, maybe on the next one....Grainger will be put to death on June twenty-fourth at seven p.m. as scheduled."

Poof! Matthew Edward Grainger is now officially a dead man.

"I hope your conscience eats a hole in your heart. Whoops, I forgot, you're heartless," and slams on the line 3 button.

She punches in four numbers, and after one ring Deborah answers.

"We're about to organize the biggest rally possible! News people, human rights activists, college students, civil liberties unions, church members, and whoever else you can find for the twenty-fourth of this month!"

"Well hello Mr. Thomas. I see you got my message. It's been a while since I've heard from you."

"It certainly has, *too* long. And please, call me John."

But sounding like he's trying to be *Rico Swa-vae.*

"So what have you been up to? How's life treating you?"

"It's okay, could be better though."

"Well the reason I called, being that you handle all those big investigations, and what-have-you; I was wondering about the murders of that couple a few days ago."

"Is that all you called to ask? That's nothing, they were just shot."

"Yes, but is there something more? You know something they didn't tell the public?"

He's on the defense now.

"Why? Are you trying to get something to leak to the press? Becau-"

"Don't be silly John, this is me. I value our friendship way too much to do anything like that. If you don't trust me, I understand. I'll just see if I can ask one of my oth-"

"I'm sorry, what was I thinking? There's no need to overreact. But you've got to promise me this is only between us."

"I won't tell a soul," she lied.

"Okay. There was a small cassette, you know the kind that goes in those mini recorders you use to record meetings and things; the old fashioned kind, not the new digital one?"

"Yes I'm familiar with them."

"Well anyway, one was left at the scene. The killer recorded the entire murder on it. You can hear a woman screaming and everything, it's bad. A man pleading for his life, gun shots and all. The whole time some kind of classical music is playing in the background. We believe it's a copycat of a case from about twelve years back."

She's at a loss for words. A million thoughts are running through her mind, an uncomfortable warmth creeps up her neck.

"I didn't mean to scare you darling," noticing her silence.

"I'm all right."

Now that she's gotten what she wants, the sexy voice is gone.

"Any leads?"

"Nothing. We discovered the man was ex-cop. His career was full of cases where he'd brought down lots of bad guys. We believe it's someone he'd put away who's back for revenge. We also think the tape is no a kind of joke to taunt us with; something they copied off the old Tangier case. The profiler says it's a white male, loner type, a real failure in life. Someone between the ages of thirty-two and thirty-nine, a career criminal; but nowhere near the serial killer level," sounding sure of himself.

"I heard he took some utility bills. What do you think that was for?"

"We think it's something he thought up at the time. Something to make it seem like more than it really is."

"One more question if you don't mind?"

"Anything you want."

"Why do you think he shot them so many times?"

"Rage. The guy's out for revenge. Shooting a person after they've already expired signifies extreme anger. In his mind, he wanted them to feel as much pain as possible. And here's something else the press doesn't know. It's kind of graphic. You sure you wanna hear it?"

"I guess."

"Well okay, you asked for it. Both of the victim's eyes were removed from the sockets, and put in their mouths. Their thumbs were severed, and stuffed into the eye sockets. The perp had to have a strong stomach to do that."

Kathy sighs.

"I probably should've passed, that was horrible. I think I've heard enough for one day."

Time to get rid of him.

"How about you give me a call tomorrow and maybe we'll do lunch?"

"Sure, no problem, I'll do just that," tone full of excitement.

"Great," with feigned enthusiasm. "I look forward to hearing from you. Thanks for the information, I really appreciated it."

"It's nothing. So what are you doing now?"
"Lots of paper work, real busy."
"Yeah me too......"
He's flying off at the lips, but she's in her thoughts. He keeps trying for conversation, and she keeps giving him one word replies. Eventually he gets the picture.
"Well I guess I let you go. It's been a pleasure speaking with you again."
They say their goodbyes and hang up.

Kathy turns her upholstered chair towards the window, and the mounting evening traffic. The setting sun has cast an orange glow over the city, a jet inches its way across the sky, its long exhaust trail in tow. From this point things seems so peaceful, so safe. But it's all a façade. In reality they aren't, things aren't all right. Somewhere out there robbers are holding up stores, men are abusing their wives, rival drug dealers are gunning at each other while innocent children die in the crossfire. Women are being sexually assaulted, shiesty hedge fund managers are swindling unwitting investors out of their life savings, vile priests are engaging in pedophilic acts with choir boys, and human trafficking is alive and well. Simultaneously, a faceless killer prowls the streets in search of his next victim.
Kathy turns back to her desk, and begins gathering her things. It's been a long day, and she's glad it's over. Her friend hasn't returned her call, leading her to shrug as she exits the office, locking the door behind her. The floor is deserted, she's worked late to finish up a few petitions. And immediately feels uneasy, hurrying past the rows of cubicles, out of the reception area, and into the lobby. As she stands waiting for the elevator, she begins hearing faint noises in the distance.
Her intuition warns her she's in imminent danger!
Bing!
The elevator startles her to the point she almost drops her laptop. She moves inside and presses the button to close. Slowly

they do.
Once she feels the decent, she sighs.

"All in due time," whispered the figure watching. *"All in due time."*

"How'd your day go?" Kathy asked, waiting in a long line of cars on the ramp to I-85.
"Not too bad, how about yours," Stockton replied from his smartphone.
"Pretty much the same until Megan started saying the person who murdered that couple is about to start a spree."
"Let me guess, she also thinks he works at the firm too?"
"Yep."
"Oh well. They've got me working third shift too, I've got to be back around eleven. "
"I'll be all right."
"I'm sure you will."
"Guess what else Megan did?"
"What?"
"She put a piece of paper on my windshield saying she's watching me and signed her name on it. I didn't take to kindly to it though. Tomorrow I'm going to tell her enough with the games."
"Right," he said. "Look, I'm about to jump in the shower. I'll see you later."
"All right. Be safe."
"You too."

"Here she comes," he announced, binoculars to his eyes watching Ms. Chase turn into the main entrance.
"Now repeat what I said to do."
"Sir, we understand what you want. We've gone over it for the past hour," Starns replied.
Gordon turns from the window and looks at him.
"Y'all better not mess this up. Now hurry round dere for y'all misser."
Stuckey's two goons leap into action.
He turns back in time to see her drive out of sight.

By the time she gets out of her car, they've made it from the other side wing. Starns and Salvo are waiting inside the visitation lobby when she enters.
"What the hell is he doing to keep her coming like this? It ain't like he's getting out," wonders Salvo.
"Fuck if I know. I just wanna stick my cock in her."
She makes it to the check-in desk.
"Good afternoon miss."
"And the same to you Mr...," looking at his nameplate. "Starns."
"We have some new rules. No purses or briefcases are permitted inside the visitation area. They can either be placed inside those lockers against the wall, or back in your vehicle."
Salvatore is busy drooling over her body. Jeans and a sweat sweatshirt is nothing special, but on her, it's more than enough to get him going.
"Okay," she agreed.
Walking to the locker, she places her purse inside, closes the door, and extracts the key.
"See, easy as pie. You're free to start your visit miss," said Starns.

Salvo screens her for weapons before buzzing her through three, heavily fortified doors. Once they see that she's seated and conversing with Parson, it's time to initiate the plan. Starns heads towards the parking lot, while Salvo moves to the locker and opens it with a master.
Stuckey's watching from his office.
Salvo opens her purse expecting to find damning evidence, but all he finds are keys, lipstick, and a folded piece of paper. Unfolding it reveals a short typewritten message:

> *Dear Asshole,*
>
> *I knew you were going to invade my privacy,*
> *so I decided to leave this to inform you of your*
> *stupidity. Your brain isn't big enough to fool*
> *me. Now don't you feel even more like what*
> *you already are, an idiot!*
>
> > *Sincerely,*
> > *Christine Chase*

Salvo's face morphs into a candy apple, his knuckles turn white as he balls his fist around her purse fighting the urge to rip it. "Yon fucking cunt!" clenching his teeth to the point that it feels as if they're about to shatter.
Once he's regains his composure, her secures it back inside, and heads to the men's room.

Meanwhile, Starns has just caught the lever with the slim-Jim, snatching it upward he unlocks the door. With gloved hands, he quickly searches the vehicle, but there's nothing to find. No trash, no old bills, no junk mail; zilch. He presses the trunk release and goes around back. It's empty except for a small piece

of folded paper. He unfolds it and reads the same taunting message. Starns slams the trunk and walks back inside feeling just as the note said. Salvo is sitting behind the control board when he pulls up a chair, and pulls a pack from his pocket. After lighting the cancer stick, he inhales deeply before releasing a toxic cloud, treating Salvatore to second hand smoke.
"That broad is really starting to get under my skin."
"You must've had a note waiting for you too," the non-smoker replied, and turns on the fan.
"How'd you think she knew?"
"I have no idea," taking a pull. "But she's up to something."
They sit in silence, as they again attempt to decode the foreign dialect, and fluent sign language.

Gordon's staticy voice comes over the radio.
"Get ready, she's on her way out!"
The crafty Ms. Chase exits the visitation area, unlocks the locker, and retrieves her purse.
"You gentlemen have an exceptional evening," her voice taunting as she makes for the exit.
If expressions can prove guilt or innocence, they'd both be hauled off to the slammer. Before walking out she turns and gives them a big toothy smile.
"Thanks for all your help. Good day."

"You. Have. Got. To. Be. *KIDDING ME!*" the warden, shaking

his jalopy head.

"She seems to always be one step ahead of us," Starns sitting before Gordon's desk.

"That broad is playin' wit the wrong one! She don't know who she fuckin' wit."

The goons say nothing.

"This fish is start'na smell real bad. She's stankin up my goddamn prison,"

Reaching inside his desk drawer, he grabs the liquor and crystal glass, pours himself a generous portion, and takes a gulp.

"I ain't gone let this lady ruin my chances of unseatin' dat big eared Yates," and returns it to the drawer.

This time it's Salvatore who speaks.

"What can she do that can possibly affect your chances? I mean, I don't see her doing anything like trying to break him out. So if not that, what else comes to mind?"

Gordon thinks for a moment. He's dealt with too many shady individuals to know when something isn't right. But what can she really be up to? All she's doing is coming to see a man who tortured and killed a social worker slash pastor. But what about the sign language and the pictures, the cold words and that briefcase?

That's it! The briefcase!

"The briefcase, we havetuh fine a way tuh get it from her."

"Yeah, but how?" Starns questioned.

"I have an idea," said the guy with mob connections. "How about we just tell her we need to search the thing for contraband? If she refuses, we refuse her visit."

"I don't think that'll work," Stuckey said, and hits the whiskey. "She'll probably make a big issuuh out it sayin' we violated her rights or somethin', some sexual harassment garbage, or some prisoner rights shit. Then here comes that Goldstein bitch. I'll have mo lawsuits on my hands. *That,* I don't need."

"Maybe she's just a regular lady who's very private, and doesn't want people in her business," commented Salvo.

Gordon leaps to his feet and slams the glass on the table, splashing booze on his white shirt!

"She, *or* he, ain't got no right to no *goddamn* privacy! This is *my* fuckin' prison! I don't give two tough turds of rat shit about her damn privacy!" with his fist balled and chest heaving.

But in a calmer tone says: "Dang, I spilled liquor on me."

And drinks the rest of what didn't fly out.

How the hell did he get to be a warden? thought Starns. *This state is doomed if he wins. I hope he never gets mad enough to put his hands on me, because I'm gonna knock his ass out. Fuck the job!*

While Stuckey sits dabbing at his shirt with a handkerchief, Starns devises a more feasible plan to discover the contents of the briefcase.

"Now that's something that can be done!" Stuckey momentarily forgetting about the stain.

The trio iron out the kinks of their seemingly perfect plan.

"Okay, that's how are going to do it! She'll be back sometime next week, which is just enough time for me to get everything in place."

Proudly leaning back in his chair, he visualizes how it should go.

"Well it's time fur meatuh break camp. It's almoss dark."

Rising from the seat, he grabs his Stetson® cowboy hat off the moose's antlers.

The group head out the office, confident they'll finally be able to make sense of all these strange meetings.

Chapter 7

Parson stands over the sink running a razor over his face, while Sheephead is downstairs taking a much needed shower. Deemed too dangerous to mingle with the others, he has to wait until lockdown to get his one hour of free time.

The host is busy welcoming a celebrity guest to the show while Parson rinses the razor, and sits down. Harry gives him the rare privilege of having his cell unlocked while everyone else's is secured. He wrestles with the thought of going down and watching TV, but decides against it remembering how angry he was when Sheep threw body waste on him. If he's wasn't so absorbed with the task at hand, Beasley would've already been in the infirmary. But he'll deal with him in due time, a special surprise awaits. Lying on his bunk staring at the twin bladed razor in his hand, he wonders how long it'll take before he bleeds to death if he slices his wrist.

He closes his eyes.

She can't any longer be called his woman because she's not. It'd be unrealistic for him to think that in the years he's been imprisoned, she hasn't slept with anyone. Nevertheless, her dedication and trust remains. This is their last ditch effort, they have no choice but to make it work. Parson knows he's next on the menu.

Every second is precious. The time to act is now.

He dozes off.

Parson's sleep is interrupted by an old rerun of *Marty Stouffer's Wild America*. Acting on her advice, he rolls out of bed and removes his homemade bit. Another step and he's standing inches from the wall, hurriedly removing the fixture's face plate. Steady as a surgeon's hand, he reaches past the live wires and removes his weapon. Unfolding it, he admires how the blade glistens in the dim light. Sliding the plate under his mattress, he drops the bit in his pocket.

Good thing Harry thinks it's all a lie. Gullible old man.

After easing the door back, the stage is set.

The king of the jungle crouches on all fours, camouflaging his body in the thick brush as he begins stalking the unsuspecting buffalo.

The guard is fast asleep with his boots kicked on the desk, slobber dripping from his mouth, hat over his face. The clock on the wall reads 3:29 a.m.

Parsons heart pounds as he moves with the coordination of a gymnast, bare feet rendering his movements undetectable. Cautiously, he observes the inhabitants of each cell before passing. The end of the tier is his destination. He'll have to do without cover if he's to get within striking distance of his prey.

The muscular body leaps before the barred door, the floor cold against his bare chest. A prison ID card is used to defeat the worn lock, the sudden release of tension causing the door to jerk backwards! A latex glove placed on each hand triggers more adrenaline to surge, and hairs to stand on end—a swallow hydrates his parched throat.

The weakest one is spotted, a huge napping male.

The time to act is now!

With athleticism, he enters the cell and sinks the knife into Sheephead's neck—ripping it upward, he nearly decapitates him! The blanket shields him from spatter, as the man begins struggling wildly! Another swing, and the blade punctures his lung; air hisses, blood turning the wool blanket a sticky crimson. Beasley attempts to scream, but the gaping wound in his neck, and the hole in his collapsed lung make it impossible. All he can muster is a bloody gurgle. A desperate attempt to live causes him to kick viciously, partly removing the blanket over his face. His eyes become the size of golf balls when he faces the bringer of his death, who slams the blade into his heart. The putrid smell of blood and feces claims the space, as Beasley's body starts shutting down.

He recovers his weapon from the dying sociopath, whose arms are flailing about, and head shaking hideously. The dance of death goes on, until the mortally wounded body completes one final jerk!

The transition from life to death took all of seventy seconds.

He steps away from the bed that is staining the floor with drops, and rinses the knife in the toilet. Absent of the slightest angst, he dusts himself off, situates his boxers, and exits the scene.

In a cold sweat, Parson awakens to the sound of banging trays and shuffling feet, instantly feeling a sticky wetness in his palm. He's still holding his shaving razor?
"Damn," getting up to wash his hands.
His entire shirt is soaked, and after pulling it off grabs a clean one. Remembering the knife, he looks at the fixture to see if he's placed it back.
It's just as he left it.
Whispering to himself, he tries to figure out why he's in a cold sweat holding a razor?
Half sleep inmates are slowly making their way down the stairs to receive their breakfast tray of grits, biscuits and sausage. Parson is reaching for his personal spoon when someone yells.
"Oh Shit!....*OOOOOOOOH SHIT!!!!!!*"
It all comes back to him.
Three men are standing at the end of the tier gawking into Beasley's cell, the new guy Billings is coming out of the tower to see what all the commotion is about. Harry's behind him holding pepper spray.
"Make a hole!"
There's a strange odor in the air.
"Sheep must be throwing shit again," commented inmate Jindle.

"TEN-TEN!.... TEN-TEN! An inmate's been killed on the row!!"
Billings shouted into his radio.
Upon hearing that, inmates stampede to see who's been killed before the Georgia Department of Corrections said so. Parson's pushed forward by instant the rush of bodies, but turns his head after a quick glance at Beasley's bloody corpse hanging off the bed.
Billings runs back downstairs until backup arrives.
"All inmates back to your cells!!!" goes the PA system.
Sirens begin wailing, red emergency lights strobe!
"All inmates back to your cells!!!"
The corridor fills with CERT team members donning black fatigues, and regular COs in blue and gray. A team of nurses follow rolling a stretcher.
"Everyone back to your cells!!! All inmates lockdown immediately!!!!!" shouts the wide, 6'5" bruiser.
Some carry shields and batons; others wield Tasers® and rifles with rubber bullets. They all have helmets.
Murders scurry back to their dens like frightened rabbits. In unison, tiny mirrors shoot between the bars, each man trying to see the show. Trays are stacked on a cart in front of the television. The news anchor is updating the public on the double murder earlier in the week, but the sound is muted.
The flood of prison staff continues in an endless stream. After about five minutes of commotion, the sea parts and Stuckey enters. Everyone becomes quiet, all movement ceases. The look on his face is not that of a happy man. He walks completely into the crime scene, and must've found a clue, because he comes directly to Parson's cell, and stone-faces him through the bars. Seemingly unaware, he continues reading *The Diagnostic and Statistical Manual of Mental Disorders,* published by the American Psychiatric Association. If looks could kill, Stuckey would've been charged with his death.
"You know anything about this?"
He plays dumb.

"I didn't know anything happened."
 Gordon studies Parson's body language before continuing.
"Somebody cashed Beasley's chips before I said so, used him for a pincushion."
"Well now I do."
Stuckey isn't buying it.
"Put the fuckin' book down, and get out here."
An officer behind him radios the control tower, and the door partially opens.
Stuckey gives the order for a shakedown. The CERT team jump into action, ransacking his cell.

After coming up empty, the entire cell house receives the same treatment. Shredded mattresses are strewn everywhere, shanks made from broken lawn mower blades to shattered light bulbs are found. Hypodermic needles, cassette players fashioned into tattoo guns, water filled trash bags uses for weight training, women's lingerie, cell phones, and illegal narcotics are just some of the things that somehow made it into a maximum-security penitentiary. Amazingly, no one thought to check the lights bolted to the ceilings. Maybe it's because they're secured with bolts the inmates supposedly can't remove.
After being subjected to a degrading cavity search, Parson is literally thrown back in his cell. While Sheephead's is photographed and inspected, Stuckey leans against the wall fuming.

Four hours later Beasley's corpse is bagged and hauled away. An hour after that the cell house is almost back to normal, except for the lockdown, and the inmates putting what remains of their personal effects back. Nothing indicates what transpired earlier. Twelve non-death row inmates are tasked with cleaning up the debris, and by 2:30 in the afternoon, lunch has been served and the box is set on the appropriate station. The only bad thing to come out of is that everyone had their contraband taken away. No shanks, no drugs, no sex toys, no tattoo guns. Things looks to be pretty boring around there for a while.

Random searches are a reoccurring part of prison life. Another part is how prohibited things always find a way to get back inside. An occasional comment about who did it is heard here and there, but minus the hoopla and excitement. Here on the death row, where killers sit packed in like church on Easter Sunday; homicide never becomes the talk of the yard. In his valley of death, today's episode of Worlds Wildest Police Chases seems a better topic for discussion. Staff members engage in the most gossip, being many of them never saw a dead body before. Officers of various ranks come to question inmates as the day wears on, not interested in finding out who committed the crime, but following protocol. There will be no funeral procession, the deceased will not be eulogized, no tears will be shed by the grieving family as the coffin lowers into the ground. Since Beasley has no relatives willing to pay for a proper burial, he'll receive a plywood box in the prison cemetery.

"Parson, let me speak to you for moment," came a serious Harry from the intercom inside his cell.

He marks his page, walks to the door, and waits for it to slide open before heading to the speaker beside the corridor.

Harry exits the tower and signals for him to follow.

The recreation yard is located on the opposite side of a reinforced steel door and a short hallway, followed by another reinforced door, another short hallway way, and another steel door. A colleague buzzes the locks as they walks through the first door into the hallway. Two buzzes and they're outside standing on the blacktop, and are immediately blinded by the sun. The sniper in the watchtower readies his rifle, though they're surrounded by two, 15 foot, electrified razor wire fences.

"Say Parson, I want to ask you a few things; man to man, not as guard speaking to inmate."

"Certainly."

Knowing exactly what's on his mind.

"Parson….You know I consider you different from the other guys right."

"Yes."

"That's why I give you privileges they don't get because I trust you."

Knowing what's coming, he cut to the chase.

"I didn't do anything to Beasley," looking him square in the eye.

Harry looks down and kicks a pebble across the pavement. Raking a hand through his graying hair, he has no doubt that Parson speaks the truth. A slight breeze begins as they stand in silence.

"I believe you, but Stuckey thinks you had something to do with it."

"What did he say?"

"He's concocted some cockamamie story about you doing this to tarnish his image, something about you trying to destroy his campaign. And some other garbage about you and your female friend having some sorta' vendetta against him and the state of Georgia…He's said he gonna use his connections to speed up your date."

"It's funny you say that, I was just reading about those people. They call them paranoid delusional schizophrenics. They're always thinking someone's out to get them."

Harry laughs at Parson's diagnosis before adding his own.

"And he's also one of those compulsive alcohol consumers too," laughing.

There they are, the philanthropist, and the convicted killer; shooting the shit like two fishing buddies on a lake.

Harry faces constant ridicule him for befriending such a violent man. Upon questioning, Harry explains he cares nothing about what he's said to have done, and can care less what they think. He's walked the gangways of Jackson State Prison for decades, and has been through seventeen wardens. He does what he wants, and there's nothing Gordon or anyone else can do about it.

"Heard anything about Grainger?" Parson breaking the silence.

"Yeah, bad news. Yates says he's not communing his sentence. Turns out she was just a lady he lived with through childhood and wasn't blood. Anyhow, the woman died a couple of years back, so there's nothing to go on now."
Parson takes a moment to let the fact soak in that his longtime friend will soon be electrocuted.
"Harry, I want to know your honest opinion?"
"Be my guest."
"Do you believe people who've killed roam the streets of heaven?"
Harry ponders for moment.
"Moses killed a man. I believe all types of people dwell in heaven. God doesn't care what man's opinion of a person is. He knows their heart and forgives whom he may. *That's* what I believe."

God also saw how Beasley was mercilessly slaughtered in his cell, and also knows how proud the person was after they tortured and shot Joseph Tangier. The culprit could care less about prayers, guilt, or God's forgiveness. His only intention is to kill again, and again, and again.
"Let's get back inside before mister watchman radios Gordon and tells him I'm trying to help you escape."
He doesn't have to, he's been watching from his office the entire time.

"So whatcha gotta taste for?"
"You decide," she replied.

"I'll be happy with a salad," she said, turning onto Mitchell St. "Don't tell me you're one of those health nuts?"

"Me a health nut, you've got to be kidding? I have enough cholesterol to give you some.......*Hay there's Mick's*, they've got great salads!"

"Sounds good to me."

Kathy parks, and they head inside for lunch. The woman who calls herself "Christie" has a plain burger, no fries, and bottled water; Kathy a grilled chicken salad.

Once they're back in the car, Christie asks: "You ever think about being a police officer, or an FBI agent or something? You know, a job where you'd have to carry a gun?"

"Not really. Why, you?"

"No, but I wouldn't rule it out. I wonder what it would be like if some lunatic takes his a teacher hostage and is threatening to kill her, and I get the ups on him; I wonder if I'll be able to shoot him to save her?"

Kathy looks at her.

"You think you'd have the nerve?"

"Yes," she said without thinking about it.

"You're a tough cookie girl. I don't think I'd have the courage to kill another human being. I'd probably just shoot them in the leg or something."

"I will if I have to....There's some wicked people in this world."

"Speaking of wicked, have you been keeping up with the murder of that couple?"

"Yeah a little."

"Isn't that horrible with some guy did?"

Christie looks at her.

"So you think it's a man too huh?"

"Come on, we don't do things like that," Kathy sounding sure of herself.

And looks away.

"Women kill.....just for different reasons."

Silence.

"My friend Megan said it could be one of the guys at the office. It scares me to think that I can be looking at the killer and not know it."

But she doesn't say anything.

"You all right?" Kathy questioned.

"Christie" turns her attention from the window.

"I'll do anything to get him out of that place, I don't care what it is."

And back out the glass.

"You never told me how you want me to help. You only mentioned a loved one behind bars that you're trying to get out."

No response.

"Christie," patting her leg.

She turns.

"I know we haven't known each other that long, but you can talk to me. It's okay, I've had good feelings about you since the store. I don't know why, I just do. Maybe we crossed paths for a reason."

Christie moves Kathy's hand from her leg.

"Thanks....I'll tell you everything eventually. Now's just not the time."

Kathy's pulling into the garage.

"You gonna to be all right?" taking the keys from the ignition.

"I'll be fine."

Abruptly, she's ready to go.

"I have to leave," urgency in her tone. "I'll call you later."

Opening the door, she jumps out.

"Christie, Christie wait!"

But she's already cranking it up, backing out, and speeding off.

Kathy's tries to figure out what happened.

Exiting the elevator, she's still bewildered. Heading down the hallway past the empty reception desk, she's spotted by Megan, dressed conservatively today.

She opens the door and sits at her modest desk.

"Damn. You look like I feel, sexually deprived."

"I'm fine. The strangest thing just happened. My friend who treated me to lunch, leaps from my car and takes off without saying anything."

"Maybe she's the killer!" Megan whispered.

"It's my friend Christie for your information."

"I've never heard of any Christie before. That's the alias I used to give guys I never wanna see again."

"She's the lady from the store I was telling you about, the one who needs the legal advice."

"Oh."

"We were talking about what she needs me to do, the minute I pulled next to her car, she jumps out. No goodbye or anything."

"Maybe she's not comfortable enough to tell you yet. You know, sometimes people need time before they reveal things. Stop being such an extrovert, and stop being so quick to think you know people. Humans will show you there representative for years, then one day they're like, *bam!* This is the real me. It took my husband eight years before he admitted he has this disgusting fetish to fuck me up the ass, then have me suck his cock."

"MEGAN!!!!"

"Sorry, but you get the point. Just be careful."

"I will, but yeah, she said she'll tell me, but just not right now......So, uhmm, what did you eat for lunch?" changing the subject.

"Let me see," Megan looking at the ceiling. "A great big plate of air. Gotta stay in shape for the career. You know what they say: The better the body, the better the pay."

"Tell me about it...That reminds me, did you come in here to get a file or something this morning?"

"No, why?"

"Because someone went through all of the drawers. And, I lock my door every evening. It was standing wide open when I got here this morning. I thought it was you so I was cool."

"No Kathy, it wasn't not me," interested in who's been snooping around.

"It wasn't?"

"No."

"That's strange."

"It is."

"Megan don't go blowing this all out of portion, but yesterday when I left, I had this strange feeling I was being watched."

"When I left, most everyone was gone. The few people still here, rode down with me. I'm not being funny or anything, but I wanted to tell you not to stay late that night. It's like I felt something wasn't right. But I knew you'd just tell me to quit worrying."

Kathy's phone rings.

After answering she hangs up.

"This is getting weird. Someone just called breathing heavily, and hung up; number unavailable," looking at the ID screen.

"Probably your friend calling to apologize."

"Maybe."

Remembering how distraught she was after her ordeal, and how she needed a helping hand.

"The next time she calls I'm going to tell her about my experience. Maybe that'll help her open up a little."

"Probably so...*Damn girl*, I've been running my mouth fifteen minutes too long. Let me get back to my desk before I'm standing in the unemployment line," and rises from her seat.

"Yeah you do that, because the boss is *watching you*. I bet a note's stuck to your computer screen, just like the one you stuck to my windshield," Kathy teased.

Megan's almost to the door.

"What are you talking about? I didn't put any note on your windshield."

Kathy's smirk washes away.

"You didn't put a note on my windshield saying you're watching me, and sign your name?"

"No Kathy, I did not!" coming back to her.

Her heart flutters, jumbled thoughts run through her mind. Megan's words interrupt her.

"Either somebody's playing games, or you need to call the police!"

Kathy puts her face in her hands, and sighs.

"Oh my God Megan."

"Or maybe it's somebody up her playing jokes."

Kathy raises her head.

"Let me slow down," and inhales. "I have a habit of overreacting."

"You're right about that," Megan chides.

"It's probably just Stu or Eric being childish as always."

Megan ponders the theory.

"I bet that's exactly who it is. I'm going to go tell them about themselves right now," and switches out.

"Call me!"

"Why would I wanna be your runnin' mate when ahm gone defeat you head up? The public don't won't someone das gone continya' to let the crime rate skyrocket. They won't somebody like me who's tough on crahm, and knows howda handle crimnulz, bring this state outta debt, ahn return the cunfedred flag to its rotful place flyin' high above the capital. Das the numba two reason why ahm gone win. You let dem blacks make a big issha out it, claimin' it's raciss. Then you up and changed it. You upset alota good folks wit dat one Yates. Thousands of Georgians died fur the cunfedracy. Dat flag is symbowlic," Gordon preaches into the phone, showing off his debating skills.

"It's symbolic all right, symbolized oppression, segregation, slavery, Jim Crow, and a whole slew of other disheartening things. What do you think the Confederate Army was fighting for Gordon? It sure wasn't to give blacks equal rights, wasn't to end slavery, and sure wasn't to let them vote. What they fought for was to continue their domination and bigotry. But you, like a lot of other southerners want to forget this particular fact."

Yates pauses to clear his throat.

"Gordon, you know nothing about politics. All you know about is the pickups, prisons, perjury, and pork bellies."

Stuckey owns several hog farms.

The statement causes his face to redden, and a slight smirk to form on his guest's face.

Gordon's brain doesn't process information quickly, so it takes him a while to come up with an equally demeaning rebuttal.

"What dis state needs iza down home cuntruh boy, not some fancy suit wearin' city slicker wita buncha degrees."

"Maybe a degree in history, one in economics, and a post-grad in common sense will do that hat rack sitting on your shoulder some good; you think country boy? I hope you're never stupid enough to challenge me to a debate, because I'll eat your corn shucking ass alive, and show everyone just how idiotic you really are. As a matter of fact, let's? Would do you say Gordo, king of swine?"

Stuckey isn't adept at controlling his anger, so he lashes out in the only way he knows how.

"Name da place and time, and I'll be dere asshole!"

Then pounds the release button, ending their conversation.

Time for a drink.

He extracts his crystal glass, and pours himself a generous portion. Upon taking a quick sip from the bottle, he places the booze back in the drawer, and after one more from the glass, he speaks.

"I don't want one word about Beasley gettin' out, not one fuckin' word, ya hear! He has no family and therefore it's no reason for him to not be buried and forgotten. By the end of tamarra I want dat basturd in the ground, no excuses. The investigation ends today! Secondly we ne-"
A call comes over the radio.
"Yeah," he answered impatiently.
"There's a lady named Seevan, See-van Goldsteed. Says she's a lawyer with some agency and wontsta speak witcha. Whudya wont meatuh tell her?"
"Tell her I'm in a meeting," holding the radio to his lipless mouth.
"Tan-Four," the CO replied.
"Now what was I about to say?" sitting the radio back on the desk.
"You were saying something about how to handle the Beasley situation."
"Yeah, we needta find out what Parson did wit da murder weapon. *And* I've davised a plan to find out what his lil whore's carryin' in that case."
"What do you plan on doing, and when do you plan on doing it?" asked the voice of reason.
Gordon grabs his glass and swirls the liquor around. Leaning back in his chair, he takes a sip, and sits it back on the desk.
"Well this is what I come up with."
But before he can continue, he's interrupted by someone beating at the door.
"Shit!" angered by yet another interruption.
"I'm busy!"
It continues.
"Goddammit! Who is it?"
It's getting louder.
Gordon leaps out of his leather chair cursing, rumbles to the door, and yanks it open, just as she was about to bang some more.

She can see the ire in his eyes and loves it.

Sivan walks in smiling.

"Well hello Gordon Stuckey!" as if they're long-lost friends.

"I'm Sivan Goldstein, and you are?" referring to Gordon's guest, offering her hand for a shake.

"John Higgins, Director of Operations," accepting her hand.

But there's no need for introduction. He's very familiar with her. Everyone from the Supreme Court, all the way down to the common beat cop know of her. There's no woman more feared than this Harvard educated warrior for human rights.

Stuckey slams the door realizing she's not leaving.

"You must didn't get my message?"

"Oh I did, but I decided this was too long of a drive for me to come back tomorrow, so I'm seeing you today. I knew you wouldn't mind," Smiling, then reaches in her purse and produces a camera.

"What are you gonna do with tha-."

As the flash answers his question. He forgot about the glass of liquor on the desk, and the top half of the bottle peeking out of the file cabinet.

"I've always been a fan of photography, especially when I can get shots of state employees drinking prohibited beverages on the clock."

Fuckin' Jew tramp!

But aloud: "How can I help you? As you can see I'm very busy," trying in earnestly to control his temper, while calmly hiding the evidence.

"It's nothing you can't handle," she begins. "I just want to personally notify you of the gathering scheduled for June twenty-fourth at 4 p.m. It'll be lots of fun, hundreds of people will be there. Reporters, civil rights groups, charity organizations, senior citizens, and lots of loud college students who love to voice their opinions. Oh and yes, I've even managed to find a few politicians and businessmen who can't wait to badmouth you and your buddy Yates on camera. *And* a very nice gentle-

man who says he knows for a fact you're using your little pig farms for illegal purposes. It should be a splendid evening for the both of you. The only thing left to decide is who's going to bring the burgers, and who's going to bring the fries; I'll supply the *punch*."
Higgins speaks before Gordon puts his foot in his mouth.
"I think that's a great idea," he begins charismatically. "That'll give us a chance to address a few concerns of our own," while Stuckey glares at her.

For the next 10 minutes Higgins attempts to defend the warden. Each commendable thing he says about him, she comes back with something to refute it.
Pleased with the results of her visit, she politely excuses herself and leaves.

They both watch the monitor as she gets in her vehicle and drives past the brick wall displaying the prison's name in red letters.
Now Stuckey speaks.
"That woman is makin' alota enemies. I'd be a real shame if somethin' were to happen to her."
"That wouldn't be a very wise move. If anything, it'd be a very stupid one," obviously a lot brighter than his superior.
"She's gonna fuckin' ruin everything!"
"Well let her ruin it, don't you go and ruin it yourself. And besides, who cares what some guy claims you're doing, none of it' been proven. People know a great deal of lies are spread during election time. Which ones they believe and which ones they don't is solely up to you. If you allow Ms. Goldstein, Yates, or whoever, depict you in a negative light, and not defend yourself by dressing the rumors, you'll never spend one night in the governor's mansion. Her rally presents the perfect opportunity for you to extinguish the fire before it becomes a blaze. Politics is nothing but a big game of poker. The higher the desired position, the higher stakes. You either bet, check, or fold. She's

already shown her hand, and it's obvious she's not bluffing. You call her bet by presenting yourself as a confident leader, someone who doesn't run from the issues; thus casting doubt on your competition, and hopefully making you the people's champion." Higgins is more experienced with wooing constituents than Gordon. Several years prior he got out of the arena after losing his senate seat in a hotly contested battle with a Montana liberal. After that, he held several mid-level positions involved in the lawmaking process, before landing the one he currently has. Gordon promised to make him director of the pardons and parole board if he wins. All he wants in return is to be steered in the right direction. Yates was correct when he said Stuckey knows nothing about politics. Higgins taught him how to hold successful fundraisers, what he should promise to do, who to speak highly of, and who to speak out against; which demographic he should target, and which one isn't going to vote for him no matter what he says. With Gordon playing the leading role, and Higgins calling the shots, it's quite possible he can wind up being the states next governor.

"You're right, I have to use this as my stepping stone. Make her little rally backfire on her."

"Precisely."

"You think ole Yates'll show?"

"Hard to say, depends on the turnout. If it's a large crowd like she says with news vans and all, I think he'll be there. But if it's just a few dozen people singing spirituals and carrying candles, I don't think it'll be worth his time. But then again, he still may not come. Either way, you'll be out there in the thick of it, flashing smiles and shaking hands. Even if they don't like what you represent, they'll remember you didn't run and hide. You stood and faced the music. And that's the type of person people will vote for. All you have to do is keep playing your role, keep telling them what they want to hear, make them believe that you're out for their best interest. Simple as that."

"Do you know who I am?" asked the young man sitting across the table.

Grainger tries to remember where he knows the face from, but years of seclusion has erased people from his memory; mainly relatives that left him for dead. It'd be a miracle if he recognizes his sister after this long. Unable to recall the face, Grainger finally gives up.

"I'm sorry. No I don't know who you are."

The young man hangs his head and nervously fidgets with his wallet. More seconds pass before he unfolds it and thumbs through it, extracting a picture of a man standing beside a boy holding a fishing pole with the tiny fish dangling from line.

 He slides it across the table.

Grainger's heart almost stops when he recognizes himself, much younger, much slimmer, and minus the gray. His head starts aching while the room swirls around him. Somehow he manages to whisper the name of the person who holds a special place in his heart.

His eyes water.

"Jason?......My son Jason?"

Speaking the name brings innumerable memories to his mind. This is the picture his wife took on their trip to Lake Lanier seventeen years ago. In disbelief, Grainger looks up from the photo, and back at him again. Both of them stare at each other while the clock on the wall ticks. He feels awkward and uncomfortable, but at the same time filled with a joy he hasn't felt in years.

"I didn't recognize you. It—it's been so long....How old are you now?"

"Twenty-one, I'll be twenty-two next month."

The weight of reality is a giant foot crushing him into the seat. The last time he saw of him was at his twelfth birthday party, two days before the incident. The boy has become a man with a goatee, an exact replica of his late father.

"It's so good to see you. You've grown a lot."

Jason shakes his head in agreement while searching for the right words.

"How've you been?"

"Fine I guess...How about yourself?"

"Pretty good for the most part," Jason replied, fiddling with his thick brown chin hair.

Grainger wants to ask what made him come after all these years, considering he's the one who made him fatherless, but he doesn't want to ask questions that bring up the past. Knowing the opportunity probably won't present itself again, he gives up wavering and breaks the ice.

"So what happened to you after I uhm........You know, came to prison?"

He had to ask. That's only one of the million things he lay awake at night thinking about.

Grainger studies the young man.

"Well....I went to live with my grandma in Cartersville. That's where I've been ever since....You remember her don't you?"

"...Yes."

How can he forget the woman who helped his wife conceal the truth from him? She got the house, the car, and everything else he owned; punitive damages awarded by the state. She must've sold his house and bought the one in Cartersville. Maybe she wanted to avoid waking up every morning, and be smacked in the face with the fact that she contributed to the obvious. It'd be difficult to eat in the same kitchen where she'd once helped prepare Thanksgiving dinner with the man she deceived. Relocation was the best option. Her conscious would've likely pushed her over the edge had she stayed.

After a brief silence he answers.

"I remember her....Did you finish school?"

"No, I stopped after tenth grade, but I got my GED. I'd missed too many days that year because I got sent to juvy a few times," drawing imaginary lines on the table with his finger.

That would've never happened had his mother not messed everything up by sneaking around.

But you didn't have to kill them both and leave him with no parents at all.

He sighs and says: "I'm really glad you came....I've missed you so much. There's not a day that goes by when I don't think about you. You're the only son I have. I loved you then, and I love you now."

Nervously running a hand over his face, he asks: "Do you hate me Jason? Is this why you came here? To tell me how much you can't stand me before I die?"

"*No!* Why would I hate you for? For what you did? To be honest with you, that man was nothing to me, and I was nothing to him, but a mistake from a good time. That man didn't give a crap about me, you were my dad! He never worked one day to keep a roof over my head, he never took me camping, or roasted marshmallows with me, he never bought clothes for me to wear, he's not the one who took me to the hospital after I broke my arm from jumping out the swing. Not once did he read me a bedtime story, or run off the boogie man hiding in my closet. And not once did he ever tell me he loved me...How can I hate you?"

Grainger turns his head to keep Jason from seeing his pain.

The low afternoon sun streams warming rays through the barred window. There couldn't have been a better day for him to hear those words. Jason's opinion of him is the only one that matters. Oh how many nights he's cried for his forgiveness, and here it is, less than seven days before he's scheduled to die, and his prayers are answered. The tears gain momentum and fall to his shirt. He turns to Jason, too rubbing his eyes.

"You don't know how long I've waited to hear you say that.

"You don't know how long I've wanted to say it."

Grainger jumps to his feet!

Jason too!

They embrace and tears flow unabated.............

".....I used to stare at this picture for hours and reminisce on how much fun we used to have."

Grainger feels the wetness against his face.

"Everybody did their best to turn me against you. Every time they talked bad about you, I'd look at it."

He doesn't want to let his son go.

"One day my grandma came in my room and found the rest of them and burned 'em up, and made me watch. She said if she ever saw me with anymore she'd put me in an orphanage. I cried and screamed for her to put the fire out but she wouldn't."

"Stop, stop crying. It's okay now," pulling from him to look into his eyes.

Jason wipes his face, and they sit back down.

"She never found this one because I carried it everywhere I went. It's kinda like my guardian angel, it kept me safe. When I asked where you were, she'd say you were dead. For a long time I believed that, until one day she must've felts guilty or something, and told me they'd sent you to some underground place in California. I prayed that someday God would lead me to you. I remember I would go to church, and after service was over, I'd go up to and ask the pastor to ask God to keep you safe. One day I got a letter from your sister in Spain saying that you here, and she gave me the name of this place."

"What's she doing in Spain?"

"She moved there after you got put in here. She came to my school and told me that if I ever saw you again to tell you that she'll always love you. She said she couldn't stay, it was too hard. It kinda made me mad when she said it's easier to forget about you than deal with the pain of seeing you in here...She named her son Matthew."

The fact his only sister moved to another country to forget about him is bad enough, but the fact that he has a nephew he's never met is too much to swallow. How can she be so selfish? How can she just run away and leave him like that and not even say good-bye? He understands the pain, but can't understand why she purposely removed him from memory? What about the strain he has to deal with from worrying if she's all right or not? What about the saying that blood is thicker than water? She doesn't have to come and see him, but an occasional letter would be sufficient.

"Do you know why I'm in this building, all by myself separated from everyone else?"

Jason looks around as if the answer is written on the walls.

"No, why?"

"This is E-house. It's where a man comes once the date for execution has been set. It's on the twenty-fourth of this month."

Jason leaps to his feet!

"NO!!....NOOOO!"

His face dark, eyes big as golf balls, mouth drops completely open.

Granger stands to embrace him.

Transforming from an adult back to a boy isn't as impossible as it's said to be. He's now the same boy who cried for his father in the middle of the night. The deep voice is gone, replaced by a bass-less whine.

"No, no! They can't! We haven't made up for lost time!!! There's so much for us to do!"

The dam Grainger's holding bursts open.

"We can't make up for the past, it's gone forever, never to return. All we can do is look towards the future, and enjoy the rest of whatever we have left together."

He never knew holding onto another man would feel so good.

He squeezes him tighter, never wanting to let go.

A cardinal appears on the ledge, and voices its approval.

Jason cries.

"Come," returning to their seats.

Reaching around the back of Jason's neck, he pulls him closer until their foreheads meet, both watching the others tears fall

to the table.
What life has done is no longer the issue, all that matters is today. The tides of change has finally turned their direction, bringing peace to their minds, and extinguishing the blaze that has inexorably burned at their souls. Closure has been brought to the book that fate authored against their will.
"Hey," Jason said, sitting up and wiping a hand across his face.
Grainger raises his head and meets his gaze.
"You're going to get a stay. Everything's gonna be fine."
"Jason, I'm not. I'm going to die."
"Don't say that!"
"Please son, you must understand. I'm a death row inmate, and my date has been set; all my appeals have been exhausted."
Jason shakes his head in disbelief, and looks at the wall.
"This isn't how it was supposed to be."
And goes silent.
"What am I going to do without a father?"
Grainger hangs his head in shame, bearing the full load of reality. Memories of that night, and the smoking gun scorch his conciseness. He feels like the lowest person on earth.
Why'd you have to do it Matthew?
"Well if that's what's going to happen, I'm going to be there for you."
"I don't want you seeing it."
"Dad look at me, I'm not a kid anymore. I'm the man you helped raise. I'm not going to let you go it alone. If you get angry at me for being there, so be it. But I will not allow my father to die like that."
Grainger feels the muscles in his neck grow taught, and knows his decision is made.
"I don't think you know what happens."
"I know exactly what happens. I'm not going to watch it, I'll be there just long enough for you to go to heaven with the image of your son....It's my turn to be your guardian angel."
"Thank you," but inside, he's shattered.

I'm really going to die.

"I'm used to hearing words like ignorant, stubborn and disobe-dient.....On my eighteenth birthday I felt I was old enough to ask grandma any question I want, so I asked her why she hates you so much, and guess what she said?"

"What?"

"Because you made her hate herself."

So there it is.

"But she did do something nice."

"What?"

"She kept your car and gave it to me when I turned sixteen. That's what I drove here in today."

"So you're telling me my old car is in the parking lot?"

"Yep."

"Let me see it," trying to shake the emotional dung.

Like death row, E-house has its own separate lot—if a gravel area the size of a tennis court can be considered such.

They both get up and peek over the high window sill.

There it is, the same pewter '69 Camaro SS 396 that his father gave him.

"I love the racing stripes."

Life's went on without you.

"Yeah, the white goes great with the interior. I get offers for it all the time. One guy offered me fifty thousand for it. I told him if he had a suitcase with ten million in, he couldn't have it."

He remembers how proud he felt leaving his graduation with the engine roaring; him in cap and gown, smiling brighter than the chrome on the rally wheels. His date, Stacy Marshall, also his first love, wanted to cruise around and show her friends her man's fancy new car. He and Butch Davis, captain of the football team raced for bragging rights. He beat the Mustang by four car lengths.

"Amazing how good it looks after all these years."

"She kept it covered in a shed, and didn't let anyone drive it."

"Do you know that's what I planned to do the night you received your diploma?"

"What a coincidence!"

"My father gave it to me on the night of my graduation."

"Man I love that car, I treat it like a baby. It never goes over three thousand miles without an oil change. Every fifteen thousand, it gets a major tune-up. One day I took it to the track to see what it could do, and it ran the quarter in thirteen seconds flat!"

"You be careful out there."

"Dad, I drive that car like Ms. Daisy, I only did that once. Take a look at this," and hands him another photo from his wallet.

It shows the vehicle's mint interior—*'Matt and Jason Forever'* stitched in cursive across the front seats.

Maybe this is his boy, and it's all a big misunderstanding. He has his heart, his compassion, and like him, very forgiving. How else can he explain that Jason, who hasn't seen him since he was twelve, possess such strong feelings for him? Maybe it's because he's too young and naïve to understand the magnitude of what's been taken. But again, how can someone miss something they never had? True indeed, she carried him for nine long arduous months, and endured seven long hours of pushing, pulling, squeezing, and releasing; tears of joy, and tears of pain, having just experienced the miracle of birth. A proud new mother, truly a blessing from above.

Only to later abandon her precious gift of life, too preoccupied with her own agenda, and not yet ready to adhere to the call of motherhood—only a mother in word. The drinking, the staying out all night, the struggle to keep up with everything that didn't involve the rearing her child; that's all she was concerned about.

"Whatcha thinking about dad?"

".....So much."

That's when Matthew Grainger become a star, masterfully playing the leading role of both parents. The mom when the script called for cooking, cleaning, instilling good values, delivering companionship and love; bandaging scraped knees and rides to school. The father when the script called for bringing home the

bacon, paying the bills, servicing the cars, repairing the house, and protecting the family. He displayed excellent poise and leadership in his portrayal of *'Mom and Dad'*, the longest movie in history; taking twelve years and fourteen days to watch from start to finish. The credits rolled two days after Jason's twelfth birthday.
"You don't know how much you coming here means, this place has taken so much from me. Seeing you is more than words can explain."
Crying's become one of his regular pastimes, doing it again as he embraces his son.

They talk for five more hours until the guard notifies them that visitation is over. They hug like they'll never hug again.
"When can I come back?"
"Every day.....until."
"Well in that case, I'll see you tomorrow."
"Deal," binding it with a handshake.
Grainger watches him exit the building, and drive away with a thumbs-up straight in the air, until the sound of the potent V-8 fades into distance.

Chapter 8

Christine stands before the outgoing mail chute double checking the addresses on the parcels. Satisfied they're correct, she sends them down. Steps away sits hundreds of P.O. boxes, of which she searches until locating the one belonging to her. Upon unlocking the door, she retrieves a stack of envelopes.

"Junk."

"Junk."

"Junk."

"More junk," tossing coupons, advertisements, and instant win notices in the trash. She comes upon one sent from the county DA's office, and opens it. On a single sheet of paper is the Georgia state seal, the official address, phone and fax number, and name of the district attorney. Below is a message several paragraphs long.

Dear Ms. Christine Chase,

Your latest request for a new trial on the behalf of Douglas Parson has been thoroughly reviewed. We found no errors in this case, nor did we find your assertions valid. Your request for this to case to reheard has been documented and denied....

Before reading it entirely, she turns the paper into a basketball, and shoots it into the basket. Next, she comes upon another letter, this one sent from the Emma Jones Foundation. A finger is used to tear it open, and unfold the carbonless stationary.

Dear Ms. Chase, Christine

We were very pleased to receive your heartwarming letter requesting our services, and are dedicated to rooting out the innocent from the guilty. The case against Mr. Douglas Parson was painstakingly reviewed by our experienced legal team, and investigators. We here at the Emma Jones Foundation are sorry to inform you that we were unable to find a single shred of evidence in this case to signify that Mr. Parson has been wrongly convicted. We assure you that this by no way means that he's guilty, only that this particular case does not warrant our assistance. We are truly disappointed that we could not help you.

Two more points.
She slams the box, and heads out of the post office. The second she enters her vehicle, she removes her sunglasses from the visor, and put them on. After cranking up, she makes her way down Roswell Rd. where she turns left onto I-285, and heads north. At the GA-400 split, she hangs a right and proceeds towards her destination. Using her cell phone, she dials a number read from a paper clipping.
"Outdoor Adventures," answered a male voice.
"Do you guys carry climbing equipment?"
"Why certainly, yes we do. What kind of climbing are you planning on doing?"
"Mountain, my friends and I are going up to Blue Ridge, and need the type of hoisting system that can be wedged into a crack, and pull a climber up. Are you familiar with what I'm referring to?" while giving the finger to a guy who wouldn't let her over.
"Yes, we carry a few of them."
"Great, can you give me directions? The ones on the advertisement aren't that clear."
"Yeah, we hear that all the time. Where are you coming from?"
"Four-hundred."
"Go all the way up until you hit Mansell Rd. Get off and go right. Three lights down on the left, big bear on the sign."
"Got it," and ends the call before he can say anything else.

She makes it to the store in minutes. He wasn't lying when he said big bear. A two-story, helium filled grizzly stands on its hind legs baring its teeth at motorists. Christine finds a space near the entrance and heads inside. But notices a man sitting in an unmarked car watching her through binoculars. Without hesitation, she goes to his window, and stares through the tint until he lowers it. Before he can say a word she flatly demands: "Who are you, and why are you watching me?"
His beer belly jiggles in amusement.
"I'm not watching you. I'm looking at that bank over there,"

nodding to it. "There's been a string of robberies. You wouldn't by chance know anything would you?" producing a badge that says F.B.I. on it.

"No," and leaves before he can ask more questions.

She feels him looking as she walks away, but doesn't turn to see.

After watching her go inside, he gets out, and lights up a cigg. Certain the coast is clear, he strolls over to her car, peeks through the dark tint, takes out a notepad, and jots down the VIN before going to the rear and getting the tag.

"I thought you're watching the bank?"

Startling him to the point he scribbles the last two letters. He turns to see a pair of Versace® shades standing inches from his nose.

The agent gives her a quick head to toe.

"Ma'am, I don't know if you know it or not, but the FBI watches everybody. Nothing personal, just doing my job. How do I know you're not part of the crew that keeps holding up the place, and is back to case again? You're *are* acting like you have something to hide, hence the need to take down your tag number. Like I said, nothing personal, basic investigative practice. Everyone's a suspect since nine-eleven."

"Why did you wait until you thought I isn't looking?"

"If I tell every perp I'm onto 'em, I'd never make any arrests? Which makes me wonder, why did you watch to see my next move? Regular people don't do suspicious things like that?"

"The world is filled with sick people...How do I know you're not a serial killer about to make me your next victim."

"How do I know you're not a serial killer yourself?"

She stands there with her arms crossed.

"....You don't."

And walks away.

"Hi, are you the guy that I spoke with about the hoisting systems?"

"That'd be me!" replied the dashing chap with an orange Outdoor Adventures shirt stretched over his less than impressive chest. "Right this way."

The charismatic clerk leads her to the back of the store, everything from kayaks to ski suits line the aisles. Tens of rifles and crossbows sit vertical in secured racks behind a long glass case; knives, fishing reels, exotic lures and costly optics. Christine passes a 15-point, trophy buck posed mid-stride. A manikin bolted to the wall with hooks and carabiners dangling from his belt welcomes customers to the climbing section.

"Here they are miss," pointing to them.

They're mounted on an imitation stone block.

"What size are you looking for," not yet retiring his smile.

"One that can lift in excess of two-hundred and fifty pounds.

"Your friend sounds pretty large. People that size don't usually scale faces."

"Well this one does."

"In that case I recommend you go with this one," their most expensive model.

"Would you mind carrying it for me?"

He eagerly obliges.

"Now I need you to show me to the ropes."

He snickers.

"I'd love to show you the ropes," insinuating.

Leading her to the aisle, ropes of various prices, lengths, gauges, and colors hang coiled like serpents around metal hooks.

"Do you know what size you'll need?"

Christine visualizes the purpose.

"I need a hundred feet, nylon without rubber core."

"How about blue? It goes with your eyes," having no idea what kind of woman he's attempting to charm.

"No it doesn't. Black will be fine," and removes 2 ropes from the hook.

"I'm ready checkout."

"Uhmmm, Sure okay."

Upon arriving at the register, he makes one last attempt at success with the stunning blonde.

"Since I've gifted you with my expert knowledge of climbing gear, would you be so kind as to recompense me by telling me your name, and possibly your number?"

"Christine," handing him three, crisp hundred dollar bills, not looking up from her purse.

"I'll just call you Christie when I take you out to dinner. Aren't you going to ask me mines?" waiting for the receipt to print.

"No."

"You sure?"

"Very."

The defeated clerk hands her the change and the receipt. She easily lifts the hefty shopping bag off the counter and makes for the exit.

"Have a nice day beautiful!" he shouts.

"You too Morrison."

"How did she know my name?" he whispered in amazement.

He must've forgotten about the tag pinned to his shirt.

She looks to see if the agent has gone. He has, but not before placing his card under her wiper. After starting the car and waiting to pull onto Mansell, she twists the knob, and sends it floating to the pavement.

Traffic on Highway 316 was hell, taking an hour and a half to arrive at Marksman's Gun Range. The lot is dotted with 4 x 4's, sports cars, SUV's, and government issue Crown Victoria's and Chargers.

Christine removes the proper licenses from the glove box, picks up her gun case and exits. The *"beep-beep"* from the alarm activation catches the attention of a bearded guy leaving the elongated, single-story building. He offers a grin as he proceeds to his white Ford® Bronco.

After paying the admission, she purchases two boxes of hollow-point shells, and goes through the sound-proof door. The repetitious, deafening crack of what sounds like machine gun fire reverberates throughout the concrete bunker. After hearing the ear shattering boom of a .50 Desert Eagle®, she places the pair of noise suppressors over her ears, loads the bullets, and sets the life sized cut-out at a distance of thirty feet. Before it even stops swaying, she plants her feet, raises her firearm, and squeezes off six quick shots; moving the patron beside her to stop shooting and watch. He voluntarily hits the button to reel the target in. Two bullets went through the same hole between the eyes, two almost took off the neck, and the remaining two are all through the heart in the radius of a quarter.

"Damn! You do this for a living?" looking at the cardboard figure in awe.

"No," she said automatically. "And I don't like being interrupted either," and removes the spend shells.

"Pardon the interruption," and returns to what he's doing.

Christine increases the distance to forty five, and reloads. With her eyes peeled, she lets off six more blasts with equal results; this time catching the attention of a dark skin guy that has cop written all over him.

"You handle that weapon like a professional," nodding at the pistol laying on the square stool.

Without acknowledging his presence, she reloads, lays it back down, and takes the unlucky target back an additional 10 feet. In a draw faster than Billy the Kid's, she snatches it up, and put six more into the cardboard head.

The officer quickly goes about his business.

This woman isn't your average patron coming to lick a few shots. For the next thirty minutes, Ms. Chase hones her lethal skills. When her practice session is over, she quietly packs her things, and leaves without saying a word to anyone.

The parking meter displays a time of 30 minutes, that's all she gets for a dollar and fifty cents. Behind the designer shades, she sees countless people footing it up and down the sidewalk: Corporate types, construction types, exercising types, and unemployed types. There's also types with nothing better to do than checker the park between Auburn Ave. and Peachtree St. Christine is incognito in her best tourist attire: Straw hat, binoculars, and eating a bag of Smartfood® brand popcorn—matching straw sandals exhibit her freshly manicured toes, drawing frequent glances from male *and* female passersby alike. A lone homeless man sits on a bench feeding stale donuts to pigeons, a gold lab twists through the air catching a Frisbee®, granite chess tables team with players in deep concentration, police officers stand guard while the sun sends heat from above, a red news chopper hovers in the cloudless sky. Commercial vehicles, city buses, cars, and cycles negotiate the daunting maze of one-way streets, and scrawny thoroughfares. The Atlanta City Jail looming in the distance, sending thoughts of Douglas to her mind. All she's done and will continue to do is for him; their accomplishments and their failures are results of their undying love—only time will tell if they'll be reunited. But first, objectives must be met. She steps from the sidewalk onto the thick grass, fescue blades tickle her toes. The building they choose is visible to the entire area, the binoculars provide a detailed view; as her eyes scan back and forth like radar searching for enemy aircraft. They both agree the side facing the park is the most favorable, the target area located equidistantly up the side of the limestone building. Satisfied with the look from afar, she begin its direction.

"Excuse me ma'am?" asked an old guy with thinning hair and ragged clothes.

"Yuh thank yuh' cud spar uh few dollars so I can get me uh hot dawg."

"Sure," automatically, but minus a smile.

They walk side by side to the stand where she purchases him two chili dogs, a bag of chips, and a cola.

"I really 'preciate dis miss. I done spunt muh lass buck ahn seventy cents......*Agrrrrh, Agrrrrh!*" a cough that sounds like gravel rolling around in his chest.

"Scuse me, bad lungs from dem damn cigarettes. But thank you vera much for muh lunch, I sho' was hongry. May God bless you fur yer kindness," rubbing his throat.

"You be safe out here. The world's a dangerous place."

After jaywalking across the busy street, she studies the entrance's alcove. Rounding the entire structure, she gives each side an identical inspection, but doesn't stay long, and avoids drawing attention. The pre-pay phone vibrating in her pocket alerts her of an incoming call.

Someone's calling from a private number.

Christine ignores the call and heads back to the car. When she arrives, she notices something has again found its way under her wiper blade. Another folded piece of paper, except this time it's not from a pesky special agent, it's from a pesky beat cop. Parking ticket.

A buck fifty doesn't buy much these days.

"What camp did you say you're from?" asked the V8® drinking CO leaning in the swivel chair.

"Atlanta Federal Pen."

"Ain't that over there by those projects that's always on the news?"

"Yeah."

"Why would you leave a sweet gig like that to come work at a dump like this?"

"Needed a change of scenery."

Anyone talking with Stockton will quickly pick up on the air of seriousness that halos over him, he routinely goes weeks without smiling.

"Shit, I guess being perched up here for eight hours watching a buncha rats run around their around their cage, making sure they don't fuck each other to death ain't much different. When I first got here, it didn't seem so bad, because I was working general pop. But back here, this shit's dead man. You feel locked up like them. The fed camp can't be this bad."

The tower does resemble a cell with all the Plexiglas®, bars, and steel door. The only difference is the computer, the control panel, and the mini fridge squatting in the corner.

"What do you know about the guy sitting over there?" Billings pointing to Parson.

"His name's Parson, first name Douglas. Doesn't talk much, doesn't watch TV, and rarely goes outside. All he does is read books: weird shit about how to control people's minds. He been here for about ten years. Jury found 'em guilty of killin' this reverend after he'd tortured him—a real freak. He's got this pretty blonde who been comes to see him every week. I also hears he's next on the list too."

"I heard about what he did. The victim was also a high ranking official with DFACS." (Department of Family and Children Services).

"Tries to say he's innocent. But with all the evidence, along with the failed lie detector tests, it's just not possible. Hell, all these mutherfuckers claim they innocent—innocent my ass. Anyway, him hand his ole girl done filed dozens of appeals, and lost every one of 'em. I think he's given up on trying to play the innocent role, and gonna sit back, and wait his turn to die."

"The guy's name was Joseph Tangier, it was a big story," stated Billings.

"Sure was, and you know the spooky part about it," pausing a before revealing the mystery. "They say he had somebody with him when he did it. They also say that somebody could've been a woman. Everybody around here says that woman who comes to see him is the one who helped him murder that pastor."

"That's a rumor."

"How do you know? You sound real sure of yourself."

"I was an officer with APD, I had friends close to the investigation; that's how," proving his knowledge superior to his. "Hold things down. I'm going talk to this Parson fellow."

When he rises from his seat, he buzzes the lock.

"Watch out, dudes unpredictable."

"Me too."

Billings exits the tower, and beckons his co-worker to open the gate. Parson is flipping a page when he sits down and disturbs his studies, drawing the attention of the other inmates.

"What do you want?"

"Everything I can't have."

"Be thankful you still have your life, now be gone.

"What are you reading?"

Not looking away from his book.

"Activities of the human brain."

"A fascinating thing indeed?"

"Quite. What brings you down? I'm certain you didn't come for the hell of it," cutting to the chase.

"Well since you asked, I don't actually have a particular reason. It's that I've heard so much about you. I was a cop back when you were the talk of the town, I even sat through a few of your proceedings, a real learning experience."

Parson watches him closely. A police officer who attends trials he has nothing to do with?

Billings is going on about a friend who was one of the dicks on the investigation when he interrupts.

"Two questions."

"But it doesn't mean I have two answers."

"Why did you follow my trial?"

Long pause.

"Who didn't, the tape and all. No killer had that trademark before."

A pause is needed to answer the radio.

"Sorry about that. But to be honest with you, I wanted to see if they would satisfy the family with the death penalty."

"Second question," Parson said without hesitation. "Why are you always staring at me? Every time I come out of my cell, before I can even shift my cock, you're looking at me. Why is that?"

"Watching inmates is a key element of my duty."

"I'm good at judging character Mr. Billings, I can't put my finger on it yet, but there's something unsettling about you."

"Funny, my wife says the same thing."

"Does she?"

"Maybe I'm a fallen angel. They say the dead walk amongst the living."

"That *is* what they say...How long have you been married."

"Three years," he lied.

"That's enough time to get a gauge on a person. If she says that, it has validity. I've noticed in a few days."

"Oh well, enough about my wife. I've heard you have a nice piece of eye candy yourself. Been using that stuff you read in those books to keep her on a leash?"

Parson smiles.

"We're not married. And no I don't practice mind control on her. Let's just say were working together for a common cause."

Billings catches the hidden meaning in the comment.

"You know, they say that you had an accomplice. Would she by any chance be that person?" finding it hard to resist inquiring.

Parson stares at him for several moments, seeing that he's not intimidated by prolonged eye contact. There's something sinister within the hazel tint. He stares face-to-face with murders, rapists, and child molesters every day. Billings possesses eyes similar to theirs.

"Have you taken a life before?"

"Unlike you, I haven't indulged."

"You're a double-edged sword Billings. It's there plain as day. But I guess we don't all share the same keen vision."

"You're letting those books go to your head," he said laughing. But Parson isn't.

"Am I?....You're a man of many secrets. It's like you have this ticker-tape rolling across your forehead reeling off your innermost thoughts....Your childhood was a painful time wasn't it?"

That's a sore spot.

"What are you a fucking shrink now?...I'm nothing like you, and never will be. Now find the hidden meaning in that," and gets off the uncomfortable bench.

"It's been interesting talking with you inmate Parson. Maybe next time we can talk about your secrets instead of mine."

He's makes it to the gated corridor before he speaks.

"Billings!" his voice echoing throughout the cell-house, drawing more attention to their exchange.

"I'm not convinced, and neither are you," he yells.

Billings continues back inside the control tower, and the gate shuts.

"What was that all about?" asked a guy fresh off the phone.

"He's like the rest of them, wants to know about my case."

"I bet he still mad bout Sheep gassing him." (Prison slang for throwing bodily fluid on someone).

"Yeah."

"Well I'll see you. Ahma go see if I can catch a short."

"Yeah."

Mail call!" yells the chubby lady standing on the good side of the corridor holding a small stack of envelopes.

Killers drop what they're doing and beeline for the front; though the majority haven't received a letter in years. But it doesn't stop them from checking. Others let announcement go in one ear and out the other.

Parson gets three letters, and two others get one.

"It's gotta be more dan nat!" said Horus Mack, a man convicted of killing a massage parlor receptionist during a robbery. A pregnant teenage girl was his next victim, whom he ran over while fleeing the scene. Miraculously, she survived and testified at his trial.

"Sorry guys, that's it," she said politely, and spins the gray cart to leave.

Mack has never received a kite. (Prison slang for letter).

Parson is use to the envious sneers and remarks. Not wanting to rub it in all the disappointed faces, he clutches his mail, and heads to his cell.

Envy quickly turns into anger if left unchecked. He's almost made it when someone shouts from below.

"You think you so much betta dan da ress of us! But you ain't shit! Let dat hada been my bother you done dat to, yo' faggot ass wooda never made it ta jail!"

That's Mack, whom he's already had several run-ins with. None have ever escalated into anything serious, but lately he's been pressing his luck.

Parson ignores him and continues to his cell.

"Yeah, das what I thought bitch! You got errbody round here thinkin' you some helleva guy! But I see right thu yo' fuck ass!"

With some people he can control his temper, with others he can't.

He calmly rises from his bunk and walks onto the tier. Wrapping his hands around the railing, he looks squarely at Horus below.

"What do you have against me? What is it?"

"I got something against every sick muthafucka like you!"

"You're waiting to die too. The jury obviously thought you're sick also," his voice revealing none of his fury, but all of his sarcasm.

Snickering spectators cause the muscles in his face to knot and contort.

"Keep runnin' dat smart mouf cracka, and ahma give errbody somethin' tuh really laugh about; you lil chain-gang tramp!"

"There you go with your racial slurs, and homosexual innuendo. Well Horace, I'm going to let you argue with yourself, I have more important things to do than stand here and contend with an insignificant gnat like yourself," and goes back inside his cell.

Once again Parson makes him look like a fool.

"*BOOOOOOOOO!!!!!*" goes spectators at another of his empty threats.

Parson's senses alert him to an individual moving hastily towards his position. Quickly, he laces up his prison brogans, and stretches.

"Here he comes Parson!" warned an inmate he can't see.

Mack must've removed his shirt along the way, because his chiseled chest, and bulging arms are visible as he stands in the doorway heaving.

"Wussup wit all dat mouth now craka!" biting his bottom lip, eyes wide with fury.

Parson stationed at the rear of his cell coolly says: "Come inside and close the door."

Driven by anger, and not rationale, Horus makes a reckless move towards Parson!

His first off-balance swing is a complete waste of energy, as Parson beautifully sidesteps it, sending Mack's fist crashing into the wall! Then swings his hand at his throat, shattering his Adam's apple!

Horace slides down the wall clutching his neck.

The fight is over as quickly as it began.

Parson's heart rate hasn't increased a beat, he didn't even break a sweat.

Calmly, he exits the cell, and goes downstairs to the call box.

"What's up Parson?" Harry answered, back from his break.

"Mack came into my room and tried to assault me, he's up there lying in the floor. You probably want to call medical, I think his larynx is broken, along with his hand."

Harry sighs.

"I'll be right down."

The spectators have gone to see Horace, and are laughing at what they see. High-fives and "I told you sos" fill the space in front of the cell. Horace has beaten up quite a few inmates, including threaten a slew of others. They're elated that he finally met his match.

Harry, Billings, and another guard make their way to his cell to survey the damage. Medical isn't far behind.

"Did anyone see what happened?" Billings asked aloud, not believing Harry's version of the event.

The inmates gladly state that Mack ran into Parson's cell and swung at him.

The medical team arrives and rolls Horace off on a stretcher. He doesn't look at Parson, or any of the other inmates; obviously embarrassed at the result of his futile attempt at dealing with Parson's mouth.

Parson's record now stands at 9-0.

Billings has returned to his post in general population, he was only there until Harry returned.

"You just can't avoid trouble huh?" he said, looking at Parson inside his cell.

"You know I don't start trouble Harry, that's not my style. I tried to avoid it, but he was bent on putting a foot in my ass. What was I put supposed to do?"

"Beats me. Where do you learn that stuff from?"

"I studied martial arts when I used to be a citizen."

"Think they can teach an old fart like me a couple of those fancy moves?"

"Sure, my instructor was fifty-one when he started training me. In a few years you can be the next Bruce Lee."

"Harry the Dragon has a nice ring to it."

"Perfect!"

"Parson you're never going to believe this. But I just came from E-house, and Grainger is happy as a lark."

"He got a stay!"

"No, but it's the next best thing. His son came to see him, and has been back every day since."

"You mean the kid from the guy?"

"Yep. Apparently the kids been trying to find him ever since it happened, but got the runaround from the relatives."

"*Maaaaaaan*, I know that makes him feel good. He loves that kid."

"He said to tell you hello too. First time I've ever seen him so happy. It's just sad that he had to wait till E-house to find him though."

"Yeah, but I'm glad he did. He needs that."

"There's more, the kid says he's coming to the execution?"

"What?"

"He says he wants his face to be the last one Grainger sees. Even brought him barbecue ribs and potato salad for lunch, not to mention a cake with both their names on it. You should saw him, it's like he's a free man again, just plump with joy."

Parson can see his old buddy laughing, finally reunited with his son after all these years.

"That's great Harry, it really is. That's going to do a lot for his spirit, and mines as well."

"I just wanted to tell you the news, I've got some things I need to take care of."

"Hey before you go, I wanna know what you think about the new guy?"

"Billings?"

"Yes."

"From what I've heard, he came from the Fed camp in Atlanta. Why, what's wrong?"

"Nothing, just wondering. He came down while you're gone and questioned me about my case. He said he came to a couple of my proceedings, and that he used to be a cop. But go ahead and handle your business. I'll tell you later."

"All right. But don't worry too much about him. He's probably just scared."

Harry waves and heads back in the tower.

Parson's perfected his personality shifting ability. Whatever the occasion calls for, that's what he becomes; epitomizing what it means to be a chameleon. One minute he can be your warm and compassionate friend, and the next as lethal as cyanide. Being considered a psychopathic genius, it's easy for him to dupe even the most noted cognoscente. During his stay, he's convinced a large number of psychologists, and legal minds that he's innocent, not to mention the majority of the inmates who think he's a great individual. Letters from all over the flooded in when an article was ran in the Sunday paper describing an interview with him. One of them contained something to help him cope with his unfortunate situation: A $10,000 donation from a rural Georgia woman. The sister of Joseph Tangier also read the article. Upset with the portrayal of Parson as a wrongly convicted man, she wrote a seven-page letter detailing the life of her slain brother, and the overwhelming evidence proving Parson's guilt. It also ran, but received little fanfare. Readers deemed her part of the conspiracy against poor innocent Parson—leading her to file a defamation suit against the paper, which was quickly dismissed. Harry's become another of his loyal supporters.

The following morning, pouring rain makes her windshield wipers of little use. The only way Kathy avoids running off the road, is to keep her eyes glued to the taillights of the car in front of her. The meteorologist predicted torrential rains, and the National Weather Service posted a flash flood warning for the entire state. Unfortunately, that wasn't enough for her boss to suspend the work day. So here she is, driving 25 down the expressway; the hazard lights of a tow truck can be seen in the distance. Amongst the noise of zillions of water droplets crashing into her Camry, an ambulance blows pass with its sirens blaring. The exit's coming up on her right, she cautiously merges.

After driving through congested streets, Kathy enters the parking garage, shielding her car from further abuse. Parking in her normal paid space, she gets out and heads inside.

The elevator doors opens with the familiar "Bing" as she steps out and makes for her office. The clock radio reads 9:33 AM;

late for the fourth consecutive day. She's usually a punctual person, but everyone falls into slumps. Kathy goes about her normal morning ritual of turning on the heater and checking her messages, and has just began prioritizing her tasks when her boss strolls in wearing an exquisite single breasted, two button suit. Ralph Prose is a decent anti-trust attorney, but his baby is liability. He's a shark when it comes to making corporate whales pay for their negligence. There isn't a doubt in anyone's mind that he's next to hold coveted title of partner. He's also great at other things needs to climb the firm's lofty ladder: He's a pathological liar.

"Good morning Kathy."

"Same to you Mr. Prose."

"Traffic pretty bad huh?" his way of letting her know she's late again.

"Yes. It's awful."

"Well, I've got some stuff material I need you to go over. I need you to find as many people as you can who worked for Tuck Lumber Company who were diagnosed with mesothelioma. Plaintiffs are claiming a chemical used to pressure treat the wood caused it. Even if they're retired or deceased, I want their names. We're talking a hundred and twenty-five million in damages."

Kathy whistles.

"All right, I'll get on it."

Prose hands her two, bursting-at-the-seams folders, and walks out.

She gets on her desktop, and begins logging information.

It's been a solid hour until Quinn, the mail clerk stops his cart in front of her door.

"Hey Kathy."

"How's it going buddy? You pass that exam?"

"I won't know the results until Monday. You know how it is when you're waiting for something," coming her way with a stack of envelopes.

"Tell me about it."

"I'm sure glad it's Friday, this weekend will give me time to relax a bit. It's been a crazy week."

"Yours too?" handing him her outgoing mail as he places hers on the desk.

"How's your brother?"

"He's the top student in his class, pretty good for a kid from the hood."

"When you two are famous surgeons, don't forget about little ole me."

"You know I can't forget about you," returning to his cart.

"See you later Quinn."

"Later Kathy."

As she focuses back on the computer screen, her attention is drawn to the stack sitting at the corner of her desk; a little brown box sits atop. She grabs it and reads the shipping slip. The absence of a return address heightens her interest. She shakes it beside her ear but hears nothing, the post-date shows it was sent Wednesday. She peels the end open, and out comes Styrofoam® popcorn onto her desk. Inside is a small piece of folded paper accompanied by a micro cassette tape. Kathy stares at it and can't help think how the police recovered one of these at the scene of the couple's murder. Unfolding the piece of paper brings an unpleasant surprise.

"A gift from someone close??..."

She picks up the phone and dials Megan.

"Hey, you wouldn't by chance have one of those hand-held recorders would you?"

"You mean one of those things people use to record meetings and stuff?"

"Yeah, but the old kind with the tape."

Megan seems to be doing something in the background.

"Sure, but it's the old kind that uses the cassette tape."

Kathy shakes her head.

"That's the one I need."

"Okay, I'll be right there," and hangs up.

A minute later she's coming through the door.

"Look at this note."

"Where'd you get it, sounds juicy."

"It came with the tape."

"Makes you wonder what's on it."

Prose walks past.

"Close that door will you?"

Megan does and takes a seat.

"Hey Kath, you remember that guy back in the day that killed the pastor and left the recordings of it?"

Remembering exactly causes her to hesitate on putting it in.

"Can you please stop bringing that stuff up?"

"Sorry," adjusting her rump in the seat. "....Okay already, I said sorry. You can stop looking at me like that."

Kathy's eye leaves Megan's and returns to the device. As she slides the tape in she looks back up.

"You think I should call the police first?" slightly frightened.

Megan can't wait that long, the anticipation is killing her.

"Nah girl, it's probably something mushy from one of your many admirers."

From the look on Kathy's face, she doesn't share that opinion.

"I shouldn't have said that. I keep forgetting how scary you are."

"And what the hell does that supposed to mean?" she shot, using a rare curse word.

"I didn't mean it like that. I'm joking."

Seeing she's angered her friend, she makes a sincere attempt.

"Don't get mad girl. You know I act a little immature at times. You know I didn't mean anything by it."

Kathy looks back at the machine in her hand, determined not to overreact.

"Be quiet, I'm about hit play."

Megan slides her chair around. They both sit in silence for a moment until Megan burst into laughter.

"Girl, we are tripping! We're acting all nervous like we already know it's something bad. It's probably some jerk beating his meat why he declares his love for you," laughing again.

Kathy laughs too.

"You're right, we are. Let's hurry up and get this over with. Ralph already walked by once and gave me the eye....Okay, here we go."

She presses the red rectangular button and hears what sounds like panting.

Kathy looks at Megan, who shrugs her shoulders, and twirls her finger beside her temple.

The breathing stops, replaced by a deep voice that sounds like it's being spoken through some type of vocoder. It brings dark memories too mind, and is impossible to tell if it's male or female.

> *"I have entered the house undetected......I can barely see as I walk down the dark hallway........There's a faint odor of bleach...I can hear the air conditioner running........Is your heart beating as fast as mines? The uncertainty of how this will end causes mines to pound with anticipation, as I move up the stairs.......The master bedroom is my destination ....I can hear the wind whipping through the trees"*

Creaking stairs.

> *"I've reached the top. It's slightly warmer..........Wait! ....Something's in the distance!"*

A snoring sound can be heard, slowly it becomes more pronounced.

> *"I'm now standing in the doorway...... Two people of*
> *known gender are fast asleep beneath the covers.*
> *They have no idea someone's in their home......"*

Kathy hits the stop button. Fear has completely enveloped her.
"What the hell is this!!"
"I don't know!"
Knock-knock!
The door startles them.
"Come in."
But Prose is already opening the door, and not pleased by the site of them hunched behind the desk, clearly not working.
"Someone sent this tape this morning. I think you should listen to it."
"What makes you think I have time for that?" irritated.
"Please, just come and listen."
He sighs, shakes his head, and pulls up a chair while she rewinds it, and plays it from the beginning; stopping at the same place.
"Sounds serious, who sent it?"
"It doesn't have a name or return address."
"I recommend you call the police."
But Megan wants to hear the rest before anybody calls anyone.
"I say we listen to the whole thing before jumping to conclusions. Then we can determine if it warrants police attention—could be just a prank."
"I guess you have a point," he agreed.
Not waiting for any more suggestions, she presses play hoping she right, and if not, she feels a safer now there's a man in the room.

> *"...I enter the bedroom, the moonlight creeps through*
> *the drapes. I wonder how they'll react to the sight of*

me standing over them with a gun in my hand?... Removing my glove, I reach down and admire the texture of the satin sheets; the misses is turned towards me, my hand is only inches from her face. The barrel caresses her hair.....My finger engulfs the trigger. She won't feel a thing, death will come easily. This is only because of her deeds. Or shall I say, it's he who has wronged, but revenge will be mines.

Now the heavy breathing is back, and continues for several moments. It grows harder and heavier, louder and steadier; quickening which each breath until reaches a fever pitch!

"But not tonight.....Now to you Katherine, I have something special for you."

Kathy drops the machine, sending it bouncing off the floor.
They're speechless!
Ralph goes to her.
"I'm calling the police," reaching for the phone. "Do you have any idea who would send this?"
She's staring at the floor, shocked by the realization that the killer knows her name, and where she works.
"Hey," Megan said, holding her hand. "Don't worry girl, everything's going to be fine. The cops will know what to do," trying to console her.
But the cops don't know what to do.
"The police are on the way, I'm going down to meet them. Where's the tape?"
"I think it fell under the desk," answered Megan.
He bends down but doesn't see it.
"I don't see the tape, but the player's right here," reaching to pick

it up. "And it's not in here either."
"Kathy, did you see where it went?"
She snaps out of her trance.
"It's melting in the heater," she said emotionless, and shuts it off.
But the damage is already done. The clear plastic cassette has turned into a black smoldering glob.
"I knew I smelled something burning," Megan declared.
Ralph grabs a ruler from the desk, and commences to prying it off.
"It's no use, it's finished," getting off his knees. "Now we don't have anything to give the cops. That could've probably helped them catch the guy, *damn!*...I'm going down to bring them back and let them decide what do," before he's out the door.
Megan unplugs it, and sits it on the desk.
"Why'd he pick me? What did I do? How does he know me? He probably knows where I live too...*Oh my God*," she sobbed, cupping her face in her hands.
"Stop talking like that. The main thing we have to do is remember as much of it as we can, so we can tell the police. I remember most of it so you won't have to say much."
"I don't wanna die Megan."
"Don't say that, nothing like that's going to happen. It's going to be all right," embracing her shaking body.

Chapter 9

Kathy sits alone in her garden tub hoping the hot water and Calgon® will indeed "take her away". She filed a police report and called it a day. Afraid to drive home alone, she had Stockton follow her. The space heater was taken to the crime lab so what's left of the tape can be salvaged, and the shipping box as well. Kathy violated the surgeon general's warning by washing aspirin down with wine; hoping the elixir will calm her ragged nerves, and stop the migraine from sparring with her head. She's aware of the dangers of mixing drugs with alcohol, but doesn't care. All she wants is relief, never mind how she gets it. The aromatherapy candles burning on the counter are making her nauseous, and the soft jazz playing from the Bose® wave radio is doing more harm than good. Trying to trick herself into forgetting what happened is proving to be quite challenging.

Giving up on her relaxation exercise, she gets up and steps out onto a fluffy floor mat. After blowing the out the candles, and turning on the lights, she stares at the pale face in the mirror. The events of today, and the thing with Christie, looks to have added years to her appearance; brought on by more than what transpired today. She dries and slips into a robe.

Stockton's in his usual spot when she comes out. He made an honest attempt at preparing dinner: A plate of Hamburger Helper®, broccoli and cheese, and garlic bread sits on the table beside an icy glass of her favorite iced tea.

He rises when he sees her; a fully loaded .44 waits atop the coffee table.

"I see you've turned into chef Boyardee."

"I wish."

Although she has no appetite, she grabs the plate anyway, and sits out on the couch.

"Why don't you put that away, there's no need to have it out like that," and sticks a fork of lukewarm meat and noodles in her mouth.

"I will, but not right this second. If it makes you feel better, I'll move it out of your sight." He lays it on the carpet.

It's seven on the dot, and ABC World News® is just starting. The ongoing conflict between the Palestinians and Israelis kicks off Friday's broadcast. Another suicide bomber struck again, this time killing twelve people in a crowded bakery along the Gaza Strip—thirty more are said to have been injured.

"Your mother called. She asked how you we're doing. I didn't know if I should say anything about what happened, so I told her you're fine, and that I'd tell you she called."

"You did the right thing, I don't need her trying to move in and bless us with her security. I'll call her later."

She takes a swig of drink and continues.

"The more I think about it, the more I think it's someone at the office. I hardly know that many people, and seldom go any-where, so it has to be someone at the firm. I haven't done any-thing to anyone," thinking about how easy it'll be for the killer to follow her.

And sits the plate down. She has no appetite.

"I don't think it's some killer. I think it's just a bad joke; maybe one of your former flings."

Kathy gives him the eyes, but ignores his assertion.

"You don't have anything a serial killer wants."

"Well then why do you have that gun out? You scared of some-thing?"

"Yeah, but it's not some made up killer."

"Who then?"

He grunts.

"For me to know, and you to find out."

"Whatever."

Stupid jerk.

"You'd never guess who I saw today, since we're on the subject of crazy people."

"Who?" rubbing her stomach, she's about to puke.

"I had to fill in for an officer who works death row; only for maybe thirty minutes, but it was time enough for me to meet the guy who killed the pastor back in the day. He's a real weirdo, thinks he's some kind of philosopher—reads books on human behavior, even went as far as tell me I have a secret to get off my chest. He's made himself out to be the victim of an elaborate set up. Guy even gets fan mail from people believing his story. If you could've saw the look in his eyes you would've turned away. I'm talking pure evil...."

Kathy leaps out of her seat and runs down the hallway leaving uneaten Helper, and garlic bread on the sofa!!

Stockton scans the area, grabs his gun, and takes off after her!!

"What Kate!"

She darts into the bathroom and slams the door! He hears the click of the metal button just as he reaches for the knob. Beating on the hollow wood, he yells again!

"Kathy open the door! Did you hear something?"

The sound of her throwing up her dinner interrupts him.

Tink!

Maybe it's his mind playing tricks on him, but he swears he hears something hitting the side door.

There it goes again!

He doesn't know if he should stand guard at the bathroom, or go investigate the noise. With his heart rate increased, he contemplates what to do. Exhibiting caution, he moves down the hall, hits the light switch, and in one long step, snatches the remote from the chair, and kills the flat screen!

Kathy must've finished emptying her stomach, because not as much as a whisper is coming from the bathroom.

An eerie silence is cast over the house.

There it goes again!

Clearer, he's only feet away.

Someone's tapping the glass!

With his cannon leading, he crab walks behind the wet bar, noticing the patio light set to come on at sundown isn't; making it impossible to see a silhouette! The ex-cop is stuck at the corner staring into the kitchen. Looking down the hall, he tries to figure out why Kathy hasn't said anything.

Another tap!

A separate noise, a loud thud!

But this time it's from the bathroom.

Tap!

"FUCK!!!"

Seconds tick away!

He makes for the rear of the house!

Bam!

Kicking the door in, starling Kathy kneeling on the floor beside the toilet.

"Someone's outside!" and snatches her by the arm.

She doesn't resist.

The laundry room is at the rear of the house beside the guest, with a door leading to the backyard.

He grabs a flashlight off the shelf.

Holding her trembling hand, he looks into her eyes.

"Stay behind me!"

Thumbs the hammer back, yanks the door open, and swings the weapon out looking both ways!

Tiptoeing through the grass, he grips her hand. Creeping like thieves in the night, they arrive at the corner of the house.

"He still there!" she whispered.

A pushy gust of wind sways the Georgia pines.

"Come on," moving under the noise of the trees to the patio— backs against the brick.

Feet from the intruder, the wind blows harder; he hunkers down and prepares to act. From here, the patio door isn't visible, only the edge of the concrete. He'll have to round the corner and spring out on whoever it is. Not about to put his beloved Kathy in harm's way, he gives the signal for her to stay put.

She agrees.

He takes a deep breath, and in one swift motion, raises the big revolver, and leaps from the side of the house!

What he zeros in on is the stuff of nightmares!!

Absolutely nothing.

But the noise is still there!

There it goes again!

Bewildered?

There, leaning against the door!

A tall roll of tightly wrapped chicken wire. One of the taught metal ties must've snapped when it fell into the door, probably from being blown by the wind. Upon closer observation, he sees that the one at the top has started it all, and one by one the others slowly followed, not able to bear the mounting pressure.

Tap!

Goes another smacking the glass, proving his theory.

After watching him lower his weapon, and let out a slight chuckle, Kathy peeks around the corner.
"It's this damn chicken wire. The wind must've blown it into the door."
"But how was it making that noise?"
He picks up one of the ties.
"These were hitting the window as the wire unraveled."
"Oh....I'm going back inside," turning back.
"Hold up."
He picks up the wire and moves it to the shed.
"All right, come on. Told you you don't have nothing a serial killer wants."

Back inside, Kathy goes back to where she was, and locks the door. Small enclosures are the perfect places for her to deal with their emotions. It's the closet usually, but she prefers the bathroom today.
SLAM!
Goes the door as she opens and shuts it, causing the framed 'Serenity Prayer' to fall off the wall.
The doctor has no explanation for her constant mood swings. Stockton never knows what to expect from her, he's just learned to deal with it.
"You all right in there?" he asked calmly through the door.
"I just want to be left alone."
"Is it something I said?"
"I just want peace."
"That always your cop-out, anytime you don't want to facing something you throw that up. I mean, why do you al-"
"PLEASE! LEAVE ME ALONE!"
CRASH!
Goes something thrown at the door.
Stockton hurt, and caught off guard jumps back. His heart aches to help her.
But anger creeps up his spine and across his face.

"I'm getting real tired of your bullshit Kate! I try to help you but you don't appreciate it! I try to show you I love you, but you don't give a fuck about me! You're an ungrateful little cunt you know that!"

And slugs a dent into the door.

"*STOP IIIIIIIIIIT!*...Why do you always do this! Why can't you just leave me alone!" she screamed.

He doesn't like being yelled at.

"Opens this goddamn door! I'm tired of playing these fucking games with you! I'm tired of it!"

He rams it with his shoulder.

"*Pleeeeeeeeeease!*"

"That crying don't work no more!"

BAM!

The door flies open!

He stands there glaring with rage in his eyes.

Kathy already knowing what to expect, sought protection in the tub, curled in the fetal position.

"Look at you down there like a fucking idiot! You think I don't know what's going on? I'm not as dumb as you think *bitch!*"

"*Nooooooo, nooooooooo*," her cries muffled by her legs pulls to her chest.

"Shut up!"

Grabbing her by the hair, he yanks her head back.

Sad reddened eyes raw from tears look up at him; begging for mercy.

But there isn't any.

She sees his lips getting ready, and closes her eyes.

He spits again.

"This what you like? You don't appreciate when somebody tries to be good to you!"

Her silence adds to his wrath.

He snatches her neck back again.

"*AAAAAAA!...*"

She can feel the heat of his breath.

"Whore!"

Stockton grabs her around the throat and lifts her upward, dragging her out of the tub, and mashes her face against the vanity mirror, smearing mucus and saliva across the glass.

"You see—trash! Nothing but a worthless skank!"

"You're hurting me," his choking hand only allowing her to whisper. *"I'm sorry."*

"You ain't sorry yet tramp!" before yanking her from the mirror and down the hallway.

"Get the fuck up!"

Kathy stumbles, burning her knees on the on the carpet—he drags her by the neck.

"Get up I said!"

Once they reach the bedroom, he slings her down, and begins unbuckling his belt.

"You wanna act like a slut, then I'm going to treat you like one."

Clenching the belt between his teeth, he unzips his pants and snatches them from his ankles. Stands over her with his erect penis, he keeps on his boots and T.

Ding-dong!

Call it a miracle, or call it fate; the doorbell rings just as he was about to rape her.

He looks down the hall?

She kicks him!

He doubles over, grimacing.

"Aaaaaaah," and kicks her in the side. *"Bitch!"*

Ding-dong!

Still in pain, he quickly removes his shirt, throws belt the belt on the bed, slips into his house coat, and walks out.

The bell rings again as he barrels through the living room, and without looking through the peep hole, snatches it open.....

To the face of Kathy's mother.

He's a great actor.

"Hi Ann," swinging the door wide.

"I hope I'm not interrupting anything. I was in neighborhood

so I decides to check on you young-uns," said the fleshy woman.
"Oh, you're not. Come on in."
Thanks you," gray curls swinging as she steps inside.
"I love the hair," he complimented, as she takes a seat on the sofa beside Kathy's uneaten dinner.
"It cost me ninety bucks. I'm glad someone likes it, because I don't. One of the bid whist girls suggested I try something new. She said my bun was played out," voice hinted with sass.
"I think she's the one that's played out," he flattered.
"Awe Stockton, hush," Ann waving her small hand.
"Want anything to drink? Cola, coffee?"
"I'll take ginger ale if you've got any."
"Vernors® or Canada Dry®?"
"Vernors® please."
He retrieves a glass from the dishwasher, fills it with crushed ice and gives it to her with the can.
"Thank you."
"You're very welcome. I'll be right back, I think she's back here taking a shower."
"All righty then."

Kathy stands at the window staring into the backyard, a twinkling skyscrapers can be seen in the distance. She hasn't washed the tears, or putrid saliva from her face, nor bandage her injured knee. This is hardly the first time she's been through this, but it's never gone to this extreme.
She's certain it'll be the last.

He walks in and closes the door.

"Your nosy ass mother's here. What do you want me to tell her?"

"......Tell her I'll be out in a minute."

Turning from the window, she comes in his direction with venom in her eyes. With a voice both resilient and confident, she says: "You ever put your hands on me again motherfucker, I swear by God you better kill me!.... *You spit on me now? Then kick me too?* What, you we're going to rape me if she hadn't come!.... Goddamn coward!" and tries to claw his eyes out, but he grabs her hands, and slings her on the bed.

Pursing her lips, she goes into the master bath, and reemerges with his straight razor.

"If she wasn't out there, you'd have to kill me, because I'd slice your throat! How *dare* you handle me like that! I'm tired of it!... *YOU HEAR ME STOW? I'M TIRED OF ALL OF IT!!!.....NO MORE!!!*" she shouted. "Don't take this as a threat, but take it as a promise!...You weak sonofabitch! I hate you!"

"I hate you too bitch."

Stockton says nothing as she turns away crying. Watching her wash her face, she falls to her knees, and slams the door!

Now that he's regained his composure, guilt constricts him. But not enough to make him regret what he's done.

Fuck her!

To him, she deserves every second of what she got, and knows she won't dare call the police, or tell anyone; not even her mother. Such a thing would tarnish her image, the one she manufactures for everyone to see, not the real one. She wants people to think she's wonderful, and everything in her life is peaches and cream. However, she's never threatened him before, but the look in her eyes tells him that he may indeed have to killer her, or deal with his own death if he doesn't heed her warning.

She ain't gone do shit!

Kathy finishes washes her face and tends to her wounds. After combing her hair back into place, a little makeup, and a few drops of Visine®, she leaves out without looking his way. She doesn't have the intimidated drag of a battered female, but the confident strut of one determined not to put up with it any more.

"Well hello there miss lady, long time no see. I began thinking you forgot you had a daughter," her voice pretending to be chipper.

"Don't be silly. Come over here and give me a hug," rising with open arms.

And that's when she feels it. Ann steps back and holds her daughter's face.

"You okay darlin'?"

Kathy feel the lump form in her throat, and wants to fall into her mother's arms, but she stays strong.

"I'm fine mother," laughing it off.

But Ann knows that's not the truth.

"I'm just making sure...You know how I worry," as she sits down.

"Why y'all got food sitting out like this?" looking at the plate.

"Here, let me take it," she replied.

Ann shakes her head.

Three people are in the room, but only two engage in conversation. Stockton reclines in his chair watching a western, while Ann and Kathy talk for more than an hour.

"It's Friday night, and you two are holed up in the house like monks. How about we go catch a movie or something, my treat. It's been a while since I've had the dickens scared out of me."

"Awe mom, maybe tomorrow. Stow's worked nights this week. He's beat, and so am I."

"Party poopers, y'all act older than me. I'd hate to see what y'all look like at sixty-one, as much as y'all lay around."

"I wouldn't mind catching that new horror movie. I hear it's pretty scary," Stockton deciding to speak.

He's knows Kathy doesn't want to be near him right now, so it's really out of spite.

She's disgusted by the sight of his face.
Piece of shit!
"Mother call and see what time it starts."

While she dresses, Ann calls the theater; Stockton takes his clothes and gets ready in the guest bath. Twenty minutes later they're backing out the driveway.

No one notices the dark sedan across the street.

"Get the popcorn, I have to run to the ladies room."

The figure sees Kathy moving through the crowd. A little boy running from a man runs headfirst into her leg, and almost falls. She doesn't bother to see if he's okay. She's a zombie who can only see one thing, and that thing is Kathy; who's just entered the restroom. The woman takes a good look at Stockton and Ann, waiting at the end of a long line.
Throngs of single men and women, couples holding hands, families with kids running ahead, and groups of teenagers looking to gossip pour in and out of the many pairs of double doors on either side of the sprawling lobby.
Entering the restroom, she sees Kathy touching her face in the mirror. Not wanting to show hers, she quickly slips inside a stall and locks the door. A rather hefty woman dressed in hot pink switches out, leaving them alone in the tiled lavatory.
"Good to see you again."

The voice startles Kathy, thinking she's alone; quickly realizing she's wrong when she notices a woman speaking from somewhere? She bends down to sees which stall has legs.
Two black boots are in the last one.
"Are you talking to me miss?"
No response.
Which isn't something she welcomes when an unknown presence is near. She repeats the question.
No response.
Assuming the woman isn't talking to her, she dries her hands and prepares to leave.
And odd sound comes from the stall, a warmness creeps up her neck!
Leave!
Without looking, Kathy backs out, keeping her eyes peeled in the direction of the voice. A young girl coming through the door collides with her.
"Don't go in there," grabbing her.
The teen's about to say something jazzy, but doesn't once she sees the black inside the stall.
They exit the restroom, the girl takes off.
Kathy heads back to the front. A cop is leaning against a wall munching M&M's®.
"Excuse me officer, there's someone in the ladies room that may be dangerous."
"What makes you think that?" not moving a muscle.
What can she say to convince him to act?
"Well a woman, I mean I think it is. But she's standing in one of the stalls doing wired things. She's been watching me or something. That's stalking right?"
"Did she follow you there?" popping another chocolate covered peanut in his mouth.
"I'm not sure."
A group of middle ages are about to go inside.

"Damn!" Kathy said, stomping her foot. "Okay, you know how when you get a gut feeling about something when you're on a call? That's how I feel. I can't explain it, but something isn't right. You'll have to be responsible for whatever happens here, especially when I'm standing here telling you, and you choose to do nothing about it."

Bingo!

"....Let's see what we can find."

He throws the empty package into the waist bin.

Upon following her to the ladies room, he pushes the door open.

"Excuse me ladies. I need to check something out. It won't take but a second."

"There, in the last one," she said, pointing to the handicapped stall.

The officer goes up to the door. A single knock causes it to swing and reveal its emptiness.

He turns back with one of those looks.

"Sorry for the inconvenience ladies."

"You enjoy your night," at Kathy, and leaves.

Not believing the woman just vanished, she has a peek, and runs to catch up with him.

"Hey, I didn't make that up! It was really someone in there!"

"No big deal, people exaggerate things. It's human nature."

And continues on his way.

Kathy stands there scanning the packed lobby for any sign of the elusive woman.

Stockton and her mother stroll up beside her hugging a bucket of butter soaked popcorn, Stow's holding a box of Jordan Almonds®, the tickets, and three drinks are in a cardboard holder.

"You looking for Carmen Sandiego or something honey?" she quipped.

"There was a lady in the restroom watching me."

"What'd she look like?" he questioned.

"I don't know, she was inside the stall."

"Probably a lesbian. Anyway, the movie's about to start, what are

y'all gonna do?"
"I don't want to be here."
"*Pssssiiiittf,*" she sighs. "We're already here. What do you mean
you wanna leave?"
Kathy sighs, and snatches a ticket from his hand.
"You see all these teenyboppers. I'll bet it's some sixteen year old
proving a dare," Ann stated.
"Let's go," Kathy said, taking a drink from Stockton.

The woman watches her mark and the two people stroll down
the corridor. She knows who the male companion is, but not the
old woman, and makes a mental note to get a shot of her before
the night ends.

Kathy sits elbow to elbow with her mother, coming nowhere
remotely close to brushing against Stockton, and welcomes the
end of the corny flick. Her stomach is full of stale popcorn and
flat Sprite®. The Jack-in-the-Box, seat trading teens, coupled
with gigantic speakers that blaring the slightest sound ten times
the normal decibel, make for a headache ridden experience. The
reoccurring notion that she's being watched by a strange woman
increases her already heightened stress level; frequent backwards
glances added extra discomfort to her already sore neck—the
more it hurts, the more she wants to hurt Stow. The events of
the last day has her feeling unsafe and vulnerable. No matter
where she goes, there's a situation. Solace has seemingly become
her adversary, but really hasn't enjoyed a peace of mind in years.

Now she's forced to be 'it' in a cruel game of tag with an invisible player; an ominous cloud has decided to use her life as a rest stop. How long it will be before the storm passes?
Well at least the movie does.
The "thunk" of spring-loaded seats smacking shut permeate the auditorium, as goers head for the exits; leaving popcorn buckets, candy boxes, and cups in their wake.

Ann and Stockton review the latest scare while walking back to the truck. The ten o'clock air is hot and heavy, the pressure is high, and the dew point even higher. Vehicles wait at the curb picking up license-less high schoolers, a man slides open the side door of a minivan as three kids and a woman hop inside—the Silverado sits somewhere in the parking lot that's quickly turning into a traffic jam.
A convertible sports car fishtails out of the entrance, leaving a cloud of smoke and burnt rubber in his wake.
"That fool's gonna kill somebody," Ann shaking her head.
As a car passing too closely almost hits Kathy. A single white female in dark shades stares strangely as she goes by, raising the window. Kathy thinks she's seen that face before, and can see the silhouette looking back as the sedan continues up the aisle.
The brake lights come on.
Ann and Stockton are too preoccupied with looking for the truck to notice.
Before Kathy has time to wonder, the vehicle speeds off.
The pickup is there just where he left it. As Stockton prepares to unlock the doors, he notices a powdery substance on the doors and windows.
"Someone's thrown paint powder on your truck," said Ann, running runs her finger through it. "Yep it's paint all right. Probably from one of these teens."
"It's not paint. It's fingerprint dust," unhappy with the invasion of his privacy.
Someone's gotten samples from them all, not to mention Alex's

too.

"Why would someone want your prints? You in bad with the law or something?" Ann questioned.

Kathy puts the pieces together.

"It was the woman who was watching me. While you two were looking for the truck, you didn't see the woman in the car. She must've did it while we were watching the movie."

"I remember seeing a dark colored car out of the corner of my eye, but I didn't pay much attention to it. I just thought it was somebody trying to find a parking space or something," Ann with hands on her hips.

Stockton thinks to himself, who is she? Why did she dust for prints, and why follow Kathy? Why come back and risk her cover being blown? Evidently, she's not trying to hide the fact that she's onto them. But she did keep them from seeing her face. Is she investigating the things he's done in his past, or the things he's doing in the present? Or does she need Kathy's for something pertaining to the past she refuses to discuss? Or is it both? Why wait until they're with Ann, or was it just a coincidence? He has to talk to Alex as soon as possible, maybe they can beat her to whatever she's looking for.

"Stow, I'm not trying to be rude or anything, but we're just standing here, and my bunions are starting to mess with me." He looks a last time, and clicks the doors.

Across the lot, using a long lens camera, the woman takes more photographs.

While he drives and pretends to be interested in Ann's conversation, Kathy ponders her recent stroke bad luck; her finger prints are now in some mysterious woman's possession. Maybe Stockton hired her, acting as if he's surprised by her actions. Does he know "all" the things she's been doing, and isn't saying?

Stow's nothing more than a live-in boyfriend, if that. That's the main reason the house, and all the utilities are in her name—

he has no clue about the secret bank accounts. For years she's misled him, though repeatedly telling him about not wanting to be in anything serious; so maybe he deserves what he gets for forcing himself into her life.

But Stockton's a brilliant liar in his own right. He's withholding key information about himself as well, he's presenting himself as one thing, when he's the polar opposite. But before the leaves begin withering, and the colors change; they'll both discover the truth. Even his childhood friend Alex is leading a double life. Nothing is what it seems when it comes to these people.

Chapter 10

Wardens don't usually work weekends, but this one has special business. It's been five days since Ms. Chase paid her last visit. Stuckey records the exact time she arrives, the amount of time she stays, and the day of the week—there's no pattern. Sometimes she shows the moment visitation starts, and others she comes an hour before it ends. Due to the large inmate population, visitation is held seven days a week. Either she doesn't work, or has a job with lots of freedom, because she'll pop up any time. Gordon had one of his buddies dig through her personal life, but there wasn't much to find. The address listed on her license is legit. The small apartment in a rough section of town was staked out for days, and saw no sign of her. There's no credit report, and all her dealings are done in cash. She's without a doubt a woman with a secret; also adept in counter surveillance techniques. Gordon has a losing record when it comes to finding out anything about Christine Chase that she doesn't want him to know.

He sits in his office with his team on standby hoping she picks today. He grabs his radio.

"C–one–s. Forty, w–one–s," code speak for get to the warden's office.

"Ten-four," Starns replied.

Gordon lays it down, and picks it up again.

"C–one–s. Niner, w–one–s."

"Ten–four."

Moments later the phone rings.

"How far are you from the row?"

Starns says he's in the D-house (one of the general population dorms) breaking up a fight.

"Let the other guys handle that. Find Salvo, and bring Parson to my office."

Seventeen minutes, and forty four seconds later, there's a knock at the door.

"Come in."

Parson steps through the door weighed down by ten pounds of chains and shackles. Salvatore leads, Starns holds the door, and five CERT's stand guard in the hallway.

"Sit down," Stuckey nodding at the chairs before his desk.

"How's things goin' in the animal house?"

"Your incompetent help keep a good handle on things."

"In case you ain't know, yo' buddy Grainger ain't gettn' no stay. He's gone die Tuesday," pausing to study Parson's face for displeasure.

There isn't any.

"Well I'll be sure the right people receive their reward."

"What da fuck does dat supposedtuh mean?"

"You'll be the first to know."

"Well let me pull yo' coat tua thing ur two. I got somethin' up my sleeve too. But guess what?"

Meaning for Parson to ask, but he doesn't, he just sits there staring.

"It's a surprise furdat bitch uh yerz," trying to anger him.

"She loves surprises. Everyone let's give Gordo a hand," beckoning Starns and Salvo standing behind him to join along as he claps, chains rattling.

Gordon hates when people bastardize his name, especially inmates.

"He who laughs first don't always laugh lass asshole."

"Anything I'm involved in is no laughing matter," saying a lot without saying much.

"Keep makin' insinuations ahn I'll have yer' smart mouf ass in da' hole!"

"We've been through the throw me in the dungeon till I tell the king what I'm doing game before. If you decide to do that it will neither win you a confession, nor prevent anything from coming to fruition. However, it will win you a visit from my lawyer, and his lovely friends. Where were you when they were passing out common sense? Let me guess, waddling around in the mud with your pigs."

Gordon is furious. He pictures himself leaping over the table and burying his glass in the side of Parson's skull.

Salvo is so amused by his comment, that he has to bite his lip, and look away to keep from laughing.

"Find somethin' funny Salvatore?"

"No," *Cough, Cough.* "No sir," clearing his throat.

"What about you?" referring to Starns.

"No sir."

He gives them both a long stare before saying to Parson:

"You ain't shit but a walkin' dead fuck! And I sho ain't scared of your lawyer, or that pissy-tramp-whore! Today ahm gone find out wuss in that briefcase; das if she shows her stinkin' cunt.

You better hope she got ESP, cause if there's anything incrimina-tin' in there, I'm gone have her prosecuted for everything I kun think of, includin' cunspearcy. Shea be right down da road in Butts County jail. That means shea havetuh go to Butts County courthouse—I too have people in high places. Shea be easily convicted and receive the stiffess penalties. You wouldn't believe what those redneck guards'll do tua perdy gal like her. I'm gone give you one lass chance ta come clean. If you tell me now before I find out on my own, I'll spare her da extras. Hell, I might juss get real nice and forgive y'all, considerin' you ain't got longta live anyway. So wuss it gone be? The ball's in yer' court. Time for you to make the call, and for her sake I hope it's da right one."
The office is silent.
Parson stares at Gordon while the others await his reply. Traffic from the radios make for a smorgasbord of bleeps, confusing code words, and scratchy voices.
Salvo lowers the volume on his.
Stuckey comes to the conclusion that Parson isn't going to an-swer, but continue sitting there with that stupid look on his face.
"Okay, I give up. You win," dropping his head in defeat, raising his arms as much as the chains will allow.
"I'll tell you, but first you have to give me your word that you won't go after her. She's the only reason I'm doing this."
Stuckey raises his hand.
"You have my word. Swear to the Lord."
Salvo has to again resist the urge to laugh at how serious Gordon looks, with his jellied body sitting erect in the chair like he's be-ing sworn in on the witness stand. His right hand on the Bible would've been icing on the cake.
"I uhm- I…I don't know where to start. Well I guess I'll begin by saying…," pausing again.
Gordon's face sweats while he anxiously awaits the unveiling of the secret plot.
"You promise?"
"Promise."

More seconds of silence.

"You're a fucking joke!"

The simultaneous release of held breath fills the room!

Stuckey's face becomes the color of a pomegranate, a crooked pulsing vein wants to burst through his forehead.

"Have it your way! That slut will never see da light of day! You'll remember this once you see how long it takes forda electricity ta kill ur ass! Yo' daddy shoulda' pulled out and nutted on yer tramp mammy's tit! Den da world wouldna been polluted with scum like you!"

"If not me, it would've been someone else. It's a dirty job Gordo, but someone's got to do it. Unlike you and your minions, me and my people are the very best at what we do."

He leaps to his feet!

"I'm gone fuck dat whore up the ass when you die!!! Get 'em outta here!"

"But I'm going to fuck you now. Along with this entire state," as Starns and Salvo grabs him under the arms, and lifts him out the seat.

"You'll get tired before I do Gordo," as Salvo puts him in a choke hold, and the CERT's drag him out.

She drives around the retention pond and continues towards the back lot. Before she can kill the engine, flashing lights appear, and a squad car pulls up and blocks her in. Another comes out of nowhere and skids to a halt beside her.

She calmly turns the car off and waits.

One man is tall slim and handsome, the other is short fat and ugly.
She lowers the window.
"What seems to be the problem officers?"
The short one ducks his head, and scans the cabin.
"There's an APB out for a car matching this description th-."
"What's an APB?" knowing exactly what it is.
"An all-points bulletin. We need you to step out the vehicle while we conduct a quick search."
"Why?"
"Please step out of your car ma'am!" said the tall guy with the stache; his partner looking very unsure of himself.
"Where's the search warrant?"
"We don't need one, probable cause has already been established. Step out of the car ma'am. Last time."
"Why did you wait until I drove on to this property before you lighted me?"
"Because we have jurisdiction over the entire county, and can pull you over wherever we see fit."
His partner reaches through the passenger window and opens the door.
Christine is skeptical of the officer's intentions, but has no choice but to cooperate. If she refuses, they'll simply detain her and search the vehicle anyway.
She gets out.
"Don't get too touchy. There's a thin line between the proper frisk of a female and sexual battery."
"I know how to do my job. But there's no need to frisk you, we just want to see what's in the car. Is there anything inside we should know about?"
"I'll let you see for yourself."
"Miss!"
"You said you know how to do your job," sensing this whole thing is a farce.
The warden and those same two officers emerge from the build-

ing heading her direction. Now she's certain it is.

"What's going on guys?" pretending like he doesn't already know.

"We think this is the same woman who ran from us a few days ago after buying dope. I would've pulled her over sooner, but I had to wait for backup."

"Go ahead and handle your business. I'm just here to observe."

So does a group of grass cutting inmates.

"Get da hell from ova' here! This don't concern y'all!"

They begrudgingly move along muttering expletives.

Her suspicions are verified when they do a twenty second search, and go for the briefcase. Gordon whispers something that triggers an approach while she leans against the cruiser.

"Ma'am I'm going to have to place you in the backseat."

She stares at him and doesn't move.

"I know this is bogus. You're going to let him cause you to lose your job; this is illegal. I want you to remember my face because you're going to see it again in court Mr.-", looking at the nameplate pinned to his shirt pocket. 'Redick' is stamped on it, but she pronounces it: "*Red dick*...You'll regret this."

"Whatever," and opens the rear door.

Before she steps inside she shouts over the roof.

"You'll regret this, *and* your two flunkies."

The officer forces her down and slams the door.

"Anybody got a knife?" Stuckey asked.

"I got one," said the tall guy returning from locking Christine in the car.

He pulls a Swiss Army® one from his pocket.

After several minutes of picking, they still haven't got it open; the Samsonite® staying true to its name. He's almost destroyed the keyholes from constantly jamming and twisting the blade into them.

Christine watches from the back seat as they huddle around the hood trying to figure out how to open the briefcase. If any of them had an atoms amount of intelligence, they would've looked for the key—it's sitting in the ashtray.

"Let me try," said Salvo.
He uses one of the other utensils on the knife, and a paperclip. And after a few grunts, picks, and turns, the steel lock clicks. He does the other. Pressing the buttons, the hardened case opens. A tightly packed clasp envelope sits inside.
"Let him open it," Gordon referring to Redick, wanting the search to look official. He doesn't want to give her anything that'll be grounds for dismissal.
They forget the dash cam is recording everything.
A quick smirk plants itself across his face, because he's positive that after all these years, he's finally about to find damning proof of some treacherous stratagem.
Redick opens the envelope and dumps the contents inside the case. One by one he begins selecting documents.
"It's a reply from the courts rejecting a Douglas Parson's appeal." He can't let Gordon look at it because he's not an authorized participant.
"Go to the next one."
This time the sheriff grabs three papers and reads them aloud.
"These are from agencies refusing to investigate his case."
Gordon is getting impatient.
"That ain't what ahm lookin' for, keep goin'."
Redick unfolds a blank piece of paper holding news clippings. Two are about the murder of the couple, and one is a front page write-up about the governor's race with faces of all the candidates. Stuckey's picture is circled, and the five paragraphs below are highlighted.
"Let dat one tuda side. Cuntinya."
Redick thumbs through a stack of cutouts about the life and murder of a man named Joseph Tangier.
"You want these put aside too?"
"That ain't nuttin'."

Another is a four-page report about the entire investigation from beginning to end, Parson's face smack dab in the center. The next one is a half-pager penned by a former FBI agent who believes he's innocent, who was also a defense witness at his trial. The last one is a four page report by the U.S. Justice Department of Justice, estimating that over nine thousand men and women are incarcerated in this country for crimes they didn't commit.

A nine page packet is all that's left.

Up to this point Stuckey has seen nothing he can use to prosecute her or Parson. Hopefully this is what he needs to nail them. Redick opens the folder, and is promptly greeted by an 8 x 10 mug shot of Gordon when he was arrested in Shelby County, Tennessee twenty six years ago. Driving under the influence was the initial charge, but after a thorough search at the jail, he was found to be in possession of three hits of rock, and less than a gram of powder cocaine—the charges later dead docketed (stored way for a later day, usually in the event the person is arrested again for a similar charge). Every aspect of his life is detailed, all the way from grade school to the department of corrections review of his job performance seven months ago. Everything he doesn't want anybody to know is in this folder, including a confidential list of how many times he's forgotten to pay his taxes, as well as reports of his dirty dealings at the hog farms. The more he sees, the tighter the knot in his stomach becomes.

Photos of his wife and son!

"Give me this shit! All of it!" and snatches the briefcase and folder off the hood, shoving them inside.

"Take her ass to jail! *NOW!!*" yelling like a deranged man.

"Calm down! There's cameras!"

"FUCK DAT FUCKIN' CAMERA!"

He storms to the squad car.

"You sleazy lil whore!" shouting at Christine through the window. "You and dat sick fuck betta' stay out my private life! It ain't none of y'all's goddamn business!" and swings the briefcase into the glass!

Salvo and Starns run up.
"Sir!" grabbing him by the shoulder.
He yanks away.
"Take dat whore to jail right dis fuckin' minute!"
"We can't, she's done nothing wrong! This was your idea in the first place, shit ain't even lawful! You lied saying she had contraband! Now all of it's on video, and there ain't no way we gonna be able to explain this! She hasn't broke the law, it's public record! We got zilch! I can't believe I listened to you!"

Christine watches the heated argument. Moments later the sheriff turns and heads her direction. After unlocking the door, he holds it open.
"I'm sorry ma'am. This has been a terrible mistake. We're truly sorry for this inconvenience," beckoning her out.
"Thank you."
But once she's free.
"Your apology is by no means accepted. You knew this was wrong from the jump, even after I warned you. I asked you not to do this, and now must deal with the consequences."
She goes to Gordon, and gets so close that her nose almost touches his forehead.
"Give-me-back-my-briefcase!" she spat, literally.
He feels the mist of saliva dampen his face.
She watches the muscles in his face and neck spasm. He's so livid that it seems his head is about to explode.
Lift off!
Stuckey erupts, raises the suitcase in the air, and begins violently banging it against the pavement.
It bursts open!
Before they can escape, he raises it again, and slams it once more, sending papers flying everywhere! A gust of summer breeze comes out of the east, but before any can blow away, he scrambles around like an insane cockroach, and gathers them in a crumpled heap!

"AHMA SHO YOU WHAT I THINK BOUT DIS BOWLSHIT!" his accent more pronounced in his fit of rage.

As if it's a shot put, he spins and slings the briefcase, sending it crashing to the pavement!

The watching prisoners, and guard are in awe!

Gordon takes off towards them!

Not knowing what to expect, the trustee begins hurriedly pushing away.

"STOP YOU SONOFABITCH!"

He quickly catches up, unscrews the gas cap, and flips the mower on its side, soaking the documents. Once saturated, he storms back to the curb, lights them, and throws them to the asphalt! The fire instantly becomes a blaze.

"THAT'S WHAT I THINK BITCH!" and stomps towards the building.

Salvo, Starns, Redick, and the two sheriffs stand froze in shock. But as he reaches the doors, he turns back.

"GET DEM AND DAT CUNT OFF MY PROPERTY!" before blowing through the doors.

"Y'all have to leave," said Starns.

"That bastard is dumb as a rock," commented Redick, shaking his head.

"I'm not going anywhere. I'm here to see Douglas Parson, and I will see him or you're going to have to call the entire force to get me out of here."

"No Ms. Chase, you have to leave," coming towards her.

"You lay one hand on me and you won't have it anymore. If you think I'm bluffing, try me."

It's the look in her eyes that makes him think twice. He's already seen how she dug up Gordon's entire life, no telling what other skills she possesses.

"First of all, I don't see any reason why she can't be allowed her visit," the sheriff coming to her rescue. "She hasn't done anything, he's the one who's wrong."

"She's a female serial killer," said Salvo. "Can't you see it?" sneering.

"No! He better hope she doesn't file charges against him. And second of all, we're Butts County sheriffs; this prison is owned by the state. Since this is Butts County, I can get in my cruiser and do doughnuts in the parking lot 'til the cows come home, and it wouldn't be shit you or Gordon could do about it! Now let's see about getting this lovely lady her visit!"

Salvo is stuck between a rock and a hard place. He looks to Starns for advice, but he looks away. He'll have to decide for himself. Deal with Gordon's wrath, which can only hurt his job, or deal with the sheriff, who can hurt his freedom. He decides this isn't his call.

"Hold on, this is his mess."

He radios him of the situation.

"He says he's coming."

Not even a minute has passed before he bursts back through the visitation lobby, and barrels up to Redick.

"You tryin-nuh threaten me Bobby!"

"You can call it what you want! But you're going to let Ms. Chase have her visit! We both know what'll happen if she decides to press charges."

He does know.

He looks at Christine standing with her arms crossed, itching to press the issue. Slowly, he realizes the impact his actions.

"Have your visit!" and walks away.

So does Starns and Salvo, like two faithful pups.

Now it's only her and the sheriffs. Redick has a wife and kids to feed; he can't afford to lose this job—it's time to make a deal. His partner is thinking the same thing.

"Look Ms. Chase, I admit this was uncalled for. All this was Gordon's idea, he lied to us. We didn't know it would escalate to this. I just want to say again I that I apologize. If you choose to file some sort o-"

"Stop," she said, raising her hand. "I'll help you if you help me, you guys are not who I want; this may be just been the break I need. If you cooperate with me, I give you my word you'll have nothing coming from my end…Deal?"

They look at each other.

"Deal."

"Okay, first I need one of you to write a report. I'll tell you what to do next."

But she didn't promise not to blackmail them. Things are about to get pretty tart in the peach state, now that Christine Chase has two sworn officers indebted to her.

Stuckey gave her a visit all right, a drastically reduced one—eleven minutes and fifty eight seconds to be exact. Coincidentally, a riots broke out in one of the houses, and the entire prison had to be locked down, including death row, including Parson. But it was enough time for her to convey everything that transpired in the parking lot. All the papers we're copies. She's also wise enough to have more than one of each of the news clippings. The appeal rejections are nothing new, nor are the agency's refusals. They both agreed that Gordon's actions only gave them more ammo. The amount she paid to have her suitcase specially fitted with a secret compartment proved to be worth every penny. If they'd been someone more experienced like customs agents, or narcotics officers, they would've probably found it. But sadly they aren't. They're small town sheriffs who rarely come in contact with people like Christine Chase.

Sitting alone at a corner table in a popular midtown restaurant; the type of establishment where predominantly white middle customers comes to feast on delicious, high calorie dishes prepares by blacks who can't afford to reside anywhere near their place of employment.

Ms. Chase sips black tea while waiting for the familiar face to pop through the door.

Waiters whizz by with plates of fattening fried meats, and butter soaked vegetables. The Saturday noon crowd is nothing like the weekday. Several tables sit empty, properly prepared with sparking silverware, tea cups, and flowerpots blooming with botanicals.

"Is everything okay ma'am?"

"Yes."

"Would you like to try a piece of our famous lemon Jello® cake?"

"No thank you."

"Okay, wave if you need me."

"I'll do that."

The woman politely walks away, stopping to grab her tip off a messy table.

Christine looks at a stack of photos, a paper with a list of names and addresses lay beside; he's pleased with the work her and Douglas have done so far. Detectives, judges, district attorneys, as well as the FBI knows of him; considering him an enemy to all of law enforcement. His organization has been repeatedly attacked, but never with any success. Dozens of charges and lawsuits have been filed, but they all turn out to be nothing but huge wastes of taxpayer dollars.

He comes through the door dressed in a yellow Hugo Boss® shirt, blue khaki shorts, and matching Ferragamo® skippers. A

Panama Straw shields his face from the sun, Versace® shades protect his eyes from UV rays—a shiny aluminum briefcase accompanies him.

He's also a fashionista.

She waves.

He rushes over and takes a seat.

"I don't have a lot of time," is the greeting, and sits the case on the table; no apologies for his tardiness.

"This is the list of them," pushing over a list of cops.

"There long shots, but it's what you asked for."

"Not for me..I don't know if I bought the right stuff or not, but I got it," she said.

"I gave you a list. The only way it won't work is if you got the wrong things."

"I got exactly what you instructed. I was just saying tha-...never mind, forget it. I don't know what I'm saying. Anyway, what else do you have?"

"All right now," going back in his briefcase. "Don't go getting cold feet on me."

"We both know that's not happening."

"That's the attitude."

Now speaking in a serious tone.

"Look," and smacks his large hand down on the thick folder laying on the table, causing the clay flowerpot to rattle, and a nearby customer to glance over.

"This is very confidential material: Pictures, internal reports, family histories, psychological tests, everything. I had to call in a lot of favors to get this. We've been working on this for a very long time, and I want it to be successful."

"Look at these. I took them last week."

She passes him the stack of photos.

"Yeah, he'll like these," and gives them back to her. "Look, I gotta to run. Read over that material and let me know what you come up with."

After shutting the briefcase, he rises from the seat.

"Failure is not an option."
And puts on his hat.
"I'll be in touch."
Gone.

Raw, arrogant, and straight to the point is Silas Rower's style; a militant radical is what many view him as. Coward, treacherous, traitor, are just a few of the adjectives used by his foes—a street savvy confidant is what she considers him. A true friend is what he's been. What she's done wouldn't have been possible if not for him, and what Parson has achieved wouldn't have been possible if not for her. There's only a minute number of people that can do what they're attempting, many wouldn't even try. Few possess the courage, discipline, and tenacity needed to accomplish a lofty goal. When confronted with the mountains that have to be climbed, the jungles that have to be entered, the sacrifices that have to be made, the fears that have to be conquered, and the pain that has to be endured, their mettle fizzles away like carbon gas; becoming nothing more than a figment of their imagination. What replaces it is often something easier, something less, something to settle for—nowhere near as rewarding. Regardless of what Douglas Parson: the convicted killer, and Christine Chase: the lovestruck blonde, believe; it's their quest. And there's only two plausible outcomes: success or death.

Kathy's locked in deep thought on a couch in a quiet house. Shooting Stockton continuously crosses her mind, she's even conjured up an entire plan; one involving a trip to Louisiana. Once there, they'd secretly hike into the swamps on a supposed nature expedition. There she'd shoot him and dump the body, hoping the alligators will leave no trace of him. She'll come back to Atlanta and file a missing persons report; explaining how he left for work and never returned. She'll cry her heart out, and plays the role of the distraught wife; going around stapling reward posters to telephone poles, and passing out fliers—a feasible plan indeed.

In a billion years she would've never imagined getting pushed to this point. She's held on for so long, but now doubt is setting in. It, and guilt have both been there since day one, but why is she suddenly feeling so horrible, so defeated? She vowed not to succumb to another nervous breakdown after the first one almost took her sanity. But over time she's grown tired and weary, unsure if things will ever work out. Life has thrown her nothing but curveballs, some she's managed to hit, but the majority she's missed.

A Blue Jay lands on the bird feeder and cautiously looks around before pecking at the seeds. At the slightest hint of danger it'll abandon its meal and fly away.

She constantly finds herself in this identical situation, always looking over our shoulder, just as cautious, never being able to relax. The slightest indication of someone uncovering her secrets sends her running for cover. Some nights she stares at the ceiling weeping while the past whirls around like a carousel.

Looking down she stares at the picture on her lap. Two people, an item; so happy and in love—not knowing what the future holds, but anxious to see it together. They were young and up for the challenge, excited that some force had brought them together. Only for that same force to send a jolting lightning bolt into their lives, disintegrating what they had. At times life can be so blissful, and others so ruthless. She'll try with all her body and soul to continue, but doesn't know how much longer she can last.

Maybe not even the next few minutes.

A lethal dose of sleeping pills sit rolled in a napkin, the letter explaining why she did it in a blank envelope on her lap. Kathy unravels the napkin and wonders how things will be on the other side. And can see her mother's face when she finds out that her only child has committed suicide. She can see Stockton standing over her grave dressed in black, she can see Megan crying and alone, overwhelmed with grief because her best friend decided to take her own life; realizing Kathy must've been just as unhappy as she.
Opening the envelope, she glances over the note written in beautiful cursive; a glass of water waits on the table.
A tear falls from eye as she takes a sip.
After counting the amount she thinks will do the trick, she one by one she places them in her mouth, and swallows.
With the framed picture hugged to her chest, she closes her eyes.

Hopefully it won't be long.

She gets up and sits the glass in the sink; there's no need to take another shower. Going back to the couch, she decides the bedroom is better.
Once inside, she removes her clothes and locks the door, barricading it with a wooden chair jammed under the knob.
Naked as the day she came into the world, she climbs into bed and closes her eyes.

Finally, she'll be at peace.

"I thought you had to work today?"

"Tomorrow, I'm off tonight," and takes a swig of beer. "You sound like you don't wanna go. The old lady won't let you out the house or something?"

"She don't dictate what I do. You on the other hand are the one that's in check. I wear the pants here," said Alex, pointing to the living room floor.

"*Psssssft...*You don't even believe that?"

"Man why you coming at me? You in a bad mood or something?"

"I'm always in a bad mood."

"So have you come up with how you wanna do it?"

Killing the remaining beer, brings a loud belch.

While Stockton thinks, he grabs the remote and flips the channel. A documentary on a man-eating serial killer catches his attention.

He knows how he wants tonight to go.

"First, we need to be out of here by no later than ten-thirty. It's Saturday night so there'll be lots of things going on. Secondly, we're going to go by each location first. The primary one we'll get out and walk so we can get a good look at what we're working with, as well as the last location; that's just as important as the firs. Things look a lot different at night. Also, we need to see how busy the street is, that'll tell us how much time we have."

Stow halts his sentence and gives Alex a dirty look.

"Chill out on the beer man! I don't need you out there drunk. It'll be fucked up if we get caught because they used your puke to get DNA."

"Damn dude! You think I don't know when I've had too much? This ain't my first rodeo you know."

He cracks another brew and takes a chug.
Stockton keeps staring.
"Dude?"
His eyes are burning into him.
"Damn, you take the fun out of everything."
Stockton leaps, and smacks the shit out of Alex!
"Pour the fucking beer out!"
Shocked, Alex cowers.
"What the fuck man!..All right, chill out. I'm getting rid of it."
While he pours the remainder in the cooler, Stockton remembers how sloppy he was on the last one. He had to keep telling him about things he should've already known, and wonders if he's losing his edge. Money problems, and call girls have taken him out of his game; the restaurant is barely holding on, and so is his marriage. If Alex doesn't get his act together, he'll be forced to turn this into a one-man show.
He sits back down.
"Hear me out...We've been doing this a while without any problems. You've gotten real carefree about things lately, and I don't like it. If you're no longer willing to participate, you're free to stop, no hard feelings. But I'm not about to rot in prison for you, or anybody else. Either you tighten up, or this is where it ends."
Alex leans back on the microfiber loveseat and runs his hands over his head. Stow is going overboard, they should've never done the last one; he's begin thinking he's invincible. But he still can't leave him high and dry. He can talk until he's blue in the face about being able to handle it by himself, but in his heart he knows he needs him. No matter how much he doesn't want to keep sneaking around after dark, he won't dare renege on his promise to always be there when he needs him.
"Naw, I'm with you bro," though his tone conveyed he's not fully committed.
"You don't sound li-"
"I said I'm in. Now let's get back to figuring out the best way to

tackle it," perturbed because he smacked his ass.

But it's too late. Stow's convinced that after tonight he'll have no choice but to do without the company of his right-hand man.

"All right. The tools, do you still have that hammer drill?"

"Yeah, but you might have to run by the store and grab a bit. I can't remember where I put the other one."

He looks at his watch.

"No problem, I'll go pick one up. Anything else you can think of?"

"What we gone do it we come across another safe?"

"Let me worry about that."

"Well in that case, I think that's it. We pretty much covered everything the other day. Also, I was wondering? How do you plan to handle the material? Being with all the tools, and how far the place is away from where we're parking?"

"Everything should fit in the trunk. The only extra stuff we're taking is two drills, the bags, and the cutting torch. That won't take up but maybe part of the corner, if that. The rest will be more than enough. It's really not that much."

"I forgot we're using cordless drills. I was thinking that a generator is going to have to fit in with everything else. I don't know what I is thinking."

"Alex! How in the hell can we squeeze that in with everything else? Maybe we'll just leave the trunk open so the police can see what we have inside. Come on man, I know you didn't think that! Tell me you're joking?"

Alex cracks a smile, imagining how dumb they'd look riding down the expressway in the middle of the night with the trunk open.

"We'd go down as the dumbest criminals of all time," laughing the statement out.

But Stockton's not.

"You need to get your head in the game....Where's the wife?"

"One of her friends had a baby shower."

"Yeah."

"After we get finished, I might hit the strip club and see some tits that don't look like a pair of socks with oranges in them. Gravity done pushes hers down as far as they'll go; them nipples be pointing straight to hell," trying to lighten the mood. "Plus I think I'd done taken a liking to black girls. You wouldn't believe how soft and round their asses are....That girl Bailey Red is the *truth*." Alex said, gazing out the living room window reminiscing about the first time he met her. For a grand she told him he could get it. He woke up the next morning after having the time his life to an empty hotel room, hung over, and thirteen hundred dollars poorer.

"Snap out of it," Stow snapping his finger.

"My bad. I had done floated off to booty-booty land...That girl was so gorgeous, I'd eat her on the rag."

"You're sick."

"*What?* You've never gotten your red wings?"

"Fuck no! I ain't eating no pussy while it's bleeding. That's disgusting."

"That's how you become a man."

"And that's why you're not one," Stockton growing increasing irritated.

"What about gerbling....When they stick a tube up your a-."

"Enough with the dumb shit!"

"Damn dude, ease up. I was just joking."

"That's the problem."

Stockton rises from his seat.

"I'll be back at eleven o'clock."

"Gotcha, I'll be ready."

He's just about to round the corner and head down the hallway when Alex says: "Hey!"

Stockton turns.

"What?"

"I won't be bullshittin' tonight."

"Hey there!" she said, Harry coming through the door of her flower shop, brass bells ringing against the glass.

"How's it going? I see you've gotten yourself some new trucks," he replied, walking to the waist high counter.

"Yep. I had to get rid of those old ones. With all the business I've been getting from the new website, I decided to start delivering statewide. Those old clunkers I had wouldn't have been able to make the long hauls, especially going up to the mountains. But wait a second! Where's my hug," as she comes around the long counter wearing blue jean overalls and an apron.

Fallon Duncan was been his mother's best friend for years. To be eighty three, she moves like she's twenty five.

Harry bends over and wraps his arms around the woman he's known his entire life.

"Where were you last week? I was worried," she said, rearranging a shelf displaying exotic flower seeds packaged in green and beige paper sleeves carrying the store's name: *Mama Duncan Nurseries*.

"I stopped by the grocery to get some because I didn't have time to make it, I was running late. I'll know next time, because the ones I got were half dead, and twice as expensive."

"See what happens when you don't go the extra mile."

And pokes him in the side.

"Tell me about it, they're nothing like yours."

"That's why they call me Mama Duncan, because I know how to raise the best flowers."

"Don't forget plants and trees too."

Anything that grows out of the ground, chances are it's here. And if it's not, she can have it there the next day. Her and his mother started the shop twenty two years ago. When they first opened, it was a one room building that used to be a tractor shed. All they carried were the usual: roses, carnations, perennials, etc.—nothing fancy, just your basic flower shop. Over time they expanded to three rooms and added more variety. But it wasn't until Harry invested one hundred and thirty five-thousand that it became a five thousand square-foot, state of the art nursery—Greenhouses, botanical gardens, bonsai bushes, hydroponic tanks, six full-time employees, and an array of garden furniture, and ceramic statues.

"You been keeping up with the race?"

"You know I have, but I don't need any sweet-talk about what they'll do if I vote for 'em. My mind is already made up, and guess who I'm choosing?"

"Hmmm..Yates?"

"Heck no, are you crazy? I wouldn't vote for that loon if he was the last loon on earth."

"Stuckey?"

"*What?* That hog riding thug...I'll go on and tell you," placing her small hands on her hips smiling.

"Okay you ready?"

"Yes."

"None of those lying fools! They're all crooked! I don't trust any of em, especially that darn Gordon Stuckey. Everyone knows he's a crook. Well I should say everyone from middle Georgia. I remember when he first started raising those hogs. He only had one little farm, then bam; a couple months later he's rich. Then he goes and gets into the prison business so he can pilfer money from the state. Now he's trying to be the governor so he can take his con game to a whole new level," misting begonias.

"There's a rally scheduled for Tuesday. A man's set to be executed."

At the mention of someone being executed, she stops spraying and looks at him. Fallon hates the death penalty, and anyone who supports it.

"What time is it?"

"Five, we need everyone we can get."

"I'll be there," her face a means sneer. "Along with everyone else I can saddle up."

Harry knows that means everyone from old classmates to the pastor.

"Thanks, it sure means a lot."

"You know if there's anything you need from me, I'll give it to you."

"Well, I need something else too."

"A kidney? You can have it."

He laughs.

"I'll remember that."

"What then?"

"Some flowers, but not my usual, something special."

"Awe Harry! I was thinking it was something specific. Come on,"

Together they pick the flowers that'll make up the bouquet: A colorful selection of red, white, yellow, and pink roses, huge sunflowers, fragrant carnations, and one Love-In-a-Mist. Fallon suggests he add a peace lily, and places them in an embroidered sorrel pot.

"This is wonderful, thank you so much Fallon," he said, lifting it off the counter.

"You sure you don't want me to pay for it?"

*"Harry!..*Get out of here so I can get some work done before it's time to close."

"Same time next week?"

"No, you'll see me Tuesday, Remember?"

Harry shakes his head in agreement.

"Bye Fallon."

The sun is almost at the end of its shift when he cranks his Chevrolet® Caprice, and makes for the cemetery. Shadows twice as long as the trees casting them lay across the highway, the sun blinking against the side of his face as he drives, blinding reflec-

tions dance across Lake Hereford as he coasts over the bridge, old shocks allowing the car to bounce as it goes over the expansion joints; a lone fisherman floats in an engine-less boat waiting for a bite. The sounds of waves beating themselves against the boulders can be heard as he returns to solid ground. Up ahead he spots a woman struggling to change a tire.
As he pulls up over, he wonders why no one has stopped to give her hand.

"Need some help I see," walking up to her car.
"Sure will be nice," out of breath from wrestling with the spare.
And uses her sleeve to wipe the sweat from her forehead.
"My brother is supposed to be on his way, but that was forty minutes ago. Changing a tire isn't as easy as it looks."
"Well let me give it a try," Harry rolling up his sleeves.

Minutes later he's removed the flat, and replaced it with the spare.
"Thanks a lot mister. I don't even know your name."
"Harry."
She reaches in her purse and hands him a crisp $20.
"There's no charge."
"No here take it, it's the least I can do."
"I'm fine, really. I needed the exercise. I'm the one that should be paying you."
"Okay, thanks again Harry. May God bless you."
"And you too ma'am. Drive safely and try not to run over any more nails."
"I won't. See you around."
He waves goodbye, before getting back in his car, and heading off flushed with pride.
God blessed me to wake up this morning....I'm thankful.

It's just about sunset when he reaches the cemetery. Elroy, the groundskeeper waves as he drives down the hill past the mausoleum. This is his favorite time to visit his wife, he loves the delicate way the spectrum of light paint the sky, hanging satin clouds over the manicured lawns resembling a divinely inspired canvas.

Engaging in conversation, a mourner kneels beside a headstone. Harry parks near the one he's been coming to for years, gets out, and removes a small shovel from his pocket. After digging out the withered flowers, he replaces them with fresh ones; a bird croons from the treetops. One engraved with his name sits beside Helen Fawell's. When his time is up, he wants to rest with his first and only love. Extracting a handkerchief, he wipes the dust from her picture framed in the stone's face.

"Sorry I'm late darling," sitting cross-legged on the soft fescue.

"This lady was stranded on the side of the road, so I pulled over and gave her hand. I know that's what you would've wanted me to do; make sure God writes that in my deed book, wouldn't want him to forget, not that he would anyway....The job is really starting to get to me, I don't think I can keep take seeing those people killed, I've been having nightmares about me being put in that chair, and sometimes wake up in cold sweats. I once fell out of bed when I jumped out of the chair before they electrocuted me....Tuesday they're doing this guy named Matthew Grainger, he's a good guy; I think God's forgiven him. If you see him up there you, tell him Harry said hello, and tell him I did everything I could to stop it. And tell him Sivan did everything she could too ....How's junior?.........I just got this nice new urn for his ashes. Tell him that I love him. I told him already once, but I want you to tell him too. Uhmmm....let me see,

what else is going on? Oh yeah, we're doing this big rally to try to stop it, I guess you'll know if it works or not. Fallon says hello, and to keep an eye on Richard."
He pauses, and starts plucking grass.
"On the nights I can't sleep, I sit in the dark and wait for you. I still laugh when I think about how you had a fit the time I spilled ketchup on the couch....I wish I could hear you scream at me now Helen. I've gotten very lonely since you've been gone, I miss you so much. I think of all the times we used to walk through the park holding hands, or the times we'd get on our bikes and take off without a destination.......I'd give anything to hear your voice again."
A sparrow lands atop her tombstone.
A wave of emotion rolls over Harry, prickling his body with goose bumps.
The bird begins a rhythmic tune, warming him with peace, and causing a tear to repel down his face. Not a single leaf on the bush beside him rustles, as a soft wind blows, triggering the sparrow to flap its wings.
"I see it Helen, I see the bird! I know it's you!...I can't wait till we hold hands again."
Taking a moment to wipe the tears, another larger sparrow joins. It's like a portrait, both their heads looking the same direction while the wind tickles their feathers.
"Thank you Helen....Thank you, this is beautiful. I'll never forget you...I'll love you until my final breath."
As if the pair understands, the smaller one chirps a reply, and they take to the sky.

For almost the next hour, Harry sits in silence reliving the moment. By this time, the sun has completely set, and the moon is partially visible.
"I'd sit out here all night and be with you, but it's getting late, and I've already stayed past my time."
Slowly, he rises to his feet.

"Thank you Helen.....for everything. I'll be back next week, and I promise to be on time. I know how you feel about tardiness.... Good night my love."
As he turns to walk away, a bird sings its goodbyes from somewhere up high.

Chapter 11

Although it's June, the late night air is cool; wind gusts with wild anger. Traffic around downtown is sparse, and most of the buildings are deserted. Surrounded by tall bushes and gated lots, the capital's building's gold dome twinkles in the moonlight—dressed in all black, a figure scurries across the lawn. Street lights illuminate the ground below, several traffic ones flash caution.

Ducked beside a tarnished statue, fatigue is an issue; the transport of the pulleys, ropes, and folding ladder proved to be a feat in itself. Adrenaline flows as the figure moves from one area to another, each time getting closer to the destination; massive columns guard the wide entrance, a pellet gun was used to extinguish the bulbs suspended from the ceiling. Good thing there's no night watchman, because they'd have lost their dinner, and maybe their consciousness, at the sight of the naked body sprawled across the stairway—rigor mortis set in, gooey red liquid has seeped from the wounds. The white corpse resembles a French fry dunked in ketchup, while items designed for scaling cliffs are stained with blood. Getting the victim there without being detected has been a stroke of genius. The figure positions the hooks inside cracked mortar, the pulley is placed and ready to begin hoisting. But progress is halted by the sight of a slow-moving police cruiser.

The Ford® stops at the intersection, and the dome light comes on.

The killer reaches for the binoculars!

The officer says something into the radio, and does something out of view.

The figure stands and prepares for a quick escape!

But the light goes off, and the car speeds down the street.

Time to expedite the process.

The throat is cut from ear to ear, and the tongue is pulled out and down. Hanging out of the lower neck, the mouth is flopped open, void of its speaking utensil. The thought of how he'll react to seeing this on the morning news brings a smile to the slayer.

In haste, the rope is tied in a noose around his waist, and pulled under the arms. Duct tape is wrapped around each ankle and wrists, before being taped to the ankles; the figure doesn't want them separating before the guests arrive—twice as gruesome now that it's been maneuvered into such an awkward position. The heavy-duty hoist turns effortlessly, cranking out revolutions with ease.

Finally, the corpse is airborne, head slumping lazily to the side. Without the help of its muscles, all the weight is placed on the broken neck; making for an awe-inspiring display—the full length of the purple tongue dangles from the wound like a tie. With speed, the figure gathers the tools, takes to the shadows, and melts into the night.

The mortally wounded man who seems to be reaching backwards holding his feet, while floating feet off the ground, swings above the main entrance with a hole in his skull.
A cassette tied to a string sways from the area where the man's genitals used to be.

Kathy's sedative induced sleep is interrupted by the ringing of the telephone, the powerful medication has her mind in a fog, and her vision in a blur. But somehow she's able to make out 6:18 AM on the clock, and wonders why someone would be calling this early on a Sunday—she thought she turned the ringer off.
The phone continues warbling as she attempts to ignore it. Upon looking at the ID screen, she picks it up, realizing the person will keep calling if she doesn't.
*"Megan..*what do you *waa-nt?"*
"Kathy, get up! The killer's struck again! Turn on the TV, hurry!"
The last thing she wants to hear is that the killer's struck again. A chill runs down her spine, as she wonders whether she's in the house alone.
The chair is still wedged under the door knob.
"....What channel?"
"Any of 'em!"
Channel 2 is the first one she comes to. A light-skinned woman

with curly hair stands before the capital building holding a mic.

*"...tigaters say a man in his early forties was killed at
his Snellville home around midnight, and brought
here between the hours of one and three a.m. His
wife and two sons were also brutally murdered.
Police are trying to gather why he was brought
thirty miles away, and hung from a rope here at
the capital's main entrance. Details are still sketchy...."*

"You hear that Kathy?" Megan blurted.
"...Unfortunately."

*".....say they believe this is the work of the same person
suspected of killing a couple at their home last weekend.
Another cassette tape was also found at the scene. Police
aren't saying whether they have a suspect at this time,
right now the death toll stands at six. We now go live to
Chief Pitt who'll give us more information regarding
these senseless killings."*

The camera is rotated to an African-American woman standing
behind a podium, she's quite pretty and seems young; a little too
young to hold the coveted title of Chief of Police. Her heavily
decorated navy blue uniform signifies that she's no rookie, despite how youthful she appears.

*"The first thing I'd like to say is for the public not to panic,
and go blowing this thing out of proportion. As you heard,*

we found a white male whose name will not be released, who was also a current member of our force; we won't be saying which branch of the department he worked. We believe the person that committed the previous homicides is also responsible for these, but will not be saying anything pertinent to our on-going investigation...At-.."

"Chief Pitt, is it true that the body was found suspended in thein the air with his hands tied to his ankles?"

Asked a WGNX reporter.

"I'm unable to verify that at this time."

"Chief, can you tell us how many, and what type of wounds the victim sustained?"

Asked a middle-aged red head.

"We believe he was killed by a single gunshot wound to the chest. Next question."

"Do you have any explanations Chief as to why the man's sex organs were removed? And if so, did it happen prior to him being murdered?"

Pitt shoots the veteran reporter a 'You weren't supposed to say that' look.

*"I cannot say with confidence whether that
happened or not. Last question."*

She knows Chan Gable will try to get her to reveal graphic details if given the chance.

*"Chief, we already know that a taped recording of the
torture and murder of the couple last week was found at
the scene, and since you have stated that this is the work
of the same person; tape found at this scene most likely
has the recorded murder, and possibly the murder of
his family on it. Why, has your department allowed
this to happen again, if a detective working the case is
heard to have said it's believed to be a known informant
out to even the score for some sort of unpaid services?
Why is it that he has not been apprehended yet?"*

Pitt makes a conscious reminder to find out how that information got leaked. And also knows the detective story is just a way to put her on the spot, and let the public know that possibly one of the PD's own snitches has turned against them.

*"That's all conjecture. As I mentioned before, nothing
will be said concerning the investigation. We will let
you know of any new developments."*

Pitt turns and walks away from the podium with her entourage in tow.

> *"As you just heard, a white, middle aged former officer*
> *was found hanging here this morning with several fatal*
> *wounds to his body, with one of them being the removal*
> *of his external se-..Hold!.....Hold on a moment!....."*

Stopping her sentence to press the earpiece with her finger, she listens attentively to an apparent new development, nodding her head every so often.

Just as she's about to say something, Kathy hits the power button, and grabs the receiver off the bed. The same news anchor can be heard talking in the back ground on the other end.

Kathy closes her eyes, and rakes her hand through her hair sighing.

The sound alerts Megan that she's back on the phone.

"Can you believe that!" amazement in her tone.

For some reason, Megan's moderately excited the killer has struck again, though she won't tell anyone.

"Yeah," sullen, and feeling yet another migraine coming on.

"They say it's maybe someone who's working for them."

"I heard, you don't have to repeat it."

"Oh sorry, I just can't believe we've got something like this going on again. I mean, this guy really made a statement by leaving him hanging at the capital. The media's gonna have a field day with this one, I wonder if he'll do it again?.....Why are you so quiet? Are you okay?.......*Kathy!*"

"....Yeah...Yes?"

"I was asking if you're all right, but you weren't saying anything."

"My head is starting to hurt, I think I need to go back to sleep. This week's been rough, and I haven't been getting much rest," hoping she gets the point.

"Well okay, sorry to wake you. I just figured you wanted to see this. But while I got you on the phone, I mines well go on and ask have you heard anything from the police yet?"

"No I haven't heard anything. But if I do you'll be the first to know."

"Kathy I know you're trying to get me off the phone, but I'm not going to hang up until I'm satisfied you're okay. From the way you sound you're not. I think I need to come over. And by the way, where's Stockton?"

"I don't know, I locked him out the room last night. He got on my nerves again. Me-.." the line clicked.

"Your lines clicking."

"I know," looking at the word 'Unavailable' on the screen.

The few people who know her home number don't have theirs listed unavailable, which means it's most likely someone for Stow, so she doesn't answer.

"It's somebody for him. But anyway, I'm all right. I just need some rest. And no you don't need to come over."

"Hey Kath?" Megan asked.

"Yes."

"I'm not trying to be funny or anything, but you might need to see a psychiatrist, or maybe even check yourself into a center for a few days. You know kinda take a break."

Kathy appreciates her friend's concern, but has already had her fill of hospitals and shrinks.

"I'll think about it."

"Promise?"

"I promise."

"Okay, we'll I'll let you go. But don't be mad if I stop by to check on you."

"All right Megan, talk to you later," and hangs up after Megan says goodbye.

Kathy lays back, the bad feelings return. Reaching under her pillow, she's somewhat comforted by the cold steel of the revolver. Not caring if Stockton's there or not, she grabs the gun and checks the house, but it's empty; although she can tell he's been there.

After eating a bowl of cornflakes, she's back in her bedroom; the chair back in the same position. The fact that Christie promised to call, but never did, bothers her. She doesn't have a way to get in touch with her, so she has to wait until she calls.

After adjusting the blanket, she rolls on her side and watches the sunrise. This is usually something she enjoys, but since her life has taken a turn for the worst, worse than it already was; all it means is the start of another dreadful day. Besides being dejected, she getting stalked by some strange woman, a serial killer has sent her one of his recordings, her unofficial husband is a walking time bomb, and she's up to her neck in legal problems; not to mention the slew of other things going wrong in her life that she doesn't care to think about. For her, pondering about death has become a normal pastime. She wakes up thinking about it, dreams about it, and sometimes wishes it'll stop by and pay her a visit.

She rolls back over, and pulls the gun from under the pillow.

"....You have the power take a life huh?"

Running her finger down the barrel, she opens the cylinder and inspects the bullets.

"...You little bastards...Look at you, just waiting to come out and play."

Her grip on reality is slipping more each day.

She flicks her tongue out at them.

"Naaaaaa-na. You can't get me."

Raising the weapon to her eyes, she peers down the barrel.

"...I see you down there."

She rubs it across her nose and down lips, before opening her mouth and putting the barrel inside—the lubricating solution is bitter.

A tear creeps down her face.

"*AAAAAAAAAAAAAAAAAAAAA!*" she screams to the top of her voice.

"*AAAAAAAAAAAAAAAAAAAAAAAAA!!!*"
Unable to resist, she turns towards the window, and just as the sun climbs over the horizon........
BOOM!!!
The deafening blasts shakes the walls.
Her hand lets go of the smoking gun. With her teary eyes still open, it falls to the floor.

Stockton has just turned off the engine, and is getting out of the truck when he hears the shot. He takes off for the front door, and quickly unlocks the dead bolt!
Kathy has the chain across it.
With no time to waste, he raises his Gore-Tex® boot, and kicks it in, destroying the frame! Programmed by the academy, he draws his weapon; having no idea where the shot came from. Peeking around the corner, he yells her name down the hallway. But it's a second too late.

The second the intruder sticks his head around the corner, she

fires.
BOOM!!!
And slams the bedroom door.

Stockton leaps back right in the nick of time! A million thoughts flood his mind, as he kneels on the carpet realizing he's in a gun battle with his wife. He yells to her again, thinking there's a reasonable explanation.

Kathy hears the intruder's muffled yells. Each time he shouts her name, it reminds her of the way he said it on the tape. Her hands are shaking so badly that she almost drops the gun! Visions of Stockton finding her dead in a pool of blood with a tape beside her mutilated body causes her to almost vomit; she winces from the sharp pain in her chest. She thinks about giving up, and letting him kill her, but remembers how close she just came to doing it herself; seeing the bullet hole in the ceiling.
Kathy feels the vibration of footsteps!
Not about to be surprised, she flattens herself on the floor and

looks under the door.
Two black boots sprint into the bathroom!

"Stop shooting Kathy, it's me! Put the gun down!"

It's a trick! Why is his face painted!
Obviously not recognizing Stow's voice.
With her vision growing increasingly blurry, she searches the room for an escape route. It takes all the strength she can muster to push her body off the floor, and beeline for the window, pushing it open—fear and a bad heart has drastically weakened her. Since the house sits on a steep hill, the back is higher than the front, making the jump more than twenty feet.
She sinks to the floor crying.
Either be murdered by a serial killer, or leap out of the window, breaking both of her legs, and be murdered anyway. No matter how she looks at it, her life is about to be over.
He yells her name again!
Fear turns in anger—rebellion; which births courage. She'll fight

to the bitter end.
"What the hell."

Stockton leaps to the floor! Bullets burst through the shower wall exploding the ceramic tiles, and shattering the vanity mirror. He's covered him in glass, and can't believe his woman is trying to take his life. But remembers what transpired the other day, and understands.
"Come on you bastard!"

Crouching beside the bed with trembling hands, she's afraid, disoriented, and has no plan; a migraine relentlessly bashes her head like a wrecking ball. The room begins spinning, and in a last ditch effort before she loses consciousness, squeezes the trigger, and blasts another hole through the door.

While sirens wail in the distance, he uses a rag to rub the paint off.

"I'm coming down the hall baby. Don't shoot. Please!"

He crawls on his stomach to the door, and pushes it; seeing through the hole Kathy slumped on the floor.

The screeching tires of more than one car notifies him of the authority's arrival.

He only has time to shoulder it once.

"Police! Show me your hands!"

Stow does as instructed.

"I live here, my wife's barricaded herself in the bedroom. Call an ambulance."

"Don't you fuckin' move!" as he's forced back to the floor.

"She needs an ambulance!" pinned down by three men in black fatigues.

"Open the door ma'am, it's the police," glued to the wall with weapons in hand.

Hearing no reply and seeing her on the floor, he gives the signal.

Four men crash through the door like the chair's not even there.

"Let me go," Stockton pushes.

"Tell us what happened first."

"I came home, heard shots, ran in the house, she thought I was a burglar, and fired on me! Now let me up!"

"What's that on your hands?"

"...Motor oil."

"Why would she be shooting at you?"

"Hell if I know. She has mental problems and probably didn't take her medicine. Now let me up!"

The officer looks at him for moment.

"Let him up," two gold bars on his shoulder state his seniority.

A guy comes out of the bedroom carrying her gun.

"Now tell me *exactly* what happened."

After spending two hours at the police station, recognizing a few familiar faces, and after she told him she believed Stockton was an intruder, the lieutenant decided not to charge Kathy with discharging a firearm within city limits, but did require her to undergo a psychiatric evaluation. The incident also gave them probable cause for an investigation. And due to the suspicious nature of the contents, Stockton's duffel bag was confiscated. No matter what he said, the Lt. wouldn't release it, but promised he'd eventually get it back.

Stockton can't believe he made such a costly mistake. Why the hell did he sit the duffel bag on the ground? As he drives down I-75, he knows it's only a matter of time before they uncover the truth—everything's in that bag.

Chapter 12

"Count time, everybody on your feet!" announced the intercom, as Harry and Billings enter the cell house.

It's 7 a.m., and Parson doesn't feel like getting up for count, especially after he's been up half the night.

The gate half opens.

He rolls out of bed and splashes some water on his face. While listening to Harry call off names, he thinks back to last night, and is mostly satisfied with the results.

"Barger......Jameison......Corson.......Kleehow..."

He stops at his cell and checks off his name.

"Morning."

"How's it going Harry?"

"You know how Mondays are. You hear about the man they found at the capital?"

"It's all the guys have been talking about," drying his face with a towel.

"Come on with the count old-timer!"

"But I still got a mean jab!"

"We'll talk," and continues down the tier.

"Addcox....Tolstoy...."

Harry stops three cells down.

"Chesterwell!" he yells. "Trent Chesterwell!" The name echoing throughout the building.

"Billings, did Chesterwell clean up last night?"

Billings backs from under the tier and looks up.

"Yes, why?"

Harry doesn't answer right away, he's not thrilled to be working with him. Billings is only there because they're short staffed.

"Everybody on your feet, IDs in hand!" Harry ordered.

This causes several comments to emit from the irritated inmates.

"Shit!"

"Damn!"

"You do it muthafucker!"

He checks the IDs of the men on top, while Billings does the bottom.

"He's not here."

"He done escaped!" shouts someone, causing the dorm to erupt in laughter, and congratulatory whistles.

Harry walks back downstairs, and is on his way to the corridor gate when something tells him to check one more area. Not expecting to find Chesterwell, he goes to the supply room, and opens the door.

He's blown back by what he sees!!

Chesterwell is hanging from a hook!!

His jumpsuit is matted with blood, and a broomstick is protruding out of his abdomen.

Harry staggers out, and grabs the table to keep from fainting,

but can't prevent his breakfast from pouring out.
Billings arrives at the scene.

Stuckey arrived from his home in minutes; after the CERT team, medical staff, and other facility officials.
Starns and Salvatore are the first people he speaks to after taking a look at Chesterwell.
"Who worked last night?"
"Billings and Upshaw," responded Starns.
Before the captain can say more, Gordon's on his way to Billings and Upshaw standing near the television.
"How did this happen...Again?"
Upshaw answers first, eager to clear his name.
"Sir I don't know how this happened, he was the only one out. Furthermore, I was running the tower. Billings was responsible for the floor."
The warden turns to him.
"Why was he out after lockdown?"
Not in the least bit cowed by his stare, he replies: "The inmate was a dorm trustee and had the job of buffing floors on Sunday nights; a practice initiated before I arrived."
"Were you not told in trainin' that all inmates, except those with special permission from me aretuh be in their cells after lockdown?"
"You obviously heard nothing I said."
Gordon steps closer.
Billings moves forward.

"......Who hired you?"

"I transferred from the Feds."

Gordon's senses something, and backs off.

He's been there long enough to know how things work, and knows prisoners routinely stay out at night to service floors. But since one has been killed while doing it, he suddenly has a problem with it.

"Who else was out with him?"

"No one," responded Billings.

He steps to Upshaw.

"Did you let anyone else out?"

"No, he was it," nervous and picturing unemployment.

"So you two are tellin' me," the volume of his voice causing the director of operations to walk over, "that some rouge ghost is runnin' round here killin' my fuckn' prisoners! Is that what you're standin' here sayin!"

"No, I'm not saying that. All I know is that I didn't let him out. That doesn't mean someone didn't sneak out anyway. We all know the inmates can screw with the locks," he clarified.

"Well if you know that, why didn't you keep a handle on the control board? It lights up beside the number of the door that's open," Higgins now joining the conversation.

"Half the sensors don't even work," Billings jumps in. "They should've been replaced years ago. So who's fault is it that they haven't been fixed?"

Not wanting to take food out of his mouth, Gordon hasn't had them repaired.

"So since you say somebody snuck out and killed em, whudya have in mind?"

But walks away and has a hushed meeting with his operations director/campaign manager.

"I want youtuh her-rup and get this shit cleaned up. Find out if he has any family. If he do and they wanna know what happened, make up somethin'. If he don't, or they don't caretuh deal wit it, I want 'em in the dirt. In exactly an hour an thirty

minutes I want you in my office wita update."
And walks away.
"Okay Upshaw, who is it?"
"I don't know sir, I haven't the slightest clue. Like I said, I was responsible for tower. Billings was supposed to handle walking the floors, and doing the count."
Stuckey gives him a dirty look.
"How long you been workin' here?"
"I reckon about eleven years."
"So you know it's both officers duty tuh watch the floor, right?"
"Yessir but a-"
"So why in the hell do you keep givin' me dat dumb excuse bout-chu bein' in the tower?"
"I wa-.."
Gordon puts his hand up and says to Billings: "How come you didn't see nobody go in the supply closet?"
"I don't have an explanation," not showing any uneasiness by the warden's questioning.
Gordon takes a deep breath and spins around.
"Y'all stop!" referring to the CERTs dealing with Chesterwell.
He radios main control, and instructs them to open all the cells on death row.
"All you sons-uh-bitches step out!"
When they're out he continues.
"I know you fucks get off on killin' people, but here, I'm da only one who says when a motherfucker dies! Personally, I don't give a rat's ass bout 'em bein' dead! If it was uptuh me, I'd line all your asses up like ducks, and fry yuh in one day! It'd save me from havin' to deal wit shit like this, and the state alota money! But since I can't, you havetuh sit and waitcha turn! But while you waitin', whether it be two years or twenty, you gone act like you got some sense! It ain't even been two weeks, and there's been two killins! Beasley first, now this bastard! Now I don't know exactly who's doin' it, but it's gone stop! You guys dat been here for a while know by experunce what happuns when I let my boys

loose! Now ahma show da ones dat don't!..This is what I wont
you shitheads tuh-dew!"
He pauses to clear his throat.
"Strip! I mean *strip!* Not one fuckin' stitch of clothin'! I don't
wanna see nuttin' but swingin' dicks!"
While they get naked, he goes to the supply room.
"Y'all her-rup and get this mess up. It stinks!"

While three reluctant CERTs prepare the body bags, two others
use germ killing agents to clean up the blood.
Stuckey stands atop a table scanning for resistance.
"W-one-s, to CT central," holding the radio to his mouth.
"...CT central."
"Ten-Ten, eighty-four, twenty CTs to death row unit."
"Ten-four."

Minutes later the corridor teams with black fatigues. Once the
massive gate opens, the commander comes over to Gordon.
"I wanna a cavity search done on every one of 'em, I wont this
whole place turnt upside down. Every bag of chips, cupa noodles, candy bar, peanut butter jar; I wont it opened and inspected. Are we clear?"
"Yes sir."
"Get to it then."
The 6'4" bruiser goes and briefs his team.
Moments later they're running around like wild bulls, slamming
men to the floor, putting boots to their necks, and yelling instructions.
Stuckey watches with pride as a CERT rams an inmate's head
into the bars. Another man is kneed in the head while lying
face down on the concrete. It's pure pandemonium, and he loves
it. Mattresses are being thrown over the railing. Popcorn, corn
chips, oatmeal pies, ready-made chili, containers of tuna, and
whatever else they can find, is scattered across the cell-house.
Stuckey smiles as a fatigue bursts a jar of peanut butter against

the wall.

Harry watches in disgust.

"When dey been searched, I wont em all hog-tied!" Gordon shouts.

A vicious feeding frenzy would be the best way to describe what's taking place. Fatigues dart from one cell to another, kicking and stepping on prisoners. Pages ripped from books float through the air; an inmate screams when a baton meets his nose.

Gordon smiles like Lucifer.

"You're going too far Gordon! This is uncalled for!"

"There's been a murder, and it's my job-duh find da weapon," not meeting Harry's teeth clenching stare.

He has fire in his eyes, and badly wants to push him off the table.

"You're no different from them Gordon, you just haven't been caught yet! But that's about to change!"

And storms out, shoving a CERT out of his way.

Gordon laughs and returns to the action; in time to see Parson getting stepped on.

"Bring that one down here!"

Bound with orange zip ties, he's snatched up; resembling a slaughtered deer hanging from a spit. Blood and saliva drip from his mouth, as they half carry, half drag him down the stairs.

"Drop dat piece-uh shit," Gordon pointing to the end of the table he's standing on.

His hands are tied behind his back, so his face catches his fall, as they sling him on the table.

"Comfortable?" looking down at him. "You wouldn't by chance know anything about what happened would you?"

Parson doesn't move.

"Answer him dick face!" one of the CERTs shout in his ear.

He still doesn't say anything.

"Did-juh like da welcome I gave dat whore? Ahm shur she told ya."

He notices Parson's feet and hands are turning blue.

"I think y'all cut the circulation to his brain. Loosenin' dem ties."

The CERT snips them with a pair of scissors.

"You betta start talkin' fore these gentlemen help ya find yer voice."

He nudges him with his snakeskin boot.

Not a word.

"Is da fucker breathin'?"

As the CERT bends over to see, he comes to life, and head-butts him in the face!

Blood pours from his nostrils, the Lt. yells and drops the scissors.

Before Stuckey can blink an eye, inmates who'd yet to be tied, rush a CERT standing beside the railing, sending him over the side. His head bounces off the floor, and seconds later blood starts seeping from his skull.

Before any of the shocked CERTs can react, Parson spins off the table, and knocks Gordon's feet out from under him, sending his out of shape body flailing to the floor.

Hearing movement behind them, four CERTs turn back, while two others take off towards the stairs shouting expletives.

Parson strikes the CERT again, shattering his Adam's apple; sending him slumping to ground in a suffocation ridden spasm.

The remaining fatigue panics and reach for his pepper spray, as Parson makes him the second victim of a broken nose, followed by a raucous uppercut that causes him to bite off half his tongue, rendering him unconscious.

Other inmates follow his lead, and begin attacking. Every convict with free hands come off the floor, and careen towards them. The air becomes hot and stale as sweating bodies, some naked and some clothed, ferociously battle; biting, kicking, scratching and throwing each other about—CERTs cry out as their weapons are used against him. The cell-house is now an out of control thunder dome; Whites, Blacks, Latinos, two Asians, and one Blackfoot Indian unite to shed blood, and wreak on havoc on their oppressors.

Parson turns to see Upshaw dragging Gordon into the corridor. He takes off like a heat-seeking missile!

BAM!!!

His body slamming into the bars, reaching to grab his shirt.

"AAAAAAAAAAAAA!" a second too late.

Furious, he stands there breathing as they go through the outer gate, and disappear around the corner.

Knowing backup will soon arrive, he grabs up the scissors, and frantically frees the remainder of the men. One by one they join the free for all, and pummel what's left of the CERTs.

Slam!!

Another fatigue tossed over the side. The way the man's neck twisted on impact, he's dead.

"Heeeeeeeeey!!!" getting their attention.

"Stop!..Stop!" then lets off an ear piercing whistle.

The noise of movement subside, as the hard breathing, sweating, and bloodied killers stare back at him.

"They'll be back! Half of you gather the mats and stack them in front of the door, all the way to the top!"

Nobody asks questions.

The condemn men round up the cheap cotton mattresses, and run them to the front of the cell house. Working in an assembly line, they're done in minutes. Sixty nine mattresses lay in five rows from one wall across the gate. The other half hog-tie the fallen CERTs, and pack them twelve to a cell. They're stripped, and in dire need of medical attention.

Wasting no time with putting on their clothes, two inmates drag a bloody faced CERT.

"They're in the tower!..*Hurry up!*"

Rifle toting officers, the warden, and nine high level staff members watch through the heavily fortified Plexiglas®, as the rip-roaring inmates move their captives—broken bodies are tossed like garbage, some landing on top of others. The fact that they're trampling barefoot through blood doesn't matter, nor the fact that many of the CERTs have life-threatening injuries. They've been inexorably treated like animals, so now they act as such. Parson grabs a pair of boots and pants, and put them on. Although he's the self-appointed commander, another inmate dons the lieutenant's crisp fatigue; a shiny gold bar pinned on each shoulder. The others find this to be a great idea, as they too begin covering themselves in black from head to toe.

Seeing this infuriates Gordon something serious. He snatches up the microphone, and begins shouting over the PA system.
"All you dogs are gonna die!! Get back in yer cells, right fuckin' now!......*PUT THAT DOWN YOU SONOFABITCH!!*" with a bloodied gauze wrapped around his head.
A baton ricochets off the glass.
"Fuck you Gordo! What we care about dyin'! We taking them with us!!"
The entire cell house bursts into shouts, yells, whistles, and screams; rallying each other to fight to the death—their battle cry shaking the tower's windows.
"All you fuckin' rats are dead!"
But they're on such an emotional high, they can't even hear him. Gordon slams down the mic, picks up a chair, and bashes it against the window.

"Everybody listen!" said Parson. "We've reached the point of no return. It's very likely that some, if not all of us will die. As we speak, armed men are on the other side of those mats. How far this thing goes is up to us. Is there anyone having second thoughts?"
No one answers.
"I'm ready to meet my maker! *Fuck* these assholes!"
Chants and yells reignite!
"Hey, heeeeey!..Let's get some order in here. Four men keep an eye on the yard, we'll work in rotations; that's direction they're likely coming from, but don't stand too close to the windows. They may use snipers, but I doubt it considering we have their

officers. But still, be on guard. Next! Demands, what will they be?"

"Food!" yells a naked man from the top tier.

"Pussy!" yells another.

"*....FREE-DOOOOOOM!!*"

"*AAAAAAAAAAAAAAAAAA!*" comes a bloodcurdling scream, causing Parson and several others to rush over.

"*AAAAAAAAAA!-AAAAAAAAAA!*"

A CERT is scooting away from another CERT whose bowels have released.

The screams echo throughout the building like a bullhorn; more inmates run up.

The terror owning his face can't be described. He loses it and starts banging his head against the bars, hysterically shaking the door to get out.

"Now you see how we feel faggot!" said an inmate, and socks him in the face.

The others smash against the wall to avoid stepping in the body fluid creeping across the floor.

Cheers break out!

Parson moves through the crowd, and takes a seat. It's going to be a long day.

"...buncha fuckin' wild apes. What da fuck is goin' on!"

"We're doing our best to find out. They've destroyed the cameras sir," stated Boyd Nelson.

"How long before we go in?" Gordon standing with him.

"It's no telling if they start killing hostages."

"What da hell you mean Boyd!" and punches the glass. "You sayin' we gone havetuh wait 'em out?"

"Our options are few. If we make the wrong move, there can be dozens of dead officers on our hands. We don't have much of a choice."

Stuckey isn't about to sit here and let no inmates tell him what to do, his gargantuan ego won't allow it. He watches with repugnance as they prance around in the officer's uniforms, the sight of the inmate sporting the lieutenant's bars makes him quake with anger. He cares nothing about the CERTs being taken hostage, or the beatings they've suffered; that's not what's bothering him. The fact they've commandeered his unit is what he can't stand. He has no intention of negotiating with a buncha fuckin' animals; he doesn't care if they kill the hostages one by one. No matter what happens, he's not making any deals. This is his prison, and he has the final say. They're going to be sorry they ever challenged him.

"Sir, there's a call on line one," notified a 12 gauge toting officer.

"Who is it," staring at Parson.

"The governor."

Stuckey spins around.

"Who the fuck called him!"

Chapter 13

By four o'clock, the death row parking lot is swamped with press vans, sheriff vehicles, SWAT teams, state police, Yates and his entourage, agents from the Georgia Bureau of Investigation, and big wigs from the Department of Corrections—a thick crowd of spectators clog the entrance. The standoff is now entering its tenth hour; reporters stand before cameras with mics. Word has gotten out that at least one guard, and possibly more have been killed.

As Parson predicted, men from the GBI's elite hostage rescue unit have infiltrated the recreation yard; readied with painted faces, night vision goggles, and assault weapons; the negotiator is working on the release of five hostages in exchange for food and water. News of the two preceding murders have also gotten out, of which Stuckey denies concealing; swearing he did nothing illegal. As we speak, Beasley's body is being exhumed; they got to Chesterwell before Higgins and his crew did. A long green tent houses the makeshift command center, as law enforcement from various agencies plot their next move.

Harry stands in the tower with the negotiator.
"If not for Gordon, none of this would be happening," he stated.
"What makes you so sure of that?" Sam Trassle.
"Because I've been here since he started, and have witnessed him do countless things to these men."
"So you're saying *he's* responsible for this?"
"You get the crap beat out of you once every couple months, and see how you start acting. You think this is the first time he's swept stuff under the rug?"
"Well if you knew these things, why didn't you report them?" Trassle questioned, wearing a tailored suit, slick hair, and make-up.
Harry thinks he looks more like an actor, than a GBI agent.
"For your information, I *have* filed complaints, numerous times; several with the DOC, and countless others with your agency. But no one cares about what happens to a bunch of condemned men."
"I don't think that's correct Mr. Fawell. I think there's just more pressing issues that need attention, and besides, they shouldn't have done the things to get themselves in this position in the first place. Let's not forget, they *are* convicted murderers. In my opinion, I don't think what happens here is of major concern." And excuses himself to speak with a fellow agent.
I wish they had you hostage, he thought, looking at the crowd of people eager to make a name for themselves.
There only concern is how to end the problem, not how it began. Hatred fills Harry's heart, remembering how his boy was

murdered by people like these.

He sees Parson sitting at the same table he's watched him sit at for the past decade, and tries to guess what's going through his mind. Looking around, he sees how confined they are, and how bad the conditions are that they live, and understands why they feel like they do.

He wonders how awful it must be for an innocent man.

"What are you over here pondering Fawell?" Yates asked. "How to save the world?"

Sarcastic chuckle.

"About how all of this could've been prevented."

"Yeah well," shrugging his shoulders. "It's wasn't, it's life—shit happens. All you can try to do is keep it from getting too deep."

"So what reason do you have to come down from your lofty mansion? Trying to show the public how concerned you are?"

"I happen to be the governor, if you don't know. And yes, I am concerned, especially when there's twenty-five lives at stake."

"What about the other sixty-nine? Oh wait, let me answer that for you: They're not the issue."

"Fawell, this is not the time, nor the place to express your views. All that matters is that this thing comes to a peaceful end."

"Well from what I see, that's not going to happen. They're devising a plan that doesn't involve peace."

"Well if that's what's got to be done, so be it. They brought this on themselves. They should've thought about the consequences of their actions first. You remember the takeover at the federal pen back in eighty-seven?"

Yates expects a response, but Harry doesn't provide one.

"Well anyway, that thing went on for thirteen days. This is not about to turn into another one of those. They've already killed one officer that we know of; how or why it started is irrelevant."

"I expect you to say something like that."

Turning away from the glass, Harry looks him in the eye.

"Your definition of right and wrong is so warped, mister I have morals. Don't come at me acting like you have integrity."

"You have a bad habit of seeing things from one angle Fawell. Would you be so concerned about their well-being if it had been your daughter they murdered after raping her, or your mother and father they shot because they refused to give up their car? And let's not forget about the uncle who spent half his life running his convenient store; that of which he used to support his family, and some thug too lazy to work decides he'll just rob and kill him. But I wouldn't expect you to look at it like that...You can't blame the entire world for what happened to your son."

"Don't you *dare* bring him into this, you understand me? Don't you dare!" drawing the attention of one of his armed guards.

"Is everything okay over here sir?" looking at Harry.

"And if it's not, *what?*"

"Everything's fine," replied Yates. "This is Mr. Fawell. He's worked death row for more than twenty years. Harry Fawell, met Stephen Daniels, my head of security."

"I'll pass," and focuses his attention back on the cell-house.

Yates smiles and waves him away.

"You're a bitter man Fawell?"

"I'm very aware...But let me clarify a thing or two. I know exactly what every one of them has been convicted of, many of whom I extremely dislike. Beasley for example, I couldn't stand the ground he walked on, I loathed the things he did to those people, loathe him as a person, I loathed everything about him. But that didn't give me the right to mistreat him, and stoop down to his level. I'd be no better than them if I came to work every day looking to punish them for their crimes. There already waiting to die, what more do I need to do."

"Well for some, it's not that simple—they're angered by the things these men have done; it's human to want revenge."

"But that's not my job. I'm an agent of the law, not an agent of ill will, and of torture. I've seen these men not feed for days, I've seen men beaten to within an inch of their life, I've seen dogs let loose on them, I've seen them stripped completely naked, and thrown in their cells while the vents blow freezing air, I've seen men forced to drink toilet water because a sadistic warden thought it was funny. Why are the people who do these things not punished, just as these men have?" pointing. "Can you answer that Yates? How come the CERTs can stomp a man to death, and go home like nothing happened? Why aren't they sitting in there with the people who do things like that?" pausing to catch his breath, and wipe a napkin across his flustered face.

"I'll tell you why: Because you and everybody else have the same effed up way of thinking. Y'all only seek justice for certain people, for certain reasons. The way I see it: wrong is wrong. And you of all people! The *biggest, lyingest, stealingest, dirtiest, sleaziest, scandalous, disingenuous, spineless* half of man this state has ever seen, has the *audacity* to form your mouth and say that I have a bad habit of seeing things from one angle! How dare you even think that you are a decent human being! The only difference between you and them is that you got away with your crimes, and they didn't!"

Yates can feel his peers' eyes burning into him, and notices the silence; sweat begins overpowering his antiperspirant. Standing with a stupid grin, he desperately tries to think of something to say, but Harry beats him to it.

"And that goes for all of you!..Looking shocked like he's the only one! Every one of you are just like him!..You're nothing but paid help—cowards with guns and badges! How many people have you scumbags stepped on trying to get the top? All y'all do is kiss ass, and pull triggers—that's your only talents in life; a buncha losers who've failed at everything else! I didn't see any of you rushing down here trying to save the day when a handcuffed man was beaten to death by same officers down there begging for mercy. Where were you then?....Look at you, all bunched in here with your guns, and your tear gas ready to enact revenge! Well guess what? They're the ones getting revenge now! Those CERTs are getting just what they deserve! Karma's a bitch!" and

storms for the door.
As he grabs the handle, he turns around.
"Oh, and just for your information, that guy who the CERT killed...He had a son in college, a daughter in high school, and a wife who loved him! And guess what else?" speaking to the entire room."
"GUESS WHAT ELSE YOU PITIFUL BASTARDS!!"
"What?" speaks Yates, limp-noodled, and embarrassed.
"He was innocent."
"Said who?"
"Said the Supreme Court of Georgia!" and slams the door so hard it shakes the walls.
Gordon didn't say a word.

After thirty sleepless hours in a mental health ward, being asked to give explanations to what black smudges resemble, and arranging red and white wooden triangles into strange shapes; Kathy's glad to be sitting in the pharmacy.
Who can she call to take her home; Stockton's out of the question.
The prison standoff is top story on the 6 o'clock news, even CNN is running hourly updates.
A neatly dressed woman sitting across from her engages in a heated conversation with the empty seat beside her.
The machine on the wall states they're now serving number Q54, though they're the only two there. The woman tells her imaginary friend she has to go, and goes to the counter to collect her prescription. The test results determined Kathy isn't schizo-

phrenic, but rather suffering from post-traumatic stress disorder (PTSD), and chronic depression. Dr. Kosterlitz prescribed Olanzapine to stabilize her mood, and Sertraline to make her feel better about living. The fact she'd been shooting at Stockton instead of an intruder amuses her, to the point she lets out a chuckle—the woman behind the counter gives her a fleeting glance.

Channel 11 news is airing a pre-recorded statement from Gordon when someone calls her name.

Kathy turns to see Christie coming through the door in a rain soaked parka.

What's she doing here?

"Hi," she replied nervously, not yet knowing what to expect.

"What are you doing here?" the question revealing her suspicion.

"I came to have my breasts examined, what about you?"

Kathy decides whether she'll lie or tell the truth.

"My coworker's mother had surgery."

Lying is easier.

"Oh, what kind?" and takes a seat.

"Uhm...I think it was something to do with her kidney," not good at lying.

Christie picks up on it, but doesn't press her.

"It's crazy how we keep running into each other huh?"

Is she the lady from the theater???

"I was about to say that."

"Maybe it's fate," Christie said slyly.

Or maybe you're up to something?........Stockton says I'm gullible.

So, did your exam go okay?" Kathy asked.

But the question falls on deaf ears. Christie's gaze is locked on the television.

A reporter is holding a mic, while Trassle updates the public on the developments.

The expression on Christie's face makes Kathy wonder why she's watching so attentively, more than the average person would be paying, and too becomes affixed when she sees the face stamped across the screen!!

The black cloud is back.

There's no hiding, it follows her everywhere she goes.

Why hadn't she seen it before? The television has been on since she sat down, but she obviously hadn't noticed.

There goes that familiar chest pain again.

The women are so hypnotized, they fail to hear the pharmacist calling her name.

Both are listening to the negotiator's words, but each for different reasons.

Unsettling visions saturate her mind!

Confusion.

Rage!

The more Trassel talks, the faster her heart beats; the more horrified she becomes.

She closes her eyes.

This can't be happening! It's not real! IT'S NOT REAL KATHY!

Expecting to see something different, she reopens them. But now it's worse than before.

She shuts them again!

Like slides from a macabre projector, more disturbing images flash through her mind

Death!

Mutilated bodies!

The faceless laughing man!

THE FACELESS LAUGHING MAN!!!

Christie comes towards her with something in her hand!

She wants to move, but fear has incapacitated her. She sees the outstretched arm about to meet her neck!

"NOOOOOO!"

Her legs come to life!

Kathy leaps from the chair, punches Christie, peels out the pharmacy, down the hallway, out the lobby, and into the pouring rain!

Unfazed by the blow, Christie takes off after her!
Kathy darts into traffic, barely avoiding being struck by a tow truck, as she slips on the pavement, and lands on her chest sliding. Quickly, she regains her footing, and is back on her feet looking over her shoulder.
Christie's hot on her on her trail.
She runs with all she has, and can hear Christie shouting for her to stop, but her brain won't let her. It's as if she's along for the ride in someone else's body.
The images keep flashing.
She cuts through a gas station, and enters a parking garage.
WHAM!
Goes her body colliding with the fender of the car, flipping over the hood.
But she's again back to her feet, feeling the burning pain in her knee, elbow, and hip. Kathy turns and heads up the ramp with her hair flying like a cape. The pain in her chest intensifies, tears cloud her vision; haunting images take shape. Christie is feet away when she shoots between two cars, and over the wall down to another deck.
Christie follows.
The humming overhead lights blur as she begins experiencing the effects of exhaustion. She looks over her shoulder again.
Christie continues like a machine!
Kathy realizes the only way to escape is over the edge of the wall she's running parallel with. Looking over the side she sees the five story drop into an empty retention pond.
Certain death.
Her steps become slow and clumsy, she makes a wild twisting motion.
The man with no face swings a knife at her!
She looks back while he laughs, only to disappear again when Christie runs through him.
"Kathy!" she shouted panting. "...Kathy!" using the last of her breath as they come to the dead end.

Christie bends at the waist and clutches her stomach, gasping for air.

Kathy stands at the corner glancing over the side with her hands on her knees, gasping too. After running full speed for more than a mile, both women are on the verge of hyperventilation.

Christie watches in disbelief as Kathy screams, and begins desperately fighting like she's being attacked by a swarm of invisible bees. Without warning, she moves for the wall!

Christie anticipating her, moves with the speed, and snatches her back, a split-second before she leaped to her death.

"HEEEEEEELP!...HEEEEEEELP!"

Kathy struggles to get away, but Christie has her arms locked around her as they wrestle to the ground.

There's no one to save her.

The laughing man again!

He raises the knife, and sinks it into her chest.

"AAAAAAAAAAAAAA!!!!"

Kathy struggles and screams, but exhaustion has her movements sluggish and ineffective. Realizing she can't get away, she lets out a last scream, and gives up; her body jerking like she's about to vomit.

"He's killing me….Please…..Let me go," she wheezes, her bloodshot eyes unable to produce any more tears.

"No one's trying to kill you…It's just us, nobody's here," she explained, out of breath.

"…He's stabbing me."

She runs her hand over her.

"Look," holding her hand in front of her face. "It's not real."

Kathy's heart is racing!

Tires can be heard screeching on the slick concrete. A security attendant pulls beside them and jumps out.

"Y'all all right? Y'all were running like two bats outta a hell! What's going on?" asked the frail man wearing a uniform with a flashlight.

"We're fine."

"It sho' don't look like y'all fine, especially with how you cradling that lady while she staring off into space."
"Well we are. Can you give us a ride to our car?"
A police siren wails in the distance.
"I don't know, I think I'll let the cops handle it."
Christie sighs and turns her attention to Kathy who has her in a sideways bear hug. Her eyes are jumpy, not believing she hasn't been stabbed by a faceless laughing man.
While the security guard returns to his vehicle, she strokes her perspiring head.
"That's the front, the cops are on their way up," he notified.
But Christie pays him no attention.
"Kathy...You're safe. It's okay," she speaks softly, while rocking her.
Kathy's heart slowly returns to its normal pace, but the throbbing continues. She lets go of Christie and leans against the wall.
"It seemed so real. He was everywhere....When you grabbed me, he came and stabbed me."
"Was it something on the television that scared you? That story about the takeover at the prison, did that have something to do with it?"
Kathy's entire body aches, her head feels like it's been hit by an anvil, her elbows and palms are bleeding, and her shirt is soiled from sliding across the pavement.
She pushes herself up and dusts off.
"It's a lot of things Christie. What did you have in your hand, and why do you keep popping up like this?"
Christie looks shocked.
"Something in my hand? I didn't have anything in my hand. And why do I keep showing up?...What are you trying to insinuate?"
"...................."
"I think you should go to the hospital Kathy. There's something seriously wrong with you."
"No more hospitals."
"You need to, plus you hit that car pretty hard."

"I'm fine...I just wanna go home."
A police cruiser pulls around the corner and parks behind the security vehicle.

After a brief conversation, they're sitting in the backseat.
"Thanks for the lift."
"Sure thing, I hope she's okay," he replied.
"She will be, thanks again."

Once they're driving, Kathy decides she doesn't want to go home.
"Where do you want to go?"
"It doesn't matter, just not there; not right now. I need time to think," watching the windshield wipers clear off the pouring rain.
"I know an excellent place for doing just that. Wanna give it a try?"
"Sure."
Waiting at an intersection, a couple crosses in front of them. The man holds the umbrella in one hand, the other's wrapped around the woman's waist.
"I want to apologize for the way I acted the other day." Christie looking at her.
"No big deal."
Both women ride in silence while in their own world, but both in one very much the same.
"You never told me what you need me to help you with," Kathy said finally.
"That's what I'm thinking about."
"So what is it?"
"...There's someone I'm trying to get out of prison. You have any experience with appeals?"
"Yes."
"Well that's the main thing that I need your help with, kind of lead me in the right direction."
"I'll talk to this guy. He's real good with that kind of stuff. I'll see

what he says, and we'll take it from there."
".....There's something else too."
It's the way she said 'else' that makes Kathy look at her. They're also heading into a remote area. And she knows Christie came towards her in the pharmacy holding something.
"Where are we going?"
"You'll see, it's a surprise."
But the expression on her face doesn't denote that. What can be on a dirt road going through a forest?
"I don't need any more surpri-."
Christie slams on brakes!
Kathy has to brace her hands on the glove box to keep from hitting the dash.
"Sorry about that."
The deer stands for a moment, and scampers into the woods. Kathy sighs.
"My heart can't many more jolts."
Something's slid against her heel.
"Is there something under the seat?"
But before Christie can answer, she sees it.
"Stop the car!!!" and grabs the door handle.
"For what, we're almost there?...... *What are you doing!*"
"Stop the car right now Christie!" and pulls the latch.
But the door won't open!!
"CHRISTIE!"
She swerves over, rocks rumbling under the tires; speechless by Kathy's outburst.
"There's a gun under the seat!"
"It's mines Kathy, oh my freaking God! What's the deal with you?"
Kathy stares into her eyes not knowing what to think.
"Are you okay?"
Then it dawns on her, and she knows exactly what Kathy's thinking.
"I know you don't thi-," cutting her sentence to hang her head.

"Kathy," she starts, in a disappointed tone. "If you're thinking that, we should just end our friendship now. That hurts my feelings Kathy," and proceeds to make a U-turn.

"......Christie I'm sorry, I didn't mean it like that," reaching for her hand. "That's not what I is thinking," she lied. "You don't understand what's been happening to me. My life has turned into a living hell! I'm so frayed out that I can't even get two hours of sleep! I'm always scared, I'm stressed beyond belief, my hands shake constantly! It's not you, it's me! You don't understand!" She breaks into tears.

"Everything's gonna be all right."

"No Christie, it's not! It's not going to be all right!"

"Kathy stop crying."

"I'm seeing things that aren't there. I–I'm losing my mind." She stops the car and embraces Kathy.

She confides in her, and why she was really at the hospital. In turn, Christie informs her about the man in prison, and other anomalous topics.

The surprise destination turns out to be a large pond with a quaint little island in the middle; whose only offerings are a shade tree and a bench, accessible by the canoe tied to the shore. Enjoying the clean air and tranquil landscape, they sit for another hour, sharing secrets and shedding tears. On the way home they stop to get a bite to eat. And by the time she wheels into Kathy's driveway, it's well past eleven.

"Well here you are."

"He's home."

"We talked about that Kathy."

"...Thanks for everything Christie, I needed that," and gives her a hug.

"You're welcome, call me tomorrow."

"All right, you take care."

When she arrives at the front door, Christie blows the horn. Kathy waves and heads inside.

The moment door shuts, she's out, heading for Stockton's truck. After doing something, she's back inside, scribbles something on a notepad, and drives off. She's only traveled three blocks when her cell rings.
"What's up?"
"You forgot to tell me the guy's name."
But Christie hadn't forgot, she deliberately didn't tell her.
"Got a pen?"
"Yes."
"His name is Douglas Parson."
Kathy drops the phone!!!

Chapter 14

The time on his watch reads 3:38 AM; all the nosy citizens are gone. A few news vans remain, but that's it. The flash flood warning has been extended for the entire area, including news of an approaching storm front. The rain continues to pour, sounding like popping kernels as it meets the top of the tent. Stuckey and his top staffers are the only civilians in the command center. After being up for twenty seven hours, his mouse brown suit is crumpled, his thinning hair is in sweaty disarray, he smells, and his temper is shorter than an ant's dick. The relentless media harassment, and rumblings of impending prosecution have done a job on him.

Yates battered him too, telling the press he's disappointed and embarrassed with the way Gordon's been running the prison; so he's understandably glad there's finally about to be an end to this mess. After two more guards were killed, the decision was made to go in.

"Does anyone have any questions?" asked the squad commander. No one says a thing.

"Well let's get this show on the road."

The armed team exits the tent.

Too bad Gordon and his cronies have to remain there until it's over. He was looking forward to seeing the inmates die.

Outside, the team heads into the woods, and emerges behind the recreation yard. Gale force winds has the temporary structure whipping like a cat o' nine tails. A thunderous lighting strike shakes the ground, illuminating the sprawling compound with white light. Being the two razor wire fences have already been cut, they'll have a straight shot to the side of the building. The team double checks their weapons and energizes their night vision goggles.

"All equipment check?"

"Check!"

Parson sits in his cell, bothered by the fact no one's in the tower, and all the lights are off. On top of that, the negotiator hasn't called since the men decided they wanted to kill more hostages, because no food and water was supplied. After that, order was lost; every man for himself. Inmates turned on each other, gang rapes ensured, defecations on the floor. The idea that setting fire to a mattresses would trigger the sprinkler system, in turn re-activating the faucets, didn't work; only flooded the cell house with fire retardant polluted water. Turds, clothes, trash, and everything else with enough buoyancy, became afloat—corpses lay stranded in the murky water like stricken vessels. The nonstop drips falling from the sprinklers has eroded the men's sanity, proving true a Chinese method of torture. The surviving hostages remain locked in cells; still naked, and still cold. No one cares to man to windows, or conduct periodic checks of the yard anymore. They're no longer concerned about them running in on them, many of which welcome an end to the standoff; an end to their lives.

Parson sits in his boots and boxers wondering how long it'll be before all hell breaks loose. The sound of an inmate sloshing through water echoes through the shambolic cell-house.

"Heeeey!" the man yells. "Who turned off the fuckin' lig-"

A mind numbing explosion blows the mattresses to shreds, lighting the building up like a fireworks exhibition! Bursts of machine gun fire blasts at will, water splashes like a tsunami—the acrid smell of gunpowder claims the air. Like a band of bloodthirsty outlaws, screaming prisoners stampede out of their cells wielding shanks, batons, sharpened broomsticks, and shards of glass! The building reverbs, and war cries trumpet, as the HR squad mercilessly mows them down—a showcase of death, taking lives stripped of their worth.

Grainger's still in a state of shock when the 7 a.m. newscast starts. Word that the hostages have been rescued, and the stand-off is over is the top story. As a result, nineteen inmates, three men from the rescue team, and seven correctional officers are dead. Thirty one other inmates, and ten guards are seriously injured. The takeover is deemed the worst in American history; trumping the infamous Attica riot of the '70s. A clip captures the destruction inside the cell-house. The walls are riddled with bullet holes, spent shell casings, and blood stains. Red splotched mattresses, crude weapons, inmate uniforms, black fatigues, and garbage of every kind is scattered across the wet floor. Both televisions are destroyed, and the cells are open and empty. The screen is switched to footage of Gordon slamming his office door on a group of boisterous reporters. Then it's Yates' turn to speak to the press. When the 7:30 broadcast begins, Matt's heard enough.

He fingers the call button.

"What is it Grainger?"

"When am I going to be allowed my visit?"

"Visitation's canceled."

"So you're saying I'm not going to get my last visit!" angrily.

"It's quite possible, sorry Grainger."

"That's crap, is there any way I can speak to him? They gotta give me my last visit!"

"With all that's going on, I doubt it. But I'm sure he doesn't have the time."

"Screw his time! I have less than twelve hours to live, and I wanna see my son!" Matt shouts, his mouth inches from the speaker.

"Calm down, let me see what I can do."

"All right."

Matt goes over to the desk, and grabs the fifty four page letter he wrote for Jason.

"And now they talking about I'm not going to see you."

The one he wrote for Parson is beside it.

"You said I'd know when it happens. You got those cowards

didn't you Doug."

Matt wants to push the button again and ask if he's still alive, but knows the CO won't tell him.

He sits down and picks up his pictures. Flipping through, he takes out the one of his parents, and the one of Jason in the Camaro. The rest go inside with the letter; seals it, and neatly writes Jason's name.

"Grainger."

"Yeah," he said, walking to the speaker.

"The deputy warden says it's off."

Matt smacks the bars.

"What does he mean it's off! I'm supposed to be granted one last visit, and I want it!"

"It's over my head. There's nothing I can do. And besides, like you said, you'll be dead in a day anyway, so what does it matter."

"What!"

He throws the remote at the TV.

"What does it matter! You!....You! fucking sonofabitch!"

"Tell Satan I said hello."

The goes intercom silent.

"BAAAAAAAAAASTAAAAAAARD!!!!"

And slings his boot at the television, cracking the screen.

Breathing heavily, he looks around the cell for something else. Snatching the sheet off his bed, he stuffs it down the commode, and repeatedly flushes it until water starts running onto the floor.

A minute later it stops, shut off by the guard.

Infuriated further, he pounds the bed.

"Is that how you did your wife?" comes a taunting voice from the speaker.

"Stick this up your ass!" shooting a bird at the camera.

"You do it. Go on and get yourself off for the last time."

Matt grits his teeth, scowling at the globe in the ceiling.

"Leave...Me...*Alone!*"

"Now when your wife told you that, you didn't respect her wishes. All she wanted to do was finish gettin' her nut."

"Leave me alone!" and covers his ears.

Grainger fights the urge to cry, but he badly wants to release the pain.

The compassionless guard increases the volume.

"CAN YOU HEAR ME NOW!"

Grainger smashes his ears.

"Welcome toooo heeeeeell!!"

The devil is standing over him. Images of blazing fire, and people screaming as they're thrown into a lake of molten lead brutalize his mind.

The officer is laughing hysterically.

"You're such a pussy Grainger."

Matt gets up and washes the dried tears. Standing in the mirror, he recalls his mother's wisdom, and goes to his bed to say a prayer.

After finishing, he goes to the wall, and looks at the many names, and last messages from the hundreds of men who've been in this cell. Some are words of encouragement, some are about the things they'd done, some are confessions, and others tell of how they passed time—the drawings are sheer works of art: Portraits of families and friends, themselves, angels with open arms, scenes from nature, and passages from holy texts. Beside the mirror is a list of names.

"Sign here if you're innocent...."

Matt reads the names again, amazed that seventy seven men claim to have been wrongly convicted; some dating back to the 60's. To the right of the message is a life sized hand drawn to match with the right one.

"Put your right hand here, and the other over your heart, and repeat these words aloud:...I swear to God, and myself, that I did not commit the crime that I'm about to die for.....Amen."

He retrieves a pencil from underneath his mattress, finds a place on the wall, and speaking aloud writes: "I am Matthew Edward

Grainger, and I am guilty. Hopefully God has forgiven me for my sins."

NOFTWA's office is buzzing with activity, as last-minute preparations are being made. Yates confirmed the execution will not be postponed due to the takeover. Sivan is sitting at her desk going over a list when Deborah communicates she has a call from Orson Webbthorton on line eight.

"Thanks," and presses the blinking button.

"Sivan Goldstein."

"Herlo miss Goldstun," greeted a man who sounds to be from the deepest part of Dixie.

"Gold-stein," she corrected.

"Oh, Ahm sarra,"

"Happens all the time. How can I help you?"

"We spoke wernce bafour, bout couple weeks ago. Ahm da guy dat werked at Gordon's farm, member?"

She thinks a moment.

"Yes, yes! Mr. Webbthorton. I apologize for not recognizing your voice. How've you been?"

"Perty gud, ha bout yerself?"

"Just working as always, trying to get everything set up for the rally. You're still coming right?"

"Wheel dats whut I cawled tuh tail yuh bout. Suh-hums cum up, anna don't thank ahm gone be able tuh mike it.

Sivan sighs.

"Are you sure it can't wait?"

"Yeah ahm shur. Ma boy over in Bama done fell of his trackter ahn got hurt reel bad; juss harpin dis mernin'. An muh plane leaves in an are. I reely ahm sarra fur not bean able tuh mike it. Baleave me, if it's sum udder why, I wud do it. But dats ma only boy, ahn I gotta be dere fur'em."

"It's okay, I understand. I know how it is when they need you."

"If ah get bike in tom, all be sur da give yuh ah cawl."

"That's a deal, let me give you my cell number."

After giving it to him she says: "You call me if you get back before six all right?"

"Oh-kay."

She says goodbye and hangs up.

Leaning back in her chair massaging her temples, Grainger's on her mind. It's something about him, he's different from the other cases she's dealt with. Out of all the men she's been able to free from death row, he's undoubtedly the one that hurts the most to lose.

The ringer for her personal line startles her. Leaning forward she looks at the number.

"Harry! Are you okay?"

He tells her he is.

"I've been worried sick about you."

He spends a few minutes explaining that he wasn't the one they wanted revenge on, and will tell her more later; he has some things to take care of and will see her at five.

"Well, see you then. I'm so glad you're okay."

Sivan dials the number she got from her contact at the phone company.

"Yeah?"

She grins at the thought of him sitting in his office pouting over a bottle.

"...Who is this!"

"Good afternoon Gordon."

"...Who the hell is this?"

She almost makes up a name.

"This is Sivan."

"......I don't know no Seevan."

"Goldstein."

Moments pass.

"How da hell you get my number!"

"You gave it to me."

He's quiet.

"....Bowlshit. You ain't get it from me, and you bet not c-"

"I have a proposition for you. I think it will be in your best inter-est to hear me out."

She can hear him breathing on the other end.

"This bet not be one of your games lady!"

"I assure you Gordon, it's not a game. But what matters is are you willing to play?"

The question has a sneaky undertone to it. He wants to hear more.

"Why would you wanna do anything for me?"

"Let's just say I thought a few things over, and came to the real-ization that we can do better as partners than enemies."

"What does it havetuh do wit?"

"I saw you on television this morning, and heard about all the trouble you've got your-"

"I ain't d-.."

"Be quiet Gordon! And don't interrupt me again! If you hold your horses, you won't have to tell *me,* or anyone else what you *ain't* done...Now as I was saying, you've gotten yourself into some trouble, and quite frankly, your chances at governor are over unless you're willing to accept what I have to offer."

As bad as he hates to admit, he's sinking and almost sunken.

He downs the rest of his whiskey.

"It depends on what it's."

"You'll be surprised at how simple it's," thinking how incredibly stupid he is for agreeing to bribed over the phone.

"You remember my last visit?"

"Yeah"

"Well here it is."
She gives him the proposition.

"Deal!" he quickly agreed. "But there's one thing I want."
"What?"
He gives her his requirement.

And hits the 'End Call' button on his cellular, and pours another drink. After guzzling it down, he slams the glass on the desk, snatches the telephone up, punches in four digits, and waits for Higgins.
"Start gettin' things ready. We gotta chicken tuh fry."

"Where am I?"
"It's so dark...."
"I can't see anything...."
"I think I'm lying down?…"
"Yeah, I am....."
"I'm lying on something hard?.......It feels like wood or something?......But really, I don't know what it is?....."
"I'm getting off this thing, it's hurting my back."
"Ouch!.....I bumped my head, I can only sit up half way???"
"What is this??????... I'm....I'm in some sort of..box??"
"A box!..How did I get in a box? What am I doing in here??
"Uhuuah, it stinks!.. Oh my God, what's that awful smell!!!... Yuck!!"
*"Heeeeeeeeey!!!......*Somebody get me out of here!!!!"

BANG!
BANG!
BANG!
"Stuckey locked me in here? I bet it was him!
"AAAAAAAAAAAAAAAAAAAA!!....SOMEBODY HELP ME!"
".........I hear something?"
"It sounds like crying?......*It is!*..More than one person!......"
"It's a lot of people crying? Where are they? Why do I hear them but can't see them......."
"This is strange..."
"HEEEEEEEEEEEEEEEEEELP!!!!"
"There's screaming now! Their screaming so loud!!"
"Something must be happening to them?? There in pain!"
"Something's hurting them!"
BANG-BANG-BANG-BANG-BANG-BANG-BANG!!!!!!!!
"HEEEEEEEEEEEELP!!!!.HEEEEEEEEEEEEELP!!!
AAAAAAAAAAAAAAAAAAAAAAAA!!!!."
"Am I dead???..*I'M DEAD!!!????.....Oh dear God I'm dead!!!!...*"
"*No,no*, I'm not dead!!............Gordon's playing a trick on me!!!...
Because if I was dead, I wouldn't be able to feel my heart beating, and I wouldn't be so scared?"
"Thank you Lord! I'm still alive!!!........."
"But......*I CANT FEEL MY BODY!!!!!...I CANT FEEL MY FACE!!!!......"*
BOOM!!!!
"What's happening???....."
BOOM!!!!
"What's that!!..Who's?.."
"Someone's moving me, I can hear them talking!!"
"They're going to let me out!....*Oh thank God!!* Gordon's going to let me out of this thing! This is horrible!! I don't ever want to be put back in here!!"
THUD!!!
"*Ouch!.*.They dropped me?"
"...Now I'm moving again???

"AAAAAAAAAAAAAAAAAAAAAAAAAAA!!! I'M FALLING!!!"
BOOM!!!
KERBLAM!!!
THUD!!!!!
"...........Oooooooooh my head!!! I think it's cracked???......."
"I CANT FEEL MY HEAD!!!!......I HAVE NO HEAD!!!"
"Something's happening!"
"The box is open!!!!......................
I'm out!!!.....The screams are gone?"
"WHERE'S MY HEAD? WHERE'S MY BODY!!"
"Something's blowing??? *BUT IT'S HOT!!!* It's hot air blowing It's blowing from under me! Oh my lord!!!I'm on a bridge?.................
THERE'S FIRE UNDER ME!!! I CAN HEAR IT BLAZING UNDER ME!!! I CAN SEE IT!!! AS FAR AS I CAN SEE IS FIRE!!! THE-THE-TH BRIDGE IS MOVING!!! IT'S CRUMBLING!!!...IT'S CRUMBLING!!! NOOOOOOOOOO!!! NOOOOOOOOOOOO!..I'M GOING TO FALL INTO THE FIRE!!! THE SCREAMS, I HEAR THEM AGAIN!!!.AAAAAA AAAAAAAAAAAAAAAAAAAAAAAAAAAAAAAAAAA!!!!!!!!!! I'M IN THE FIRE!!!!I'M IN THE FIRE!!!I'M BURNING, I'M BUR-NIIIIIIIIING!!!!"

WHAM!!!!
Heavy breathing!!!
A plastic cup bounces across the floor!!
Grainger opens his eyes to a blurry ceiling! Extremely disoriented, his heart is trying to burst out of his chest, and his entire body is soaked! He can't swallow, and his mouth feels like a barren desert.
How'd he get on the floor?
He sees the cracked television with his boot on the floor beside it.
Dear Lord that was horrible!
Realizing he must've just fallen off the bed, he pushes himself of the floor, and washes his face. Patting the throbbing knot on the

back of his head, he looks at the mirror, and sees lines from the blanket crisscrossing his cheek. Upon further inspection he discovers a cut under his neck that's crusted with blood. His heart's just beginning to return to its normal cadence when he's startled by the sound of a slamming door.
"Get ready for your final visit."

Grainger has returned to his cell, and the tears won't stop. The entire facility is on lock down, and he's the man of the hour. Though he's presently alive, he's already experiencing the cessation of his mobility; he collapsed on the way back, and had to be rolled on a stretcher. And due to security protocols, he wasn't able to give Jason the letter.

They've already returned.

"Beautiful day ain't it?" Stuckey, holding a plate of steak and potatoes, with a devilish grin.
"I don't want it."
"Why not? They say you should always eat before a long journey."
"I don't want it okay."
"Well I guess I'll go back up front and give it to your boy, he looks pretty hungry, specially since he came all this way to see his paw die."
"You're gonna rot in hell Gordon."

"But not before you," laughing. "Now here, take your food,"
and shoves the tray through the slot, spattering it over the floor.
"It'll taste better if you eat it that way; animals don't use plates."
Matt grabs the 16 oz. T-bone, and chucks it at him—narrowly
missing his face as it smacks the wall.
"*Heeeeey,* that ain't nice. Is dat how you show yer appreciation
for me deliverin' you such a wonderful supper?"
"I wish they would've got you too!"
"Well they didn't. But now I'm boutuh to get you," rubbing his
palms together.
"Get away from me!" Matt shouts, and quickly throws the po-
tato, catching him in the shoulder as he attempted to dodge it.
"You fuckin' dip shit!"
Gordon unzips his pants.
"I got somethin' fer you tuh take witcha....I call it dick colonge."
And tries to urinate on him though the bars him.
Matt leaps to the rear of the cell while Stuckey urinates—all over
the floor, walls, and on the food. Then turns sideways and shoots
some on the mattress.
"Be sure not-tuh use too much. You don't wanna over do it."
And walks away zipping up.
Halfway down the hall, he yells back.
"Be ready in an hour cuz we startn early! You never wanna be
lass to a barbecue!"

The time is 5 p.m. when the rally kicks off. Evidently, the inhu-
mane treatment the inmates have suffered drew extra attention,

because people are showing up in droves—news vans, reporters, and police are near the entrance. The lot is packed with cars, trucks, and buses; colleges students, human rights organizations, ex-prisoners, families of current prisoners, senior citizens, and countless others are present to protest capital punishment. Alice and her three busloads of church members, the pastor, choir dressed in canary robes, employees, relatives, and friends are walking toward the stage NOFTWA erected. Police barricades surround the lobby so witnesses won't be assaulted as they go inside to view the execution.

Sivan stands behind the podium shouting like the leader of a fanatical movement, Harry and several others sit in folding chairs behind her. The twenty three-hundred plus crowd cheers and applauds as she gives a gripping speech about America's love of the death penalty, and how carelessly it hands it down; even exercising it on the mentally ill. Yates' former accountant explains how he accepted hundreds of thousands of dollars in bribes from businessman, nursing home directors, farmers, state and private university presidents, hospitals directors, government officials, wardens, politicians, and even kingpins—for preferential treatment. After she's finished exposing the governor's unsavory business practices, Harry, Alice's pastor, and a few others speak, but are interrupted by a scuffle between a prison guard, and a young woman who claims he pushed her, so she hit with the wooden pole of her '*State Sponsored Murder*' sign.

After the angry crowd calms, Sivan is back on the mic.

"I have a special guest I'd like to introduce," and hands the microphone to the young man.

"My name is Jason Grainger, Matthew Edward Grainger is my dad; and I have be permanently scarred by his absence. My mother never worked a single day the entire fifteen years she was married to him, but had the finest of clothes, cars, jewelry, and home to live. But above all, she had the finest example of a human being for a husband; he sometimes worked eighty hours a week to provide for us. My father is a kind, gentle, and loving man; a man and a father in every sense of the word. Every weekend that he wasn't working, he'd take us on family trips. We used to go to all kinds of places: camping trips to the mountains, everything. He did things like: Go to PTA meetings, made sure I had lunch money, bandaged my knee after I fell off my skateboard, made sure I had regular checkups, and dentist appointments, ran away the monster I thought is in my closet, and cooked for us. I remember the night the furnace went out, and he got up at two in the morning to chop wood in the freezing cold so we could stay warm. Or the time all we were coming out of the grocery store, and a woman with a child asked for some money so she could buy food for her family. He took her in the store and bought her four bags food, then paid for a taxi because she didn't have a car."

Jason pauses to hang his head, and wipe a tear from his eye.

"I want to tell all those people who think my dad is some kind of monster or psycho; he's not! He just made a mistake, and I love him for how he treated me.......And I hate my mom for doing this to us!"

And walks off the stage heading for the building.

The crowd riotously cheer and applaud.

Sivan gives an overview regarding the unconstitutional way of which Grainger was convicted.

After she's finished, the choir moves towards the stage, and the lighting of white candles begin.

Chapter 15

Matt sits on the bed holding the letter, staring at the same passage on the wall. His face is clean shaven, mustache neatly trimmed, hair combed and parted in the same fashion his father wore his.
After cleaning up the urine, he asked God to forgive Gordon for being so evil.
The prison boots he's worn for over a decade shine with six coats of polish; his two favorite photos are in his pocket.

The sound of dragging chains let him know it's time.

Stuckey, Higgins, Boyd Nelson, Chaplain King, Captain Starns,

Lieutenant Salvatore, and eight CERTs stand before his cell.

"Well Grainger," Gordon smiling. "On your feet."

While the door slides open, Matt realizes this is the last time he ever has to hear that sound.

"Hands on the wall!"

Starns pats him down.

"Turn around and take one step forward," he instructed, and pulls milk crate full of chains inside the cell.

Matt is chained and shackled in every imaginable way.

"What's that for?" Stuckey referring to the envelope on the bed.

"I'd like to get this to my son Jason, he's waiting in the observation booth. This is the only the request I ask of you sir...Please."

"Fair enough, you have my word. I'll see to it that he gets it."

"Thank you sir."

"Okay, let's go," and grabs the envelope.

Grainger baby steps into the hallway.

Eeeeent!

Buzzed the lock, as Starnes pushes the heavy steel door open.

The convoy heads down a short hallway where Grainger passes a barred window overlooking the yard he's spent many years pacing around.

Eeeeent!

Buzzed another door, opened by a CERT, leading to a long, window-less corridor. Four CERTs, Higgins, Nelson, and Gordon are in front. Starnes, Salvo, the chaplain, and four CERTs bring up the rear.

With each step he musters, the chains clank with tormenting cadence.

The closer he gets to the red door, the faster his heart pounds!

"Though I walk through the shadows in the valley of death, I shall fear no evil. For the Lord is with me. Thy rod and thy staff, they

comfort me. Thou prepareth a table before me in the presence of thine enemies. Thou anointed my head with oil, my cup runneth over. Surely goodness and mercy shall follow me, and I will dwell in the house of the Lord forever.............."

By the third silent reciting of the prayer, he's standing before it.

"You know there's a thousand people out in the parkin' lot rallyin' for ya, they even got ole Fawell out dere wit em. Don't dat make yuh feel special?"
"Yes sir it does."
"Well I'm glad, but it ain't gone stop nothin'!"
Gordon radios main control.
Eeeeent!
He pulls it open.

Matthew's heart sinks!!!

It's cold and white; people are looking at him through the observation window.

Jason!!!

He's turned around while the chains are taken off. Another CERT unfastens the leather straps that will bind him to the chair.
Slowly, he spins, as two CERTs guide him back into the seat.

They imprison him to the wood......

While memories rush through his mind, his heart punches with thunderous strokes!

Jason raises his right hand, and pledges allegiance to his father for the last time.

After the belts around his wrists, forearms, waste, chest, biceps, ankles, knees, thighs, and neck are double checked; Gordon walks to the wall, and turns the intercom on so the audience can hear.

"Matthew Edward Grainger," in a loud and clear voice. "You were found guilty of the brutal murder of Nancine Grainger, and Jeremy Springfield. For your punishment, the state of Georgia sentenced you to death. On this day, the court imposed punishment shall be carried out....Do you have any last words?"

The observers can't see Gordon's face because his back is turned. If they could, they'd see him smiling.

"I do....I'd like to say I'm sorry. I'm really sorry for the mistake I made that night....I took two people's lives, and for that I am truly sorry.....And to my son-"

"You bastard, you ain't sorry!" screamed a lady on the front pew. "You ain't sorry for killing my nephew! I hate you-I hate you-I hate you!!"

Before the man she's with sits her back down.

Matt tries his best to hold back the tears.

"And to my son Ja-"

"That ain't your son I said! He ain't yeers!" jumping up again.

"Ma'am I know it's difficult," Stuckey begins. "I know how much pain you're in. But don't let this monster see that you are hurting. And please, remain respectful of our other guests."

"I apologize warden. But not to *that!*...And I don't have anything else to say to that *MURDERER!*"

"I have something to say," Jason stepping to the glass and placing his palm against it.

"He *is* my dad. And I *am* his son—no matter what anybody says..And I love him...I'll always remember you dad. I'll never forget the fishing trips," he cried.

Matt sees the tears rolling down his face.

"I'll always remember what you did for me. I'll never forget you," and holds up the picture of him as a little boy with the tiny fish hanging from the rod.

"I'll see you in heaven dad."
"................" Matthew can't even speak.
"Is there anyone else?" Stuckey anxious to get things underway.
"Okay then....Matthew Edward Grainger, your face will now be covered, and a metal device placed atop yer head."

I will not be afraid!!!!!
I will not be afraid!!!!!....
The Lord is with me!!!!..........I WILL NOT BE AFRAID!!!!.

"WAIT!" finding his voice just as the hood is about to be pulled over his face.
"Jason...We'll meet again."

Are his last words.

The hood comes down, and it's impossible to see; it stinks something awful—his heart is beating five times its normal rate! He starts hyperventilating, the belts squeeze without mercy!
"Yuh boy just ran out da room cryin' like a *bitch!*....Get ready asshole!"

I will not be afraid!!

Scenes from his childhood shoot past!
His mom!
His dad!
His childhood pet!
His sister!
Their house!
His high school graduation!
The woman he loved!

2,500 VOLTS OF WHITE HOT PAIN!!!
"*AAAAAAAAAAAAAAAA---*" the volcanic explosion of current

clamps his mouth shut!
His eyes roll backward, he can taste the electricity cooking his tongue! Superheated blood burbles forth from his nose; his entire body bucks and convulses like a demented Bronco!

SECOND CHARGE!!!!1,000 VOLTS!!

The belts pop and stretch, the electricity unpityingly slams his body like a ragdoll; his roasting head shakes hideously in every direction!
He hears his skin sizzling.
Blood comes out of his ears, as the drums are fried to a crisp; his teeth crack like thin ice, and his gums becomes hard as stone. One by one, they dribble from his mouth like forlorn Chicklets®.

The irate woman covers her mouth in shock!

It's feels as if his skin is being raked from his flesh, while simultaneously drenched in acid.

THIRD CHARGE!!!!! 1,000 VOLTS!!!

Finally, his heart overloaded by the alternating current ripping through its ventricles, bursts like a microwaved grapefruit—his brain rendered to papier mache'.
Beet red, and severely blistered, the molten brass courses through his veins until his muscles are mush. Well done, his tongue is hard as a brick, his hair brittle as burnt paper.

The dance of death is complete.

Under the hood his eyes hang like weary pendulums from there sockets. Grainger's smoking corpse scents the room, the once screaming woman lay unconscious on the floor.

Gordon reneged on his promise to deliver Jason the envelope. Later that night, it's reduced to ashes.

Chapter 16

*T*oday is the second consecutive day Kathy's missed from work. Finding out Douglas Parson is the man Christie wants her to help is more shocking than the tape, *and* the stalker lady put together. Christie's called repeatedly, and even came by, but she's too disturbed to answer.

How can they both be connected to the same person; and to him of all people. With all the things Christie's claimed to have done, and with all the things she's done; you'd think they would've crossed paths before.

Why'd he involve another person without telling her? How much does Christie know? Maybe she's up to something else; he's never spoken of her before. Maybe he purposely didn't mention it?

Things aren't adding up. The mystery about why she broke into tears, and jumped from her vehicle now has new meaning. Was it all an act? And the woman at the theater, could she be that woman? From their conversation, she knows Christie isn't above disguises. But that still leads to the same unanswered question: why? What reason would she have to follow her, and dust Stockton's truck for fingerprints? And how did she so conveniently appear beside her car in traffic that morning? There's too many unanswered questions. No matter how much she doesn't want to, she'll have to speak to Christie.

Maybe she'll answer the phone the next time she calls. But since she's sitting in her car in the parking lot of a drugstore, it'll have to wait.

Kathy opens the two pill bottles, and shakes one from each. After washing them down with flat cola, she opens the door, and upon seeing the beauty supply store realizes she needs a few items. Before detouring for the store, she makes a scan of the lot for stalkers.

The door opens with a chime, alerting the Korean woman behind the counter to the presence of a customer—she waves as Kathy heads to the back of the store. After a quick walk down the aisle, she has what she needs.

"How are you today?" asked the short woman, as she rings up the items.

"I'm living."

After paying, she goes back out the same way she came, and is almost ran over by a man running by! He avoids colliding with a couple exiting an erotic toy store, and disappears around the corner!

Now she's really on edge.

Hurrying to her car, she thinks she sees Stockton's truck across the street, but can't be sure as it pulls away when the light changes. But thinking of her previous hallucinations, she lacks con-

fidence in her perception. Before opening the door she makes
another look around the area.

That car wasn't there before.

Keeping her eye on it, she gets inside and sits on something
hard.
She knows exactly what it is.
She jumps out and spins around!
Combing the area, the only people she sees is the couple getting
in their van.
"Leave me alone!"
The shout draws the attention of several guys in front of a liquor
store.
Kathy stands feet from the flung open car door, holding a brown
paper bag in the middle of the parking lot looking mean.
One of the men across the street yells that he has something she
can do to earn some wine money, and laughs.
Considering the way she's dressed and acting, it's easy to see how
she's being mistaken for a drunk. She's standing in the middle of
parking lot yelling for no apparent reason.
Kathy ignores them, snatches the tape off the seat, and slings it
as far as she can.
"I don't want this!" drawing more stares and laughter.
Finally, she gets in her car and peels off.

The black car eases out after her.

Traffic on Boulevard is bumper-to-bumper, normal for this area,
even on a Tuesday night. Numerous sports bars, nightclubs, and
restaurants are hosting their usual activities for those who don't
want to wait until the weekend to get their party on; the adult
entertainment lounge attracts a crowd no matter what day it is.
Kathy sits at the light fuming, while bass from the SUV beside
her shakes her windows. It's then that she notices the strange

sound coming from her speakers, and before she can react, sub-tle piano melodies fill the cabin.

There's a CD spinning inside the player?

Confused, she sits there until a horn rescues her from her trance. The light has changed, and people are looking strangely as they go around. But she still doesn't move—gets flipped off by an agitated granny.

The tail not wanting to be spotted, pulls in with a line of other vehicles, and watches the Camry sit in the street.

Oblivious, she's fixated on the CD player.

From behind the piano melodies comes the same type of whispering that she encountered on the tape. But this time, it's several whispers speaking at once. They're so jumbled she's having trouble making out what they're saying.

A man appears at her window asking is she okay. But she's too preoccupied to acknowledge his presence.

He walks away dialing into a smartphone.

The whispers get louder, and seconds later, drop to where she can barely hear them; all the while staying in perfect harmony with the composition.

> *"…This my whisper-whisper-whisper-whisper……*
> *Listen to my whisper…..Listen……Listen*
> *carefully……..Enjoy our ballad…But listen!"*

The music grows angry, the keys banged with reckless abandon!

> *No Please! Please don't!……I'm sorry!!"*

It's the unmistakable voice of a terrified woman—the overture chants with sinister intentions.
Screeching tires!!!
A car almost rear-ending her frees her from the spell.
She pulls into a gas station.

The tail casually slips off the busy street, and into the gas station too.

The whispers lower, and children cry for their mommy and daddy not to be hurt. The music dictates the coming event, as it exhibits even more annoyance, the choir whispers louder and faster; the volume setting has no bearing on the level.
The rear view mirror vibrates.
BOOM!!!
The gun blast quiets the choir, the piano returns to its normal tempo.
"AAAAAAAAAAAAAA!!!"

Screams become bloodcurdling, hairs on the back of Kathy's neck stand on end, a trail of sweat runs down her side!!

The woman's erratic breathing becomes more defined, the microphone is being held to her mouth.
Sniffles.

> *"......Listen to their pain...Listen to their anguish.*
> *But what about the pain they caused?"*
> *".....I've never seen that before.........Please no more!"*

The choir returns, angry and intense, the whispers clamorous and swift—the piano is being abused!
Kathy holds her breath!

BOOM!!
The woman is muted, the children go into a fit of horror!
The music displays its unapologetic rage..............

Silence!

> *"This is the arrival of the hour, that of which you knew not...
> You will all bear the fruit of his deeds."*

BOOM!!

Like a cunning wolf, the piano creeps back into the fray; whispers slink in the backdrop.

Kathy's frozen to the seat, unable to discern what's real and what's manufactured!

Instruments materialize, they're quiet at first: Snare and bass drums, French horns, trombones, violins and cellos, cymbals and xylophones—they too become wicked! The piano bullies its way to the height of the heap; assaulting and pissed off!

Kathy's trembling finger fights for the eject button.

BOOM!
BOOM!
BOOM!
BOOM!
BOOM!
BOOM!

The disc player shrikes like nails on a chalkboard, and the disc shoots out on the floor!!!

"What have I done to deserve this," she sobs. "*What?...*"

And bangs her fist against into the dashboard.

"Why are you doing this to me!!!" and throws it out of the window.

Kathy slams the car in gear, and stomps the accelerator!

The V6 reacting accordingly, lunges forward, spinning the front tires!

Yanking the wheel left, she sends the Camry sideways, narrowly missing a person walking to a pump. Biting her bottom lip with tears in her eyes, the car jumps the curb; slick grass causing the car to skid left, then right!

BANG!

Goes the steel frame, coming off the other curb, and into on-coming traffic!

Headlights swerve, and horns blare, as vehicles part around her. With her hands positioned at 10 and 2, she jerks the car to the right at the intersection, flying past a police cruiser doing 45 up the wrong side of the road. Another snatch and she's back on the correct side. Weaving in and out of traffic, Kathy doesn't give a damn about being pursued by a cop! Jumping the median, she challenges an 18-wheeler to a duel.

"COME ON!..COME ON!"

The truck vigorously flashes its high beams and blows the air horn; the engines Jake brake sounds like rapid fire!

At the last second, the skilled operator slings the big rig off the road.

Flooded with adrenaline, she gives the engine more gas, and rounds a curve doing 30 over the speed limit.

A police car is blocking the road.

Thinking she's about to careen into him, the officer leaps from the car, and dives for the pavement!

Kathy bounces the sedan back over the median, side-swiping a Volvo® station wagon.

Like a veteran Formula One driver, she dips in behind one car, and out around the other; cutting off a cop trying to block her from getting on the expressway. She zooms down the on ramp, and by the time she merges into traffic, she's doing well over 90. But has to slam on brakes, and rumble through the shoulder to avoid a slow-moving car hauler.

Another swerve and she's back on the highway, leaving pebbles and bits of glass in her wake.

She glances over her shoulder and sees a sea of flashing lights, which only add to her rage, encouraging her to tempt fate. Recollections of Stockton beating her, and images of Douglas being executed bring more tears to her eyes; visions of Christie trying to kill her plays tricks on her sight.

The faceless laughing man appears!

With no regard for safety, she wheels the car left onto the exit ramp; determined to make the light before it turns red.

But it does.

She's seated at a crap table with God and the Devil. In her hands are two red dice, floating above the table is her soul.

She throws them!

As if it's happening in slow motion, tilted on two wheels, the Camry skids sideways! Smelling burning rubber, she hears horns and blaring sirens.

While the dice flip, Satan takes shape in the passenger seat.

Ready to die, she lets the violently shaking wheel go—jerked in an unknown direction, centrifugal force throws her into the passenger door! Shattering glass bedazzles the cloth confines as the car bounces like a fractured piston, and goes airborne!

One dice is 2 skulls, the other 5 bones.

Now there's only darkness.

Tap!
Tap!
Tap!
"Get up inmate."
Parson gets up and looks through the tray hatch.
"For what?"
"Don't ask any questions. Just turn around and put your hands behind your back," said a man in business attire, a brass shield clipped to his belt.
Four CERT's, and another similarly dressed man accompany him.
Parson stands and allows the guard to cuff his wrists through the hatch.
"Tower, open J-twenty-six."
The seven foot hunk of steel slides open.
The CERTs enter first, followed by the suits.
"We're from the GBI, and are here to inform you of the new charges brought against you."
"What kind of charges?"
"Charges stemming from the riot you incited that cost twenty-nine people to lose their lives, and another forty-one to be in-

jured."

"I didn't incite the riot, the warden did."

"Well according to him," and flips open the thick manila folder he's holding.

"You started it by head butting one officer, breaking his nose. Then broke another's nose, and ruptured his liver when you kicked him in the stomach."

"Hold it right there. All of that's true except the part about me kicking him in the stomach. He had his men beat me up, and hog-tie me, and throw me on a table naked. After they cut me loose, that's when I kicked his feet from under him, and he fell off the table into the wall. I never touched his stomach."

"Well it's all the same, it's all assault: Two aggravated and one simple, plus the incitement charge. Once we get enough evidence to nail you with the murders of.....," looking back at the form again. "Gus Beasley and Trent Chesterwell, you'll be charged with those too. The warden is adamant you killed them, and several of the hostages as well."

"Well since you're on a mission to discover who did what, what are you charging the warden with? Off the top of my head, I can think of two murders he never reported and buried with no investigation. Not to mention the ones that *were* reported, of which the CERT team beat to death. I'm sure you're looking into those too?"

"We're aware of the things that have been taking place here. And those responsible will be prosecuted; whether it be the warden or whoever. Now as I stated before, you've been charged with the-"

"I heard you the first time."

The detective doesn't like the interruption.

"And something else if I may: What more can these charges do than what I already have?"

"You're right Mr. Parson, there isn't anything more that we can do. But it's our job to investigate crimes, no matter what the situation is."

"The staff have been committing crimes here for years, you must've been on vacation then."

"We can only prosecute what we're aware of, and unfortunately, we didn't find out until recently that there's been violations here. And that's the last I'll say about anything that doesn't pertain to the subject at hand."

"I see."

"We're told you're a leader amongst the inmates, can you tell us what reason will any would have to kill Beasley and Chesterwell; since you say it's not you?" asked the other agent.

"No."

"I find that hard to believe Mr. Parsons."

"Parson. No s."

"As I was saying, I find it hard to believe that someone who's been on death row as long as you have wouldn't know about all that goes on."

"Believe it."

"We've been told you and Beasley we're enemies."

"Bitter."

"Were you happy when he was killed?"

"Didn't matter one way or another."

"What about Chesterwell?"

"What about an introduction?"

The agent looks confused.

"Your name, what is it?"

"Morales."

"Ah, like the Bolivian socialist."

"....So?"

"Didn't matter."

"Didn't matter what?"

"Didn't matter to your question."

"......Mr. Parson, what are you talking about?"

"Never mind."

"So are you going to answer my question?"

"I did."

Morales sighs.

"You're definitely not like the Bolivian socialist, you're kind of dumb."

The agent's expression is priceless.

"....Had any of the officers killed during the riot ever assault you?"

"I don't know which ones were killed."

"Okay," he inhales. "Let me put it this way, did you see any of the guards that allegedly assaulted you in the building that day?"

"Yes."

They both write on their notepads.

"Did you mention in any way, to any prisoner, that any of the hostages should be killed?"

"No."

"Are you and a woman by the name of..,"

Thatcher flipping to another page in the folder.

"Christine Chase planning to do anything that will be considered detrimental to anyone or anything?"

"Why do you ask? That has nothing to do with the subject at hand."

"The warden says you two are up to something. Says when she comes to see you, you all communicate through sign language and code words. He also said she shows you things for your approval. Would you care to elaborate?"

"No."

"I see you like playing hardball," said Morales.

And steps to Parson.

"I say what pertains to the subject, not you. Understand?"

"No."

"We can see to it that you spend the remainder of your time in solitary confinement," comments Thatcher.

"Wouldn't matter to me, it's not like the cell-house is any different. If you think I'm going to give you something, you're mistaken."

"What something would you have to give?" Morales, who lights a cigarette.

"I don't smoke," informed Parson.

"Neither do I," and blows it in his face.

Parson rises to his feet triggering the CERTs to step between them.

"Sit down!" pepper spray in one hand, Taser® in the other.

"I'm getting a drink of water," he said innocently, standing within striking distance.

"Not until they're finished! Sit! Down!"

Looking at Morales.

"No problem," with a grin on his face.

"I can see the fear in your eyes," boring into him with a stare so penetrating, it makes the veteran agent look away.

Parson lets out a chuckle, then kicks his feet up, and starts whistling.

"Where do they find you shmucks?.......Here I am, a man convicted of searing a man over ninety percent of his body with an iron, including his face, then blowing a hole in the side of his head, emitting brain matter everywhere; all while recording the act on a cassette, and leaving it for the cops listening pleasure. The other day I broke two correctional officer's noses, knocking them unconscious; in conclusion, *and* retrospect; I sweep the feet from under poor Gordon, causing him to bump his empty head—all in a matter of seconds."

And lets out a wild, yelling laugh that resounds throughout the building.

"I wonder what kind of looks you talentless rejects would have if my hands magically came from behind my back, *un-cuffed?*"

The CERTs back away, pointing pepper spray and Tasers.

Morales caught off guard, is plastered to the wall, not knowing what to do..

Being he's the closet to the door, Thatcher wisely slips out the cell.

"Hey! You left your partner, you're not supposed to do that."

The CERT supervisor radios backup, the others prepare their

shields and batons.

"You gentlemen do realize I have anything to lose?"

"Don't do anything you'll regret Parson," advised the aiming officer.

"Well get this coward out of my cell before I do something I *won't.*"

Morales unthaws himself from the wall, and scampers away like a frightened fawn.

The CERT's back out, slamming the heavy door behind them.

"You forgot something," and slings the hand cuffs through the hatch.

"Have a nice day gentlemen. My office is now closed."

Just as a stream of pepper spray shoots through the hatch.

"I'm immune to it jerks! Ummmn, smells like honeysuckle! Would you happen to know where I can purchase a can of my own? Money-House-Blessing®?...Airwick®?...Glade®? *FEBREZE®!* Tell me which one you ass wipes!"

After they'd cursed him out, and are long gone, he takes a wet towel and wipes it up, not in the least bit fazed by the solution that has bull stopping power. After rinsing his hands and face, he sits on his bed pulling lint balls off the blanket. That, a mattress, two sheets, a sink, toilet, and two towels are all he has to keep him company—oh yeah, the jumpsuit. Everything else that belonged to him, and any other member of death row, was destroyed. He tried to smuggle a few cherished items, but they were found and discarded. Photos that men had for decades, old letters from families and friends when they cared, essential legal documents, books, and any other mementos, are now gone—revenge for what they did to the guards.

He desperately needs to speak with her so he can find out what Silas's next plans are; the mail isn't an option, the phone either. Harry told him long ago, the second he enters his inmate identification number his calls get recorded, and any mail with his name on it is opened and read. But he's confident she'll find a way to see him, even if she has to go through Gordon to do it.

The jingle of keys causes him to sit up.

"These came out of your fuck buddy's pocket," said a familiar voice, and throws two charred photos on the floor.

The squeak of a wheel turning follows, then a heavy piece of metal hitting the floor.

Parson spins off the bed and laces his boots, determined not to take any more beatings. Before he realizes it, a fire hose blasts him with cold water, slamming him into the rear wall, stinging his body, and flooding the cell in a matter of seconds.

"Shower time!"

After he's finished with him, he shuts off the valve, closes the flap, then proceeds to the next cell and does the same thing.

Out goes the light.

Parson's left in cold wet darkness.

Feeling his way to the soaked bed, he peels out of his clothes and stands there shivering, wearing nothing but soggy boots and dripping boxers. As if things can't get any worse, the air conditioner kicks on.

Covered with chill bumps, he sits on the floor, pulls his knees to his chest, and hopes he doesn't die from hypothermia.

Kathy was charged with reckless driving, five felony counts of alluding a police officer, twelve counts of improper lane change, excessive speeding, seven counts of running a stop light, four counts of failure to yield, improper use of an emergency lane, endangering the lives of motorists, two counts of misdemeanor criminal damage to property, not wearing a seatbelt, and one felony count of criminal damage to property for destroying a fruit stand.

After passing three different sobriety tests, and one urine analysis, she was jailed until a judge granted her a $77,000 bond. Ann put up the house as collateral, and by 4:19 a.m., Kathy is free to cause more mayhem. Her passing the tests almost had her sitting with no bond, because she had no explanation for the way she was driving; was even grilled about being a terrorist. Had they been aware of the other situation, there would be way she'd be standing at her front door waving goodbye to her mother, after literally begging her not commit her to a mental institution.

The Camry's totaled, and astonishingly, she has minimal injuries. Since the gun was registered, and having no felony convictions, she wasn't charged with illegal gun possession, but the police confiscated it anyway.

She fishes the keys from her purse, opens the door, and flips on the light.

Stockton's sitting in his recliner with an empty bottle on the table.

He gets up and comes towards her with a cold stare.

She wishes she had her weapon.

But he walks past, and disappears into the dark hallway.

She doesn't feel safe around him anymore.

Turning, she sits her purse on the counter, and exhale with high tension.

Danger.

She spins around to him standing behind her.

Chapter 17

Of not for Officer Fawell, it's quite possible inmates could've died. The A/C was set so low, that when he arrived, the thermometer displayed a reading in of 42°, 10° from freezing. He had dry mattresses, blankets, sheets, pillows, and clothes given to them. The heat was turned on, and they were allowed to take respectable showers.

So now at fifteen minutes after midnight, he sits in a dark cell staring at the floor; light from the hallway streams through the open hatch. With things back to normal, the heat's off, and the air blows at a reasonable level.

The inmate gets off his bed, and squats to look out; a tray of un-eaten meat loaf and mashed potatoes sits beside his knee. With-the coast clear, he tries for the ninth time to defeat the lock; the doors of J-building aren't as easy to open as the ones on death row. Since he doesn't have his favorite tool, this will have to do. He meant to get him during the riot, but he sought protection with the same man who raped him; knowing he was out to get him.

"Shit," he hissed, the tool popping off the latch, bouncing across the floor loudly.

He snatches it up, checks the point, and goes to a rough spot on the cinder block wall, and hones it back to a point.

Satisfied, he returns to the door and recommences trying to jim-my it open. With one hand, he grabs the bottom of the door and wiggles it, using the other, he jams it inside the track.

Click!

The steel slab cracks an inch.

To fool the sensor, he stuffs a wad of tissue and a section of the roll into the jamb—adrenaline surges as he prepares to make his move. Preparing to emerge from the cell, he slides the door back, but is halted by someone at the end of the hall quietly closing the tray hatches.

He jumps back to his bed leaving the door conspicuously ajar.

When the boots get to his cell, they stop.

He sees the shadow through the crack, and knows the person is looking at the door.

Amazingly, they continue on.

After several minutes, the remaining flaps seem to have been shut, because he doesn't hear any movement; a distant snore is all he can detect.

Now the boots are coming back.

He runs back to the bed just as they reappear.

A gloved hand reaches between the jamb and pushes it open, bringing their entire body into view.

His eyes haven't adjusted to the light so he can't see their face, but can see the blue shirt and gray pants.

He plays sleep.

His eyes are closed, but he can tell the door is being shut from the inside.

He stirs and yawns as if he's just awaken.

"What's the problem officer?"

In a flash, the guard is on him, and snaps his neck; the crunching sound is nauseating!!!

While the inmate convulses, the killer bends down and proceeds to stab him, but the dying man's arm shoots up and grabs his shirt! The guard sinks the blade into the man's chest, while trying desperately to free himself from his clutch. But his death grip is too strong.

He stabs him again!

The man releases his final breath.

With the knife protruding from his forearm, it takes both hands to grab his wrist and pry it loose, ripping his shirt in the process. Angry that he's bloodied his uniform, he retrieves the knife and pounds the man's torso, decorating the white garment with maroon stains.

Hearing his name over the radio startles him!

"Pedophiles merit nothing but eradication."

The killer straightens his clothes, eases out, and slowly shuts the door.

The flap closes with a subtle click.

"You counted that fast?" inquires Officer Couch with his boots propped on the control board.

"Yeah," sitting with his back to him.

He gets up and goes into the restroom.

After spending quite a while, he reemerges with wet areas on his leg and shirt, and sits back down. The stains are partially visible, but not enough to tell they're blood.

"I see you had a little accident in the john," nodding at it.

"Something like that."

Couch shrugs, spins back around and props his boots back on the board. A buzz from the board causes him to reach over and turn a small lever. The door swings and the shift supervisor enters.

"How's it going gentlemen?"

"Pretty good," replied Couch.

"What about you over there?"

"All right," without looking up.

The sergeant reads, and signs the count sheet.

"What happened to your shirt?" looking at the tear.

Still not making eye contact.

"My dog ate it."

Couch spins around!

"What's your name son? The dog must've ate your name tag too."

He stands up patting his chest, eyes searching the room.

"I *said*, what's your name son? Did you not hear me the first time?"

"Doe, Officer Doe."

"Well Mr. Doe, I think you better find that tag, and do something with that shirt before I come back for the next count. If not, you can spend a few days at home figuring it out."

And turns the lever on the control panel to let himself out.

After he's gone Couch mentions: "You've got balls smartin' off

at Sarge like that."
"Fuck him, let me out."
"You'll never make rank with that attitude," as he twists the lever.

Back to the scene, he unlocks the door and goes inside; using his flashlight to avoid the puddle. Aiming the beam at the corpse's hand, he sees the glisten of his nameplate, puts on his gloves, and bends down to open the hand. Having little success, he lifts his boot and stomps it, crushing the bones. Pulling the knife, he moves the grotesquely smashed fingers out of the way, and retrieves his bloodstained pin.
In three long steps he's back in the hallway.
"One of the inmates have your name tag?" Sarge, sarcastic and coming towards him.
Doe knows he's caught!
"Eat shit and die coppers," someone shouts.
"Shut up before you don't eat at all!" Sarge standing before Doe.
"Find it?"
"No."
"So why are you down here then?"
"Checking the toilet, he said he needed a plunger."
"Well?"
"It's clear now."
Sarge stares with an odd look.
"...You wanna tell me what's going on?"
"Nothing's going on."
Sarge raises the radio.
"J-one, open J thirty."
.....Click!
Sweat beads are running down his face!
"Let me see your light?"
Doe gives it to him.
"Step aside."
SARGE SEES THE BODY!!!

Doe slams the blade into the side of his throat, and kicks him inside the cell—blood squirting from the wound! Stumbling, Sarge grabs his neck, and drops to his knees, gurgling—the flashlight echoes of the floor!
Doe slices his esophagus!
Does stabs him in the temple!
Sarge wheezes and kicks, until the remaining vestiges of his life are gone.
Breathing heavily, he calmly shuts the door, while blood flows from underneath.
"What y'all bitch guards doin' out dere!"

Halfway there, he heads back, red liquid now staining the gangway.
"Opens this shit up'!" shouts the same guy, and kicks the closed tray hatch.
Back for a third time, it's everywhere!
He pops on the latex, grabs Sarge by the arm, and situates him in an assuming manner. Repositioning the inmate's corpse, he places the knife in a fashion insinuating Sarge was killed by the prisoner; being sure the inmate's prints are on the murder weapon.
Voices are difficult to recognize over the radio.
"J-one, this is SK one." (Sarge's call sign).
"J-one, go ahead," answered Couch.
"I'm twenty in H-house. (Which is on the other side of the prison). Did I leave my clipboard over there?"
After moments of searching.
"That's a negative sir."
"Ten-four."
Doe secures the door, but he's stepped in the blood.

"You seen Sarge's clipboard?"
"I didn't see it in the break room...Have some?" offering him the bag of microwave popcorn.

"Nah, I'm burnt out on that stuff."
"Guess where I found it?" holding up his name plate.
"Your dog's mouth."
"In the other restroom, I found it when I goes to get this."
"That's a lot more than three letters. Come on tell the truth, Doe isn't really your name, is it? You told me once, but I can't remember it."
"Maybe Sarge will take it as a joke," pinning it on.
"He's pretty cool, probably just laugh it off. He ain't no tight neck like Gordon, just a regular guy who wants to do his eight and go home."
"He married?"
"Yep, a wife and five kids, if I remember right."
"That's unfortunate."
Couch leans over and reads the name.
"Billings! I knew that was it."

Parson sits straight up terrified, perspiration abounding!
He wipes his face.
The reoccurring dream has been haunting him for weeks, the one where he sneaks out at night and kills the inmates he doesn't like. The first time he had it Beasley, was found dead, the sixth time, it was Chesterwell.
He pushes the blanket off, praying no one will be found dead this morning. Washing his face, this one was different: After getting Billings, he magically appeared at Stuckey's home dressed in star spangled spandex, and a weight lifting belt, and stabbed him

as he fed a sty of hogs with kick stands for legs in the center of his living room, surrounded by rows of shape shifting bleachers. An auctioneer holding a glowing clarinet with a plate of eggs benedict for a head, tried to warn Stuckey, but it was too late.

After being around killers for so long, he's began thinking like one.
Out of habit, he glances at the light switch remembering his buck knife. Although he's not in his regular cell, he can't understand the need to hold onto it. When he first arrived on death row, he didn't know what to expect, so he stole it for protection. Why?
Because Douglas Parson is not a murder, he is not a psychopathic monster, and he's definitely not the merciless killer of Joseph Tangier.
He's spent 4,035 days living in hell for a crime he didn't commit.

Each day, he looks at the mirror and wonders how this has happened to him, for years, he's stared at the same mildew covered ceiling, and asked the same unanswered question: why?
Words can't remotely explain the endless suffering he's endured at the hands of an incessantly cruel warden; made possible by a judicial system rife with corruption.
Parson squeaks off the faucet and returns to bed.
With no books, no one to talk to, and no light; there's nothing to do but interrogate fate.
Closing his eyes, he sees the face of the woman he loves, then the seared one of a dead pedophile, who moonlighted as a social worker, and pretended to be a pastor—a tiny cassette floats tauntingly into view. Visions of a youthful Kathy sitting on the front row crying causes him to shake the agonizing memory from his mind, and get up.
Pacing the small area between the bed and the bricks, there's no way to determine the time, or whether it's day or night; but guesses it to be close to breakfast.

The sound of radio traffic gives him something else to focus on.
Noise from the flaps opening and closing get louder.
They stop.
He estimates the location to be five cells down.
"TEN-TEN!" yells the panicked man. *"TEN-TEN! J-BUILD-ING! TEN-TEN!"*
It's happened again!!!

Moments later, boots are running down the hallway; his head throbs, trying to recall who is in the last five cells.
Since he hasn't paid much attention to who went where, he hasn't the slightest clue.
Now there's a stampede echoing down the tier! And from the shuffle of feet, he can tell they're taking turns looking through the tray hatch.
More boots in the distance.
Parson tries his best to listen.
"I don't want anybody going in there!"
Seconds later, someone says: "Their dead."
So evidently there's multiple fatalities?
A chill comes over him, realizing how close he was to death.
Unexpectedly, the lights come on, and a female voice is close by.
Playing it smart he, pushes himself off the floor and gets back on his bunk. If they come asking questions, he'll play like he just woke up, and doesn't know anything; several murders are already trying to be pinned on him, he doesn't need anymore. In the event his appeal is granted, he'll still be in prison fighting the new charges.
What's Stuckey going to do when he finds out this time he has multiple homicides to deal with?
The thought leads him to remember that chilly March morning. And as much as he doesn't want to relive that dreadful day, his brain does anyway.

Someone speaking on behalf of his good friend Renée, called the office of *Evans Loch* apartment homes requesting maintenance come repair a gushing water pipe. He dropped the reading of his college course material, and went to Cottage Q, and knocked on door #9. After receiving no answer, he used his master to disengage the computerized lock. Since it was raining, and his hands were already wet, he didn't notice the liquid on the inside of the handle. Almost immediately, he noticed something burning, and heard what sounded like a wailing smoke detector, plus the lights were of, and classical music was blaring from a portable CD player sitting on the counter. He flipped on the foyer's light switch, and turned the volume down. Holding his tool bag, he asked if anyone was home.

There wasn't.

A soiled rag sat feet away, wasted Maraschino cherries, canned vegetables, and soy sauce was everywhere. Someone attempted to clean the spill, smearing it badly. As he made his way through, he knocked over a mop, getting liquid on his work pants. That's when he came upon an iron burning atop a shirt, and without hesitation, lifted it upright, and pulled the plug from the receptacle. He then silenced the smoke detector, drops were on it also; a wooden chair with a compact disc sitting on the edge blocked his path. He moved it aside, causing the disk to slide off and land in a small puddle that seemed too conveniently located.

He radioed the office about the mess, but was instructed not to bother it, make the repair and leave.

Before repairing the leak, he took out his micro-cassette recorder so he could listen to a lecture while working. He replaced the cracked pipe and left.

Framed, he's convinced the anonymous caller is the culprit. With his fingerprints everywhere, eye witnesses placing him at the scene, found with the micro-cassette recorder in his pocket, blood on his pants, shabby detective work, and motive fabricated by a vainglorious district attorney; he was charged with murder; only to later have it upgraded to capital—the commission of additional felonies during the crime as the basis. His only defense was the discovery of an unidentifiable pair of shoe and finger prints, which they claimed belonged to his accomplice; and with the size, shape, and type of pattern said to be from a woman's running shoe, but later rebuffed, when it was discovered the shoe also came in a male variety.

The evidence against him was so well engineered, that investigators chose not to put much effort into searching for the other suspect, especially since it took the jury only two hours to reach a unanimous decision.

The sound of the door causes him to forget the past, and focus on the present, and the men hastily coming towards him.

Chapter 18

"*H*ello Christie."

"Kathy!..I been worried sick about you! Why haven't you been returning my calls?"

"To be honest, I haven't been in the mood."

"That's mighty inconsiderate! I drove all the way over there to check on you, and you're in there avoiding me. Huh, I'll know next time."

"I needed time to think."

"Let me guess, about me right?"

"About everybody...and yes, you."

"Here we go again with this. Well you know what Kathy, I don't have time for this. Have a good day."

"Christie wait."

She sighs angrily.

"I'm not in the mood."

"Can you calm down please, I'm just trying to understand some things."

"You're selfish Kathy."

Silence.

"Why are you being so rude?"

"Because you act like you're the only one with problems, like you're the only person who's dealing with struggle....What is it so I can get some sleep."

"It's about what you asked me to help you with."

"What about it?"

"About the guy. I don't mean to pry, but it'll make things a lot easier if I know the involvement. If I'm going to assist you, I need to know the facts."

"He's my brother."

Kathy almost drops the phone, again. She's taken aback!

"He's your what!!!!"

"He's my brother Kathy! Is there something wrong with that? Judging by your reaction, I'm getting the feeling I shouldn't have told you."

She's speechless!

"Hello."

"......Hello!"

"Hold, hold on for a second!!"

Out of breath, Kathy sits the phone down; her mouth's dropped completely open. She runs her hands through hair that's seen better days.

He doesn't have a sister.

Angered by her deceit, Kathy picks up the phone.

"How is he your brother?" hostility in her words.

"Why? And I don't exactly like your tone."

"Just answer the question Christie, why all the secrecy? How are y'all related.

"Who do you think you are? I'm about to hang up before I say the wrong thing."

"Please Christie, I need to know!"

"What does it matter to you? He's *my* brother, he has nothing to do with you!"

"You don't know what it has to do with!"

"We have the same dead parents okay!"

Kathy's hand smacks over her mouth! The room, the bed, the floor; it all seems to be spinning—she can't tell which! But he never mentioned anything about having a sibling.

"Kathy!!"

She's too overcome with disbelief to speak.

"Kathy! If you don't start talking, I fucking swear...."

"I–I just can't believe what you're telling me."

"Why would you care?..Do you know him or something?"

Her pause seems to last an eternity.

"Yes...for quite some time. And he told me he was an only child."

"What!! How do you know him!"

"First tell me how he become your brother, then I'll tell you how I know him."

"Have you taken your medicine?"

"Come on, I'm not joking."

"My mother had me as a surrogate to a couple, well not really as a surrogate. When they had me, my parents were very poor and going through a lot of hardship. To keep me from having to live in a bad situation, they gave guardianship to a family friend until they got on their feet. At first everything was fine. My mother spent time with me, took me to the doctor and stuff. Then my dad got killed, and she just kinda fell by the waist side, and disappeared. I never saw her again."

Kathy's in a complete state of shock!

"Kathy."

"Huh."

"Are you there?"

"Uh-huh.....So you're saying that Douglas Parson is you're bio-

logical sibling?"
"Yes. "
It can't be....It just can't.
"This is like something out of a book, I'm mean what are the odds of me stumbling into his sister in a city of five million people?"
"You act like I'm not amazed. I'm still not sure where talking about the same person yet," Christie.
Kathy thinks for a moment.
"Why haven't you gone to see him?"
"Well, because I've been afraid to. I mean, I don't know how he'll react. Gosh, I don't even know if he'll believe me. How would you react if some strange woman popped up and said: Hi, I'm your sister? Every day I think about going and telling him, but I never have the courage. He has no idea that I've been working to get his case overturned, or the lawyers I've hired to get him a new trial."
"How'd you find out that you have a brother?"
"I found out when I got a letter from a lawyer saying I was bequeathed an estate by my uncle. When I met with him, he told me my younger brother gets the other half, and that's ultimately how I found out."
"Does he know about the money?"
"I don't know, I've never spoken to him."
".......Christie, this is a lot to swallow. I can't believe what I'm hearing."
"Now it's your turn. How do you know him?"
"It's a long story."
"I've got nothing but time."

For the next two hours, Kathy explains how she came to know the convicted murderer known as, Douglas Parson; shocking Christie just as much as she has her. Upon disclosing a particular piece of information, Christie doesn't believe her, so Kathy invites her to come see for herself. Minutes later she's ringing the doorbell.

"It's open."

Christie rushes in, and closes the door.

Kathy's standing in front of the couch holding a suitcase in one hand, and a backpack in the other. Christie embraces her in a bear hug. Moments pass while they hold each other tightly; tears squeezing through tight eyes.

"Fate brought us together Kathy," holding her shoulders, looking at the tears on her face. "I'm so happy I found you."

"God made this happen, not fate."

Christie smiles and embraces her again. "This is unbelievable," releases her. "Now let me see it!" breathing with anticipation, wiping her tears.

Kathy wiping her's too says: "He told me to get this one."

Then unzips the backpack, and places the .38 revolver on the table. Looking at it Christie says: "Hollow points."

"Let me show you something else," and hands it to her.

"Is this real?" Christie asked.

"Yep," and hands her a document.

"How did you get this stuff?" impressed.

"It's not what you know, but who you know."

The name on the license and the birth certificate is none other than the infamous and indispensable, fastidious, and ferociously feminine, Christine Chase.

"Would you by chance know sign language?"

The FBI profiler is adamant the killer's a male.

The ride from Summer Hill to the Lakewood Village apartment complex takes approximately nineteen minutes—Kathy drives her "other car". The guard gives them a stare down as they enter. "What could you have to show me in this place?" asked Christie, suspicious of the group leaning on a car.
"There's nothing to worry about. We don't look as odd as you think."
"I don't know what two white women getting out of an old car with tinted windows looks like then."
"Looks will fool you."
"It still looks unsafe."
She parks in front of is a two-story brick unit in the very back. She kills the engine and gets out, but before she closes the door, a woman appears.
"Hey girl!"
"Hi Dominique, it's good to see you! How've you been?" and wraps her arms around her.
"I've been pretty good, how about yourself?"
"Me too I guess. Meet my friend Christie. Christie, Dominique."
As the two women speak, a little boy wearing a red #23 jersey, and matching shoes runs up.
"Wuss-up?"
"Uhuuah, you're getting heavy. What's your mommy feeding you?"
He sticks out his green tongue, and shows her a Jolly Rancher®
"Can I have one?"
"Mommy she wants one too," holding out his pudgy hand.
"Come on, it's almost time for granny to get here. Go on back in the house and watch TV. I'll be there in a minute."
Kathy puts the little fellow down.
"See ya later Ms. Kaffy," and runs off.
Kathy asks has anyone been snooping around.
"Nope, I haven't seen anyone. But you know I'm moving next month. I got the job."
"So you got it!"

"Yep!"

"Congratulations!"

"Girl who you telling! Guess I won't be able to keep an eye on your place anymore?

"Don't you worry about that. You just tell me what day I need to come and help pack."

"Girl I ain't about to be loading no truck—get my brothers over here, and pay them some chicken and beer."

"I hear that. We'll look, we're going to run inside. I'll come say goodbye before I leave."

"Well let me give you another hug, because I might not be here when you come out. I'm taking night classes at GSU now."

"I better watch out! I may be working for you some day."

"We can work together. It was good seeing you again girl."

"It was."

"Nice meeting you Christie."

She waves and smiles.

They hug and say their goodbyes.

"She was pleasant," commented Christie.

"I told you we're good," unlocking the twin deadbolts.

"I know, but haven't been around that many black people; I get a little uncomfortable."

"People are people Christie. You should be uncomfortable around anybody."

The moment it opens, an overhead flood light comes on, drawing the attention of a man working under a hood.

Kathy dashes inside, disappears down the hallway, and reemerges.

"Only have eight seconds to turn the alarm off. So what do you think?"

The walls are bare, the carpet is clean with crisscrossing vacuum lines, and the living room is empty as the refrigerator.

"Come on," Kathy said, and leads her to the only bedroom.

After unlocking another dead bolt, the solid metal door opens. Boxes packed with files are stacked midway to the ceiling. Another wall holds a bookshelf packed with burgundy law books, and related material. Beside it, a state-of-the-art computer, a fax machine, and a copier sit on a table. A small safe squats in the corner with a silver camera atop.

"This is where I search for ways to get him out. For the past twelve years, ten months, and three days, I've searched for the one loophole that'll bring him home....The district attorney, the judge, nine of the jurors, and all the detectives were white. Don't let the color of someone's skin lead you astray."

"I get the point Kathy."

"Good."

A picture of a young Kathy riding Parson's back sits atop the monitor—a furry magnetic teddy bear sticks to the frame. The suitcase that Gordon destroyed is tossed in on the floor.

Christie pulls a book titled: *"Language of the Deaf"* from the shelf.

"Is this how you learned sign?"

"That and a few classes. I sent him that same book, he mastered it in two months; it took me fifteen with a teacher. It's the only way we can communicate without everyone in our business. The warden swears we're up to something, and has these two guards watch me like a hawk. You wouldn't believe all the hassle I have to go through just to see him. And that's after I've told Stow some cockamamie story about me going to a seminar, or to the gym or something. I don't know how, but he knows something is up—accuses me of having an affair and stuff. I guess if trying to get Douglas out is an affair, then I'm guilty. I kind of think he's hired a private detective too."

"Yeah?"

"Every so often he sneaks out at night, and does God knows what. Other times he just gets up and goes, not caring whether I'm sleep or not."

"You think it's a woman?"

"It's something else. But I could care less what it is."

"I just realized something. You told me he sometimes works

death row. What if he finds out you've been visiting Doug?"
"There's nothing I can do about it now. I begged him not to transfer from the other prison, but he said he'd had enough of working there; I almost had a heart attack when he told me. The day we got into the fight in the bathroom, or should I say the day he knocked me around; he came home talking about how he'd met the guy who killed that pastor, and how sick he was. I ran in the bathroom and threw up. He got mad and kicked the door in."
She pauses to stare at the floor.
"You should've sees how scared he was when I was shooting at him, I really thought he was someone else. Even now, I don't understand why he had that stuff on his face, and wearing that black outfit."
"....Do you mind if I ask you a personal question?"
"You don't have to say that Christie, just ask."
".....................Why did you get involved with another man?"
Kathy doesn't answer immediately
"He pushed me into it. He didn't understand when I told him I didn't want to be involved with anyone, he wouldn't listen; kept forcing himself into my life. After they sentenced him, I literally almost went crazy; even tried to kill myself. Honestly, if not for him, I would have. He paid for the psychiatric treatment, the therapies, the medicines, the programs; everything. When I had financial trouble, he helped me out, and never acted like he wanted anything in return; wouldn't even accept the money when I tried to repay him. He was the perfect friend, and that's what we agreed to remain. But then he started wanting more. And the next thing I know, he's out of work saying he needed a place to stay—months later he pressuring me to marry him. He knew I only liked him as a friend, and would get angry when he'd tell me he loved me, and I wouldn't say it back. We never even had sex; he couldn't understand that he couldn't force me to love him—my heart was with Douglas. I pleaded with him to move on with his life. but he wouldn't. Then he became

obsessed with this common law marriage stuff, started telling people I was his wife....I felt so indebted to him, that I let him stay around. It's hard to turn my back on people who've been there for me; I don't like to use people.........Also, I got lonely." They apartment is silent.

"Has he ever asked you what happened?"

"Yes, but I won't tell him. I just say I can't remember, then a couple of months later he'll ask me again. We've got into some heated arguments because of it."

"You might need to get away from him before he ends up hurting you. Love can quickly turn into hate."

"I think about that every day, even have nightmares about him strangling me to death. But really, I can't see him killing me, he's not the type to take someone's life."

"You'll be surprised what bitterness and resentment will do to a man."

Kathy nods in agreement.

"What would you do if my brother did get out? How would you break the news?"

"I haven't figured that out yet. I guess I'll just deal with it when it happens, or should I say *if* it happens."

"You say this plan you guys have is the last straw, but you never told me what it was."

"Well, it involves a few things. One is getting that corrupt warden put behind bars; I have a serious vendetta against that man. Three months after Douglas got there, he damn near starved him to death, not to mention caused him to catch hypothermia, and almost die. And that's after he sat in the county jail for three years fighting the case. Another time, his arm and two of his ribs got broken because he wouldn't say yes sir when the warden asked if he was he a piece of shit. I'm part of the reason he's under investigation today. Me and this guy, Silas Rower-"

"Oh I've heard of him. He's that ex-CIA agent who blew the whistle on the agency for some drug operation they were running in Columbia?"

"Yes. Now he runs an agency that investigates wrongdoing in all sectors of law enforcement; the government hates him. He just finished a case where he proved an incumbent sheriff had the new sheriff assassinated because he lost the election. He's the only one besides me and my mother who believes Douglas is innocent."

"And me," Christie raising her hand.

Kathy smiles.

"Last week he gave me some new information, something we've been trying to get for years."

"What is it?"

"A classified file of the hundreds of potential suspects who could've killed that pastor. That's what they call him, even though we worked for DFACS—I guess that's better for the media's profit margin. But anyway, Silas says the real killer's in-."

Kathy gets up and kneels at the safe. After entering a six digit code, she presses a button, and it opens under its own power. She extracts the thick folder, and hands it to Christie.

"There."

"This feels like a cinder block."

"He says it'll take months to go over every person in there. Some of those cases date back forty years, even though Tangier didn't start working there until the last ten or so. He says it could've been someone out for revenge, or someone at the department— Tangier lived a double life. A teenager under his case load accused him of being an sex trafficker, saying he preyed on troubled girls by tricking them into becoming prostitutes. And also claimed girls were being placed in the custody of johns posing as foster parents, who paid kick-backs—permanent sex slaves."

"No Kathy, tell me things like this aren't happening in today's society?"

"They are, and at an alarming rate."

"That makes me sick to my stomach. America spends billions of dollars fighting wars, and on foreign aid, but lets its own citizens, *children*—the purest form of life, fall by the waist side....

That's why I've unplugged from this world Kathy. Things are just so wrong, people are so evil; and they take pride in being such. At every juncture, people are looking to benefit themselves at someone else's peril; everyone wants money, trying to get rich any way they can. And if they do, society praises them for it— something as insignificant, and morally useless as money; like they've really accomplished something. It would be different if they used it to make the world a better place, but all they do is hoard it; self-gratification and ego coddling. Those kinds of people are shallow, and I'm glad I don't suffer from that sickness......Sorry about that, I go on rants sometimes."

"No you're fine. I agree with what you're saying, you're a lot like your brother; he's a man of principle too. He once told me a story about how this guy got rich by doing shows where he'd eat anything the audience supplied. He ended up making a ton of money, but died from a bad stomach infection. That just goes to show: Having money doesn't make you intelligent. It just means you'll do anything to get it, even if you kill yourself in the process," and laughs.

Christie laughs too.

"This one guy I dated, all he did was brag about how much money he had, he was *sooo* obnoxious. And to boot, I could barely see his little wiener. He would've traded all that money just to not have me laugh when I saw his...*penis;* if it could even be considered such."

Kathy bursts into laughter!

"Girl you're a hoot. I've heard men with small ones are the hardest to deal with."

"Yeah! That's *if* you can deal with them at all!"

More laughs, they both enjoy the joke.

"But yeah, let's get back to business...Oh look, this guy here was fired because he raped four prostitutes, but doesn't say anything about him serving jail time."

"The majority of officers that commit crimes are never prosecuted."

"But if it was a civilian, they'd be in prison. They say the police protect their own."

"Yep," and receives it from her.

While Kathy locks it back in the safe, Christie picks up a letter."

"You've got accounts in that name too?"

"Yes."

"What for?"

"Paying legal fees and stuff."

"Is Kathy your real name?" expecting her to say no.

"Catherine with a C., Royce is the name I was born with, but all most people know his Kathy Billings-Easterbrook," and opens the closet door.

"Isn't it funny that my real name is Christie, and your fake name is Christine?"

"Pure coincidence. Now close your eyes."

Kathy ducks her head inside, does something, and comes back out.

"Okay, you can look now."

Christie's hand flies over her mouth!

"Lace front, I like it! You make a good blonde. How come I never see you wear it?"

"Because I only wear it when I'm Ms. Chase," and strikes a pose.

"Girl you're too much! Let me try."

Christie slips it on.

"Is it me?"

"Better than Marilyn Monroe."

"Liar!"

Christie takes it off and gives it back.

"You're right, I am." Kathy's mood suddenly losing its luster.

"Come on Kathy, don't start going in the tank again."

"....They've got him in isolation, I hope he's all right. I wish I could see him, but the warden's canceled visitation; only attorneys."

"It's probably because of the riot."

"Yeah......Did I tell you I got another tape yesterday?"

"You mean like the other one?"

"Yes, I came out the beauty store and sat on it. I knew someone was watching me. I keep telling myself it's just some joke, and not the killer, so I won't lose it. But in my heart, I think it's really him."

"This is bad Kathy. You're acting real coy about it, what's on it?"

"You don't wanna know."

"Well give me the edited version."

"It's a recording of people getting killed. I think it's the guy they found at the capital and his family."

"Are you serious!!!"

"I wish I wasn't."

"You they have these music production programs where people can make things sound real? You think that could be it?"

"I don't know Christie, I don't know what to think."

"Did you call the police?"

"No, but I probably should've though. I threw it out the window."

"*Kathy,* you're acting like it's no big deal that a person, possibly the same one that's killing these people, is dropping you tapes. Have you forgotten, he also left tapes at the murder scenes too?"

"Yeah."

"Which means the same person who killed Tangier could be doing these too."

"The police say it's a copycat."

"I don't believe that."

"And besides, the cops already know about the first one, but it fell in the heater under my desk and melted before they got there. I don't think they believed me, because they haven't called back check-up on it. And what more will telling them I received another do? It's not like it's going to make them catch him. What it *will* do is make them lock me in some witness protection program, and ask me a thousand questions, or either put me under surveillance. No, that's okay. I'll pass."

"At least you'll be safe."

"If he sees fit, the Creator will keep me safe."

"I suppose you've got a point....Things *have* gotten bad. With all the stuff I've learned, I can see why you wanted to jump off that parking deck."

"You know, I don't even remember that."

"Oh it happened. You were almost a goner."

"Lately I've been feeling like giving up, wishing God will just take me in my sleep or something; life doesn't appeal to me anymore. Things with Douglas aren't working out, some maniacs stalking me, my conscious has me feeling like crap for how I'm doing Stockton—I've turned into a basket case. I'm tired Christie, really really tired…I'm living in a fantasy world, wishing on a star that Douglas is gonna get out someday. Look at all this stuff," swinging her arm around the room.

"I'm in my own little dream world, and I need to wake up and face reality. And the reality is: My life is screwed and it's never going to change."

"Don't say that Kathy, change will come; you just have to believe it. Nothing good comes overnight, and anything worth having isn't easy. You remember the little train that could, that's how you've got to be; you have to keep trying until you make it over the hill. You make it Kathy! You hear me, you make it; don't you ever give up. And if something happens to you, who's going to fight for my brother?"

She shrugs her shoulders.

"I guess I've lost hope…The other night I went on a death wish; drove into oncoming traffic with my eyes close, hoping that when I opened them, I'd be in a better place. All I ended up doing was destroying a fruit stand, totaling my car, and getting arrested."

"Kathy you need help. I'm not saying this to offend you, but because I'm your friend. You can't see how bad it is, but others can. Have you looked at yourself in the mirror lately? You don't look like the same lady I met in the store that day. You have bags under your eyes now, and your skin is pale; you look like you've

aged five years in three weeks. For God's sake Kathy, you need help. You're gonna run yourself into the grave!"
"That doesn't sound so bad," staring blankly at the wall.
Christie kneels and holds her hand.
"You don't mean that."
"Yes I do."
"No you don't!"
"Whatever you say.....Let's get out of here, I'm starting to think the walls are closing in," and pulls her hand away.
"You can't keep brushing things off Kathy, that won't make them go away."
"Christie let's go, please. I'm for real, I haven't taken my medicine today," and walks out of the room.
"Come on, pull that door up tight," waiting to press the '*Arm*' button on the keypad.
It begins beeping as she flips the hallway light.
The apartment becomes pitch black.
"Kathy I can't see."
"We don't have but ten seconds," holding the front door open, light from the overhead flood guiding her way.
They walk out and proceed to the car.

"Your friend left you a note."
Christie pulls it off the windshield.
Kathy takes the piece of yellow paper, and gets inside.
Dominique's car is gone, and as she backs out, she hands it back to her.
"Would you mind reading it for me? I've got a headache."
Christie unfolds it.
"Dear Kathy, I finally found your hiding place. I hope you enjoyed the recording."

Chapter 19

Kathy, and everything that was inside her hideaway, is now in Christie's living room—they're taking no chances. Sitting at the dining room table, the doors are locked, the security system armed, and pistols on cock. Kathy feels responsible, with Christie's life now in danger, and possibly leading the killer to her residence. They've been holed up since yesterday, having no idea on how to handle the situation. Kathy finally broke down and asked for Stockton's help. Glad to be of assistance, he sits on a bar stool with his cannon standby; her belongings are covered with a sheet to keep his wandering eyes at bay. What's not covered, because boredom leads Christie to keep bothering it, is the bag with the climbing equipment Kathy purchased as a gift for a relative—she's not concerned about him seeing that. However, he's become quite curious as to why she doesn't want to go home. Each time he suggests it, she comes up with an excuse as to why she's not ready. And still hasn't yet decided what to do about all this stuff—taking it home isn't an option. Her only choice is to leave it there. Stow has to be to work by 9, and wants to get some shuteye before going in.

Kathy thinks he could care less about some tape he's never seen, and that she's probably making all this up, when in all actuality it has something to do with the affair he's convinced she's having. He probably feels she's getting what she deserves.

The sound of a revving engine causes her get up and run to the window.

"What is it?" Christie reaching for her weapon.

"Just some kids," walking away from the blinds.

"I thought of something. It's harsh but something to consider."

"Go ahead, say it."

"Well...being that if this *is* the killer, and he's been following you for a couple of weeks, I recall you saying that on the first one that he was inside somebody's house watching them sleep; days before those people were found dead. I think if he wanted to harm you, he would've done it by now, especially with all the opportunities he's had. I personally don't think he wants to, I think he's chosen you for another purpose?"

"But I'm not looking at it that way. I think he's going to wait until he drives me good and crazy, and right before I blow my brains out, he does it for me."

"I don't think so. If I'm correct, all of his victims have been cops and families of cops; past and present. You're n-"

"But Stow is. He used to be an Atlanta police officer."

"But they say the people he killed made lots of enemies. Stockton doesn't seem like that," glancing at him. "Did you make any enemies while you were on the force?"

After taking a swig from his drink.

"I didn't know until it was too late."

"What does that mean?"

"I was set up, fired for something I didn't do," emotionless.

"I'm sorry to hear that. Do you think any of them will try to come back and kill you?"

"I think they were quite happy with their initial one," and takes another sip. "It's likely just a bad prank."

"I don't know anyone who plays jokes like this," Kathy avoiding eye contact with him.

"How can you be so sure?...People aren't always who they seem," Stockton not looking either.

"You'd know wouldn't you?"

He ignores the pointed remark.

Kathy feels a vibration in her pocket and rises to her feet.

"I'll be back," and dashes down the hallway leaving Christie with him.

"Excuse me also." Christie heads for her room.

After closing and locking the door, Kathy flips the exhaust vent switch, and pulls out her cellular. The screen shows '1 Missed Call', and a message marked 'Urgent'. Keeping an eye on the bottom of the door, she sits on the toilet and listens.

Silas has extremely important information!

"I think I found the guy who killed Tangier."

Her hand begins trembling, she presses the speed dial button.

He answers on the first ring.

"Where are you?"

"At a friend's house," whispering.

"How far are you from the zoo?"

"Twenty minutes."

"Be there in thirty, main parking lot."

"Okay."

Her hands are shaking to such a degree, she has a hard time pressing the 'End' button. The seriousness in his voice only adds

to her anxiety.
She stands, flushes the toilet, gives the faucet a quick on/off, and
opens the door.
Stockton calmly walks away.
Christie's coming out of her bedroom.
Wondering what he heard, she thinks of a way to get out.
"We must've had to go at the same time," said Christie.
Kathy grabs hers before she goes by.
"I've gotta go."
"Kathy!" Stockton standing at the end of the hallway.
Heading towards him she remains calm.
"What?"
"You ready to go?"
"Not really. I guess you can go ahead, I should be fine."
But she sees he knows her intentions.
"All right," a tricky smirk on his face. "I'll see you later then,"
and walks out without saying another word.

Looking out the living room window, she watches him crank up
and pull off.
"That was Silas! He think he's found Tangier's killer!" getting
her keys.

But Kathy didn't notice the sheet had been moved.

"Don't lose em!" and tosses the radio on the seat.
The way the suspects left the house, he knows he's onto some-

thing.

In his regular clothes, he pulls into the driveway of the single level townhome, and gets out. Being a working-class neighborhood, few people are home. Other than the mailman, the street is void of activity.

Casually, he walks to the door and extracts his keys. With his other hand, he pulls out his pick. Simultaneously using the one on his key ring, and the other in his hand, he defeats the lock in seconds.

Moving quickly, he performs a warrantless search. Upon finding nothing of concern in master, he breaks into the locked second room, and rummages through the desk drawers, coming upon a myriad of material concerning a man named Douglas Parson. He reads files, takes notes and pictures, places everything back, and exits. Entering the living room, he returns to the things covered with the sheet, and hurriedly, but thoroughly goes through each box—he can't get inside the safe though. After checking the kitchen cabinets, pantry, and laundry room, he slips out as smoothly as he slipped in.

Now armed with vital pieces of information; Christina Lythgoe is somehow Douglas Parson's sister, Kathy Billings, born Catherine Royce was Parson's woman when he was sentenced to death fourteen years ago for murdering a man named Joseph Tangier, and also has another identity in which she goes by the alias: Christine Chase—she and Ms. Lythgoe are trying to get him out. He starts the vehicle, radios his partner, and backs out.

"You might wanna slow down before we get pulled over," as Kathy guns the engine through the red light.

"Let's just hope that doesn't happen."

Boulevard, a street named just that, will go from six lanes to four in the blink of an eye, then thin down to two.

She floors the accelerator again, and swerves around a motorist; her right tire almost striking the curb.

"Kathy!"

"Sorry."

"I'm sure he's not gonna to leave if you're a little late."

"I'm eight minutes now, and still have a ways to go."

A yellow light is up ahead.

"You're not gonna make it!"

"Yes I am."

The light turns red.

"Kathy!"

She skids to a stop, milliseconds before colliding with the school bus. More tires skidded behind them, an SUV avoids rear-ending them.

They look over their shoulders!

It pulls around, and goes into a gas station. It's not until a horn blows that Kathy takes her eyes off of it.

Back focused on the road, she mashes the pedal, spinning the front wheel, but eyes the rear view as she continues down Boulevard.

"What's wrong?"

"Just making sure we're not being followed."

"Who can follow us with the way you're driving?"

"You never know."

Her cell vibrates.

"I'm one minute away," she answered. "Okay......Okay......Gotcha," before hanging up.

"I told you he wasn't leaving."

But that doesn't stop her reckless driving, as the car goes airborne over a railroad crossing.

Christie realizes she'll have pray for their safety, because Kathy's only concerned with getting there.

The green *'Atlanta Zoo and Cyclorama Up Ahead'* sign causes her to ease off the gas; the entrance guarded by a cop directing traffic. Kathy plays like she doesn't see the stop command he's signaling, and pulls down the hill into the lot.

Christie looks in the rearview to see him glaring at them before speaking into his radio.

Silas's heavily tinted BMW® sits under a tree, as she wheels in beside it, getting out while the car's still rocking.

With a patient look on his face, he wastes no time on greetings, or questions about her tardiness, and hands her the 12 x 9 legal envelope.

Kathy stares at it like it's a priceless diamond, palms sweaty and wondering whose name she'll see inside.

"How did you find out?"

"From the retired chief, who knew the truth all along."

Extracting the contents slowly, her heart thunders with wary anticipation.

Their name and birth date is the on first page.

For the seemingly eons it takes her brain to absorb what she's seeing, her body becomes paralyzed, her breath grows short! She tries to say something, but has no speech to convey it with!

Her mouth is moving, but nothing's coming out!

After over a decade of searching, she's unsure whether she can handle the weight of knowing the truth. In a diffident motion, she turns the page and looks away, hoping the image in her mind isn't the one she's see on the paper.

She looks back down.

The more she stares at it, the more implausible it becomes!!!!

The more she thinks about him, the more her eyes burn.
Now tears—pouring down her face, compromising the mint quality of the glossy photograph.
Dizzied and dismayed, enervated by utter disbelief, she lay her forehead on the dashboard.
Many years of pain to flow.
Silas slides the envelope from her lap, and places a comforting grip on her shoulder.

She cries, and cries.............

"Are you sure? she sobs. "I mean," sniffles. "I-I mean this can't be," sniffle, sniffle, sniffle, and more tears.
"Yes. Gene Primrose called me yesterday. How he got my number, and why he chose me, is anyone's guess. He said it was a deliberate cover-up, they didn't want the embarrassment of the public knowing a vigilante officer was killing sexual predators. According to him, not only did he do Tangier, but nine others. And that the charges accusing him of police brutality we're a way to distance the department from the situation; was even forced by the mayor to keep quiet."
"So they let an innocent man take the blame to avoid them from being *embarrassed?*"
"I'm afraid so? I met with him this morning, and he gave me the file; the proof's there plain as day. But before he let me take it, he wanted my word that I wouldn't mention him, or how I got it. He also said he let someone else in on the secret, but wouldn't say who. I took a few hours reading over it, and called you."
Kathy's comprehending what he's explaining, but not the fact she's been living with the killer she's spent years trying to find.
The migraine is returning, she hopes she doesn't start seeing things, she hopes her heart won't fail.

Anxiety is flattening her like a steamroller, the truth, crushing like a demolished building; proverbial boulders of hate pulverize her psyche with unbridled restraint.

"So he's the one killing these latest people too then?" looking at nothing through the windshield.
"Most likely. All the victims, excluding their families, were either internal affairs people involved with his termination, or regular beat officers."
Slowly nodding her head. "He always said he'd get them back for what they did to him. But I never imagined he meant like this......All this time.....I've been living with a murderer, and didn't even know it."
She snatches open the door!
Silas looks away while she vomits on the ground.
Christine hops out to offer assistance, but Kathy waves her off.
One she finishes, Silas hands a bottle of water after.
She rinses her mouth out, and sits back with trails of tears staining her face.
"You remember the abandoned house you took those pictures of?"
".......Yeah."
He takes a folded piece of paper from the envelope, and hands it to her.
"The house changed owners four times after this man owned it."
The deed has Stockton's father's name printed across the top.
"Take a look at this," and passes her an old report on his father's death.
"Says that him and someone named Alexander Zarbin were suspected of the murder, but since they were juveniles, and minus hard evidence, the case went cold."
Kathy's downright blown away.
".....How could I have not seen it....He always told me he knew who killed his father."
"I'm going to have you escorted you to an undisclosed location, you'll stay under twenty-four hour security until he's apprehended. Hopefully, CID can get a warrant signed immediately,

or at least within the next forty-eight hours. With all the infor-mation in the file, I don't see it taking that long."

"What about the murder weapon?"

"In a case like this, he'll be arrested, then a search for the weap-on will be conducted. If we do the search first, it'll spook him, and he might run. Being he's likely the one killing these latest people, nine times out of ten, the gun and everything is either somewhere in your house, or with this Zarbin guy."

"What if he has it somewhere else?"

"Even if it's not found, he can still be convicted. There's been hundreds of cases where no weapon was recovered, and guilt was still proven. But don't concern yourself about all that, you've worried long enough. Let me deal with this, the hard part is over. You just sit back and think about what you and Douglas are going to do when he gets out."

Hearing those words brings chills over her body.

"I'm suing, I'm suing the whole freaking state."

"Wasn't that the plan."

Taking a deep breath, she lowers her gaze—Alex's face comes into focus!!!

Staring through the windshield as he coasts by, sticks his arm out, and points his finger at her.

"Who's that!" Silas tight faced, and reaching for his Mini-14.

Before she can say, a camera appears, flashes a few times, and speeds away.

Silas's hand is on the shifter, the other on the trigger!

"No," grabbing his arm. "Let him go...let them go."

They watch the vehicle gas through the parking lot, and out onto the street.

"Who was that!" pissed.

"Alex."

"Are we talking-"

"Yes, his adopted brother."

"He followed you!"

"Stockton must've put him up to it. He thinks there's an affair,

he'll just think you're the guy."
Letting out an angry sigh, he puts the assault rifle back behind the seat.
"Who's the lady in the car?"
"Doug's sister."
"His sister? Since when?"
"She was born first, and adopted before he knew; still doesn't. I'll explain the rest later," massaging her temples.
"Silas I need a few hours to sort things sorted out, and I wanna take the file with me. Before eight I'll call you, and we can go to place. But make it for two, she's coming with me. Will that be too much to ask?"
"Yes!"
"Silas, please."
He doesn't want to let her, or the file out of his sight.
Silence.
He always follows his gut.
"Do you have your weapon?"
"No, but she does. We'll probably ride to the park or something, I won't be long, I just need to go think."
"Give me your word you won't go home, or near that Alex character, or anywhere else you know I wouldn't approve of."
"You have my word."
"...Okay."
Kathy leans over and hugs him.
"I don't know what I would've done without you."
"All right now, enough of the lovey-dubbey stuff," patting her on the back.
As she opens the door, he says: "Call me in an hour and let me know you're okay."
"I'm a big girl Silas, but I'll do it. See you later."

She closes the rickety door; reduced back to sitting on hard, cracked vinyl, no longer in the luxurious confines of the BMW.
"Was it something you ate?"
"I'm fine."
"Oh...so what did he say?"
She doesn't immediately answer.
"That bad?"
Kathy hands her the envelope.
"Stow's the killer."
Christie thinks she's joking.
"That's not funny Kathy."
"You're right, it's not."
Christie stares at her.
"...*What*, that's ridiculous."
"That'll answer all your questions."
Silas honks the horn as he drives by.
Waving back, she puts the car in gear, but doesn't take her foot off the brake.
Christie's dumbstruck when she sees his police academy photo.
"Where did he get this!"
"From the former police chief who set him up."
Kathy takes her foot off the brake, and wrestles the powerless steering to the left.
"What do you mean set him up! What did they do! Wait a minute Kathy, this is too much to take in at one-time! I'm not understanding how Stow's the killer! This doesn't make any sense!"
"The department knew he killed Tangier, but didn't want the public to know; pinned it on someone else. Douglas happened to be in the wrong place at the wrong time."
"Why, why?" baffled and confused, "Are you sure Kathy? I mean

Stow, *come on*. That's not possible!"
"It's true."
"Why'd they pick him to frame?"
"Probably coincidence, they didn't care who it was."
Christie takes a deep breath, and laughs disbelievingly.

Across the street, beside a dumpster in a drugstore parking lot, sits an SUV waiting to pull out. When she does, the big Ford slides from its hideout, and emerges eighty feet back, with seven cars and a concrete truck between them.

"This is unbelievable, they've got his entire life in here! Oh yeah, who was that guy with the camera?"
"His adopted brother."
"Why was he taking pictures?"
"Stow probably told him to follow us."
"So he's gonna know you were with Silas."
"I don't care what he thinks. I just want him to stay far away from me. The more I think about it, the more I realize that he was going to kill me next."
The comment moves Christie to look back.
In the distance she sees the midday sun reflecting off the hood of something big.
"Kathy, I think that SUV from earlier is following us."
She grabs the rear view mirror, stares momentarily, then looks over her shoulder.
"Get over two lanes and see what it does."
Seconds later it does the same thing.
"Get off on the next exit, I know where a police station is," Christie reaching for her gun.
Out of nowhere, Stow's truck pull from behind the SUV, not trying in the least bit to be discreet!
"There's Stockton Kathy!"
Kathy swings around!
He's coming up on her right, close enough to be seen through

the windshield. Veering over, he advances one car behind her.

"That Alex guy's back there too!"

"I see him."

With their attention on the vehicles, they pay none to the exit.

"Damn, that's where we were supposed to get off!"

Kathy gives no reply, her eyes switching from mirror to expressway.

The blue tail picks up speed, whips in front of Alex, comes around a yellow moving truck, pulls up two cars behind her, and one behind Stow.

"Kathy!"

"I see it!"

Alex makes another move, but doesn't pass the SUV.

The I-85 turn is coming fast, three lanes on the left.

"Put your seat belt on, hurry up!"

The second the buckle clicks, Kathy's slings the car right, around one car, then left, around another, narrowly missing the motorist—leaning to the side, hugging the sharply curved ramp.

Christie holding onto the door, looks back!

The Silverado is locked in a hard turn, coming across the emergency lane, barely avoiding a head-on collision with the point of concrete a wall separating the exit lane.

Alex doesn't make it, he's trapped in a tire smoking 360, cut off from view as they enter the tunnel.

Reemerging seconds later, she swerves into a reckless merge, slices across four lanes, and straight into the fast lane. But bad luck strikes again; the vehicle dipping hard in the front, as she slams on brakes!

Traffic jam.

Stow and the other SUV cut people off, as they jostle for position. Stockton gets over five cars behind her, but the SUV doesn't move; occupying the lane adjacent to theirs, in case she gets smart.

"Where'd you learn how to drive like that!"

Poised, and eyeing the rear view, traffic comes to a halt. For as far

as they can see, there's gridlock. Blurry heat waves float off the baking asphalt like lethargic phantoms, people sit parked with their legs hanging out.
Without hesitation, she cuts over two lanes to the right!
Stockton, and the tail copy.
"GO!" Christie looking back.
Another lane, and she's behind a welding truck, another whip of the wheel, and another lane is taken—bruising the front bumper, she pays no attention to the gasp of the driver.
Stockton superseding her maneuver, beats her to the far lane, the SUV one car behind, waiting for her next move. Sensing trouble, the vehicle in front of them voluntarily moves, leaving no one between them.
And that's when Kathy sees the mysterious woman again. Not trusting the rear view, she turns around and looks.
The bulky Ford® pushes closer, putting the menacing chrome grille right on her ass; the woman's face expressionless.
"Kathy!"
She turns back around and hits the brake, hands preventing her body from hitting the steering wheel!
The SUV takes another lane, almost side-swiping a motor home.

Twenty feet is all she has!

Stockton knows she's going to go for the emergency lane.
She cuts the wheel, stomps the bare metal accelerator, and darts onto the shoulder; pebbles, trash and bits of glass rumble, while the orange needle climbs!
20!
30!
40!
She thinks she's getting away, but he's back on her in moments, the truck having no problem with the rough pavement.
Dodging a large tire tread, Kathy wishes she would've listened to Silas—the envelope clutched in Christie's lap.

Going almost 60 down the narrow lane, vehicles swoosh by like comets!
A delivery van pulls into the lane!!!!!
She tries to avoid it!!!!
The vehicle runs over an *'Adopt-A-Highway'* sign, and takes flight off the side of the embankment!!!!
CHRISTIE SCREAMS IN HORROR!!!!

IMPACT!!!!!

Word of the latest prison murders, and the casualties of the riot days before still own the airwaves. The killing of the sergeant, and the inmate is the only incident commanding top story status on all local news station. Facing an impending FBI arrest, Gordon has been forced to withdraw from the race. Also, the infamous death row inmate: Douglas Parson, known for the slaying of an up and coming bishop, is somehow orchestrating the murders from inside—by way of a woman named Christine Chase.

The effects of stress, disappointment, and weeks of sleepless nights cling to him; his disheveled hair looks to have been victimized by a windstorm. The top of his shirt unbuttoned, exposing his sweaty shaggy chest—there's a liquor stain too. With a full stubble beard, sitting in the office of his arch enemy, he's accepted the fact that he's hit rock bottom. Slouching on one of the cushy leather chairs holding a square metal flask, he stares through bloodshot eyes at Yates.

"So how's it going?" leaning in his high backed chair with his legs crossed.

"Shouldn't you know?"

"Wouldn't have a clue," knowing exactly.

"So, what brings you?"

"Why-yuh think ahm here for?"

"I honestly do not know Gordon. No call, no appointment, just bam, and my secretary says you're here demanding to speak with me. I assume it's something important, that's the only reason I allowed you in."

Gordon takes a drink.

"You assumed right.......These killins ruinin' yo campaign too?"

"They sure aren't helping."

"Well I'm done, my shits over. You gotcher wish."

"Gordon, you still don't get it do you. This was never about you, it was never personal—business, a show for the public; or shall I say a play of who can shoot the most smiles, do the most promising, and be the most convincing. *You* made it personal. Politics can never be that."

Stuckey looks around the spacious office, with its oil paintings of past governors, mahogany furniture, and picturesque view of the city behind the desk.

"Whutcha know bout Douglas Parson?"

"I know enough, why?"

"He's behind the murders, inside and out."

"I've heard the rumor."

"It ain't no rumor."

"Well it's not proven. You must be the one leaking that to the press?"

He doesn't answer.

"Like I said, it ain't no rumor. I been dealin' wit dis guy way before you knew what dis office looked like. He's behind 'em, and dat broad who helped him kill da reverend is doin' it."

Yates laughs and sits up in the chair. Laying his forearms on the desk, says: "Where's your proof?"

Gordon hits the flask.

"When's da lass time two men were executed in the same month?" avoiding the question.

"Anywhere, or just Georgia?"

"Don't matter."

"Well in this state, it's only happened once?"

"So dat means it can happen again?"

"There was a reason for it."

"Why?"

"It doesn't matter, but it has on purpose in other states. Extremely uncommon, but not impossible."

"So if you wonted, wit you bein' da governor and all, you could schedule one in the next week huh?"

"Cut to the chase Gordon."

"If dese killins weretuh stop because of some move you made made, it wud make you a hero, you'd win by a landslide. Dey say dat Autry cat's gonna force you into a runoff, and possibly win; goin' by da latest poles."

Yates sits back and studies him.

He's been trying to manufacture a strategy that'll guarantee victory, knowing he's only leading by a slim 3% margin over Autry; nothing when voter's minds change like the weather. Maybe this buffoon has come up with a feasible plan.

"So you're saying that executing Parson with stop the killings?"

"And you can take all da credit; gotta stay hard on crime right?"

"It can also backfire, making me look like some kind of power struck who's obsessed with executions; that Goldstein woman would have a field day."

"It'uh also show da public you ain't afraid tuh take charge; theyuh respect yer courage and leadership. She rallies and whines at evruh execution? Do it ever stop anything? Did da public hatechu? No. This is Georgia, da original penal colony. People here ain't into all that human rights, cruel and unusuh punishment bowlshit. They love how we da only state wit da balls tuh still use duh chair. Dis can be yo chance tuh prove yer worth tu duh state. Oppertunties like dis don't come evruh day."

Gordon is convincing, knowing just what to say to get Yates to bite. He's betting his obsession with power and fame, coupled with the fact he's in jeopardy of losing it will lead him to take drastic measures.

"Tell me Gordon, why have you become so interested in helping me?"

He screws tight the cap on his chrome flask, buttons his suit, and leans forward.

"Politics. You game or not?"

Then stands and tosses a bulging envelope on the desk.

"Consider it'uh campaign contribution."

"So you think you can waltz in here and throw money at me? Bribery is a crime, or have you forgotten?" and pushes the envelope on the floor.

Gordon looks down at it, then back to him.

"*Ha-ha-ha-ha-ha-ha-haaa!!*...Come off yuh fuckin' high horse Hal, save da good guy shit for the cameras. Ain't nobody tryin' tuh set-chu up. We both know you on thin ice. All I'm requestin' is a service that'll in turn help you. Either yuh do it, or yuh don't, but save da act."

This pig farming, half of warden is giving him advice on how to prevent his political plane from crashing, and he hates it. But the fact remains, and after forty minutes of discussion, the decision is made. No matter how much he loathes him, he knows what Gordon proposes is in his favor. If getting the Department of Corrections to accelerate an execution means him keeping in his seat, so be it.

But he still has to protect himself.

"You familiar with J. Johnson Welch Properties?"

"No."

"Well find out," writing on a sheet of paper. "Get in touch with this guy. Drop him your package, he'll see that it gets to the ap-

propriate place."
Gordon takes it, picks up the bribe, and heads for the door.
"If everything works out, I may have room on my staff for some-
one like you."
Holding the knob Gordon turns.
"I'd rather die."
And walks out.

The woman in the SUV turned out to be an FBI agent, believing her to be a part of a robbing crew. Kathy listed in stable
condition, sustained broken ribs, a broken nose, and a substantial amount of lacerations and bruises. Christie sustained a fractured collarbone, broken wrist, dislocated shoulder, and several
other injuries. Kathy recovers in the mental health ward until
it's determined which psychiatric facility will best suit her needs.
Stockton is laying low, but did find a way to get her purse, cell
phone, and classified documents.

Alone in his truck, Stockton stuffs the material back inside the
envelope. Now privy to Kathy's secrets, and any day will be a
wanted man, he's surprisingly calm. The information was no
shocker, although he did find it interesting the police suspected
him of killing his father, and knew he killed Joseph Tangier, but
chose not to prosecute him. Discovering it was the chief who
arranged the whole set up was the best part. He suspected him
from the beginning, but didn't want to believe the man he ad-
mired and trusted would stab him in the back, and throw him

to the wolves. He also wants to understand how the he came to know Kathy, and why he gave her the files? After all these years, was he going to hand it over to the district attorney? How long had she had them? Why hadn't she gone to the police already? His heart warms at the thought that maybe she actually loves him, and doesn't want to see him put behind bars, but is quickly erased when he thinks how she duped him—secret bank accounts to pay for Parson's legal fees, the apartment, the aliases, and all the visits.

Stockton shakes his head, disgusted by the guards' envious comments of Parson's beautiful blonde.

How much of his money did she use to help him? The truth finally comes out: Her fiancé being sentenced to death was the reason she almost lost her sanity—all the money he spent to keep it from happening.

He lashes out at the steering wheel!

He wants to drag her from his truck down the roughest road he can find.

Stockton cranks up, and squeals out.

Driving up the one-way aisle, he crashes through the black/white striped arm, snapping the wooden board in two. After running a red light, he heads towards the expressway. A press of the preset button, and the cabin is fills with the gripping classical piece: *Hungarian Dance No. 5 in G Minor.*

A glance at his timepiece shows the hour hand on the 8, and the minute hand prickling 23—the sun has already set. Protracted dashes of vermilion, magenta, periwinkle, and gold stretch across the cloudless sky. Making way down the I-85 S. ramp, he violates the two-person requirement, and moves into the HOV lane.

About to pass the sign, he foots the ABS brake, and gets in deceleration lane. Stopping a car length pass the neighborhood's entrance, he guns the 5.7L engine reverse, and speeds into the neighborhood. Having no regard for being seen, he backs into the driveway and gets out. Having disabled the alarm system on his previous breaking and entering,

BAM!

He kicks the door in.

And commences to ransacking the place; going through boxes, emptying things on the floor, kicking shit over. He takes the safe and pushes it to the door, the framed photo of Kathy riding Parson's back is crushed. Searching the kitchen, he finds what he's looking for: foil, and a wrench.

Storming through the living room, reaches the backyard by way of the patio. Aggressively unscrewing the propane tank from the grill, he takes it, and the additional one inside. Stockton goes into Christie's room, a glistening machete is mounted on the wall, *Made in Panama* is engraved in handle. Grabbing it, he makes sure all the windows are shut.

Now to the office.

BAM!

Another door down, three brass hinges dangle from the frame. Taking a marble paperweight in his hand, he cocks back, and slings it into the monitor.

Sparks and broken glass fly everywhere, destroyed circuit boards, and busted transformers scent the air!

Now the garage.

Where's the gas can?

He douses the entire dwelling: The walls, the carpet, the furniture, everything—nothing is spared. Before going to the furnace, he sits the machete on the counter, and pulls the oven away from the wall. Squeezing behind it, he kneels beside the counter, and unscrews the flexible hose. The odor quickly becomes overwhelming, as he slides back pass holding his breath, and grabs the blade.

Now to the furnace.

He yanks off the service panel, and covers the flame roll-out sensor with the foil; leaving the burners exposed to the air. Being late summer, the unit's not in heating mode, so he goes to the digital thermostat, switches the setting, and fingers the button to 90°.

He hears the inducer fan kick on.

Moving faster, he hurries to the propane tanks, and completely opens the valves.

Knowing time is of the essence, he moves as quickly as the safe will allow.

Now beside the truck, he opens the passenger door, and with a final lift, heaves it on the floor, and gets in.

Looking around, he starts the engine, and pulls out. But doesn't heading out—the cul-de-sac at the end.

Parked in front of a home with a *For Sale* sign in the yard, he lets the engine run and waits.

Twenty minutes elapse.

Thirty.

Then thirty five.

He begins thinking he's done something wrong, and is about to go back when his attention is drawn to a slow-moving vehicle pulls into Christie's drive.

He sits up!

As the reverse lights go off, and the car begins moving forward, the townhouse detonates, lighting up the late evening sky like the 4th of July!! The gray vehicle becomes bright red, as the flaming mushroom cloud reaches into the heights, raining glass, wood shrapnel, shingles, and pieces of furniture down onto the neighboring houses!!

Stockton is astounded by the scale of destruction, as one of the propane tanks falls from the sky ablaze, and crashes into the car, cratering the roof! Pleased with the results, he puts the truck in gear and drives off, ignoring the screams for help.

Chapter 20

Away from the keen ears of Alex's wife, Stockton tells him the news, but he refuses to believe the police suspected them of his father's murder, until he sees the file. While he reads, Stockton decides it's time to tell him about the duffel bag.

"Why are you just now telling me this, they can be watching as we speak! That's fucked up man!"

"Shut up! Quit whining like a fucking pussy! Ain't no way for them to connect you, your prints aren't on anything, it's my truck they got it from. How can they find out about you!"

Alex stares at his un-blood brother.

Would he give him up? There's only one surefire way for him not to be implicated.

"That look is giving me bad vibes. It's saying you can't be trusted," said Stockton.

His statement has an unsettling undertone to it, insinuating what Alex is already afraid of. If he knew back then things would culminate to this, he never would've tagged along when he killed his father.

"Alex."

"What?"

Stockton doesn't saying anything.

"What's up?" uneasiness in his voice, body tensing up.

"....So you're quitting, time for you to run and hide huh?"

"Who said anything about quitting?"

"That's the feeling I'm getting: That you don't want to go."

"Go where?"

"Visit the chief."

"You didn't say anything about seeing the chief."

"I thought you knew."

"How was I supposed to know?"

"I didn't think I had to mention it, you know how we work. It is still we, isn't it?"

"....Yeah," hating how sheepish he sounds.

"Well okay then," his demeanor suddenly bright, letting go of the something he was holding.

"How's the restaurant?"

"Fine."

"That's good to hear," flashing a smile. "You scared to die?"

"I've never really thought about it. Why do you ask?"

"Just a thought."

"You?"

"I'm ready to see what all the fuss is about."

".....Do you believe in a higher power Stockton?" realizing he's never asked him before.

"I believe in me, I control what happens; no one else. But do I believe there's a supreme power who presides over the universe?" tilting his head to look at the stars.

"No. I'm the supreme power of my world," and opens the door.
"Let me go say hi to the misses, I wouldn't want to be rude," smiling.
Alex gets out and walks to the door. For the first time in his life, he doesn't not want him in his house, especially around his family.
Stopping at the steps, Stockton says:
"On second thought, let's go to the shed. I've got more things to tell you about," and wraps his arm around his shoulder, forcibly spinning him around.

As they walk in silence through the fence, and into the backyard, Alex envisions Stockton killing him, before going inside for his wife—wishing he'll remove his arm.
A gust of wind blows open the gate, banging it into the post!
A hound dog howls in the distance.
Stockton waves at the misses looking from the window.
The shed doors are swung open, displaying the back of a green ride mower.
"You know my days are numbered."
"You shouldn't think like that."
"The cops are coming for me, it's inevitable," taking a seat on a paint can.
"If I knew life would turn out like this, I would've started earlier; perfected my craft. I now understand why my mother used to say the things she did, I know exactly what she meant. My entire life's been shitty, I wonder why I got dealt such losing cards....
Ha-ha, God did it right?....Tell that to somebody else. The only good thing I had was taken from me; I wish I could bring him back so I could kill as ass again. I'd do it over and over until I'm satisfied he paid for what he did to her....Since this fucked up world, with these fucked up people, and these fucked up laws made me the way I am, there just going to have to deal with what I've become.....Jesus wept," and snickers.
He gets up and goes inside the shed.

"I might nail the chief to a cross," speaking from inside. "Crucify him like he did me. The Bible does say eye for an eye."
Standing with his hand in his pockets, Alex understands why there's so much anger in his heart.
"Did you know King James was a pedophile who raped and killed the choir girls he accused of being witches?"
"No."
"Yep, so basically the Bible was translated by a murdering, paranoid, pervert, schizophrenic, fag."
"Did you know Mary Magdalene was a slut whore?"
"No."
"Well she was. Jesus was just like any other man, he liked having his dick sucked; he liked pussy."
"You shouldn't be talking like that."
"Why not?" his back turned, searching.
"It's wrong."
"So you saying Jesus was queer?"
"You're gonna get struck down for joking like that."
"I've already been stuck down, don't you know a fallen angel when you see one?"
Alex says nothing.
"Maybe I'll drink the blood of the lamb for forgiveness."
"What are you looking for?"
"This," pulling up a roll of metal wire.
"And this," grabbing a weed eater off a hook.
Afraid to ask what he's planning to use the stuff for, Alex watches him fill the tank with the gas, and fit the wheel with a spool of the wire.
"Let's see how it works," he said, walking past him.
He pulls the string, and the motor comes to life. Revving it, he goes to a small bush, cuts part of it, and turns it off.
"Works like a charm. Look, I'll be back in a couple of hours. While I'm gone, maybe you can go find me some of those salvation crackers they pass out in church.....*Be ready.*"
And disappears around the side of the house whistling the tune

from the Andy Griffith® show.

While crickets chirp offbeat, and slow floating lightning bugs blink through the air, it was a night similar to this when they ambushed his dad.
The truck door slams, the start of the engine, light beams shine into the forest beyond the fence.
Now the woods return to darkness, and the sound of the engine fading into the distance; inhaling the warm country air, Alex looks at the twinkling stars, hoping that wasn't the last time he saw his brother. But not because he's looking forward to seeing the chief.

It's not much Parson is looking forward to either. He no longer has Kathy to look forward to seeing—she's been officially deemed a security risk. It could be months, or even years before he sees her again; or never. It doesn't look like his hundredth appeal is going to be granted, nor does it look like he's going to see the outside of this cell until it's time for that dreadful walk to E-house. Sixteen inmates wrote statements against him, claiming he convinced them to participate in the riot. They also stated he killed two CERTs, bragged about murdering Beasley and Chesterwell, and saw him running from Chesterwell's cell in the middle of the night holding a shank. Benito Gomez, rapist and murderer of his neighbors' twin autistic girls, even went as far as to say: He woke up one night to him attempting to break into it his cell, but he got scared off by a guard making his rounds. And that the reason he didn't tell anyone before is because he feared for his life after he told him he'd kill him if he did.

The governor is striking deals with anyone with information. Harry has been suspended until an investigation into whether he encouraged the riot is complete.

Throngs of detectives have been coming and going. A forensic team examined each cell for traces of blood, focusing more so on his, and confiscated all of his clothing for evidence.

Muffled conversation, and deliberate movement can be heard, as the dicks continue hunting for clues.

Parson's stomach growls.

The meal would've been nice had it not been seasoned with dirt, saliva, and other particles—the bread soggy with an unknown liquid.

It's probably close to midnight, as he prepares to enter his third consecutive day without food, water is the only thing keeping him alive—his commissary privileges have also been striped. He sits, stands, squats, or any position comfortable at the time, in a room where he can't see his hand in front of his face—giving him more time than he wants to think. For the last week, his brain has begun preparing for death, realizing there will be no happy ending to this story. There will be no waking up to Kathy in his arms, no children to take to school, and no career.

There's only the chair, and it offers only one thing.

Presently, death seems better than life; hopefully there's no Stuckey's or CERTs in the afterlife. Since he's going to be executed for a crime he didn't commit, why not go on and kill Gordon, snap his neck or something. At least that way he won't be dying for nothing.

The light comes on?

Squinting, his eyes burn—who's about to harass him now. He spins off the bed, throws the wool blanket aside, and stands barefoot on the cold cement floor buttoning the paper jumpsuit he was given. Leaning against the rear wall, he readies himself for another round of interrogations.

But after minutes of waiting, he arrives at the conclusion that Gordon is being his normal malignant self, and lays back down. Covering his eyes with his arm, thoughts of Kathy return to his mind; he pulls the cover over his body, and rolls on his side. Comfy, hungry, angry, depressed, suicidal, and beat from the day's events, he dozes off.

Clank.

Bang!

He see the bricks, the sound of the bolt sliding back startles him from his dream!

Looking over his shoulder, he sees him first.

Then his entourage.

Then the chains dangling from his hand, and the smile on his face.

"Douglas Parson...it's your turn."

Perplexed as to what Gordon means, he lays there as ten CERTs in full riot gear step into the cell, while four more, Boyd Nelson, Salvatore, Starns, and the assistant warden man the hallway. From his brain solving the equation, and him not wanting to accept the answer, his heart starts striking heavy blows to his chest, irksome sweat beads perturb his armpits.

"Dis beautiful state of Georgia has made you the newest resident of E-house," Stuckey announced provokingly. "Whudya be so kind as tuh remove yourself off dat bunk, and stand up so you can be escorted tuh yer new, temporary home?"

Parson is defiant.

"This ain't no joke boy! Now getcha ass off that bunk!" he barked. "Yates knows you and dat cunt is behind these murders; got da okay from the senator to fry yo ass asap. Now you wanna make dis easy, or yuh wanna make dis hard?"

Buying seconds, he gradually pushes the covers back.

The CERTs tightened their grips on the batons!

His feet touches the floor.
They trigger the Tasers®!
With elbows propped on his knees, and his hands interlocked, Parson stares at the concrete.
"Dis is your last warnin' boy!...Get up!"
His eyes roll upward, and lock onto Gordon's. The scowl, and his fists say it all.

Unbattered and unabated, he sits on the same mattress, minus the blankets and sheets; which are heaped on the floor with his jumpsuit. After succumbing to a strip-searched, and deciding against assaulting more officers, he opted not to put it back on. For the umpteenth time, wearing only boxers, he reads Grainger's inscription—a crescent moon and star adorns the ceiling, a green book with open hands provides the backdrop. He'd heard the stories about the drawings of this room, but hoped to never see them.
His senses detect something!
He turns to see Billings holding an envelope, the remote and a compact disc in the other.
"I see they've set your date."
He ignores him, and turns his attention back to the wall.
"I have something to show you."
"You have nothing I want to see."
"I sincerely doubt that."
Parson cuts his eye.
"Leave."

"But it's from someone we both know."
Maybe he's doing favor for Harry?
"What?"
"You'll see."
Billings steps out a view.
Hearing squeaking wheels, he rolls a television on a stand into view.
"Back to back executions? You must've really pissed someone off."
"What does this have to do with?"
"Everything."
Billings slides the CD into the built-in player, steps back, and points the remote.
The screen becomes a noisy hive of black and white bees, silenced by the mute button. A press of the TV/Video button, and they vanish, replaced by a black screen with a number 3 hovering in the top corner.
Billings extracts a photo from the envelope.
"Do you know this woman?"
"Should I?"
"She's your sister."
Parson is immediately annoyed.
"Or yours, incest wouldn't surprise me."
"By her not wanting to associate with a murderer: A person who tortured a pastor to death, she hates you."
Parson walks to the bars and inhales.
If Billings comes any closer, he's going to send a fatal blow to his carotid artery.
Oblivious to his intentions, Stockton digs through the envelope.
"This is her with the people who didn't want her."
It has to be a mirage, or a figment of his imagination!! Billings can't be really holding a picture of his mother holding an infant girl, with his father beside them!!
He lowers that one, and raises another.
"And these are the people they sold her to," he lied.

Parson's knees are weak! Dazed, he slowly reaches for it, but Billings snatches it away.

"Let..let me see that," his voice low, using the bars to stable himself.

The emotional toll the realization is taking on his equilibrium has his chest constricted.

"This is the woman who calls herself Christine Chase."

Seeing the old snapshot of he and Kathy at an amusement park doesn't make sense????!!!!!

In a millisecond, Parson releases the bar and reaches so fast, that he knocks it from his hand, instead of grabbing it. As it floats to the floor, his arm vigorously lashes to catch it. Dropping to one knee, his fingers inches away from it; he slams his shoulder into the bars to grab it!!!

Stockton watches him go horizontal, chin on the floor, face mashed between the bars, and just as the tip of his index grazes it, he stomps it away.

"AAAAAAAAAAAAAAAAA!!!"

And grabs the cuff of Billings pant.

He kicks Parsons wrist, and retreats to a safe distance.

"I'm going to kill you, you fucking cocksucking vermin filth!!!"

"If you think that was something, wait'll you see this," and taunts him with more.

"It's a.k.a. Ms. Chase again, better known as Kathy Billings, pictured here with her husband?"

Adrenaline rockets through his veins!!!!!!

Hot needles of fury stab him like acupuncture!!!!!

Vats of jealousy and rage pour over him like acid rain!!!!!

"*What?*..You were expecting her to put her life on hold; wait for some miracle to happen? Well I hate to burst your bubble, but this ain't thirty fourth street, and it damn sure ain't Christmas… You remember the secret you said I had? Well you were right, I did: her. Every time I saw your pitiful face, I'd think of all the times I fucked her brains out, rammed my dick up her ass. Meanwhile, you pranced around here thinking you're some kind

of righteous genius."
Parsons lays on the floor destroyed.
Stockton hits the play button.
"The answer to all your questions."
The blank screen transformers into a room, the date displayed in the bottom left-hand corner, 1:13:09 seconds and counting beneath it.

There's that all very too familiar piano melody!!

......A door opens.
His heart flutters!!
A man bound to a chair!!
He sees the naked body, the ankles tied around the legs, the slumping body, the hanging head, the runaway strands stuck to a neck wet with sweat!
Then he see Billings round the chair and stand before the captive!!!
Parson feels the burning reflux in his throat!!!
"State your name for the audience."
His heart pole vaults wildly out of his chest, and slams into the pit of his stomach, pounding so unnaturally that he can hear it.
Those words!
That tape!
The ruin of his life!
The sadistic music, it's exactly the same—the voice, the same hunting tone that terrified the jury, and made him a monster.
Perspiration dampens his body, shockwaves rip through his soul.
He can't move, cemented to the cold floor!
Billings pick up an iron.

"AAAAAAAAAAAAAAAAAAAAAAAAAA!!!!!"

Parson's starts twitching uncontrollably; the bloodcurdling shrill debilitating!!
Billings reveres it, increases the volume, and presses play again.

The piercing, pain induced outcry blasts from the speaker, echoing throughout the building!!!
Puffy, puss-shined, iron shaped burns are stamped across his chest, abdomen, shoulders, neck, and face—badly beaten, a bloodstained rosary drapes his neck.
Parson knows what's next!
BOOM!
BOOM!
BOOM!
And already knows what the aftermath looks like.
Billings ejects the disc.
"Be sure to watch the news. I've got something special in store for my wife."
And rolls the television away.

Alex fully clothed, lays in bed beside his wife, pretending to be reading; hopefully she's sleep. Staring at page 7, he wonders why Stockton isn't back yet.
Have the cops has gotten him?
Are they about to kick down his door waving guns?
After a half hour on the same page, he turns it.
"You're under arrest"
Is the sentence he reads.
He closes the book.

Startled by the low hum of a vehicle pulling into his driveway, he slips out of off the bed, and sneaks out. Not touching the

blinds, he peeks.
The Silverado.
Swearing under his breath, he grabs the heavy bag off the floor, fingers the red button on the keypad, and goes out the front door—the temperature's low.
Stockton signals for him to hurry.
"What took you so long?" Alex shutting the door.
"I had to stop by the job. Look, you're not going tonight, I'm doing this one alone"
A wave of relief comes over him.
"Why, I mea-"
"It's not up for discussion, I can manage on my own."
"Well at least tell me where you're going?"
"No need. You just go back inside with your family, I'll be fine."
Alex stares confusingly at his brother, realizing he doesn't want to see him leave."
"Well let me be the lookout then."
"Alex, go!"
He sighs.
"Go on, I should've never involved you in the first place," holding out his hand.
Disappointed, Alex shakes it, then pulls Stockton over.

A long embrace.

"If anything goes down, you call me. Give me your word."
"You got my word."

Alex can feel it.

"....You sure man?"
"Yes," putting the truck in reverse.
He takes a deep breath and gets out.
"Be safe bro."
Stockton nods, and Alex shuts the door.

He watches him back out, the bright headlights blind him as he wheels onto the street. Stockton honks twice and drives off. His eyes follow the red taillights until they become two glowing specs, then vanish.
He's left with only the sound of the wind, and the certainty of he'll never him again.

Chapter 21

Using binoculars, Stockton peers at the house from the woods behind the yard. Inside, a man sits asleep in a recliner; the television flashing against his face.

Having been confronted with this situation before, he taps the fence.

The Belgian Malinois pokes his head out of his house!

Another tap, and it's coming to investigate.

But before it reaches the fence, he tosses a handful of jerky over.

The canine sniffs twice, and devours at once.

As his hand moves to get more, it sees him and starts barking.

Stockton tosses more, but this time within arm's reach.

The dog growls; cautious before moving forward to eat those

too. Now it's expecting more.
Holding a fistful before the fence, he drops a piece.
It disappears in a single chomp.
The snout meets his hand, his thumb pushes a piece forward.
When the Malinois nibbles it away, and starts licking his hand, he has him.
Stockton jumps the fence, dumps the entire bag, and makes for the house.
The grass is patchy and the yard smells like poop.

Hunched beside the dining room window, the chief looks just as he did back then; sporting the same bushy mustache. His shirt's off, his unshapely chest is hairy—man's best friend wants another treat. Stockton moves down, clips the phone line, and to his luck the window above is ajar. He takes a look around, and climbs inside.
The dog's head tilts questioningly.
Standing in the bathroom on a fluffy floor mat, there's a fruity smell in the air. In mere darkness, he lowers the window and readies his weapon. Holding his breath, he opens the door, exhales, looks both ways, and steps out—the sound from the television apparent.
A move to the corner.
A glance around.
The snoring man.
He creeps back down the hall, and tiptoes upstairs.

His eyes open abruptly!

The audience applauds.

Sweating capaciously, the blades on the ceiling fan fade into view. Using the back of his hand, he wipes the drool, scans the room, and thumbs the power button.

Silence is now abundant.

The ex-chief pushes his heavy frame off the recliner, flips the lights switch, stretches, and heads to the kitchen barely able to see.

Opening the refrigerator briefly illuminates the area, as he stares at the Shepherd's Pie the misses cooked before leaving to visit her sister. Two beers, a half-eaten watermelon, and a hunk of lunch meat is what he sees before closing the door.

He settles for a granola bar.

Tearing at the shiny wrapper, he walks barefoot out of the kitchen.

"*Dat-burnit!*" banging his knee against the island.

Stockton watches "Mean Gene" Primrose pass by him chewing something, then turn the corner, creaking the floor.

Seconds later, the sound of running water—light from the bedroom reflecting off of the wall.

Weapon in hand, he steps from his blind, and into the hallway.

The lady of the house is about to become a widow.

He sees Gene's shadow move across the carpet, and peeks half of

his face around, looking down the hallway.
A closet, a wicker chair, and the light from the master bath is
what Stockton sees.

Standing in the doorway, Gene contemplates the idea of getting
another snack; tasting the strawberry, and bits of grain rolling
around in his mouth, he can't resist gluttony.

Stockton hears him coming and plants his foot.
But the move causes the floor to creak.

There's no movement!

He can hear Gene's suspicious breathing, but can't see what he's
doing.
SLAM!
Goes the door, fluttering Stockton's heart.
He's now in complete darkness, he sees the sliver of light shining
under the door.

In three long steps, he's up against the wall.
Behind the door he hears him ask himself where he put the re-
mote.
Stockton reaches for the knob!
And that's when he hears it.

He scoots to grab it off the nightstand, unplugs it from the char-
ger, and answers.
"Hi hun," sitting on the edge of the bed.
"Why aren't you picking up?"
"I just heard it."
"We're you sleeping or something?"
He yawns.
"Yeah, I fell asleep in the recliner."
"Well you probably turned the ringer off again like I keep telling
you no-."
"I didn't turn the ringer off sweetie."
Knock.
Knock.
His eyes jump to the door.
Ignoring what his wife is babbling, he gets up thinking it's ju-
nior; he loves popping up unannounced. But when he opens it
seeing nothing but his own shadow, he farts, and focuses back
on what she's saying, thinking he's hearing things.
Knock.
His spins around, sure he heard it that time!
Now his officer instinct kicks in.
Pistol!!

He hears the unmistakable sound of movement!
Fear paralyzes him when a shadow pulls beside his own!

The pricey phone hits the floor!!!
He's staggers backwards with his hand clutching his chest!!

"Remember me?"

Chapter 22

This end of East Ponce-de-Leon Ave. consists of mostly smoke shops, questionable gas stations, and restaurants with low heath department scores; the occasional crime-ridden apartment community, outdated office complex, and risqué hotel waits here or there. Even at 6:13 on a Sunday morning, this area isn't as deserted as one would think.

A bus passes a burned-out nightclub—a huge eyesore on the once proud and prominent street. Across the street, Kroger has raggedy cars scattered across the lot; another is pulling in. Rising, the sun sends incandescent rays slicing between the trees, and obtuse angles across the pavement.

The shopping plaza is their destination; driver: manager, passenger: assistant—both are employees of the office supply. And late for its 9 a.m. opening.
A frail shirtless man jogs in the opposite direction.
"Hand me that coffee please?" the manager asked her sister-in-law.
"Be careful, it's hot," handing her the piping hot joe.
"Aaaaaah," after taking a sip.
Her sister rattles through the recycled paper bag in search for a jelly to put on the dry biscuit.
"Damn! Bitch didn't even put no jelly in here. Go back," said foul mouthed trailer-trash.
"Can't you just use what's in the break room?"
"I guess...but I'd rather have the strawberry kind I asked for."
"Well you can get it another day. You're ain't gone to die if you don't have it."
The assistant mumbles something slick.
She snaps her head at her!
"I don't have time for your shit today Ashlyn," cancer stick teetering on her lip.
She makes a left into the shopping center, and notices a person sitting in the middle of the parking lot.
"Look," nodding.
"Yeah, so what."
Looking, she drives by and parks in front of the entrance, far away.
They get out, both wearing flips flops, and both keeping their eyes on the mystery.
"Looks like they've got some kind of uniform on."
"Maybe it's your husband, ain't he a security guard," the manager smarts.
"Ain't yours unemployed, and hooked on crank?"
"He's your brother heifer."
"I don't even claim that sum-uh-a-bitch."
"Awe yes you do. Shut up, look."

"....Maybe the motherfucker's sleep."
The supervisor thinks for a moment.
"I bet it's a homeless person. You think we should go see?"
"Damn that bastard, I'm ready to eat."
A street sweeper turns off the main road, heading their direction with a flashing light bar mounted to the roof; apparently not noticing the person.
He waves at them, and starts circling the lot.
The two women are quiet.
"Hey!" the manager yells. "...You okay buddy?"
Nothing.
"Let's go see?"
"I'm gettin' out my mace, just in case he jumps up, and horse kicks your ass."
As they walk, they see things they weren't able to from a distance.
"Looks like their hands are tied."
"Yeah, I see it. Something's sure ain't right."
The sweeper does a U-turn, and starts coming towards them, but slows to take a look.
The manager sees something under the chair, and something weird about the way the person's leaning against the light pole.
That's when the man starts yelling.
"Call nine-one-one! Call nine-one-one!"
They see the something under the chair is actually a puddle of blood; the back of their head is missing, and insects are obliging themselves to a meal.
The coffee hits the asphalt, her hand goes over her mouth!
Lost for words, and feeling herself about to puke, she's frozen in a state of disbelief!
Ashlyn no longer wants her strawberry jelly, but can't resist taking a closer look.
The man is shouting into his radio!
Leaving her boss behind, and still holding the bag of breakfast, she goes in for a closer inspection. But that's until she sees the full extent of the damage. The face has ripped muscle tis-

sue hanging like tattered curtains from a rod, teeth are visible through the whole in his jaw, there's severe chest trauma, and the grotesque, crusted organ he's holding has a badge stuck in it.

She collapses.

Chapter 23

A week ago the mutilated body of a retired police chief was stumbled upon by two women; increasing the body count, and the slaying's notoriety—officially named the *'Atlanta Cop Murders.'* The fact that local icon, Chief Gene "Mean" Primrose was slain, and left on display across from his old building, was a crushing blow to the entire law enforcement community.
Investigators are still working to determine the origin of the heart found in his hand.
The ATF has now joined the FBI, and GBI, in an effort to track down the newly known suspect. America's Most Wanted aired a two hour special on the fugitive, sending his face into over twenty million homes; including a host of other prime time specials.

APD officers are on mandatory 12-hour shifts—roadblocks are everywhere. Yates is all over the television and radio expressing his extreme sympathy for the victims and their families, promising the person responsible will be hunted down, while at the same time seizing the opportunity to fuel his campaign—his hardline, pro-death penalty approach is what the state needs to prevent further occurrences like this from happening.

The murder of Joseph Tangier has regained its steam, in turn, opening wounds from the past. At a time like this, the public wants revenge, they want justice. And Yates gave it to them in the form of Douglas Parson. His mug-shot is seen daily on morning and evening newscasts, the expedition of his execution date winning an 88% approval rating by a recent poll, sky rocketing Yates' popularity. They want to see Parson fried as soon as possible—Yates basks in the undeserved praise he received for unmasking the suspect.
The lieutenant who found the duffel bag of blood stained murder weapons, and torture devices, received a medal, a handshake, and a bunch of empty promises.
"Serial Stockton" is now public enemy number one, and Douglas Parson number two; about to die for the slayings of Beasley, Chesterwell, Sgt. Northcutt, another inmate, and of course Tangier—five lives taken by Serial Stockton, five lives the police have no clue he took.

Parson sits in E-house hoping, wishing, and praying that the authorities don't kill Billings before they found out the truth, or the state kill him, and discover it after he's dead.

Meanwhile, Catherine Royce sits in a mental health facility; taken there after being discharged from the hospital. Ann is allowed to see her for an hour a day, that of which Catherine is under such heavy sedation, she can barely talk; and doesn't know how she got there, or how she got the stitches on her face, or how her ribs got broken. She spends her days muttering: *"I gotta save him. I gotta to save him."*

Seeing her child in this condition: dark ringed eyes, nose puffy and swollen with stitches across the bridge, and badges on her arms and legs; Ann is devastated. The 500 mg sedative had her drugged to the point that Ann had to explain that she's her mother; which caused her to throw a fit, demanding they release her baby so she can take her home and get her well. But all she got was her visit cut short, and physically removed when she began fighting, and screaming obscenities at the staffers.

After sitting in the parking lot crying, she attempted to reenter the building, but the police arrived and instructed her to leave, or be arrested.

Later, the agent Catherine encountered in the parking lot of Outdoor Adventures, and the one who chased her in the SUV, tried to get something out of her, but failed, just as they did initially. All they got were slurred pleas that they let her go so she can save him. When she saw his face on the news yesterday, she had to be restrained after she started throwing chairs, and tried to go out the window. To prevent her from assaulting more staffers, a higher potency sedative was administered into her buttocks. Every so often a nurse comes to wipe the drool off her chin, whatever she doesn't get is caught by the bib. Once a day, after her lunch is intravenously fed, she and several other patients are strapped into wheelchairs, and taken for a walk around the compound.

They know she's a rumored serial killer, and all about her many identities. Therefore, no one is taking any chances with Catherine Royce, slash, Kathy Billings, slash, Kathy Easterbrook, slash, Christine Chase.

The modern-day Joan of Arc sits at her desk looking across W. Paces Ferry at the marble Roth & Stan Investments building, with its lot full of sumptuous German automobiles. A stylishly dressed woman with a white flying saucer tilted on her head struts out of Lenox Mall with two bags in each hand.

Why not quit trying to rid the world of its wrongs, and tell Harry she's had enough of fighting this useless war. That way she can return to her old job, and make tons of money representing CEOs who rape their secretaries, and titans who have their spouses killed. At least that way she can live the good life, hoard her dirty money until she finds some superfluous status symbol to go squander it on—to hell with dedicating her life to helping the disadvantaged.

Sivan discards the thought, and turns back to her cluttered desk. Laying her chin on a stack of manila folders, she stares at the *Star of David* ring her mother gave her, and rotates it around her finger. She wishes people weren't so absorbed with their own agendas, and cared about the well-being of others. She's had this same talk with herself many times before, asking the same exact question: *What more can I do?*

And her heart giving her the same answer: *You're doing all you can.*

Despite having a wall covered with plaques, ribbons, medals, certificates, trophies, and pictures with some of the world's most influential people; not to mention three degrees from arguably the best university on the planet, and graduating summa-cum lade in a class that consisted of many of the country's most gifted minds, she feels something is missing. There's still a burning desire to achieve more—an achievement that benefits more than just herself.

Sivan Goldstein: The compassionate rebel with a worthy cause, raises her head, pushes her hair back, takes a deep breath, and returns to the battlefront.

With all that's going on—mainly because of the biased media—the public isn't feeling very sympathetic. The two recent demonstrations at the capital yielded a low turnout. At one, police arrested several protesters, and forced the crowd to disperse because they became hostile; Yates encouraging officers to make more arrests. The message has been sent: They've had enough of her pesky rallies.

Back from the restroom, Harry comes through the door holding a bundle of mail.

"Where do you want this?"

She looks up from her vintage Rolodex®, and points to the seat beside his. The tray on her desk is already overflowing with yesterday's mail.

He sits the bundle on the seat and takes the other. Unshaven since being suspended from work, he wears the same clothes he had on the day before, and the day before that.....and the other day. Signs of sleepless nights are etched into his face, grief and disappointment wrap him like a straitjacket—the color of stress has completely overran his thinning hair.

Noticing he's not saying anything, Sivan looks at the old man she loves like a father; he's staring at the floor massaging the back of his neck. She knows the hurt he's feeling, and would give anything to take away the pain in his eyes.

"You all right?" knowing he's not.

No answer.

"...Harry," she calls in a soft voice.

"Harry."
She startles him.
"Yeah?"
"You all right?"
"Yeah," and returns his gaze to the floor.
"You don't look all right."
"I'm okay," speaking in a tone that's told that lie many times.
He's such a sweet man, her heart aches for him.
Sivan pushes from her desk, goes around to the back of his chair, and hugs him. Resting her chin on his shoulder, tears roll down his face.
"All right already," and quickly wipes them away.
"You should stop trying to be so tough," smiles, and squeezes him tighter.
Gasping sounds.
She laughs and kisses him on the cheek.
"Sentimental Sivan," he said, as she walks back to her desk.
"But thank you."
"You needed a hug."
"And you sure did give me one."
"I've been eating my Wheaties....and baklava."
"So what do you suggest we do?"
"I have no idea, my mind's too clouded right now. I want to believe things are going to turn around, I'm praying something's gonna happen to stop it. We need a miracle Harry."
"Miracles do happen," and drops his head. "I'm getting too old for this stuff, I can't keep going through this. You see a guy every day for years, you learn so much about him, you hear his hopes and dreams, you watch him sit at the same table every day, you see him play the tough role in the day, only to walk past his cell at night and see him crying. Then he's dead....A quarter-century of working at that place has taken its toll on me. I feel guilty for even working there."
"It's not your fault."
"Then why do I feel like it is? Why do I feel so bad inside?"

"Because you're human."

"All of them aren't bad people. And I don't care what anybody says, some of them haven't done the things they're imprisoned for. That's how they did my son, killed him for no damn reason!"

"Harry, sometimes I think it happens my mistake, other times, I do believe they know the truth and hide it, or either don't care to reveal it. Some people are so evil, they'd rather see a man put to death, than lose a case; conviction rates directly correlate with pay. These prosecutors and judges are literally enriching themselves by killing innocent men. There committing murder—nothing but judicial war criminals."

"Those men have wives and kids, mothers and fathers that love them. How do they keep getting away with it over and over again?"

"No one knows there doing it, they keep the citizens in the dark. Sports, reality shows, music, material things, smart phones, misinformation, propaganda; anything to keep the public thrown off. As long as you keep a carrot dangled before a rabbit, it'll never realize it's already in a carrot patch."

"You remember that Clifton guy in Virginia who sent seven innocent men to prison?"

"I do. But what's even worst, is that many of the states won't even compensate them once they've been exonerated. They take years of their lives, then release them and say 'Oh, we're sorry. Good luck on getting back the thirty years we took from you."

"Goddamn government sucks! I'm mean this American justice system makes me sick to my stomach! They got all this human trafficking going on, all this expensive heath care, cops killing unarmed men, and all they want to do is fight wars, and hand out bail-out money to these sleazy corporations."

As he said that, his eye notices a large envelope laying on the floor with no return address; striking him as odd.

Sivan sees him move to take a closer look.

"What is it?"

"I wonder why this doesn't have a return address?"

"Let me see it."

He hands it to her.

She examines it.

"It sure has a lot of material in it. Maybe the sender just forgot," and grabs the letter opener.

After a quick slice, she extracts the contents.

The first item is a hand written letter.

While she retrieves her glasses from the drawer, Harry gathers the remainder of the mail off the floor. And by that time, Sivan is attentively reading the letter. The more cursive handwriting's of the guilt ridden Gene Primrose she reads, the faster and her heart beats! With each line her eyes traces, the more awestruck she becomes!

"Something important?"

But she's too spellbound to respond!

Perplexed, he watches her hands let the paper go, and snatch another; reading it with speed!

Another!

Her lip drops when thumbs through a group of photos.

As if a spider bit her rump, she leaps to her feet, and voraciously corrals the stack!

"Let's go!"

On the other side of town, another urgent matter is unfolding. A man whose days are numbered, has decided to make his stand. Since death is to be his portion, nothing will prevent him

from receiving it—he's ready to die.
After checking his guns and ammo, the martyr for his own cause sets his sights on the building.
Click-clack!
And converges on Unit-8.
The security guard made the fatal mistake of trying to stop him.

Serial Stockton is here.

Steadfast in her defiance, Catherine sits in a semi-circle with other Unit-8 residents—only she's restrained to a wheelchair. Nearby patients each meander in their own world, not paying much attention to the TV they're unblinkingly gawking at. A slow moving woman sits cross-legged in a corner trying obsessively to get more than three dominoes to stand at a time. A short distance away, another has expended a 1/2 an hour completing the task of placing two paper tiles on each of the six roundtables. Due to the difficult time she's having tearing them along the perforated line, she still has seven to go. Those deemed unacceptable are balled up and fed to the trash bin.
Showers from last night have carried over into the day, and are continuing to soak up the afternoon; thus canceling their daily walk. The remaining patients are somewhere engaged in a psycho-therapeutic session, or maybe not engaged at all.

A female staffer keeps a keen eye from the nurse's station; the remote on standby, ready to change the channel the second Douglas Parson, or Serial Stockton come across the screen.

Mrs. Elliott stands at a cart dispensing meds into plastic cups—those are for willing patients. Catherine's dosage will be injected into her bag of liquid dinner. No longer beautiful and brunette, long voluminous and illustrious; her hair's a dull, discombobulated mass of tenacious split ends, and wayward locks. Although the topic on the talk show has nothing to do with her merciless husband, or her greatly abhorred former lover; Stockton remains on her mind, but it's Douglas' plight that's causing her the most anguish.

Today is the day that he's to be executed, the day that was suppose to never happen.

The hour that will change their lives forever is almost upon them.

With each passing moment, her glands secrete more salty fluid from her body. While the credits roll, and the predominantly female audience applaud in unison with the shows familiar tune, and the nicely dressed African-American host walks through the studio hugging and shaking hands; the other half of the patients are coming through the double doors.

Bringing up the rear is something resembling a stainless-steel refrigerator on wheels, but is actually a cart for transporting food.

A young lady waves to Catherine as she walks to the sink to wash her hands—the middle ages amble down the hall to the restroom.

The male orderly is busy strapping 'Francis' to a wheel chair.

BANG!

He spins around!

Knowing what the problem is, the specialist dashes out of the nurse's station.

Ms. Elliott prepares a syringe in case the woman has to be tranquilized.

Behind the clamor are the barely audible words of the reporter, and the face of the man she loves.

BANG!

The woman kicked over the trash can, angry the paper towels wouldn't cooperate.

But the action goes completely unnoticed by Catherine, her attention is focused on one person.

The screen changes, and there it is, the place she's visited for the past tenth century, the place that holds the key to her happiness. Now the face of the man who's brought her so much misery. Her eyes water as an old clip of Douglas being escorted from the courtroom in chains is shown; even catching a glimpse of herself sitting on the front row.

A tear falls from each eye, her heart defies the medicine; spears of pain pierce her chest.

A live feed of him sitting in his cell is shown, now Gordon stands beside the device that'll take him away forever.

The woman is physically restrained and given a sedative.

As the commotion comes to a halt, the camera is switched to a reporter holding an umbrella at the *Jackson State Prison* sign. With the room quite again, the woman's words are audible.

> *"Douglas Parson will be put to death at five, fifty-five p.m.,*
> *unless the governor orders a stay, and he's already made it*
> *clear that isn't happening........Monica Kau-"*

The nurse has makes her way back to the station, and changes

the channel.
But it's too late, the damage is already done.
Catherine hears the beat of her pounding heart.
Beat-beat!
She painfully squeezes her hands through the leather cuffs.
Beat-beat!
She undoes the strap.
Beat-beat!
Grimacing in pain, she pulls the IV out of her arm.
Beat-beat!
Her feet touch the floor, trying to shake off the powerful sedative
Beat-beat!
Her legs push her sore body off to seat, rising to her full stature!!

The staffer yells for her to sit back down!

The male orderlies are busy down the hall wrestling the table setter into 4-point restraints. She and Ms. Elliott are the only ones in the day-room.

She orders her again to return to the chair!

Ms. Elliott watches the unruly Catherine walk towards the eating area; her balance off, but moving.
Beat-beat!
Catherine she's her approaching with a syringe!

DEATH WILL BECOME HIM!!!!!!!!!!!!!

She takes off towards the tray cart!
The staffer bolts!
But by the time she rounds, the corner it's as if she's ran onto a movie set!
Catherine is running with the cart in front of her! And the only

thing in her path is a floor-to-ceiling window.
With adrenaline surging, and Douglas on her mind, the down-
ers are rendered ineffective! With the strength of desperation,
she races the car packed with the evening meal across the carpet,
and sends it through the window!

The domino lady knocks over her three dominoes!

Elliott drops the tray of medication on the floor!

A woman who hasn't spoken in months shouts!

Before any of the shocked people can think, the
"WHAM!!"
of the cart slamming into the ground sends them further into
wonder. While droplets of summer rain, and falling bits of glass
sparkle; she stands on the ledge looking over her shoulder at the
stunned audience behind her.
The gray sky breaks.

Like an angel about to return to heaven, the sun casts its brilliant
rays upon her body.

The orderlies run back, and are taken aback by what they see! As
if Catherine has the power to control the elements, she turns—*a
beam of blinding light immobilizes their vision!!!*

When it returns, the rain has stopped, the once mute patient is
singing, and Catherine Royce is gone.

Two relatives coming to have their loved one transferred to a private hospital just turned into the entrance, missing the dead man on the floor of security booth.

Meanwhile, Stockton just forced the Unit-8 receptionist to tell him where "Kathy Billings" is, and is waiting for the elevator to arrive—weapon in plain view.

The cart crashes to the pavement, trays of food goes flying in every direction!!

The receptionist cowering in the corner screams bloody murder, thinking the blast came from his gun!

Stockton doesn't give a fuck. That's not what he came for.

The elevator doors open, and there stands a professionally dressed man looking down. He first sees the gun, then the man blocking his path, and freezes when he recognizes Serial Stockton. His legs becomes rubbery, he falls back inside grasping the handrail, clumsily drops to one knee, and begins begging for his life!
Stockton grabs his tie, snatches him up—a radio falls from his pocket—and smashes the barrel into the man's face. Looking into his petrified eyes, Stockton's index finger pressures the trigger. The hammer cocks back, and is about to hit the firing pin! Out of the corner of his eye he sees something else fall from the

sky.

He turns, and to his surprise sees a person lying the ground. Concerned with only one thing, he turns his attention back to the man.

"Kathy Billings! Take me to her!" and shoves him into the elevator doors.

Using the gun barrel, he pushes the call button, now seeing the person is limping away.

Bing!

Stockton turns back to the man, and kicks him inside.

"Emergency! Emergency! All staff! Patient Kathy Billings has escaped out the unit eight window!"

He thinks his ears are deceiving him, until he hears it again.

The receptionist knowing what he's about to do, presses the button that automatically locks them down, and scrambles through a door behind her desk.

Realizing what she's done, Stockton turns to see them slam—the man inside the elevator is frantically jabbing at the 'Close Door' button!

Stockton leaps, but before he can cover the distance, the doors shut.

Kathy is limping away.

He raises his weapon.

BOOM!

BOOM!

Clears out the glass, and steps through.

Hearing gunshots, Catherine looks back and sees a man climbing through the entrance doors.

From a door at the rear of Unit-8, the two orderlies, Ms. Elliott, and another man she doesn't recognize are coming—out of the adjacent Unit-7, more people are running. Atop the hill, Units 6 and 5, each produce staffers of their own. In the distance sit 4, 3, and 2, followed by the main building near the entrance.

She has no idea where she's going, but is certain she has to get away from the developing mob! Pain from her broken ribs, and the ankle she fractured from jumping out of the two-story window, and the knee she shattered from it banging against the ground when she landed, course as she wills herself to move faster; feeling the irregular beat of her heart worsen as it tries to make complete contractions.

She grits her teeth, fighting the crushing pain in her chest; shortness of breath, and the sudden urge to urinate progresses as she runs for the wrought-iron fence. The closer she gets, the more lightheaded she becomes; her heart can't take much more. If Douglas is going to die, so is she—death is the only thing that can stop her from getting to him.

Her throat becomes chafed and sore, the saliva in her mouth thick and difficult to swallow. She stumbles and almost falls, one of her shoes comes off; the hot asphalt burning the bottom of her foot.

She darts between a group of cars!

Behind her people shout, others gawk from windows; with each step, her ankle punishes her—blood continues escaping from her wounds. She reaches the grass, and is only feet from the fence, when three orderlies appear out of nowhere!

Attacked by fear, confusion, hyperventilation, and the agony of defeat, she tries to perform the breathing exercises. Struggling to keep her balance, she exerts the last reserves of energy, and makes it to the fence. Wrapping her hands around the poles, she attempts to get over, but falls to her knees! Fighting earnestly, Catherine pulls herself up, and slides down again. Wincing, she

rolls over and sees the sky.
Cumulus clouds turn into blurry whirlpools above her.
Not wanting to quit, she roll on her side, and through the blur, sees the orderlies are almost upon her.
But they skid to a halt, and takes off back the other direction!
BOOM!
A blast knocking one off his feet.
BOOM!
BOOM!
BOOM!
BOOM-BOOM-BOOM!!!
Ear bleeding screeching tire sounds!
A loud collision!

Now people screaming and yelling from everywhere!!!

She sees the gap in the fence, and crawls for it.

Then she hears it again, but with more rage and anger than the first time!

Someone is calling her name!

She drags herself faster!
Through her fatigue and disorientation, she recognizes the resonant voice of the last person she wants to see. It's her mind playing tricks on her—grass and blood stains on her pants.

As she reaches the gap, and is pulling her body through, she hears her name again!
But this time it's from another person.

A rapturous scream sends chills down her spine!

With half her body through the fence, and for the first time since leaping out the window, she stops and turns back.

Her entire world comes crashing down!!!!

Her mother is at the side of a wrecked car on her knees with a gun pointed to her head. Facing her, is Christie on her knees with a different gun pointed to her head—between them Stockton stands looking directly at her.
Kathy pulls herself upright.
Slumping against the fence, sweat runs down her face while she sits under a Weeping Willow.
Crying and trembling, her mother wears the sun dress and matching skippers she gifted her for Mother's Day.

The time between heartbeats become father between.

He comes and grabs her by the hair, and pulls her to the curb. Gasping for air, she tries to regain her footing, but is dragged like a rag doll; rocks, twigs, and whatever else in the grass rakes across her arms, chest, abdomen, and side. With a final yank, he snatches her neck backwards, and positions her on her knees with the others.

A public execution.

Seeing her mother's hand ensnared in a hideous claw by an arthritis attack fills her with a hate exceeding any she's ever felt. Christie stares at the ground saying nothing. .
"When you got up this morning, you didn't think you'd be seeing me......These," referring to the pistols. "Them," meaning her mother and Christie.
"Or the act that I'm about to commit...Let it be known that I have no regrets, nor do I wish to have changed any aspect of my life—this was my destiny. Who I am today, is what I was at birth: A born loser with nothing to lose, a misfit with nothing to miss.

Who would've ever guessed you and Parson....But who would've guessed me and Tangier?"

Sirens can be heard, an advancing chopper dots the sky!

"If people could've walked my walk, wore my shoes, and feel what I have I felt, looked through my eyes, and see what it is that I see, maybe they'd understand why people like me do the things they do.....They say God creates life......but man makes death."
Minus haste or hesitation, he steps forward, and presses the barrels hard against their skulls.
They squint, tremble, cry, and plead for their lives!
He thumbs both hammers back.

Catherine raises her palm and tries to speak!

But can't, as she falls to one hand, the other clutching her chest. Lacking the strength to even hold her head up, she knows it's finally over. It's nothing she can say or do to stop him from doing the unthinkable!!!
Squad cars skidded to a halt, officers draw weapons—the chopper is almost overhead, snipers take rooftop positions!

Regrettably, they're all too late, their response a moment too slow.

Catherine watches in horror as he closes his eyes, raises the revolvers over their heads, and pulls the triggers!!!!!!!!!!!!!

Before the slugs hit home, her heart has already stopped. Her body falls forward, smacks the pavement, and lands beside her mother's knee.

Chapter 24

Standing alone in the emptiness, the pain in her chest is gone; no beat of her heart can be felt. She has no sense of direction, nor can she tell whether she's upside down, or right side up. She doesn't know the size or circumference of the area she's in, or if she's hot or cold. This temperature is unexplainable, one she's never experienced before; one that can't be measured in Celsius or Fahrenheit. Feeling naked, she touches her body, but nothing's there. She knows she has feet, but upon bending down, she feels nothing there either. She knows she's standing on something flat, but upon reaching down discovers, there's no floor. When she stands back up, she's suddenly standing in a room void of color. It has no walls, flooring, or ceiling; but does have light, and she's now wearing some indescribable garment—

plus her body's visible. To her right, a woman stands—it's her mother. But before she can say anything, a door appears, and out comes a man she's never seen before, and takes her through. She wants to follow, but it vanishes. She tries to move, but can't.

A BLINDING BURST OF LIGHT!!!

Now she's prone on her back surrounded by endless people in vast rows. As far as she can see, there's people dressed identically as her. Looking to the right and left, she tries to get their attention, but they act as if she's not even there.

A VOICE STARTS SPEAKING FROM EVERYWHERE!!!

It's extraordinarily beautiful and reassuring, speaking a language she's never heard, but somehow understands.
People began rising to their feet smiling with joy!
Others are paralyzed with fear, reeling in agony!
She attempts to stand, but is unable. Crying and screaming, her mouth isn't moving, and there are no tears.

THE VOICE SPEAKS DIRECTLY TO HER!!

So potent and so full of meaning, yet so consoling and reassuring; words that no human can fathom, or begin to define—speech so intricate and magnificent, it's impossible for to repeat or remember, but easily comprehendible.

Catherine's eyes open.

After being comatose for the past month from being struck by the massive heart attack in the parking lot, her vision is blurry. Seconds from the dream, she realizes she's not dead, but alive; lying on a bed surrounded by machines, monitors, gauges, pumps, and other contraptions. An IV is in each of her arms,

padded things are stuck to her chest, some sort of warm squishy bag with liquid inside is between her legs, tubes are running out of her mouth, and some device keeps beeping in unison with her pulse.
What is all this is stuff, and how did I get here?
Stockton!
Her mother!
Christie!
Her heart flutters!
The machine starts beeping faster!
Douglas!!!!!!!
Her head begins aching.
She begins to panic!!

There's a man is in the room with her!!!

When she sees who it is she, knows she has to be dead; heaven is the only place that she can be!!!

She stares at him in disbelief, this can't be real.

Tears well up in her eyes, the heart monitor goes beeping mad, her tongue can produce no words—astonishment has disabled her brain from thinking! All she can do is hope what she's seeing is no illusion, and she really is looking into the eyes of the man she loves.
Gently, he uses the back of his hand to wipe the tears from her face, and uses his lips to bless her with a kiss.

She breaks down.........

Everything she's endured over the past decade has all for this moment. Every subterfuge imaginable was used to keep this re-union from happening. Finally, the long awaited day has come. Douglas and Catherine have been made whole again.

Epilogue

After Douglas was found to have been yet another unfortunate victim of a faulty, and corrupt judicial system, it stunned the entire country. Many refused to believe that Douglas Parson, the convicted killer of Joseph Tangier was actually innocent. The fact that the Atlanta Police Department knew that one of their own was responsible for the murder, and covered it up, then went as far as to frame an innocent man, caused mass outrage. Protests erupted from coast-to-coast, it was the top story on every newscast, and the topic of discussion at every dinner table. Douglas and Catherine Parson were specially invited guests on all the major talk shows; people wanted to hear their compelling story. Even Ms. Winfrey herself did a two hour, prime time exposé on the matter. The case also gave Sivan the push she needed to bring national attention to all the cracks, holes, and just plain lies in America's court system. Thousands of men, women, and three hundred and sixty two juveniles turned out to have been victims of reckless prosecutors. Out of the three thousand-four hundred and sixty two people in the U.S. on death row, Sivan proved one hundred and twenty two of them were not guilty—some having served as many as thirty one years. As a result of the Douglas Parson case, the state of Georgia abolished its use of the death penalty.

Four years later, Sivan was awarded the Nobel Peace Prize for her stunning display of legal excellence, and her indefatigable devotion to the promotion of human welfare.

In the bowels of Henry County, tucked away in the back of an abandoned building, a man sits alone. On his spree, Stockton not only killed the chief, but also his son. Leaning in a chair, holding a revolver, Alex tries to figure out why Stockton did all of that just to end up blowing his own brains out. Now that his wife has divorced him, leaving him lonely and broke, and his restaurant seized, he finds himself contemplating the same thing.

But for the time being, he has other things in mind. From off the desk he picks up a small rectangular device, and presses the button.

"Please state your name for the audience...........For I bring the coming of the hour."

There are two primary choices in life: to accept conditions as they exist, or accept the responsibility for changing them.

-Denis Waitley

Pierced

By

A

Rose

Harrison Charles

Prologue

"Excuse me sir............."
"Sir!...................."
"*SIR!!!!!* "
"What do you want?" mumbled the man.
"You can't sleep here. You'll have to find somewhere else to go."
"Yeah?.......Go to hell," he spat, rolling back over chasing sleep. The sound of screeching tires, blaring horns, and a woman's scream yanks his attention away from the trespasser. Adding to his bewilderment, engines rev and shouts of profanity begin. Assuming there's been an accident, the suited man runs from the awning covered entrance, and dashes across the parking lot. The second he makes it to the street, he sees him. Known around town as "Doc", he was once a highly respected surgeon, but al-

cohol has beaten him out of everything he owned. Stripped of his medical license, he wanders the streets of Atlanta in an intoxicated daydream wearing his old lab coat telling stories of how his shaking hands used to save lives. Being nine in the morning, he's already so inebriated, he's collapsed on the side of the road with his feet hanging in the street. The group of people at the bus stop gasp laugh and gawk—out come the camera phones. The city bus operator stops and throws the
hazard lights on; packed with commuters rubbernecking and pointing.
"He was stumbling in the street yesterday when I saw him," the driver begins. "I thought he was going to get hit for sure today. Remember when he used to be in the papers? Messed up how life did 'em. Let me see if can get nine one-one on the line," said the suit.
The club bouncer lifts him with care. Working this strip for the past twenty years, he's encountered Pearl on multiple occasions. Being the city's premier district for seedy entertainment; nightclubs, new-age speakeasies, hotels, and lounges sit buddied like beetles and dung balls.
Pearl has a deteriorated stethoscope around his neck with a flask in his back pocket. Soaked in his own urine, he smells like a
liquor haul. The tragedy of him losing his family to a drunk driver the night he was to accept an award from the American Medical Association plunged him into an abyss of heavy drinking and deep depression, and before he knows, he's sleeping behind a laundromat without a penny to his name.
"Instead of taking pictures, why don't y'all help!" he yells to the people huddled around.
A gentlemen gets off the bus and runs to assist. After pulling him to the sidewalk, he stands to his feet and shakes his hand.
"Thanks brother. People suck nowadays."

Thirty minutes later an ambulance arrives to take the former surgeon to the hospital.
The bouncer returns to his post, irritated the homeless man has the audacity to still be sleeping there. He hurries his stride,

reaches down, and pulls the wool blanket off, exposing his frail body to the mid-fall chill.

"Why don't you get out of here? How many times do I have to tell you these people don't want you sleeping in front of their business?"

"They ain't even open. Do whatever you want. I don't have anywhere else to go. So like I said, go to hell," and uses a section of the tattered cardboard he's lying on to fling over himself.

A folded blue tarp masquerades as a pillow, the backpack tucked between him and the brick holds his scant possessions.

The brute in the suit promptly grabs the makeshift bed and begins dragging.

"HEEEEEY!"

He's rolled off, the bed thrown aside.

"Why don't you go find yourself a shelter or something? This is private property, act like a human being. I don't want to physically remove you from the premises, but you're leaving me no choice."

"Go to hell I said," pushing himself off the ground.

Reluctantly he begins gathering his possessions.

"What's your name?"

"Vagabond."

The bouncer snickers.

"Say,…I've got a couple warrants. Go on and call the cops so I can get a few hot meals and a cot before the winter sets in," holding out his wrists.

The doorman looks at the fresh slashes and responds: "…Go to hell," and prepares to leave.

As he unlocks the door and ambles back inside he turns.

"If you really wanna die, quit playing with yourself and run out into traffic. If not, you should find a way to get in touch with your higher power, find something to lift yourself out of this hole you're in. I'm sure something gives you a reason to live; go find a purpose or something," and slams the door.

The adult entertainment megaplex doesn't open until two o'clock, and it's barely nine twenty. The man with no destination heads off the property. A stray dog locked in a zigzagging pattern sniffs the ground for edibles, a putrid mound of decomposing squirrel flesh merits a slight wag of the tail, but deemed ineligible for a meal.

The iridescent morning sun warms the side of his face, a breeze sneaks coolly up his leg. He feels the greasy film encapsulating his sock-less feet, and can only imagine how bad they'll smell once he takes them off.

A series of buses-planes-trains-and-automobiles drive, fly, rumble, and speed by in-route to deliver occupants to the unknown. Meanwhile he traverses the busy thoroughfare seemly oblivious to the reckless abandon of the frenzied morning rush, equally oblivious a wanted fugitive is brazenly walking down the street in broad daylight. The dusty duffle bag hangs lazily over his shoulder while his wrinkled trousers are falling down. Up ahead, the intersection offers a bench riddled with three unsanctioned advertisements, two traffic control devices, and one path to obscurity; regardless of which way he wanders.

A rush of blood to courses thorough his veins! Something resembling a crumpled green back seesaws precariously on the edge of the bench. Excitement quickens his pace, and much to his surprise it *is* a green back, and a twenty dollar one at that! The day seems to be turning for the better! He's fallen a long way since his days of blowing money on strippers and owning a successful restaurant. There was a time when he would've turned his nose up at someone chasing a dollar, but now he's being sneered at. Only a second ago he found the money and it's already burning a hole in his pocket.

Some old habits never die.

His stomach is telling his brain it needs some filler, his brain is telling his stomach to shut the hell up; this twenty dollars is going on his habit.

"Fucking prick talking about finding God, finding a purpose. Screw him! He don't know anything about me. He don't know what I've been through, he don't know why I'm out here."

The Waffle House diner across the street is pumping out aromas of things being scattered, smothered, covered, and chunked.

His stomach growls.

Hopefully the owner won't throw him out this time, considering he'll be a paying customer instead of a restroom sleeper.

Preparing to commit the petty crime of jaywalking, he steps off the curb and onto the boulevard, and is almost hit by a vehicle rounding the corner at high speed!

Looking through the windshield, he thought he recognized the female in the passenger seat of the fast moving Chrysler® 300. The notion he saw the infamous person from his past only pushes him further into remembrance of his former life, the one of a little boy who grew into the adopted brother of one of the nation's most prolific villains. There's not a second that goes by where he doesn't think the authorities are about to arrest him. That's the reason he's been condemned to the life of a homeless drifter. It's the only way he can afford to hide.

Occasionally, the thought to go to the precinct and spill his guts crosses his mind, but is quickly discarded. Especially since they haven't proven anything yet. The warrant states: Sought for questioning. They have no hard evidence proving he's involved in anything, only hunches hearsay and suspicions. What they're really after is a mouth swab, or a lock of his hair. Since he's not a convicted felon, the state crime database has no profile of him. Broke, destitute, and ostracized from his family, hiding within the city's homeless community made sense on many levels. Alexander Zarbin and his *Fat Man's Bar and Barbecue,* are both shells of themselves; with the latter being sold and leveled to make way for the new *AMP Motor Sports Complex.* As Alex reaches the other side, he notices an outstretched arm hanging out the window of a burgundy '92 Camry. Telling from the look of the car, they're in no position to be giving away anything. But he bows his head and takes it anyway.

The elderly black woman offers a warm smile and grabs his hand. "Trouble don't last always baby…You just make sure you do something good for the world when the lord delivers you from this tribulation."

"Yes, ma'am. Thank you, and may God bless you too."

She pats his hand and drives away.
"Hell she talking about God, I believe in me."

The closer he gets to the entrance of the 24-hour eatery, the clearer the image of the passenger in the car becomes. Now on the property, he can see the people inside looking his way hoping he's not about to come in. Opening the swing-glass door he's mugged by the smell of fresh coffee, creamy grits, and sizzling meats being cooked to perfection. The woman at the register gives him a stale glance before reading of a long list of shorthand words from the yellow ticket she's holding. Somehow the burly cook understands every word, because the more she yells, the quicker he grabs items from the fridge and pantry. From the looks on the customer's faces, and the way their eyes burn into him, he isn't exactly a welcome sight. The man driving the 300 is sitting facing him, the woman has her back turned so he's yet to verify if she's indeed the woman from his past. He'll have to play it safe if he's going to find out, because if he doesn't produce some money fast, he'll be tossed out. Holding the twenty dollar bill in plain sight, he grabs a menu and sits the money on the counter. Taking a seat he can smell the odor hemorrhaging from his shoes and knows others can too. He'd caked a mound of baking soda under his armpits, but still, the stench has grown quite overpowering. Obviously the patron beside him thinks so too, because she grabs her plate and relocates to another booth. "Is this for here or to-go?" asked the clerk who appears out of nowhere. The tone of her voice tipping her hand to what she's hoping.
Despite the body odor and hard stares, he can't leave until he looks at the woman. But the guy she's with keeps glancing in his direction. He'll have to come up with a way to get close without getting ejected. The fact that he's a paying customer comes with certain legal protections. As long as he's spending money and isn't causing trouble, he can't be forced to leave. But he's a fugitive so he doesn't want to take any chances. Alex decides to make himself comfortable by taking of his jacket, his partially white shirt gives the impression it's clean, though he's been wear-

ing it for the past four nights and three days. Sleeping with his clothes turned inside out hides the stains that come from lying on the ground. It also keeps people from seeing just how dirty he really is.

"It'll be for here," he answers with pride.

She rolls her eyes. "What?.....You ordering coffee?"

"*Yes!* For right now, that'll be all."

"Well you probably don't wanna' wait too long because we're real busy this morning. You sure you don't want it to-go?" hand on her hip.

Glancing over the top of the menu he hears the waiter's words, but he's focused on the woman who's preparing to get up.

"I'll take a waffle and a chicken breast *with* a coffee."

"Yeah? You sure about that?"

"Anything else?"

"Yes. Let me get a glass of water too please. Since you asked."

She sucks her teeth. "Sure," but not before seizing the money from the table.

The woman is now standing speaking to the guy. Judging from the rear, it seems like it could be the same lady, the wide hips and ample bottom are evident.

The moment she spins and starts walking his way, their eyes meet.

Her strut is unmistakable! Her perfume is a rush of jasmine and juniper as she passes looking at him as if he's just another thirsty admirer.

Those hypnotizing brown eyes are unforgettable! *It's her!*

As she proceeds to the Jukebox to select a tune, her male companion keeps a close watch on him. A slick smirk appears on his face as he retrieves a cellphone from his pocket and answers.

The waitress returns with his water.

He requested a glass, but before him sits a Styrofoam cup with a plastic lid.

"Maybe the glasses are reserved for the unsoiled customers," he smarts as she walks away.

Though it's been almost four years, he still remembers the night he and his late adopted brother Stockton decided to forgo the night's reconnaissance mission in favor of a more stimulating assignment.

Atlanta, GA, staked in 1837 by a Zero Mile Post, it marked the founding of its original name: Terminus. Though a beautiful and sought-after city, it also has an ugly and long standing history with strip clubs, prostitution, and government corruption. *Dream Kings* has some of the nation's preeminent female offerings, even people from abroad come to oblige themselves to the plethora of beautiful women, many of whom are underage runaways trafficked from around the country. Atlanta, GA ranks as the world's #1 destination for human trafficking. A recent report commissioned by the Justice Department estimates that between 100-200 girls each day are sold into slavery in the city, far outpacing established heavyweights like Miami, Washington, D.C., Oakland, CA, and Queens, NY.

The plan was to have a few drinks and get a dance or two, but that was before he met this exquisite vixen who called herself *"Bailey Red"*. Ms. Red claimed to be twenty two years old, and a transplant from Toledo, OH. After hiring her for the normal run-of-the-mill partially nude teases, "Tim" elected to get up close and personal, and joined her in the secluded VIP room. Admission to this reserved area set him back two hundred and fifty dollars, and the cost of dances increased from ten to twenty five. Once there, she dazzled him with suggestive exhibitions of her anatomy, and after being fondled to near ejaculation, she proposed an erotic tryst off site. For thirteen hundred she offered to spend the night with him. He accepted, and subsequently had the most memorable night of his life. Fittingly, he wanted a replay and returned many nights thereafter, but it was like she vanished.

Now here she is, walking back past him after selecting a jam from the juke box. But she's looking nervous like something's wrong? It's obvious she's completely forgotten him and has no clue why this white man is staring so strangely at her.

The man she's with whispers something in her ear,
causing her to glance over her shoulder at him and shrug. A waiter stops at their table with two glasses of orange juice. The man says something to her and moments later she's heading his direction.

"Sir! Some of our customers are complaining about you looking them down."

Alex doesn't say anything.

"I'm not trying to be rude, but you have odor! Why don't you just wait outside and I'll bring your food?"

He smiles.

"Well I guess the sooner you get my food cooked, the sooner I'll eat and be out. But I won't be stepping outside. I think I'll just wait right here."

Agitated by his refusal, she sighs and spins away, before entering an office behind the kitchen. After about a minute a man sticks his head out, looks at him, and fans her away.

She shoots Alex another dirty look, and returns to refilling customer's glasses.

Seeing his message has been delivered, the man continues his conversation on the phone.

While Alex's brain works on a way to speak to her, his peripheral vision notices sun reflecting off the roof of a slow moving luxury vehicle. Black in color, and heavily tinted, it shines with waxed brilliance and doesn't seem to be your normal type of automobile; its gait is much too regal for this side of town. As the car continues past the building and around the side, the man with Bailey Red catches a glimpse of the car and his face changes.

In the seconds it takes for Alex to pick up something from his body language, the waitress returns with two steaming plates of food, places them on the table, and slides the condiments to the center.

BAM!

He slams the phone to the table, sending orange juice splashing in the woman's face, drenching her apron. She jumps from the sudden shock of the cold liquid against her skin! Spoons and plates drop, the startled cook scalds himself with hot grits!

For a second it looks as if she's about to lose her temper, but remembers her tip, and her $7.25 an hour, and her two children. With no support from the deadbeat father, she's on her own— swallows her pride, flashes a smile, and everything's okay.
"It happens all the time."
He on the other hand offers no apology, not even the recognition of what he just did, only scowls and whispers a quick word to the lady with him, takes a moment to situate himself, and heads for the exit without even looking her direction.
She blots the mess and heads to the office with her head hung and tears in her eyes.
A highly decorated war vet who flew with the Tuskegee Airmen, sits in the corner booth glaring with disgust at the sight of the rude young punk. The fact he's black just like him only further infuriates the honorable senior citizen. It's stupid thugs like this who make it hard for upstanding blacks, and to him, there's nothing worse than seeing a black man acting ignorant.
Alex watches the athletically-built dipshit head through the door and disappear around the side of the building.
He turns his attention to her. He'll have to think fast, but rationally. It's no telling what'll happen if an altercation ensues and the police are called. His adrenaline surges as he realizes this may be his only opportunity to make a move! But what's the move? What's he doing? What's he hoping to accomplish by speaking to a stripper he copulated with years ago? What can he possibly offer her?
But what can she possibly offer him is the question?

Being sure not to walk too fast as to seem overly submissive, but not too slow as to come across as nonchalant; he regains his composure as he prepares to meet the boss. The slime known as, "Troy Merciless" possesses the keys to Atlanta's shadowy under-world, one which consists of wealthy businessmen, mega-star athletes, an exploding film industry, and captive sex workers. Merciless guards the gate to this evil empire, but the being inside the air conditioned vehicle is the one who rules the realm. As he makes his way around the curved alleyway, he locks eyes with the familiar 6' 8" behemoth holding the rear door. At four hundred pounds, he's one big S.O.B. Wearing a tailored suit, single-breasted, with size 23 Italian oxfords, he has the nerve to be fashionable. The twin Glock .40's holstered under each arm seem redundant. One would rather get shot twice than get hit once by him. With fists the size of bowling balls, they're sure to cause sudden death.

Once again making certain his cocky persona is in check, he definitely doesn't upset his superior. Taking a deep breath and a hard swallow, it's always a hairy situation when dealing with him. He's the headmost vulture in a self-eating world of rats maggots and roaches.

"Zeus," he greeted, before ducking inside.

He nods and shuts the door.

The confines of the limousine are dark and uninviting, the leather seats are comfortable and goose bumps prickle his skin; partly from the abnormally cold temperature, and partly from the extreme fear he has of the person he's sitting beside. The power he's emits is incapacitating.

Merciless keeps his head forward, it's against policy to walk ahead of him, or to initiate conversation without his permission. So he looks down at the long, gaunt, white fingers of the chairman, wondering why he popped on him like this. On his pinky is a ring said to allow the wearer intersection with the universe's dark forces, his hands are tightly interlaced with each nail neatly manicured. The mere sight of them, the way they seem to radiate terror spurs him to look away; he's well aware of the atrocities they command. To the outside world he's Troy Merciless, but now he's Terry Bostic, a two bit street chump who rose from crack head auto mechanic to an "esteemed" position. Despite being utterly reprehensible, the position affords him tremendous amounts of latitude and privilege. Fortunately, more than he knows what to do with. Getting there by proving his loyalty when he accepted a virtually impossible assignment no one else was willing to. No one knows how, but he proved victorious and claimed his prize. However, he as well as the other "help" know, they will never become fully vested members. It's no cleansing to be undertaken, no challenge to complete. To higher-ups they're only pawns, expendable tools used to protect and serve the ilk. In return for their loyalty, they're thrown a few scraps of sirloin, and a complementary seat at the table. But the prized filet, and the reins of power reside with *them.*

Only his breathing can be heard, and he wonders why it seems so forced. Though he's exhaling as softly as he can, it still seems loud.

"Why are you sweating archon?" asked the abominable figure.

He didn't know there's perspiration dripping down the side of his face, and quickly uses his wrist to wipe it off, being sure not to make the fatal mistake of accidently elbowing him in the face.

"I apologize my lord. I was unaware," he responds, still looking ahead.

Staring at the back of the driver's seat, and the side of Zeus' leg, he hears the rustle of movement and cuts his eyes to see him reach inside the center console. His heart begins racing! He tries to remember if he's done anything that can get him killed! But grew at ease when he notices a manila file folder has found its way on his lap.

"Do you recall our recent conversation and the instructions?"

"Yes my lord. I remember exactly."

"Inside are your new ones."

Without hesitation he opens the file and begins viewing the photographs and reading documents. Blueprints of a guarded shipping port, shift change times, banking information, medical histories, etc. Bostic has risen through the ranks of the minions by being fearless in his approach of managing the boss's minor affairs. But this latest assignment has him wondering if this is really a ploy for his assassination. He'll have to exhibit extreme caution if he's going to question his superior.

"My lord, if I may be so kind as to speak freely?"

The man-like being studies him.
"Proceed."
"Thank you my lord. To be sure I am following your exact order. The information you've provided are pictures of the objectives?"
Pausing, he expects an explanation. But there's nothing but the low hum of the 8 cylinder engine, and the
outside chatter of the a.m. commute.
He continues.
"I also don't see any in the instructions altering the method of extraction and termination. Are they still the same as follows?"
Nothing.
It's a widely understood that Mr. Denmark has never been witnessed engaging in smiles or laughter, and he almost never answers questions.
Denmark penetrates his soul with his piercing pupils. Within the silence is his answer.
Terry looks away.
"Yes lord."
The managing partner of 'Super Firm' *Denmark & Perminter*, the premier full-service practice in the Southeast, lightly thumbs his cufflink.
The door swings open! The instant rush of sunshine is both startling and delightful. Zeus stands to the side staring down at him with frost in his eyes.
"Good day my lord," and steps out without out saying
another word. Without straightening his back, or popping his lapels, he clutches the envelope of new orders and starts walking like a puppy with his tail tucked.

By the time he rounds the side of the building and traverse the short alleyway, Zeus is already inside the flagship and driving away.
In ten more seconds, an insect as insignificant as a house fly can beat its wings up to two thousand times, twice the time it took for Terry Bostic to shape-shift from subservient finger puppet, to Troy Merciless, the murderous street king who wants to be feared by all.

In ten more seconds, his back stiffens and his chin returns to its arrogant form. The tough guy shtick is back as he pops his sport coat.

Another ten seconds and eighteen more people have died around the globe, the universe expanding ninety two more miles.

Drunk with ego, he snatches the door open and sneers at the homeless man. Moving with purpose and even more attitude, he treats the waiting customers to a wisp of his designer cologne as he speeds past their tables throwing looks of daggers. Bailey Red is scarfing down her food like she's on military time.

"Get up bitch! We gotta go!" he shot.

Having missed his grand re-entry, she looks up strangely. She's so hungry she didn't hear the bells clanging against the door when he entered.

Reaching in his pocket he extracts an obscene wad of cash, peels of a hundred, and palm-slams it on the table, bouncing the silverware like dominoes! Before she has the chance to savor another morsel, she's lifted out of the seat by her arm.

The old P-51 Mustang pilot boils with anger. Jerks like this are part of America's racial tensions. Cuffed inside his jacket is his Saturday night special on stand-by. He's waiting for him to make a false move so he can "stand his ground". Though it's Friday morning, he badly wants to bust a cap in his ass.

Merciless passes directing the lady by the arm, and is almost out of the door when he turns and looks at the homeless man. All twelve of the patrons, including the Waffle House staff are pissed. He pushes Bailey Red forward, rudely spins her around, and showcases her assets to the man.

"Now you have a close-up view," and grabs a hand full of her buttocks.

A woman gasps and covers her mouth!

"Everything in this world costs muthafucka!"

Extracts another crisp hundred, and tosses it on the floor.

"Go take a bath."

And walks out with his fingers dug into the woman's arm.

But he doesn't notice what she drops on the floor before he hurries her through. He was too busy mean-facing the dude who sleeps on the street.

But Alex saw it—it's laying on the inside of the doorway. The draft coming under the door is like angels breath, swooping the white tear of loose leaf paper up, skimming it across the floor where it comes to a rest somewhere under his table.

But he'll come back to it. For now he watches the man go to the passenger side of the car, shove the woman inside, go around the driver's seat and get inside. Seconds later he's gassing off, the high performance six liter Hemi blowing loud as he accelerates down grimy Stewart Ave.

For as much as his pride is hurt, so is his pocket. It infuriates him to have been subjected to that kind of treatment, but it burns even more that he's fighting the urge to bend down and take up money. Well if he's going to swallow his pride, he better get to swallowing fast! There's free money on the floor in plain view of needy people. He panhandles daily so he understands the hunger, but this is different—like bending over and taking a shaft of humiliation while everyone watches.

Obviously not different enough, because he leans over and snatches it, and stuffs it in his pocket.

Now he feels like shit, but glad he has the assuring weight of it in his possession.

A lady shakes her head in sympathy.

The fiery fighter pilot raises from his seat, and goes to the counter to inform the waitress he's footing the bill for the homeless gentleman.

The waitress wipes a tear from her eye and accepts; feeling the sting of how she too treated him.

The kind gesture is completed, and the kind-hearted man exits the restaurant with his appetite gone, and day thoroughly ruined. He wishes he was God so he could've struck that god-awful bastard down!

With the money on his mind he turns back to the note. Looking under the table, he becomes startled when a sense of deja-vu flashes over him like a Polaroid camera from his past life! The way the note is fluttering against his stinky shoe, is like a hitch-hiker flagging for a ride—it's begging to be noticed.

He reaches down and grabs it, and sees someone has used a torn piece of notebook paper to tally their work hours. But when he flips it over and reads the haphazardly scribbled message on the back, he knows the urgency in the misspelling is a message in itself.

Me an my cihild are n dagner, plesse help!!!!!!

Un.

A book claiming to be open may not be open at all. Perhaps, a curtain closed is not the end, but rather the precursor to the defining scene. There's an old wives' tale of a fisherman who every morning would travel to the same spot day after day with the anticipation of securing his bounty; the premier fishing point in the area, one that many other fishermen depend on as well. Being he has the luxury of owning the best equipment, and the nicest boat, he always secured the largest catch. But things take a turn for the worse, he starts bringing home less and less fish. He begins complaining to his wife that he doesn't understand why his most profitable location is no longer paying dividends. She explains the fish won't return until they've eaten the store they already have. After coming home with only one fish in his net,

she suggested he take his lone catch of the day back, and maybe it'll birth new fish. But he disagrees with her assumption. Upset his wife is considering herself to be wiser than him, he waits until she's fast asleep, loads their entire stockpile onto the boat, and the following morning returns to his favorite cove.
Pretending to have fished all day, he prepares to return home, plump with pride he'll prove her theory wrong. But before he could, a giant wave turns the boat over and spills the fish into the sea, where they miraculously return to life. Fishermen from all around eager to finally have something to eat pour in. Sea gulls, pelicans, seals, and dolphins come to share in the feast. The reef transforms from barren wasteland to abundant oasis. He's mind-blown by the sheer scale and awe of activity, and understands the point his wife was trying to make. Feeling like a fool, he goes home empty-handed. Expecting to find his wife in an uproar, he arrives to find a huge sack of fish sitting on the kitchen counter. He asks where the fish came from? She says a friend dropped them off, saying there were so many fish available today that he had enough to give away. From that day on he understood the danger of continuing to eat once you've already had your fill.

Upon having his fill two days ago, Alex's stomach has long consumed the calories from earlier, and is now reduced back to hunger, and once again contemplating his next move. Had it not be almost two forty in the morning, he could make an attempt at visiting a church food or maybe work his cardboard sign. The hundred dollar bill is now three twenties, a five, a dime, and nine pennies. Every precaution is being taken to prevent losing his newly attained financial standing. He can always rent a cheap room at one of the many roach motels up and down Stewart, but can't afford the thirty five dollar charge. Instead, he broke into an aquatic center in a gated apartment community and took a free bath. Sitting four miles away his hair is still damp. The funk between his legs is gone and his feet are clean, but the chlorine from the pool has parched his skin. As time passes he becomes increasingly itchier, but despite all of his troubles he's in surprisingly good spirits. Lying atop the roof of an after-hours social club, looking at the sky, seeing the expanse of stars takes him back to science class and Galileo. Centuries later, here he is pondering about the accomplishments of a person he never met.

He thinks about all the horrible things he's done, and wonders are these the only type of contributions he can make to the universe? While the low hum of liquor, music, and sexual energy rumbles below him, his mind wades through a proverbial cesspool of past bad deeds. How did he go from easily intimidated son of an onion farmer, to wanted man? The one guy deserved it, he was scum and no one cared. But all the others are now starting to attack. They're in his dreams, they're in his reality, and still fresh on the minds of the investigators. He's wanted, and ten grand is nothing to flick your nose at. But if he keeps a low profile nobody will recognize him, he's found the perfect ghillie suit to keep him camouflaged within the undergrowth of Atlanta.

What was lost however, was his self. The one that got away when he accepted his role in the crimes. He's a coward who was ruled over so absolutely, he felt he had no choice but to submit to Stockton's will. Now he's gone, and he's left trying to pick up the pieces. It's no way to justify those things, they went overboard with evening the score. He learned long ago life isn't fair, and neither is fighting. In modern combat, the scarecrow sits far from the battlefield barking orders while the real heroes give their lives for a cause that lacks both merit, *and* justification. To him, the honor lies in each man's valiant effort to die for what he believes, not in the loss of life itself. That is a travesty.
But for the time being he'll have to keep his psyche in check, and his demons at bay. There's a meeting, and the *Coming of the Hour* is almost upon him.

When her handler left out of the Waffle House, he made the risky move of going to the table and explaining who he is. After making her privy to a few details regarding their one night together, she remembered him. At first she was nonchalant and standoffish, but after a minute or so her attitude took a drastic turn for the better, and she became very willing to talk. Out of desperation, he disclosed information about his current situation, and how he became homeless. She in turn explained she's a victim of human trafficking and in grave danger. The frantic look in her eyes spurred something in his soul. He's destitute, and she's talking life-changing sums of money. They outlined a scheme they believe will get him paid, and at the same time rescue a mother and child from the clutches of an international sex ring. She even gave him a cheap pre-pay phone and promised to be in touch. Contacting him later that next day, she offered him an update to the proposition. He accepted and began making preparations for the move.

Now fully prepped and partially rested, he awaits her late night call while talking to himself.
"If you had any courage you wouldn't be sitting on some freaking roof waiting on some stripper prostitute to throw you a life preserver, you wimp! Why couldn't you have told him to go fuck himself? Now you've let this lady sweet talk you into getting in some more mess. You're one pansy-ass guy Alex. I see why your wife left you. I see why people take you for a joke. Goddammit *dude,* when are you gonna *man up!!!*"

If it was this easy, the wildebeest would tell the lion the jungle is now his, and it's he who's now the prey.
One's an animal, and one's a man, but they're both
vertebrates that'll get their heads ripped clean off if they dare challenge the established order. It'll take a princess of epic proportions to kiss this toad into a prince.
He begins letting doubt slip into his mind, and has become certain she's playing him for a fool...............

Until the phone chimes. A text lists an address, a time to be there, and the number to a cab service?

His heart skips a beat and begins racing! Both energized and filled with butterflies, he rolls up his trusty tarp and places it inside his backpack and gets to his feet. In about twenty steps he crosses the roof and climbs down the ladder.

Back on solid ground, he moves towards the tree line behind the building, a short distance away is the club's back door. He's in the back alleyway with five cars and a group of men standing talking and laughing. A hint of something's in the air. It reminds him of how he and his late brother used to sit in the back of his restaurant and get stoned. It's been almost seven months since he's been on the lamb, and seven months since he savored Mary Jane's uplifting flavor. His cerebral palate badly desires a toke.
"Maybe I'll go find a bag once all this is over."
Alex has a habit of talking to himself.
Hunching in the brush, he dials the number to the cab, and after eleven rings someone answers.
"Uhmn...Yes. I'd like to request a taxi at...twenty -two eighty Covington highway, it's the Club Sandcastle."
The dispatcher asks him how many passengers, and what's his destination?
"Just me, and the address is six seven zero Woodcrest Manor Dr., zip code three-zero-three-three-one."
She asks how he's paying?
"Cash."
She says the estimated time of arrival is in eighteen minutes, the cost is forty five dollars, and asks if that's all?
"Yes."
And lastly she asks for his name.
But he hasn't even considered that part of the equation. Before she has the chance to repeat herself, in a very clear and confident voice he says: "Paine Bogart," having no idea where it came from.
She thanks him for choosing their service and ends the call.

An odd sense of certainty comes over him, and in a peculiar way feels driven by a sense of meaning, a sense of justice; *purpose.*

But he knows he's a weakling, and his gusto meter is on zero. Where that name came from and what it means is pointless. All that matters is how powerful it makes him feel when he says it, and how much better it sounds than a diminutive name like Alexander Timothy Zarbin II. He says it again.
"*Paine Bogart!......P-A-I-N!* I think I'll drop the 'e'."

"*Wow!!*" He feels like somebody. What a difference a name makes!

For the next ten minutes he visualizes the most favorable out-come to tonight's mission, he envisions this fearless capped cru-sader who swoops from the shadows to free women and children from the grips of ruthless oppressors.
He imagines it morphing into a total disaster, falling from his fantasy into an acid rain of hot lead. After weighing the pros and cons of one versus the other, deciding there's no way this can have a good ending, and is about to chicken out, the phone chimes—except this time someone else is calling. He silences the ringer and stares at the number. It's a different one.
Taking a deep breath he answers.
It's the taxi driver calling to say he's out front.
His heart starts pounding again!
"Okay. I'll be right out."
The big mean gorilla is back, having characteristically comman-deered his back, and is firmly weighing him down once again. He was just beginning to feel like he's getting over the hump, but this species of primate seems to possess special powers, and no matter what it is he attempts, he never seems to be able to do it without feeling the burden of inadequacy. He was just at a high point, but now back in his typical lull of pessimism and self-doubt. The shot of bravado has worn off, replaced by the insecurity that controls his life. If Stockton were here he'd know just what to do.
Out of confusion he starts smacking himself in the face!
"Come on Alex. Stop being a bitch!......Pain Bogart!-PAIN BOGART!!.....*PAIN BOGART!!!*"

He bangs his head against a tree several times until one of the men pointing his direction saying something.

Realizing he better go, he emerges from the brush and begins stumbling as if he's drunk.

One of them yells something but doesn't move. He continues with his manufactured gait until he rounds the building and is out of their line of sight.

Now clear he adjusts his style and dusts himself off, the noise and excitement of inebriated club goers calling it a night is suffocating. A warm gust of air brushes his cheek, and a fallen limb almost trips his feet; his well-worn *Braves* cap shrouds his face in mystery. Vehicles sit jammed into every available parking space, and even on the curbs. Though his back is turned and head down, he's still made uneasy by the squad car lurking a ways down. He scans the area but doesn't see the cab, looks over his shoulders, and it hits him like a jab! Right pass the officer, and straight through the teeth of the crowd. With no conviction his plan is sound, he makes for the sedan while scratching his balls wishing he was well endowed.

He catches the attention of a parking attendant.

"*Hey!*...Get the hell outta here!" the man yells coming towards him.

Moving for the sidewalk, Alex waves meekly and nods, but is now exposed to the throngs of cars and people congesting the lot's exit. He's prime rib for any wasted douche bag looking for a laugh. Expectantly, he becomes the court jester, but doesn't first get a laugh, but rather a kick, a swift one right in his ass! *Now* comes the laugh—a howling one from two faux tough guys.

The blow is painful, the guy's booted foot meeting his glute causes him to grimace.

Fortunately they don't stop, just get their kicks and keep going.

He does too, and with a little more fervor now, and can now see the cab. The driver is looking around, he still has a ways to go; and much to his horror, sees the sedan shift into gear and begin rolling.

Alex quickens into a jog/walk and is in the process of cupping his hands to shout when he hears the whistle of someone else trying to hail the cab. As it stops, a couple hurries to get there. Alex takes off running and reaches the car just as they're about to get inside.

"Excuse me sir," he begins, breathing hard. "I called for this taxi and ran from over there to try and catch it!"

The man looks at him strangely, up and down at his appearance. For several moments they stare at each other until the woman reaches for the man's arm.

"Go ahead sir, we'll get the next one...............Go ahead," she said politely, obviously sympathetic to his destitute look.

"Thank you miss."

He scoots around and gets in.

The driver who looks to be of foreign decent looks back at him as he sits behind the Plexiglas partition, in what's apparently an old police cruiser converted to a taxi. How fitting, considering he's in route to do God knows what. The cabin light goes out the second he shut the door, and the pale blue Dodge Charger pulls away. Alex looks over his shoulder. The guy is saying something to the woman, but she puts her arm around his waist and strolls him off.

Alex turns to see the eyes of the driver watching him in the rear view.

"You live around here or something?"

"No. I was just doing a job."

"Oh? What kind of work do you do?" asked the man with a Middle Eastern accent.

"....I'm a painter. I paint houses."

"Oh! You should make good money from that I would think."

"Not that much, work's kinda slow now."

"Aaaaaaaaaaaaaah."

He turns down a side street, cuts through an alley, and pops out four blocks down. Clear of the gridlock, he punches the destination into the G.P.S. bolted atop the dash. Once they're moving at a brisk 72 M.P.H., the driver situates the rear-view and returns his gaze to him.

"So where's all your paint and brushes?"

"...I leave my tools at the house I'm painting, the people I work for flip houses." Alex isn't a good liar.

The man's eyes brighten and reaches for the radio. An energetic pentatonic scale piece blasts from the speakers, while a woman sings quick rhythmic blips of sharp words and tones, while someone in the background vigorously plucks what sounds like a banjo. Another musician slaps frequencies of varying octaves from a hand drum, and some type of wind instrument croons back up.

"I saw something about that on television the other night," he shouted over the music. "I was telling my wife after we have our first son I want to start my own company. If Allah blesses me with this, I will be very grateful," he explained.

"I'm sure he will."

"Me too," and looks at the road singing with the song.

Maybe it's the fact he's from a third world country and doesn't understand American culture? Maybe it's the fact he's more concerned about being robbed than his passenger's fashion prowess. Whatever it is, he doesn't seem to pay much attention to his dress.

In the dim light of the bulky sedan, Alex does his best to look at the small, no-frills analog phone she gave him. No new calls and no new texts. The ride is smooth, but his nerves are ragged as barbed wire.

In the distance there seems to be a vehicle trying to keep up with them?

You just sacred! Ain't nobody back there!

At this hour traffic is non-existent, and there isn't much to see other than the highway, the stars, and the green exit signs.

The driver has evidently acclimated himself with the operation of a motorcar, because he seems to be under the impression he's Aryton Senna. There's hardly anyone on the road, but for some reason he feels the need to routinely change lanes, and search for the apex of every curve. Currently, they're stuck in a curb-weight-increasing turn over Spaghetti Junction, the sedan shoots down the on-ramp, and jets onto Chamblee-Tucker Rd.

Alex decides it's time to put his seat belt on.

The click must've caught his attention because he reaches and turns the volume down, even though the steering wheel has its own controls.

"Ha-ha man! You scared or something?" he laughs.

"I'm good."

The driver snickers and turns the music back up, continuing his fun.

Alex should consider himself lucky to have run into a woman from his past. She seems to be an honest person who's only try-ing to do what she needs to survive. The fact she's so beauti-ful, and even seems to be somewhat educated causes him much confusion. Maybe it's because he's from rural Georgia and hasn't dealt with many women outside of his race. Since he can no longer use his adopted brother Stockton as a guiding light, he's falling back on the advice of his father. His pops was a good man who taught him the world is better with variety, and raised him to deal with people on a case-by-case basis.

He said to never allow racism to ruin him as it has so many others.

There's something magnetic about this woman of color. She's his exact opposite, and is convinced that helping her will put him back on his feet. He doesn't know where this will lead, but since he's a born follower, he'll follow his new leader. He should be euphoric, suspended in a state of bliss. He's been sleeping on the streets for the past eight months, and now about to have to chance to take a real shower and lay in a warm bed. Maybe it's his gut, or maybe it's his sixth sense, whichever it is, it's mak-ing him quite uneasy about the whole situation. The uneasiness increases when he looks at the G.P.S. and sees the destination is less than three miles away. The driver turns down a side street and drives for about two more minutes.

The device starts beeping!

After pressing a button it ceased.

"You must do pretty good painting. You live out here with the sheiks man." He doesn't have to be born in America to recognize the lifestyle of the rich and famous.

In terms of price and privilege, the area is quite high up the scale but not in the 'showy, new to money, look at me, I want to make people think I'm rich when I'm really not', kind. But the wealthy, 'I've been raking it in for a long time, don't want any of you broke-asses to know', kind. The comfort that generational success brings. "Old money".

The aggressive driver pulls the well-worn Charger into a Shell gas station and locks the doors.

"After you pay me I'll take you the rest of the way."

The jovial attitude is gone, and the cash tray attached to the Plexiglas partition pops open. *'$45.00' is* glowing red on the black box mounted on the dash, and his eyes are in the rear-view peeled on him.

Alex doesn't hear any music, out of the corner of his eyes he sees a gray GMC Yukon pull into the lot, and roll to a halt beside them.

The attendant inside the gas station watches through the window.

Like an underhanded Washington lobbyist rearing its ugly head, from inside the dark expanse of the crime free neighborhood, emerges a van. Like a cunning wolf slinking out of a cave, it stops at the intersection and scans the street. Moments later, it runs the light, and sprints into the distance.

The cab driver looks over his shoulder.

"You don't live around here do you?" having determined his attire and said occupation doesn't match the neighborhood.

Alex extracts the money, unfolds the two twenty dollar bills, and pushes them in the tray.

The man retrieves it from the other side, and clicks the locks. As

he prepares to put the car into gear and proceed to the address,
something happens.

The passenger side window lowers and a face appears.

The cab driver looks strangely at them, and back at him.

"Are these your people?"

Alex is stuck. He's never seen this man a day in his life and sees
no sign of Bailey Red.

Leaning over he lowers the window.

"Are you with Bailey?" sounding green as a pool table, and twice
as square.

The man plays along.

"Yeah."

But he doesn't come across as an errand boy. *He's* an errand boy,
so he knows the type. This guy is not in any way a peon, well at
least not in the physical sense. He's afraid and the guy can tell.

"Okay."

Chump!

The cab driver looks at him again, his unspoken words are intense. Danger has a universal way of presenting itself.

Alex grabs his backpack and exits the vehicle.